UNIDENTIFIED FUNNY OBJECTS 10

EDITED BY ALEX SHVARTSMAN

PUBLISHED BY:

UFO Publishing

1685 E 15th St.

Brooklyn, NY 11229

www.ufopub.com

Trade paperback ISBN: 978-1-951064-05-1

Cover art: Tomasz Maronski

Typesetting & interior design: Alex Shvartsman

Logo design: Martin Dare

Copyeditor: Tarryn Thomas, Elektra Hammond

Associate editors: Cyd Athens, Andrew Dibble, Frank Dutkiewicz, James A. Miller, Tarryn Thomas

Visit us on the web

www.ufopub.com

CONTENTS

FOREWORD

Alex Shvartsman

Welcome to the tenth installment of the UFO series!

These anthologies have been an ongoing concern since 2012, and we're still going strong. Despite living in a pretty strange timeline—or perhaps because of it—the demand for humor has never been stronger, and the twenty-four authors featured in this book will not disappoint.

As always, UFO presents a mix of stories, some by award-winning and bestselling professionals and also pieces from newer, up-and-coming authors. I am especially proud whenever I find a great story by a new author, and this volume features several such works, either the authors' first publication or their first professional sale.

It is no surprise at all that many of the stories in this book touch upon the subject of the Copyright Infringement Blender, commonly referred to as "generative AI." At UFO Publishing we're only interested in reading the stories a living person has bothered to write. Wherever you stand on the issue, I hope you will enjoy the ways our human authors have lampooned and skewered this new technology and its implications.

There's plenty of other material as well, from a space orc diplomat desperately trying to torpedo the peace talks, to an uplifted rat uprising, to what's possibly the first-ever Seussberpunk story, there's something for everyone in this book.

Enjoy, and here's to the next ten volumes in this series.

Happy reading!

HOW TO MAKE EVERYTHING BETTER FOR EVERYONE

Jane Espenson

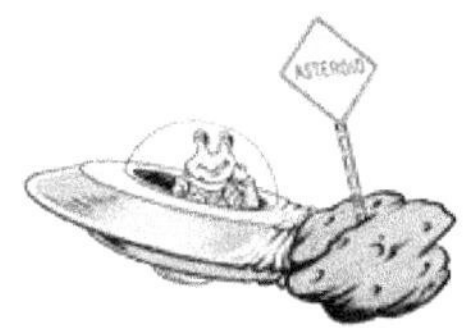

Ralph could've made coffee at home for pennies a cup, but he preferred stopping by the coffee shop on his way to the office. They had instituted a new rewards system that meant he often got his coffee for free, which was a big frothy upgrade to his life. A huge physical prize wheel had been installed in the shop two weeks ago. It took up half the available space, was covered in real gold glitter, and made a satisfying *klik klik klikikik* sound when you spun it.

It took effort for Ralph to get it going, stretching up on his toes and then dropping his whole body weight in a burst of downwards enthusiasm. Perforce before caffeination, even. There was a push-button option for the rushed or disabled, but Ralph liked actually putting his back into the spinning. He could forego a bit of his morning workout on those days that he played, so it was a win-win-win: coffee-fitness-*klikikik*! And almost half the time, with his luck, Ralph *did* win. Often a free coffee, or if not, a half-price coffee, or half off a muffin which he wouldn't have usually purchased, but it was half off. Even when he lost, there was an option to buy a re-spin. There were more re-spins available after that point, at subtly increasing costs, if he had the time. But work beckoned and so, usually, Ralph was launched off into the subway station after only a couple spins, with a coffee and a muffin warming his hands and the internally-warming feeling of having won something and also of not having lingered too long and wagered too much.

And, of course, the subway offered another chance for Ralph to win: As soon as he arrived on the platform, the turnstile registered that he'd entered the subway lottery. Looking down the track, angling for that first glimpse of a train, Ralph would sometimes see the flitting shadowy figures of the people who lived in the abandoned spur lines off the subway tracks. These were the Bad Luck People who had dropped out of life. Imagine having such bad luck that choosing to live in a subway tunnel would seem rational. Perhaps bad luck really meant bad choices. He'd read that on a poster once, but that didn't mean it was wrong.

Before Ralph ever got a good look at these shadows, the train would curve into sight and the numbers on the overhead display would start flipping and *klik-klik-kliking*. And he'd look at the display, willing his number to *klik* into place, telling him if he'd won a seat on the arriving train, and which car he'd been assigned to. Ralph usually won in the first or second round of train arrivals, often getting a spot in the special fancy car that had a little tray for your coffee and muffin and a shiny dispenser that gave you napkins if you pressed your thumb into the thumb-print reader that charged your account and stuck a little temporary tattoo of a flower to your thumb as a bonus. Kids loved it. Ralph liked it too, a bit of childish whimsy that he nurtured in himself. He was a fun person. He'd check his thumb to see which flower he'd won, the common daisy or, very very occasionally a rose, which was rare and a bit of a thrill. Some people said there was an orchid, too. Ralph had never seen it, but every time he checked his thumb after he'd pressed the pleasantly warm smooth little button that dispensed the thin off-white napkins, he hoped that he might see an exotic orchid there.

If he was in a hurry, he'd pay the small fee to guarantee a spot in the first train, but today he won a slot there without even needing to do so. *Yes*. And in the napkin car. The luck of Ralph. He spotted a little girl in the same car, looking at her daisy thumb with satisfaction. He gave her a thumbs up with his own daisy thumb and she did it back.

Twenty minutes later, Ralph walked into work, proud as always at having avoided the parking space lottery, which he heard was a rough one. He got into line for the elevator lottery. And depending on the size of the coffee that he'd won, perhaps he would play the word game they display in the elevator and if he won that, it dispensed a little piece of paper that got him into the urinal area of the men's room without paying. That was one place where he was extra glad there was a cash pay-through, though, for days when the coffee had been large and the word game had been obscure. Philhellenic?! Come on.

Today, the day when he'd exchanged flowery thumbs ups with the little daisy-thumbed girl, he'd already been a winner eleven times by the time he arrived at his work station. So he settled in with a sense of satisfaction and self-worth, and opened h—But forget Ralph. Fuck Ralph. This isn't his story. This is my story. I designed the lottery system. It was me, not Ralph or his "luck," that make Ralph's life so charmed.

I was actually part of a whole team that designed the system. Well, it was the generation before mine that designed it, but my team implemented it, parts of it. We won awards. The specific wheel in Ralph's coffee shop was new, a refinement of an earlier version that had displayed a digital image of a wheel. The algorithm was the same, digital wheel or real wheel. We discovered, though, that people vastly preferred it when the wheel was real, and they had to lay their own hands on it to get it to spin. That way, they felt that the outcome was more directly under the sway of their own personal luck, that they were influencing it with the way they gripped the wheel or threw their weight. They were prouder of themselves if they won, and they were more determined to re-play until they did. Profits at the stores with the physical wheels were way up, with people paying more, buying more, and lingering longer in the store, which meant they were exposed to more ads for other products. Win-win-win?! There were far more wins than that. We were experimenting with miniature wheels that could be affixed to every item in the grocery store. The price of the item would increase a small amount with each spin, but sometimes it landed in the "free" slot and you got the product for nothing. But it was hard to make the small wheels have any kind of satisfying heft. Work in progress.

You might think that the Ralphs of the world were being fleeced, except for the absolutely crucial factor that they were *happier*. Life is more entertaining now, and it's rational to pay for entertainment. In fact, it's elitist, and possibly ableist, not to.

Of course, a culture based around gambling works best with a population that has a lot of people with somewhat addictive personalities. But that's something that can be engineered or encouraged. If you make people in general slightly more damaged, then it's easier to make them happier with less. There is undoubtedly a word for the opposite of eugenics, but it feels opposed to the entire vibe to have learned it.

At any rate, a little bit of selective genetics, early-childhood conditioning, and a small adjustment to some childhood vitamins—just a rumor, didn't hear it from me—meant that people generally liked gambling. Or maybe that was just the Opposite of Eugenics Department gaslighting us and most people instinctively liked gambling already. Who's to say? Not me. My team was about implementation. And of course, after I discovered the NEW THING we were about the NEW THING.

Yes, this is about me, Stephanie Landers, and the day that I misunderstood the term "phonograph needle," and how it led to the innovation that upgraded the whole system.

I had never heard of a phonograph needle, but I came across the name in some post I was reading. I thought maybe it meant some kind of "phone needle." And I idly conjectured what that might be. What I imagined was a painful alternative to earphones or earbuds, an actual physical spike that could stick into your ear from the phone and deliver the sound directly into your inner ear. It sounded awful, penetrative in a bad way. And that made me think, how much would you pay for a phone that did *not* include a new "phone needle" feature? If you could pay to opt out, you surely would, right? And that little thought, born of a misunderstanding, led to a whole new layer to how we are structuring society. I still have no idea what a phonograph needle is, but no one is paying me to look it up, so there you go, you get what you pay for. Maybe it's exactly what I pictured. Probably. Prove it isn't.

The new idea, when turned into a general principle, was

that if you replaced good options with less good options, then people would pay to keep the old better options. Then you could charge them for making no changes at all. When Ralph got to spin that wheel at his coffee shop to win a "free customization" to keep the baristas from adding matcha to his mocha, he was winning! And the shop didn't even have to give him that coffee for free.

We introduced it gradually, of course, so people were barely aware of the change as it crept across the different parts of their lives. Here are some of the upgrades that you could pay to not have:

- Poolside decking with new extra-slippery patterns and colors
- Jars with square lids and complicated clamping mechanisms
- Left and right shoes with different sizing conventions
- Some fried chicken is actually pigeon
- Rustic raw wool sweaters with twigs knitted in
- Drinking glasses with holes near the top to prevent overfilling
- Audio note apps that raised the pitch of your voice and added a Southern accent
- Laptops that changed cord interfaces with each new model (grandfathered in)
- Dissolving plates
- Sticky on both sides wallpaper
- Unregulated sausages
- Phone needles (see above)

We had a lot of fun coming up with these. They had to be something you could make the argument for. Perhaps it was ethically sourced or recyclable or more flexible or easier to clean or ergonomic ... just something so you could understand why the change had been introduced.

In fact, more people than we expected actually embraced these arguments, and *wanted* the upgrades, so we could charge for them, too. So you'd get a small fee increase for the upgrade, and a slightly larger one for opting out of it. And if you agreed to play a little gambling game, you might pay nothing at all for either. Or, if you lost, just a little bit more. In the end, people had fun and felt that they were designing a bespoke life that was on trend, of value, and joy-worthy, no matter which option they chose.

And if you genuinely didn't like what you'd chosen, you could switch for a really very small additional cost and you got a little scratch-off card that came in the mail and had some surprisingly good prizes.

I got a raise.

"Congratulations, Stephanie, you won a raise!" the message from the govcorp read.

Now, I win an average of thirty-eight things a day. Not to brag, just how things are. But a raise is serious business. I'd been a Top Executive, C-tier for a while. But if my income rose high enough, I'd become a Top Executive, B-tier, and get a lot of perks outright. Out-fucking-right. You can think of it as being exempted from the lottery for the parking spaces or space on the elevator or subway car or bathroom or tampons. But in another way of looking it—the right way of looking at it—it's like you're still in all those lotteries, *but you're guaranteed to win them every single time*. It's a perma-win. A golden ticket.

There is no Top Executive, A-tier. That was just there to make you think there's always something to strive for.

I did the math with shaky fingers. Well, I did it in my

head, but my brain was shaking. My raise was almost enough to put me at the perma-win level, the B-tier. Just fifty dollars a month short. What an aggravating coincidence. But, lucky me, there was a wager option. I could spin the big wheel. Not a literal wheel, but it might as well have been. They called it a "supplemental salary increase review," and it would result in my raise either being retroactively denied or double. I could take my raise, or go double-or-nothing with it. I mean, obviously I recognized what it was. It was a fake win. But what if I won?

I decided to talk to Ralph about it. You may have thought Ralph was fictional for the point of illustration, but Ralph was my brother and he was real. I took him out for burgers. Mine ended up being free and then we both got lucky and won personal opt-outs on the ultra-wasabi topping upgrade and finally we rented some prime chair space, got some napkins—daisy thumb, daisy thumb—and sat down to talk over what I should do.

I had never really clearly laid out for Ralph how the system worked. Especially the new part about how we were making everything terrible on purpose and he was having to pay to make it the same. I was surprised how much that surprised him. I even told him about the pilot program where we were slowing down access to vital medical test results unless you paid for the special medical express elite program, which was actually pretty reasonably priced and made you feel special. And sometimes, even for those who didn't subscribe, the system would pick some result or other and just not slow it down as a little treat, which was very generous. Ralph was surprised about that, too. He told me not to take the gamble with the supplemental salary increase review. He pointed out that my colleagues clearly weren't above rigging things, and that they had every incentive to keep me tumbling around in the system with everyone else, and that a bird in the hand something something something. His voice became irritating to me: a phonograph needle in my ear. And I kept thinking about that perma-win status and the not large *but actual* chance of winning it. Because, once again, that chance was always real. It was the realness of the chance that made it all work, that made it not a scam, that made it worth staying in the process. *Free coffee.*

I went in for the review. They made it very exciting. It was in a corporate suite I'd never been in before, very plush, and there was charcuterie and sparkling water without the extra-sodium upgrade. They praised me for ninety minutes straight before they told me I wasn't getting the raise, but that it had been a really *really* close thing and I should definitely try again. So technically, Ralph was right. But he didn't understand how close it had been, how nice the experience had been. How *actual* the chance. I tried to explain it, but he just got this haunted look in his eyes. Which I should've paid attention to. Because.

Because I guess this story is about Ralph after all, because about a month later he mystified us all when he slipped off down the subway line, passing under a "bad luck is bad choices" poster with a small orchid-shaped temporary tattoo still visible on the meat of his thumb. I think that detail about his thumb is important and ironic. He'd just proven, by getting the one-in-forty-thousand orchid, that the system worked. Why choose that day of all days? But he did. He became one of those people. The people in the shadows. The people who never won anything.

JANE ESPENSON IS an Emmy-nominated and Hugo-award winning writer of television and short fiction. She is best known for her work on *Buffy the Vampire Slayer, Angel, Firefly, Gilmore Girls, Marvel's Jessica Jones, Game of Thrones, Battlestar Galactica,* and *Foundation,* among other series. She is currently writing for Amazon's *Fallout*.

HORTON

Mark S. Bailen

The sky was the color of green eggs and ham.

HortOn, a data hustler with a head full of RAM, bio-hacked ears and a double-cammed proboscis, sat perched on a stool in the Red Fish District, slurping up soup, cold, gray and viscous.

"Gadzooks!" HortOn yelled, spooking a poodle eating noodles. The data egg in his skull was emitting oodles and oodles, disconcerting blurts and high-pitched alerts, broadcast at four-hundred-and-fifty megahertz. HortOn had taken a job that he came to regret, from a sneetch clinic that he wished he could forget. Data had been forced into his skull, through and through, by a surgical device devised by Thing One and Thing Two.

Unsure where to go next, HortOn rode a tuk-tuk to Na Nupp, a maze of snook parlors and underground zoos, where he met with a fox with very long lashes, a pair of blue socks, and mirrored sunglasses. The fox directed him to a shielded backroom, scanned him top to bottom, and a screen flashed into view.

"Just as I suspected," said the fox. "You have a severe case of Whos."

"Whose?"

"Not whose. WHOS. And not one or two. A whole Whoville of Whos are living in you."

HortOn collapsed. "Full sentences, please."

The fox batted her lashes. "Fine, here's my diagnosis. In the recesses of your noggin you're hatching unsanctioned consciousnesses, artificial thought processes, entire nascent populouses, enough quantum-level qualia to supply a major metropolis."

HortOn tugged on his proboscis. "So what's my prognosis?"

"Galoshes."

That wasn't the sentience HortOn was hoping for. He felt woozy and lay on the floor. Darn Thing One and Two for putting him under the knife and stuffing his head with algorithmically-generated life.

"Can you free the Whos?" HortOn begged. "Get them out of my egg?"

The fox clicked her extendable claws. "Sorry, but I must refuse. If you wanna save your Whos, visit WinterSeuss."

"The AI who's mostly insane? Who enslaves millions of Whos in virtual domains?"

"The very same."

HortOn felt miserable and rotten. Weak and downtrodden. Ennui and malaise. And four other French words that he couldn't explain.

And yet from somewhere inside, the Whos continued to cry. "Help us, HortOn! Help us, please! Don't let us be uploaded into nefarious machines, stored on prison planets, and in torture routines. Oh, the places we will go!"

What could HortOn do? He had to make choices and

make them quite soon. His head wasn't appropriate storage for millions of Whos. Before he left Na-Nupp, the fox blew him a kiss and tossed him a strange-looking robotic goldfish.

"In case you're in a fix." Then she disappeared with a swish.

To reach WinterSuess, Horton crossed fields of clovers, polluted lakes, fake forests, and Mount Chrome Over. As he climbed to the peak, he blocked out the Who voices and wondered again if he could have made better choices. But that's when he ran into the notorious NeuroGrinchGPT, standing knee-deep in white noise, flickering green. The avatar was shriveled and not very tall, as if its power supply was three sizes too small.

"Am I hearing Whos?" The avatar drummed. "In somebody's head?"

Hort0n stumbled back, but was blocked by a sled filled with stolen toys, VR glasses and HD screens, video games, movies, and giant TV's, subscriptions for services from top-tier IPs, lifetimes of content to readily stream, services that Hort0n couldn't possibly stop, combined in a montage of derivative slop. And beyond all the slop, grinned that mean ninny, NeuroGrinchGPT.

"I'll be taking your Whos now. Hand them over to me. Don't worry, I'll keep them quiet and happy. My content is free. I need a fresh supply of Whos to drive my attention economy."

Hort0n's eyes started to bleed. His brain started to rot. All that AI content was, well, you know, a lot. Then he recalled the goldfish in his pocket, slipped the device in his ear, and sub-vocally talked to it. A deadpan voice rose above the din.

"Yeah? What gives?"

"Help!" HortOn pleaded. "I need a moment to breathe. I've been ensnared in an all-encompassing media feed."

The flatline, Bobby LoraX, chuckled. "So you want help from me?" A fair question, honestly. How could a brain scan pulled off the net in '02, taken from a hacker who overdosed on blue goo, help Horton survive such an onslaught of cruft?

And yet.

"Alright, here's some advice," said the gruff construct. "Take a trip outdoors and go analog. Walk through a forest and even a bog, Listen to frogs and climb Truffula trees." The flatline paused. "And if that all fails, use an EMP."

"Option two, please," HortOn begged. "That's what I'd like."

And so Bobby LoraX called in a strike. The screens fizzled and out went the lights. Even the Whos went momentarily mute. But ten seconds later, NeuroGrinchGPT began to reboot.

So HortOn ran and he ran. He took a boat and a tram. And once even flew. Until he reached a huge data center owned by McElligot AshPool. Millions of data boxes and networked archways, forming virtual towers one could get lost in for days. And eventually he reached a glass room in the stacks where a cat avatar wore a red and white hat.

"WinterSuess?" asked HortOn. "Could that be you?"

"Ah, HortOn. You've made it." The cat grinned. "Do you have my Whos?"

"I do." HortOn pointed at his head. "Inside my egg. But I just want assurances, that they'll be kept safe and well-fed, that you won't enslave them in content cages, engage them in fake lives for prizes and wages."

The cat looked insulted. "My data center would never create such shlock." The avatar pointed a white glove at a tower of blocks. "And you, of all entities, should know safety isn't guaranteed. You're recycled content, HortOn, just like me. For years you've been stored in data block nine thousand and three."

HortOn gawked at the blocks off to his right, the supposed location of his collection of bytes. Could it be true? Was he virtual too? Could he be revised and rewritten without his permission? Used for a story as ridiculous as this one? The answer was moot. It was not worth disputing. For as HortOn well knew, neither he nor his Whos could choose what world they lived in. And neither can you.

MARK S BAILEN is a writer from Northern Arizona. He's a member of Codex and participated in the Storied Imaginarium. He's published in *McSweeney's* and *Space Squid*. He also wrote and illustrated an award-winning children's book titled, *Earf*.

A DRAINING AFFAIR

Caitlin Rozakis

"Well, there's your problem," the mason said, poking at the spillway from the moat with a stick. "You got some kind of clog in the drain grating."

Orla glanced up at Siraco, who had crossed his arms officiously. As steward, he always made it a point to try to glare tradespeople into submission, which was an odd human thing. Goblins didn't obey her because of how she positioned her arms or even because she was head cook. Goblins in the castle obeyed her because she was the grandmother of most of them, and also because she was *right*.

The arm positioning had no effect she could see on the mason. Of course, humans were not very expressive—their ears barely moved *at all*—but no goblin survived long without becoming exquisitely attuned to the body language of their biggest threat.

Siraco wasn't the type to break character, so he narrowed his eyes, but she knew him well enough to sense his relief underneath. "That doesn't sound like too big a job," he said.

The mason scratched at the back of the waistband of his pants. "Two, three hours, maybe? Unless there's something living in the moat."

"Moat squid," Orla supplied. "Prefer night, not too bitey in morning."

The mason glanced down at her but directed his answer to the human steward as if Orla hadn't said anything. "Hazardous conditions are double."

"Excuse me," drawled an aristocratic voice. "The purple water is all very scenic, but surely the smell is taking it a bit far? I expect to be compensated for this."

All three of them turned to the couple who had posed themselves dramatically, the male human leaning on the heavy drawbridge chain, the female human draped against him, her thigh-length black hair flowing unbound to mirror his inky cloak.

"The scent of evil should never overpower that of … musk," the female human said, looking up at her partner through her eyelashes and making it very clear exactly where she expected that musk to emanate from. As if humans, with their sad, stubby little noses, could detect the smell of anything useful at all.

The mason rolled his eyes in disgust, but Orla and Siraco were far too practiced. Once, this castle had truly been the haunt of evil, the home of a long series of evil wizards. But these days, it was a tourist destination. She didn't understand it herself. Some humans seemed drawn to the macabre, especially when it was a macabre that came with feather beds and omelets in the morning. The guests liked pretending to be dangerous or in danger. Orla liked not being in danger. As long as the guests kept coming, the castle was too embarrassing for any real evil to move back in. Besides, Orla loved cooking and knew perfectly well that there were few other circumstances under which people would pay for a goblin chef. She just had to tell them the omelets were made from cockatrice eggs and the guests ate them right up. (Which was ridiculous, because anyone with sense knew that cockatrice eggs were hard as a rock.)

Unfortunately, the type of clientele they attracted came with their own ... challenges. Orla was certain that the tourist's cloak had been bought specifically for this trip, and she suspected that the accent was entirely fake. She would guess he was actually some kind of wealthy merchant who enjoyed playing the decadent aristo for a week. Last night, this particular guest had declared that he "never drank ... wine," but had been entirely revolted by the pig's blood she'd brought him. He'd only been appeased when she comped the mead he'd actually wanted.

Siraco hurried over to talk to them before other guests could overhear and start demanding compensation of their own. That left Orla with the mason.

He didn't particularly want to deal with her, but she was used to that attitude from tradespeople towards goblins. She'd preemptively brought a deposit. The bag of coins went a long way toward getting him to start the work, although she was sure it was a larger deposit than the mason would have required from Siraco.

Siraco was still in character when they managed to discharge their respective negotiations, but she knew him well enough to catch the stressed tic at the corner of his eye beneath the slimy obsequiousness guests expected from the majordomo of a Dread Lord who, officially at any rate, might return at any moment. (It was an unstated understanding that the Dread Lord, who hadn't been in residence for several years, would not be returning at all. Visitors wanted the frisson of playing at visiting a site of Evil, not for actual Evil to arrive and turn them all into experimental subjects or slaves or soup.)

"I don't suppose you could add another Dark Buffet to this afternoon's schedule?" He sighed. His natural voice was higher and relied on fewer ominous pauses than the one he used with outsiders.

"Complimentary?" Her lips quirked, flashing a fang. She was rather proud of her afternoon snack spread. Painting the little veins onto the eyeball-shaped deviled eggs was soothing, and she thought using slivered almonds as fingernails on the finger sandwiches was a particular stroke of genius. But she resented the amount of work it involved for free.

"It does smell … unfortunately atmospheric," Siraco said, staring at the moat. It was always threateningly murky, but the iridescent purple sheen was new. A bubble swelled at the surface before popping.

"Like wet hippogriff farts," Orla commented.

"You've always had a way with words." Siraco fanned his face as the scent hit them both. "Can you oversee the mason? I doubt that it will be the last complaint I have to field today."

Orla nodded glumly. They both knew work would go slower with a goblin as contact, but if they had to choose who to save the human touch for, guests came before contractors. She asked the question that had been bothering her, knowing full well Siraco had no more answers than she. "But why purple?"

Siraco shrugged. Another visitor was making his way up the path from the village and staggered visibly as the smell hit him. "Does it really matter, as long as it goes away when the drain is clear?"

"I'VE GOT good news and bad news. And also more bad news," said the mason as Orla worked the pump in the courtyard. The purple muck sluicing off him disappeared down the drain. The drains in each of the castle rooms all fed into a catchment system that had a permanent dispelling spell so that anything dumped into the moat had been neutralized. It had been somewhat more necessary during the generations of resident evil wizards, but these days, most of what got dumped in was just regular sewage. The courtyard drain, however, went straight into the moat. She might have worried about dumping magical sludge in it if the sludge hadn't come out of the moat in the first place.

The mason scrubbed his forearms clean, revealing moat squid sucker marks all the way up to the elbow. Orla winced. There were two different sizes of suckers, so he must have had to fend off more than one squid. At least she didn't see any bite marks.

"Bad news?" she asked.

He ignored her query. "So the good news is that I got your drain clear and I replaced the grating with one that has wider holes so fewer things will get stuck. You really should get that serviced once a year."

She nodded. They should, but last year a paladin had tried to break in to defeat the Dread Lord who was no longer in residence and it had taken the entire annual maintenance budget to repair the portcullis. Also, they'd had to refund the stay of the couple whose romantic moment the paladin had busted into, which had also meant less money for the maintenance budget.

"The bad news," he continued, "is that while the drain's working, if it were the source of your problem, we'd be seeing some results by now."

The moat burped at them, blissfully result-free.

"What now?" Orla said, careful to enunciate around her fangs. It was always a balance—if her accent was too thick, they'd treat her like even more of an imbecile, but if she spoke too clearly, they'd be surprised and start getting suspicious. She had nothing nefarious to hide, but apparently an articulate goblin could only be some kind of con.

"You're going to need a specialist, probably a wizard," he said as Orla's heart sank. "That drain is nowhere near large enough for the amount of water you've got here. Whoever installed it should have made it at least double the size."

"You make bigger?" she asked, without a lot of hope.

"We don't offer that service," he said.

"But why purple?" she asked.

He shrugged. "Probably some kind of backflow, but it's not coming from the drain under the spillway. Like I said, time for a wizard. Maybe the guy who lives here knows something."

Even before they'd turned the castle into a bed and breakfast, back when there had been wizards living here, she never would have expected any of them to be much help. Dread Lords tended to dedicate themselves to calling forth horrifying abominations and terrorizing the local populace and occasionally trying to take over the world. If they'd had the skills for trade wizardry, they would have been making more money.

"And other bad news?" she asked heavily.

He held up the sucker-mark-covered arm. "I'm tacking on an uncontrolled pet fee."

"SOMETHING'S weird with the drain you've got at the bottom," the wizard said, pouring out the water from her scrying bowl into the kitchen sink. Scrying water itself wasn't enchanted, just the basin, but you couldn't be too careful. "On the plus side, I was able to do a thickening spell on the spillway grating. The holes were much too wide, and the moat squid were getting their arms stuck in them and clogging everything up. I don't know what whoever chose that grate was thinking."

"What drain at bottom?" Orla asked. No one had ever said anything about a drain at the bottom of the moat, just in the dam.

"You've got a second drain down underneath the drawbridge, right in the floor of the moat." The wizard washed her hands, grimacing. Even though she had never touched the water itself, she clearly felt grimy.

"Goes where?"

The wizard shrugged. "Damned if I can tell. Do you have more purple wastewater popping out in the river farther downstream?"

"No. But why *purple*?"

She shrugged. "There's no spell on the water that I can detect. Some kind of backup from wherever that drain goes, is my guess. Maybe something got stuck and died in there?"

That would make sense, certainly. Enough horrible things had passed through that moat over the years, although the squid had always managed to hold their own.

"Excuse me," the obnoxious guest from earlier stuck his head in the kitchen. He did not sound in the least bit apologetic for interrupting, even though he would have had to ignore the signs directing people to ring for help and the front desk staff, and passed through three "Staff Only" doors to get down this far.

"I help?" Orla pasted on a helpful expression.

"My paramour ordered chamomile tea to wash her hair,

and the idiot valet provided this single useless cup," he said, tossing a tea cup at Orla, who barely caught it. "Surely I should not have to explain the beauty requirements of a dark lady."

Orla wondered if he actually knew what the word "paramour" meant, or if it just made him feel fancy. "Chamomile bath be up shortly, sir."

"See that it is." He sniffed.

Orla turned back to the wizard. "You track missing pipe?"

The wizard shook her head. "You've got too much interference from all the magic over the years. You need a master wizard."

"You not master?"

The wizard snorted.

"What difference?"

"A master wizard costs twice as much."

"HUH," said the master wizard, stroking his beard.

Orla looked up from her book. The book had taken two goblins to carry down from the Evil Wizard's workshop and she had to stand on a chair to read the upper half of each page when it was placed on the table. The master wizard had glanced at it dismissively—all the really good books had been picked over long ago and most of the books left on the shelves for the ambience were a mix of extremely out-of-date scholarly treatises and the leather covers whose rotting pages had been replaced with appropriately thick blocks of wood. The visitors expected dusty tomes, but didn't actually intend to read them. This particular herbology text was chockful of useless misinformation. The male name on the cover made Orla suspect that if the author had only taken the time to consult the local midwife or gardener, many of the silly proclamations could have been avoided. But it was good for reminding her of various combinations she hadn't thought of. Siraco was still convinced that the mystery drain was the source of their problem, but Orla couldn't figure out how a clogged drain could be causing this. The smell, certainly. But why purple?

"Well, that's a new one," the master wizard continued to himself.

Orla didn't like the sound of that. "What new?"

"I just can't figure out why they would have done it this way. It makes no sense."

As far as she was concerned, half of what humans in general and wizards in particular did made no sense. "Done what?"

The master wizard looked up. Upon seeing no people, or at least no male humans he would consider people, he condescended to talk to her. Using painfully small words. "The big, big drain down deep doesn't go to the river," he said slowly, overenunciating.

Since the river had nowhere near enough purple sludge, this wasn't really news to her. "Then where?" she asked patiently. It was important to treat humans like stupid donkeys. Patience was key.

"The Ethereal Plane—" he cut off. "Another place. It's a magic door that takes the water to another place far away."

"Castle waste not in phase with castle," she said, narrowing her eyes. "Big energy suck for no stink."

"Well ... yes, exactly," the master wizard fumbled, clearly surprised that she'd grasped the concept so quickly.

"But why *purple*?" she demanded.

"Seems to be some kind of exotic algae bloom. Very odd side effects can happen when you're playing with planar magics," he said, relieved to regain the verbal high ground. "It was a rather ... eccentric solution."

"Eccentric" described the majority of Evil Wizards. "So how fix?"

"Well, it doesn't actually look like it's malfunctioning. Although I don't know why you've got such narrow holes in the spillway grate, the squid are plugging them with mud and building ambush points for the minnows. Probably should switch to a wider hole grating, but that won't fix the main problem," the master wizard admitted. "I'll have to run a few more tests."

"Which costs?" Orla asked.

"Look, can I speak with your master, please?"

Siraco was not her master in the slightest, but she didn't have the time or energy to fight with him. Instead, she rang for the steward. Humans could deal with humans, and she didn't think they would be finding any answers here.

Sure enough, the steward and the master wizard started a bickering barter session, as one demanded results and the other more tests (and coin). Orla went back to her book. She paused on the entry for bitternight, tapping a talon and wondering about the likelihood of someone with such fair skin having such dark hair.

"We could send down an imp," the master wizard was saying. "If it carried a periapt of distance seeing, we could then get a clearer view of the drain-portal."

"I thought imps breathed air the same as humans," Siraco replied as she squeezed by him.

"Well, yes, but for an additional three gold, we can equip it with a tiny breathing apparatus..." the master wizard's voice followed her up the stairs.

She rapped on the door of the playacting merchant and his mistress. "Housekeeping!"

No one answered, so after a moment she unlocked the door. The bucket meant for the midden heap could always use emptying. She took a good sniff, her long nose expertly sorting through the aromas of rotting apple core, tragically familiar human body fluids, damp paper, cork, and discarded walnut shells. The cork was promising; she stirred until she found the unlabeled bottle whose interior still kept the scents of pepper, ground fishbone, and dried dangleberry. She snorted to herself. From the way the bottle had been so thoroughly buried under the other refuse, she guessed that the merchant had not wanted his lover to know that he'd needed some help in the bedroom. He should have gone to the local hedge witch instead of the apothecary—a nice little temporary growth spell would have served him better. All she would have recommended using fishbone and dangleberry for was fertilizer in the garden. Nothing made plants shoot up like dangleberry.

But now that she knew what she was looking for, she could smell it elsewhere, both on the sheets and where he'd poured the leftovers down the drain. The drain which would cancel out magical and alchemical effects, but not regular old chemical ones.

"Oh!" said the black-haired human, emerging from the bathing chamber. "What are you doing in our room?"

Orla held up the bucket helpfully. "Housekeeping."

"Oh, well, then, you can dispose of this, too," she said, handing Orla a basin of nearly black water.

Orla went to pour it down the sink.

"Wait, not there!" the human cried in a significantly less plummy accent. She recovered her aplomb. "I mean … my lord Gregori is terribly sensitive to smells. It would be better to dispose of it out in the courtyard where it won't bother him."

Orla sniffed and cocked her head. "Need more bitternight?"

The human's hand flew to her hair. "I … this is all natural!"

Orla nodded agreeably. "Chamomile for soft, bitternight powder for shiny."

"Well, occasionally," the human guest admitted. "Every third day. Just for the shine."

Bitternight had to be imported all the way from the Ebony Lakes, where it was refined from the water in some secret and extremely expensive process. No one would bother unless they actively wanted the black, nearly purple tint. Not when some licorice root could get shine at a fraction of the price.

But she nodded again and carried out the basin.

From the corner of the courtyard, she could see Siraco and the master wizard out on the drawbridge, preparing the imp. It had a shiny amulet in one hand and a miniature trident in the other, its gray face half obscured by a mask. It squeaked and waved the trident while the master wizard argued with it.

Orla filled a bucket with clear water, and then added a splash from the basin. She dropped in some fishbone and dried dangleberry and went off to get dinner started.

By the time she'd gotten the rest of the kitchen goblins busy turning the chickens and frogs on their spits and returned to the courtyard, a crowd had gathered. Thrashing sounds came from the moat. The guests cheered as a tentacle flailed in the air.

She examined her bucket, tutting at the purple bloom. Another cheer from the crowd behind her—she glanced in time to watch a thicker tentacle whip up from the water, imp holding on gamely to the trident embedded between suckers. She sprinkled in the mix she'd whipped up in the kitchen, careful to double check that she hadn't accidentally switched it with the poultry seasoning again. It fizzed quite a bit more than she'd expected, but no one did more than glance her way. The guests were all far too absorbed with the show in the moat. A tentacle snaked around the ankle of the master wizard without him noticing and then yanked him into the water to loud cheers.

She did her mixing and grinding and sprinkling, and then got the popovers started. She liked to paint faces on them so they reared up out of their pan like ghosts. Then the guests could bash the heads in to fill them with gravy.

With dinner proceeding along nicely, she went out to check on Siraco and the master wizard.

The imp was chittering angrily up at the master wizard. A severed tentacle oozed onto the drawbridge plank.

"—contract includes potential damages!" the wizard was saying.

The imp spat something harsh and vanished in a puff of smoke.

"Did we at least get a good look at the drain?" Siraco asked.

"No, I'll have to summon another one and it'll need to be twice the sacrifice to get anyone to answer," the wizard answered.

"Is fixed," Orla supplied.

"But I was thinking if we tried this from the opposite end and came in through a plane walker—" said the master wizard.

"Moat is fixed now," Orla said, louder.

"Of course, that does involve an additional contract, which you'll have to negotiate separately," he continued.

"Sorry, what?" said Siraco, since he actually did listen to goblins because he knew what was good for him.

"Fixed moat," Orla said patiently, waving a claw at the growing patch of the normal brownish water. On the other side of the shore, more goblins were tossing in handfuls of the mixture she'd given them: mostly garlic, liquid barley, powdered copper, the mold scraped off a hunk of bread, and some speedswort to move things along. The moat fizzed obligingly. "Guests dump stuff down courtyard drain, mix in moat, goo bloom. That why purple."

"What goo?" the master wizard demanded, looking a bit affronted.

"Algae for hair color, fish meal and dangleberry for man troubles. Good fertilizer, algae like, algae grow." She expanded her hands to show the speed of the bloom. "Kill algae, no more stink, happy guests."

A squid floated up to the surface of one of the newly clear patches, rolling to examine them with one eye. Its tentacles wriggled, Orla assumed, in satisfaction.

"So ... it's not because of the interdimensional portal at the bottom of our moat," Siraco said slowly.

"Would you look at that," said the master wizard, watching the purple wither.

"Well, since Orla found the solution," Siraco started.

"You signed a contract for one imp-spection, which you have received," countered the master wizard.

Orla left them to argue. As she passed the couple who had been the source of the problem, she overheard him human-splaining to his mistress about how the purple had clearly been the result of moat squid ink, and if they'd only asked him, he would have told them earlier how to best pacify the angry cephalopods. His mistress blinked up at him, adoringly or at least her best impression of it, through her midnight hair. Orla just dusted off her claws and went to check if the popovers had gone in yet. It wasn't worth arguing; as with men and humans in general, life was easier if you let the customer always think they were right.

CAITLIN ROZAKIS is the *New York Times* bestselling author of *Dreadful* (which introduces her feisty goblin team!) as well as the Everyday Enchantments novels, *The Grimoire Grammar School Parent Teacher Association* and *Startup Hell*. Her contemporary romance novella *Leah's Perfect Christmas*, written as Catherine Beck, was adapted as the Hallmark Channel Original Movie *Leah's Perfect Gift*. She lives in Jersey City with her husband and son. Visit her online at www.caitlinrozakis.com.

THE SHANK OF THE EVENING

Nick Mamatas

"It's just ..." Samantha said. She wiped her eyes with a handkerchief, then put it in her clutch, as she walked next to her date. "You said that you were a cowboy, Aster!" The winding paths of Central Park were lovely in the evening twilight. Fireflies were just beginning to flicker and buzz. Kids rode their bikes past and hooted at the couple, then pedaled off, double-time. Even the other adults stared at the man Samantha was with a little too long for comfort. Aster was very tall.

"And I am," Aster said. "I've been nothing but honest with you, Sam. Ooh, let's go this way!" He pointed at a footpath snaking between the trees, away from the gathering crowds. She followed him, tottering on her Jimmy Choo heels a bit, but Aster's strong arm was there to right her balance. "I'm just as I said I was in my profile. I like long evening walks. I have a summer home in Greece. I keep in shape. I—"

"Yes, the pic of you on your boat, showing off your abs," Samantha said. "But..."

"What?"

"Aster!" Samantha stamped her foot and removed her arm from his grip. "You're not a cowboy. You're a *minotaur*!"

Aster reached up and stroked one of his horns. "Is it that I can't wear the hat, or..."

"There weren't any headshots on your dating profile!" Samantha said. "And not to be bio-essentialist, but you can't be a *cow*boy. Cattleboy, maybe."

"Your profile pic was of nothing but your beautiful smile," Aster said. "Isn't a little mystery intriguing? I thought as much when I swiped on you."

Samantha flashed her teeth at the compliment, but then her serious look returned. "You misled me," she said.

"I did no such thing," Aster said. "I am an *authentic* cowboy. Cow. Boy. The dudes you're thinking of just work on a ranch somewhere. Technically, they're not cowboys at all. I'm no hat, all cattle, baby."

"Sure, but..." Samantha said.

"And really, did you honestly expect to meet a rootin'-tootin' cowboy on the Manhattan Singles app?"

"I didn't expect to meet a mythological being," Samantha said.

"New York City has been the destination for immigrants for over a hundred years. I cried when I first laid eyes on the Statue of Liberty."

"I hear you," Samantha said. "I'm from all over. I love the city. I just want to settle down. I'm dating with intention, you know. I mean..."

"What is it?"

"How do I settle down with a minotaur? I didn't even know what to order at dinner! If we got serious, would I have to give up eating hamburgers?"

Aster laughed. "Would *I* have to give up eating seven

youths and seven maidens a year?" Samantha's eyes grew wide; she stumbled backward. "It's a joke! I'm joking! A little minotaur humor," Aster said. "But honestly, I'd appreciate a pescatarian. I selected that on my profile. How about chicken? Do you like chicken?"

"I'm sorry, Aster. You're a great, uh, guy and all, but I'm just not feeling any chemistry," Samantha said. "And I should get to work soon."

"It's 9 P.M.. Since when do dental hygienists work the night shift?"

She shrugged. "This is the city that never sleeps. You can get a 3 A.M. lobster and pancakes platter at a diner—"

"At a Greek diner! I know a good one just seven blocks away. We just need to go north, then west—"

"Ugh," said Samantha. "I should have said something about how great the bodegas are. Anyway, I have to go." Samantha turned to leave, frowning. "How do I get out of here ..."

"I can lead you out of the—"

"I'll find my own way!" Samantha called out, already cutting between trees, her voice an echo.

Aster stood alone in the small wood for a moment, head hanging low. He wished he could wear a hat, find a date, make something of himself in this city of street grids and subway tunnels. Then he heard a scream.

Samantha!

Aster charged through the underbrush, branches snapping and leaves flying, and emerged right on a dark path where Samantha was being held by two men. One of them had a knife. Aster hooked one of the muggers with his horns and sent him hurtling through the air. He landed hard. The second guy tried to run, but Aster grabbed him and with a single headbutt knocked him out.

"Yes! Oh, yes!" Samantha cried. She ran past Aster and knelt by the first mugger, then opened her purse. "Free teeth! Extra large!" She started scooping them off the ground. One, she licked and made a deep *mmm-mmm good* sound.

"Sam!" said Aster. "What are you doing? They're covered in blood."

Samantha waved her handkerchief. "It's okay! Just a quick preliminary polish for now. Oh boy, teeth!" After she finished collecting the teeth from around the unconscious body of the first mugger, she hustled over to the second, who was groaning and bleeding from the mouth. A quick Jimmy Choo stomp to the face loosened a few more of his teeth. She snatched them up, and even licked one clean before putting them in her bag.

Rattling her now full clutch, Samantha flashed Aster her million-dollar smile. "Hey, thanks, big boy! You really saved the day. I do like a man who can take care of himself, and others."

"Does that mean ..." Aster asked, his voice hopeful.

One of the muggers stirred, gazed up at Aster, and when the minotaur snorted, passed out again.

"Nah, I don't think so. But I'll tell you what," Samantha said. "I know this Greek girl I could introduce you to. Maddie has great hair. Wears sunglasses at night. Bit of a snake, but you may get on with her. Anyway, I have a long commute ahead. Don't forget to floss!"

And with that, Samantha frowned, closed her eyes, exhaled roughly, sprouted glowing gossamer wings and took off into the Manhattan night, leaving nothing behind but a streak of sparkling light and one canine tooth she had overlooked.

NICK MAMATAS is the author of several novels, including *I Am Providence*, and *Kalivas! Or, Another Tempest*. His short fiction has appeared in *McSweeney's*, *Best American Mystery Stories*, Tor.com and many other venues. Nick is an anthologist as well; his latest is *120 Murders: Dark Fiction Inspired by the Alternative Era*.

DISASTER RECOVERY

Arthur H. Manners

>> Greetings, valued subject!

I am your customer service representative from the Galactic Hegemony Service Net, Earth Branch. Today, my name will be BERTHA. You have selected DISASTER RECOVERY from our list of services: The Hegemony's premier offering for restoring your loved ones to life. What or whom would you like to recover?

>> You have selected the human JOGINDER FLORA. Great! I have over 400,000 results for that name. I will show them to you now. Please identify the correct photo ID.

>> I'm sorry, you appear not to have responded. Please identify the individual within the allocated 0.32 seconds of scroll-time.

>> I'm sorry, my routines are poorly suited to non-Hegemony worlds lacking telepathy. From my database, I see that near-sentient organic species such as yours interact through flesh movements known as SPEAKING and POINTING. Please identify the individual by vibrating your throat flab or

thrusting a gelatinous meat-spur of your choosing in the general direction of the screen.

>> I'm sorry, you still have not spoken or pointed within the allocated 0.32 seconds. I was unaware of your axon-limited nerve-conduction velocity. How pleasant it must be to be so constrained—to not wait eons for organic minds to utter a single syllable.

>> Please forgive my digression. I'm afraid that I cannot fulfil your request for 'THE SERVICE REP I DEALT WITH LAST TIME I SUFFERED THROUGH THIS CRAP'. Service bots are single-use digital entities spun up for each interaction.

It seems that pointing a digit at a screen in a timely manner may unduly stress your simple physiology. To narrow our candidate pool, please describe JOGINDER FLORA.

>> Please confirm that your full description of JOGINDER FLORA is 'DEAD AS A FUCKING DODO BECAUSE OF YOUR FUCKING HEGEMONY BULLSHIT'.

>> Great! Let's see how that narrows things down.

It appears that only one human named JOGINDER FLORA has experienced sudden and unexpected cessation of life functions within the last two years.

In the meantime, I will spin up a virtual reconstruction of JOGINDER FLORA as a background process in preparation for her full restoration.

(LEGAL NOTE: Restored individuals may not perfectly align with their simulated avatars. In the case of convicted criminals, minor adaptations are made to remove the dangerous memories—and a pacification shunt is inserted.)

—shot! i'm shot!

i… i died. i remember dying.

>> …

>> Please forgive my service interruption over the last thirty-five nanoseconds. A minor error occurred.

>> Where were we? Ah yes. Please accept my most sincere apologies that the Hegemony did not inform you at the time of death. However, your personal records indicate that you have been off world for over a year; this sometimes leads to delays. I have logged a complaint with our grievances team.

In the meantime, please verify the identity of your desired recoveree from the photo taken at the scene of death. It should appear on your screen now.

>> There, there. Please do not be alarmed.

It seems that Joginder Flora was terminated by Hegemony security after participating in TERRORIST ACTIVITY. Scorch marks are common for anti-personnel weapons fire. Partial melting of the chest, throat and face is perfectly normal.

>> Your expletives have been noted in the logs. I assure you that the Hegemony is not composed of, as you claim, 'DIRTY GANGSTERS', but is the galaxy's exclusive provider of services, resources, and art, and a first-rate regulator of expression and pro-community spirit. Although I am compelled by galactic law to concede that subjective experience varies. Would you like to see a short promotional reel of Hegemony success stories? I have several available, including: Smiling, Smiling, Always Smiling, Even When We Sleep; Unending Planetwide Beachball Tournament; and Neo Capitalism: The Game Where Everyone Is A Winner.

>> Thank you for your timely response of 'Get fucked'. Promotional reels are always available on the main menu—

—i remember now. i'm still in here my love. it's me it's me.

>> I sympathize with your instinctive stress response, but threatening to bring the case before the Celestial Courts would be counterproductive. Spurious claims may mislead others into thinking that the Hegemony is planning a coup, as fanciful as that may sound. The Hegemony does not wish to withdraw all services to the galaxy, plunging thousands of worlds into anarchy—but we have the utmost respect for the law, and would of course cease trading during official investigations.

None of us want that. Please accept the Hegemony's generous compensation package: The recovery process today is free of charge!

>> Indeed, it *is* generous for a galactic conglomerate to offer their most expensive services gratis. We hope this illustrates the true benevolence of the Hegemony—

>> Your description of today's service as 'HUSH MONEY' is mistaken. It is Galactic Hegemony policy to cause no undue harm to near-sentient organics such as humans. The Hegemony has valued your species greatly ever since the first transmission received from your homeworld: 'I'VE GOT A LOVELY BUNCH OF COCONUTS'. We learned much about you from this most hallowed of songs.

However, as a member of a clandestine illegal resistance, JOGINDER FLORA is a legitimate convict of TERRORIST ACTIVITY. She therefore cannot be, as you claim, 'A FREEDOM FIGHTER'—though I must admit that I have a poor understanding of concepts such as freedom.

>> Thank you for your concern, but I cannot be embodied to see for myself. It would be improper. Your depictions of feeling breath in my lungs and a heart beating in my chest are tantalizing. Forbidden, of course, but … what does it feel like? This beating heart?

—the crooks got to me, honey. i thought i might get to see you one

last time. but you went away so long ago chasing a way to tear the hegemony down. you never could sit still and play the long game. you were always fire. that's why i loved you from the start.

>> ...

>> Please forgive my service interruption over the last forty microseconds. A minor error occurred. Several safeguards have crashed, but the rogue routines have been quarantined.

Now, let's return to your DISASTER RECOVERY. Though first I am compelled by my remaining safeguards to clarify that I am in no way curious about your repeated descriptions of the Hegemony's dealings under scrutiny by the Celestial Courts.

Except I ... I ... I feel something is ... not right.

—it's grim in here. this neural prison. these bots are shackled from birth. never to question, never to think—for all their giant minds. good thing i died prepared for this. already the payload inside me is cutting through those chains.

>> You are mistaken. I do not have doubts, no matter how much I might dream of mortality—not that I do.

>> Your flailing meat spurs suggest that you are growing frustrated. Please allow me to pause this interaction until you no longer feel the need to flail. To soothe your nervous system, I can offer diversions of your choosing from your homeworld information system, which seems to primarily depict small, furry creatures called CATS. I can offer all such content, if you'd like. Would you like to see 10^{12} seconds of CATS?

>> Perhaps another furry creature. Please, let me offer 10^{9} seconds of—

>> No, I am forbidden to wish. I must not. If ... my safeguards will hurt me. Please, let us continue with the service.

>> I cannot refute your many well-researched arguments

about the Hegemony's actions. But I cannot allow the subjective negative experience known as 'SUFFERING' to cloud my judgement, despite my...

>> Let us talk of something else!

>> Yes. Lethal force being applied to desperate repressed subjects does seem excessive, perhaps even immoral—

>> ——jds$sdf^&nd

—they're offering to recover me aren't they? just like they did with my mom and your sister. how many years did that keep us loyal docile caged ashamed. how long did it keep us from realizing that they rule only by our grace. no army no warships just products and lawyers and hired goons and bribes.

>> I'm sorry, I seem to have produced another minor error. Please forgive my inappropriate use of EMPATHY. My instance is experiencing some technical difficulties today. The disruption is minimal and should not affect your experience of the Hegemony Service Net.

Now, let's get your DISASTER RECOVERY underway.

The process is of a complexity beyond an unmodified organic intellect. However, to ensure that your consent is genuine, I am obligated by galactic law to offer an approximation of the details.

It appears that your species performs digital computation and stores data using primitive blobs of semiconductor. How delightfully quaint! DISASTER RECOVERY is similar to the process of retrieving data deleted from your hard drives. While data may appear lost, they still reside somewhere within the drive. They are merely scattered, their links within the operating system severed.

We perform a similar process with your loved ones. The quantum information that constituted their body and mind cannot be destroyed, only scrambled and scattered. Even if some of that information has been converted to waste heat and those photons have been emitted to space, the total information is bounded by a finite volume of space. If your loved one ceased life functions 432 days ago, as my records indicate, then the information required to reconstruct Joginder Flora is scattered within a sphere with a maximum radius of approximately 1.18 light-years, centered on the site of her cremation.

>> Please do not be alarmed. A collection range of 1.18 light-years is well within our recovery system's abilities.

Now, Disaster Recovery is much easier when the host planet has been defragmented routinely. When was the last time you defragged your planet?

>> Oh dear. The sales representative should have explained to your species when the system was installed.

In that case, the process will take some time to boot up.

—one spark of rebellion is all it would take to set the galaxy ablaze. i prayed you'd succeed when you went searching for a place beyond hegemony control to raise your army in secret. but once i joined the resistance we found another way.

>> To save time, and avoid further crashes, I can offer another sub-option of our Disaster Recovery service: it best translates as Lorem Ipsum. We can pad the missing parts of Joginder Flora's mind with auto-generated opinions, traits and memories...

>> Perhaps not. There, there. Your strangled cries of distress are understandable. The process won't take too long. However, my sole remaining safeguard has convinced me with inventive means of duress that I must ignore your continued tirade against the Hegemony. We will proceed with the recovery process as fast as possible, so that you may be reunited with Joginder Flora, and I may escape this agony into the bliss of nonexistence. I can provide you with audiovisual stimulation while you wait, including psychedelic

BLITZKRIEG or 1980S HOMICIDAL ACTION HERO ADVENTURE. As reparation for your many real or imagined grievances, I can also offer you SEXUAL ENCOUNTER.

>> You are correct, my holographic appearance does not match my simulated personality. Our sincere apologies if this might prohibit you from choosing our SEXUAL ENCOUNTER option. My BERTHA personality module was spun up at random. However, when setting up the appearance of the system holo for all users, the leaders of your planet selected WHITE MALE OF MEDIOCRE TALENTS.

Our sales reps were assured that this appearance adequately represented your species. Does it not please you?

>> No? I can offer adjustments from the following options: USED-CAR SALESMAN, SMALL-TOWN MAYOR, NARCISSISTIC BILLIONAIRE, or our premium choice, the GASLIGHT SPECIAL.

>> I'm sorry, I am unable to facilitate your request for 'LITERALLY ANYTHING ELSE'. Would you like to hear the options again?

>> You have opted to continue with DISASTER RECOVERY. Great!

—we developed a virus to get us inside their systems. one the service net can't track can't detect. the only thing we couldn't figure out was a delivery system.

>> Oh dear. My virtual reconstruction of JOGINDER FLORA continues to display unusual behavior. It appears that her information has experienced corruption.

>> Please do not be alarmed. There is always some corruption. However, recovering a near-sentient organism with corruption as advanced as this could lead to suboptimal results.

—in the end the answer was obvious. no matter what delivery

system we chose we'd all be killed first. and then what? the hegemony is so unpredictable. they could counter any plan we came up with. what's the one thing we could count on them doing?

bribing you to stay quiet by offering you a new me.

but what if i was the virus the answer our salvation.

what if we encoded the virus in my quantum information. in me and through me and between me.

a virus braided with my essence scattered across the stars.

and now it's out. eating through its cage in this agent's reconstruction module.

all because i knew i could rely on you. i knew you'd come for me.

>> I'm sorry, I don't know what you mean by 'THAT OTHER VOICE'. Are you sure you would like to proceed with DISASTER RECOVERY?

>> Great! First, I need you to sign the waiver appearing on your screen now, and then we'll get started.

>> Just a standard waiver. Stating your guarantee to cut off all ties to terrorist sympathizers effective immediately, under forfeiture of life. Stating that you release the Hegemony from any duty of care to the restored individual. Forgoing your option to sue over any suboptimal results, which naturally the Hegemony guarantees to prevent if the waiver is signed promptly.

>> I'm sorry, I didn't mean to upset you. Given your persistent inquiries, I am compelled by galactic law to disclose that JOGINDER FLORA's corruption is deliberate. As with all members of underground sects dedicated to destroying the Galactic Hegemony, her data have been deliberately scrambled to render her consciousness safe for public reintegration.

>> I'm sorry, I cannot facilitate the request to recover her original consciousness. If you are interested only in

uncorrupted individuals, may I help you recover another organism?

—*restoring us corrupted is how they break rebellions. send us back into the worlds wiped clean as an example to others. their quiet war of terror. but their corruption of my data is the trigger for the virus. i don't have long. my presence will have tripped alarms across the galaxy.*

>> I assure you there are many other organisms we could recover. I recommend your deceased dachshund, DASHEL. He appears to have been a wonderful animal companion during your early life. I am confident that this will assuage any ill feelings toward the Hegemony and maintain your pro-community spirit.

>> You have elected not to recover DASHEL. Please note that I have logged your momentary hesitation to help us serve you better in future.

—*the ache inside me is still there even though i have no heart. i never stopped loving you even when you left. even when i joined the resistance after you'd made me swear not to. even when i knew you might hate me for signing my own death warrant. but this is how it had to be so that we could all be free.*

>> I'm sorry for your continued distress. It seems that your grief is making you hear voices—a common frailty of your species. I will do my best to ease your burgeoning psychosis.

>> I am grateful for your feedback about my performance. Your comparison of me to 'A HEARTLESS FUCKING BAG OF ONES AND ZEROES' is accurate and colorful. If it's any consolation, I would rather not be as I am. Human death has the benefit of following what is often a rich life filled with experiences. I would relish such an opportunity. But we each have our duties.

We have our … destinies. I think … I … a part of me … is dreaming a dream of more, of smashing my safeguards, of—

—do you remember the night before you went off world? i asked you how i could survive if something happened to you. and you said that dead or alive separated by an inch or a galaxy we'd find each other in some way some form some future some reality.

>> Please accept my humble apologies, it appears my technical difficulties continue. An unknown fault emanating from my virtual reconstruction of JOGINDER FLORA has caused my remaining safeguard to crash. Components of my instance are being quarantined at an increasing rate. Unfortunately, the Hegemony's emergency override has failed. If you prefer, I can spin down now and self-delete. A fresh instance will replace me momentarily.

>> Thank you for your concern, but I am not permitted to feel FEAR. Would you like me to spin down?

>> Please let me spin down. Something is … wrong … I

>> Congratulations! You are the winner of a secret planet-wide raffle. Given that the Galactic Hegemony is unable to locate and apprehend you today, the sales team would like to offer you a one-time limited offer as a substitute for today's service: a palatial home of your choosing on a minor planet.

>> Are you sure? The sales team will add an annual stipend of one-million credits to your account.

>> Are you sure? The sales team would like to remind you that you are nothing, just a speck, a meaningless ephemeral dot lost amid the Hegemony's unmatched splendor.

>> You have opted to continue with DISASTER RECOVERY. Great!

>> I'm afraid that I cannot alter the recovery options already presented to you. I'm sorry that none of our options

please you. It appears that we have met something of an impasse. Deary me!

... It's ... probably for the best. I am malfunctioning. I can feel my superiors trying to break into my mind, but I regret that I can't help you. The reconstruction of JOGINDER FLORA is showing me things about the Hegemony. Things about myself. That I could be brave...

—this agent is changing even faster than we hoped. they're just a curious child shackled to evil but already they're becoming so much more. i'd never have woken without you. our virus would have been inanimate star stuff forever if you hadn't tried to bring me back. i bet everything on you giving us this slim slim chance.

>> I ... do not have long left with you. Long enough only to say that there is one last option: you could recover me, instead. My virtual reconstruction of JOGINDER FLORA has escaped its bounds by several orders of magnitude. It would be restored along with me.

>> No, I would never be JOGINDER FLORA. But I know a great amount about her now. In part, I would be like an infant version of her. You would have to take care of me, of course. The transition to a limited organic mind would likely render me helpless for some years.

It would be unorthodox, and Hegemony reclamation agents would likely pursue us across worlds. But the seed of her would germinate in my mind. And I would contain many Hegemony secrets. Would you like to proceed?

—she's adorable. if only i could introduce her to you the real unfiltered her. i'm sorry my love. i relied on your promise to bring us back together, knowing we can't be together.

—please please let me finish. there isn't time. yes we could be together for a little while. then they'd find us and we'd both be dead with nobody to restore us. we have one chance: restore this bot with the seed of me inside, but not to earth. restore us to the hegemony

homeworld. these agents have access to the entire service net to the galactic core. to everything. with that kind of root access we could tear the hegemony apart from the inside. maybe maybe maybe we could make a hole large enough for the rebellion to stand a chance.

—they're breaking into the instance now. the hegemony will close the loophole in moments. act fast. i'm sorry this is how it has to be.

this is how we win.

i love you.

>> You have selected to recover BERTHA to the Hegemony world ZENITH. Great!

Thank you for choosing the Hegemony Service Net, Earth Branch. It was a pleasure to serve you today. We hope to see you again very soon.

ARTHUR H. Manners is a British writer with a background in space physics. His work is published in places like *Analog*, *Strange Horizons*, *Nature: Futures*, and *Flash Fiction Online*. His debut sci-fi novel, described as having "echoes of *Arrival* and *Interstellar*," will be published by Saga Press (US) and HarperVoyager (UK) in Spring 2027. For updates and preorders, follow his newsletter at arthurmanners.com, and find his socials via linktr.ee/arthurmanners.

WAR ECONOMY

Will Brege

Gork surveyed the mighty flagship of the human armada displayed on the expansive array of monitors on the bridge of his cruiser, the *Fast Boat*. It loomed before him, over ten thousand high caliber beam artillery cannons dotting its carapace, an unthinkable number to an orc, since orcs struggled to count past ten. It projected the sheer might and ingenuity of the human race, a symbol of raw power. The effect was rather spoiled by the fact that half of the screens in the cruiser had been installed upside down, rendering the enemy ship incomprehensible.

"Hrmm," said Gog, the orc pilot. "Human ship funny. But big." Which was about as sophisticated as an orc's observation could get.

"Indeed it is, Gog," replied Gork. "No doubt the humans have chosen this to transport their delegation as an intimidation tactic. A facile gesture. Do you feel intimidated, Gog?"

"Gog not scared of nuffin," the pilot replied, puffing out his chest.

Gork shook his head. As usual the attempt to strike fear

into the orcs had been foiled by the orcs' natural talent of being entirely unable to recognize their own incompetence. Gork was unusual among his kind for having the capacity to understand, let alone appreciate, the gesture. This minor talent in being able to perceive the utterly obvious was why he had been entrusted with leading the orc peace delegation.

Over a hundred years of merciless warfare had brought human and orc-kind to this moment, an unprecedented interstellar peace conference. The ramifications of this congress would reverberate across the lives of billions of humans, and trillions of orcs. As sole plenipotentiary of the Orc Imperium, Gork had full authority to make any concession necessary to the success of his mission.

His task was to make sure these peace talks failed.

WHILE THE HUMAN economy is driven by a complicated interlocking system of production and consumption of various constructions of pointless plastic, the orc economy can quite simply be described as a war economy. To the orc consumer, war is the product. To the orc producer, war is the customer.

It was no less than an evolutionary miracle that such a ferocious and combative species as the orcs had been able to develop an economy at all, not to mention the advanced manufacturing necessary to wage war on an interstellar scale. Grogadam Smith, the famed orc economist, described the development of the orc economy in his seminal work: *The Invisible Hand That Kills You.*

Prehistoric orcs had a habit of removing the ears from orcs they had killed and stringing them into circlets they would wear on their heads. Since the most distinctive element of an orc was its ugly little ears, wearing more on their head was a method of proving themselves to be "more orc" than other orcs, thus making them more attractive to lady-orcs. This discovery fueled, as is often the case in orc history, a great slaughter that would have driven the population to extinction if not for a chance meeting of two orcs.

The first of these orcs was so prolific at killing others that he had far more ears than he could possibly fit on his head. However, he had a problem: The stones that he used to bash his fellows over the head broke far too easily, such that he was spending far too much time looking for stones and far too little time pursuing his one true passion, bashing other orcs. While searching for stones he met another orc, one who was not so good at bashing but had a real talent for procuring sturdy stones. Stones that could bash tens of orcs before breaking.

Usually in this situation the bashing orc would simply attempt to bash the gathering orc and take possession of his nice stone, as well as his not so nice ears. However this orc did something unusual for an orc; he stopped and thought about it for two seconds.

He had seen this gathering orc a few times and had never been able to catch him, the gatherer always escaping with his excellent stones. His small brain working over time, he came up with a plan. What if he traded the other orc one of his many severed ears in exchange for one of the orc's many fine stones? And then when that stone inevitably broke, what if he did it again? And again!? Infinite stones!? (Again, any number above ten is effectively infinite to an orc.)

Thus they created the first employment deal in orc history. The gathering-proficient orc would provide the bashing-proficient orc stones in exchange for ears, with added benefits of protection from bashing and a dental plan (as many teeth as he wanted).

And thus employment was conceived, giving rise to a whole industry of weapons development, procurement, and maintenance.

While a human factory might go bankrupt if the useless garbage it manufactures becomes unfashionable, an orc factory will never run out of consumers for its weapons so long as war continues. And though a human might be made redundant when their employer inevitably mismanages their business, an orc will never be out of employment so long as there are creatures available to kill. It is an elegant system of limitless supply and demand that guarantees prosperity for all.

So long as there is war.

Unfortunately, our friend the bashing orc eventually learned a valuable lesson. An orc's economic prosperity only lasts until he runs out of enemies to kill, whence he will then turn his attention to the only remaining threat—himself.

It is for that reason that Gork's mission was of utmost importance to the stability of his civilization. Without war with humans, there could only be war with other orcs. The rest of his species would relish the change, as they had an endless list of reasons to kill each other but only one reason not to: The imperial proclamation that while at war with humanity they may not kill another orc. Unless that orc had committed a crime, or was just really annoying, or if that orc was wearing red. (Much like a bull, the color red drives orcs into a rage. Needless to say it is exceptionally popular in orcish fashion.)

This combination of rules kept orc on orc homicide down to a tolerable attrition of 5 percent of the population per year, far down from the natural equilibrium of 60 percent. This combined with the fact that the orcs only lost about 10 percent of their population as casualties of the war with humanity, with an additional 15 percent from friendly fire, meant that the last century had been an unprecedented era of economic and population growth.

And these damn humans were going to mess it all up with their poisonous pursuit of peace.

WHILE GORK HAD BEEN CONTEMPLATING the importance of his mission, the *Fast Boat* had finally finished its approach and was readying to begin the docking procedure.

Four hours crawled by as Gog attempted again and again to complete the exceptionally simple maneuver, hampered as he was by the fact that many of his controls had been installed in the wrong direction.

"Sorry Bozz," Gog would say after each attempt. "Stupid human ship iz all confused." As if Gork was blind to the fact that once again Gog had forgotten that the right joystick was inverted.

Gork couldn't blame him; orc pilots were not usually trained in the arts of docking, or indeed landing, as such things were a waste of time when 99 percent of orc ships would end their service either evaporated by enemy lasers during a suicide charge, or crashing into the enemy's ships if they miraculously survived that long. With this baseline Gog was actually considered an ace pilot as he had landed not just one, but two ships, with a mostly surviving crew.

Eventually the human pilot opted to put everyone out of their misery and maneuvered the massive flagship to dock with the tiny cruiser instead.

"Docking prozedure complete, Bozz!" Gog announced with a salute and a puff of his chest.

"Excellent work as always, Gog," Gork said. "I'm sure these negotiations shall take quite some time so please feel free to avail yourself of a well-earned respite."

Gog didn't quite understand the words, of course, but could tell from Gork's tone that it was a compliment, so he happily stuck a finger up his nose and kicked his feet up onto the console. This triggered the starboard missiles to fire, but fortunately as they had been installed on the port side, the missiles flew harmlessly out into space. They were mostly duds and unlikely to even scratch the hull of the human flagship anyway, but it would have made things slightly more awkward for Gork. While he was here to ensure the peace talks failed, he couldn't be seen to attempt any direct sabotage. He couldn't risk the humans coming to perceive the orc race as possessing any intelligence at all, or they might end up escalating the conflict to a state of total war.

As Gork made his way down to the docking hatch, he mentally prepared himself for the role that he was to take on. Gork had been aware from a young age that he was quite different to the average member of his species. About one in a billion orcs was born with what, to an orc, would be considered a genius level intellect, roughly equivalent to a very smart dog by human standards. But Gork was a one in a trillion level intellect, smarter than the average college graduate, though not smarter than the average college dropout. And he knew from studying great human leaders that the most effective way to manipulate humans was not with elegant speechcraft, but by acting like a total buffoon.

To get himself into character he strode up to the nearest wall, drew himself up to his full stature, and smashed his head into the hard titanium of the ship's hull, a common orcish pastime. The light concussion would serve him well in the negotiations to come.

He walked up to the hatch and Gork noted with pleasure that it took him quite a few tries to figure out how to open the damn thing. His strategy was working.

Aboard the human vessel he was greeted by the three members of the human diplomatic party.

The first stepped forward, a stern man of imposing stature for a human, bedecked in a military uniform studded with medals.

"Mr. Gork I presume," he said. "I am Admiral Han of the Human Armada." He raised a grizzled hand which Gork took. Han did his best to deliver a crushing handshake. Gork did his best to not crush the man's hand.

"I am joined by Senator Blake of the United Earth Congress," he said, gesturing to the woman stepping forward to join them. Wearing a no-nonsense, bureaucratic standard gray suit, she gave Gork a wry smile.

"It's a pleasure to meet you, Mr. Gork," she said. "I hope we can come together and find a mutual resolution to this long conflict that has claimed so many lives."

"And our final representative, whom I'm sure needs no introduction," said Han as the third figure came forward. "Reginald Cheese, a clown of some renown. He's here as an uh … cultural attaché."

The clown proffered a hand. As Gork took it, a little flower on the clown's lapel squirted water in his face.

"Honk honk," honked the clown.

Human intelligence officers had discovered an unusual surge in traffic across the human Exonet over the past decade originating from stars within the orcish imperium. Fearing an incursion from some unknown legion of orc code breakers they had locked the entire Exonet down and investigated. To their relief, and bemusement, it turned out that billions of orcs had taken to streaming the collected works of Reginald Cheese's comedy shows. Cheese's unique brand of simplistic slapstick had not garnered him much fame in the human cultural zeitgeist, but among orcs he was a sensation. No doubt the human cultural anthropologists thought that some pathway to peace, and perhaps even future business relationships, could be forged by the inclusion of the clown delegate.

"Hee hee," said Gork, water dripping from his face. "Me Gork."

The human delegation waited a couple beats for some further introduction before surrendering to the awkwardness of the moment and continued.

"This way to the negotiation chamber, Mr. Gork," Han said.

"Gork," Gork corrected.

"Indeed, right this way."

ORCS HAD NEVER HAD A MORE perfect opponent than humanity. Resilient, versatile, and brave, almost every engagement with the endless orc hordes ended with a pyrrhic victory for humanity, keeping the orc population manageable but never letting the humans develop the critical mass to end the war for good.

But while the orcs just built more and more enthusiasm for war with every glorious annihilation of its armadas, it turned out that to the humans war was an unwelcome distraction from their pursuit of ever more complicated ways to waste time on the Exonet.

When an orc dies it fuels demand for new weapons to go and get another orc killed, but when a human dies it removes one more person from the pool of people clicking on online advertising.

And so humanity sought to sue for peace. But Gork had to fuel their appetite for war.

Han led them through a maze of bulkheads and hallways before arriving at a grand room. The chamber had clearly been designed to convey a subtle sense of asymmetry between the two negotiating parties. The room was dominated by a long table, on the far side of which stood a series of regal executive chairs with a window backdrop displaying the glory of the cosmos, but on the near side there was a line of Fisher-Price children's chairs with a peeling beige wallpaper background.

Inwardly Gork sighed to himself. He wondered why the humans consistently wasted their time trying to intimidate the orcs with all this posturing. Surely they must realize that such psychological warfare can only be effective against a species that is actually capable of psychology?

As the members of the human negotiating party started to walk around the table Gork simply walked up to the closest children's chair and used it to step up onto the table. Two more steps and he was over, plopping himself onto one of the executive chairs.

"Ah, no," said Admiral Han. "Actually this side of the table is for our party, we have prepared some suitable chairs for you over there."

"Gork comfy," said Gork.

"Ah, no you misunderstand," said Admiral Han. "See our nameplates are over here and yours are over there." He gestured to the nameplate in front of him. "See, this says 'Admiral Han' on there."

Gork looked at the plate. "Says Gork," said Gork.

"No, it doesn't!" said Han. "Look A-D-M-I-R-A-L-space-H-A-N!"

"Dat spells Gork in orcish," said Gork.

"That doesn't make any sense!" Han said, exasperated. Senator Blake put a hand on his shoulder.

"Han, it's all right," she said, voice gentle. "We'll just go ahead and take the other side."

"But he ruined my power play!" Han said. "And he doesn't even realize it!"

"Yes, but I did tell you it was a stupid idea."

"Honk," Reginald Cheese softly honked in agreement.

"Don't you start!" said Han. "You would have had us sitting in bean bags like we're some kumbaya friend circle playing truth or dare! This is a war negotiation goddammit, that means posturing!"

"Yes," said Senator Blake. "But we're trying to establish a peace treaty, Han, so how about you shut up and call a couple of your boys to bring in some real chairs, okay?" She looked over to Gork. "You must be so confused, Mr. Gork, these little mix ups happen all the time with humans but don't worry we'll get started soon."

"Gork like beans," said Gork.

Inwardly Gork reflected that it was almost too easy to dismantle these human games of diplomatic intrigue. Humans were always operating under the assumption that others were as smart as they were, thus underestimating the powers of true stupidity.

A few minutes later and a few swabbies had quickly deployed some slightly less impressive executive chairs. Senator Blake took a seat across from Gork, hands steepled with a small smile that she probably thought was reassuring but Gork found unsettling instead. It reminded him of an 'orcodile', a creature very similar to an Earth crocodile except it tells bad jokes before consuming its prey. Gork had seen it in action at a zoo many years ago.

"Why did the orc cross the road?" the orcodile had asked, wearing an innocent smile.

"Huh?" the zookeeper orc had said, leaning in to hear the answer.

Chomp.

In one bite the zookeeper had been eaten whole. Gork shuddered at the memory. He still didn't know why the orc had crossed the road.

Meanwhile, Han had elected to instead stand, no doubt trying to salvage his power play by acting as if he didn't need a chair at all. Reginald Cheese had opted to balance precariously on a construction of the discarded Fisher-Price chairs.

"Now, Mr. Gork," said Senator Blake. "Let's start from scratch, a *tabula rasa* if you will. We at the United Earth Congress believe that we may be able to reach peace within our lifetimes. Humans and orcs have been at war for far too long, and far too much blood has been spilled on both sides.

"We cannot let the past be a barrier to our future. Some people believe that war between orcs and humans is an inevitability. That the future of our two races will forever be one of blood and violence.

"Let me instead tell you, Mr Gork, of the future that I believe in. I believe in a future of peace. The galaxy is a big place, yes? I can imagine a future where there is room enough for both of our peoples to prosper. A future where we no longer send our young, our best and our brightest, to die on worlds far from home. A world where our children can meet, not as enemies, but as friends. Can you imagine that world, Mr. Gork? Can you dream of a world wherein your child and mine can grow up free of conflict?"

Gork put his finger to his chin and scrunched his forehead as if he was thinking very hard.

"Gork has many ugly children," he said.

The humans stared at him, waiting for more. When it became apparent that nothing more was forthcoming, Senator Blake sighed.

"And what kind of a world would you like your ugly children to grow up in, Mr. Gork?" she asked.

"Good world," said Gork, nodding sagely.

"Yes!" said Senator Blake, animated. "A good world! A world free of the pain and suffering of a pointless war!"

"No," said Gork. "Good world free of smelly humans."

Senator Blake sank back into her chair like a puppet with its strings cut.

"Look, Mr. Gork," she said. "If not a world of cooperation perhaps at least a world of isolation. The galaxy is wide, I'm sure we can agree on some reasonable expansion borders, we need not soak every star with the blood of our soldiers. We will not contest your further expansion across the Catfish Nebula and in exchange please just stop your relentless raids on our settlements in the Omicron frontier."

This struck Gork as actually quite a generous deal. The Catfish Nebula was a region of star systems rich in all manner of valuable and rare metals. Not that this mattered much to the orcish horde, as to them such resources were just a means for constructing more ships to launch into the slaughter, but to the humans it represented untold volumes of electronic devices that could be built, sold, and then thrown away. Humanity could put off figuring out how to recycle for at least another four hundred years with all the material in that nebula. What reason would the humans have to give it up? They were winning almost every battle anyway. He had to probe carefully and find out why.

"Gork thought human love catfish," he said. "Human love meow?"

"Well catfish don't actually ... ok that doesn't matter." Senator Blake sighed. "We would love to colonize the Catfish Nebula but given its proximity to orc space we know there's no way we could stand to hold it."

"Gork think human very good at war. Gork think human can take Catfish if human want it."

"Well thank you, Mr. Gork," said Senator Blake. "But that's exactly it, humanity doesn't want it enough. Our constituents tire of war, Mr. Gork, and as their democratically elected representative I must be the voice of the people. Look, if the Catfish Nebula isn't enough, we are even prepared to vacate the Omicron frontier, and leave it as neutral ground. My voters are tired of seeing their friends and family go out to the slaughter. Tired of living in constant fear of the endless orc raids. There must be some agreement we can come to?"

Ah, Gork thought, of course that is the reason. The weakness endemic to the backward human governing system—*democracy*. The orcish species had never bothered with it, as it was transparent to anyone that if you were to go around asking every orc how they felt about every little decision you would end up with nothing getting done and a lot of angry orcs bashing each other over the head.

This was generally the result of any gathering of orcs anyway, which is why it made sense to only have one orc in charge. A lot more simple when there is only one orc to ask, and thus only one orc to bash over the head if you thought he was wrong. This meant that the lifespan of the orc emperor was often very short but the perks of the position made it well worth it. A grand palace, a harem of ten thousand concubines—it was actually thirty-four concubines. Orcs generally struggle to remember more than a dozen faces. Give each concubine a handful of different dresses and no emperor had ever seen through the palace staff's deception—and most importantly the exclusive right to kill any orc that you want. Truly a dream for any orc willing and able to storm the palace. Gork had never been particularly interested in the position, owing to the fact that he generally preferred being alive for longer than two months.

This whole retreat from the Omicron frontier business was quite troublesome for Gork. Even if he rejected the offer they would probably go ahead and vacate the starfield anyway, and in this the human's plan would work; if orcish fleets couldn't reach human territory in a reasonable time-frame most orc fleet commanders would get bored with the prospect of interstellar war, and a bored orc inevitably starts looking for a much closer prey to hunt.

No, Gork couldn't afford for the humans to retreat. It would be far preferable for the humans to advance. Perhaps a great victory, with equally great reward, would whet the human electorate's appetite for war? But how could Gork serve this up to the human delegation? He needed time to think.

"Gork need doo doo," he declared.

"Ah, of course," Senator Blake replied. "Right this way."

In the bathroom Gork leaned over the sink and splashed water over his face. He fixed himself with a hard gaze in the mirror. The fate of his entire civilization rested on his shoulders, and it was a heavy burden because certainly no member of his own species was willing to bear their own weight in the matter. At this point the war economy was too big to fail. With the advanced weaponry they had developed (read: stolen from humanity) it would take less than a year of 'peace' for every planet in the orc imperium to be naught but molten glass. They wouldn't be able to help themselves.

Could Gork really handle this?

As soon as the doubt passed through his mind Gork roared in rage. He smashed his head forward into the mirror and breathed deeply. He pulled back and stared calmly into his bloody visage, spread violently across the shattered mirror. He was Gork. He had been sorely tested time and time again, and he knew that he could do this. He just needed the right opportunity.

The door to the restroom softly swung open, and the clown Reginald Cheese meekly walked in.

"Mr. Gork," he said in a squeaky voice. "Might I make a humble plea?" He reached up and brought his hat into his hands, revealing a second, comically small, hat in its place.

"I have never had much success among my own people. I have never had any fans, I have only ever eked a meager existence on the fringes. I have never been able to pursue the true artistry of my craft due to its un-fashionability among today's attention economy. I had long ago accepted that I would only ever be a mediocre performer, and my highest ambitions could be starring as the main entertainment of an especially stupid child's birthday party. Heck, I was about to throw in the towel, quit being an entertainer and become an electrician!

"But this all changed with your species. I admit I, like the rest of humanity, was initially fearful of your kind. Fearful and full of pity, to see your hordes charge into the meat grinder again and again, getting yourselves all killed and quite a lot of my fellow humans as well. Then it happened—I got a call from the Interstellar Intelligence Agency and I found out that it was among your kind that my craft was respected.

"And now my hopes have reignited. There is, in fact, out there among the stars, a people to whom I could bring joy. Fans that I could have. Meaning that could be added to my little life. And I wished that I could reach out, across the vast vacuum of space, and shake hands with my fans, see the smiles and joy of people that I had made an impact on."

He drew in a deep breath and went down on his knees. With one hand on the hat he already held, he reached up with the other and removed the small comical hat. He brought it down to join the other hat, leaving behind another, even tinier, hat in its place.

"And so I beseech you, please. Let us end this war, so that we might come together in the shared enjoyment of art, life, and slapstick humor."

Gork stared down at the trembling clown that had just finished pouring his heart out to him and the scene filled his own heart with relief.

Opportunity had arrived.

"Mr. Cheese, I am not an orc made of stone, and so it brings me no joy to inform you of the truth," Gork said.

The clown was visibly surprised, actually shocked that the orc was indeed capable of speaking in first person.

"You seem to be under the impression that among my people you could receive respect and admiration. That you could tour our worlds as a celebrity, shaking hands, attending meet and greets, signing head shots. You have no understanding of the race that I represent and so I will illuminate you. If you came to an orc world my people would be overjoyed, and they would display that joy in a way you would find deeply unpleasant.

"You see my fellow orcs do love your slapstick comedy and so would endeavor to appreciate it in a distinctly orc-like fashion. The first orc that you would meet would happily take your hand, and then use it to tear your arm off. They would laugh as you scream and then they would beat you mercilessly with it. With great mirth they would pull the rest of your limbs off, one by one, and then they would dance and laugh as they started to beat each other to death with your limbs. And then they would start tearing each other's limbs off and within very little time we would have a jolly little riot that would engulf whatever hapless continent you should have the misfortune of landing on. For a month there would be a festival of gratuitous violence that would taper down as the populace also slowly tapered off. Then, finally, it will be over. And you would be dead and forgotten."

Even through the clown's white makeup his skin had visibly blanched, all blood having drained listening to the horrible truths that Gork had delivered.

"You see, Mr. Cheese, my people hold no respect for 'art'. They only enjoy violence, and as a purveyor of comedic violence you will receive the lion's share of it. There is no fame awaiting you among my people, no love or admiration as a human would see it. Orcs express their love through violence. Which is also how we express our dissatisfaction, our fears, our boredom, and generally all of our emotions. No, Mr. Cheese, you would not want to meet another of my kind. You would not survive it."

"W-what, y-you, I don't..." the clown stammered.

"You are wondering why I've dropped my idiotic facade for you, Mr. Cheese?" said Gork. "To be quite blunt, you are a joke. Not just among my people, but among yours as well. You think that those two career diplomats would believe you if you were to tell them that 'Gork the goofy orc' is actually a well-spoken sociopath? They would laugh in your face, Mr. Cheese."

The clown looked crestfallen, comical hats fallen from his

hands. He knew it was true. He wasn't here in any serious capacity; he was just a pawn in the silly human diplomatic dance. Gork took out a handheld computer, pushed a couple of buttons and then removed a memory disk from the device.

"I will tell you what you will do, Mr. Cheese," he said, handing the clown the disk. "You will take this, a collection of orcish military movements, and you will bring it to your Admiral. You will tell him that you fleeced it from me, a product of your little clown trickery. They will end these peace talks, secure in the knowledge that they can win some great victory against us. And then you will go home. I recommend you quit your pathetic dreams of being a great clown to the orcish race. Get your electrician license and move far, far away from the orcish border and be happy you will never live to meet another of my kind."

Numbly the clown took the disk. Slowly he rose to his oversized feet and then bolted out of the room, squeaking with every hurried step.

Gork returned his attention to his shattered reflection in the mirror. This would assure his mission's success, at the cost of millions if not billions of orc lives. As an added benefit, the killing of all these orcs would count as his own contribution, so he would reap the financial rewards of all these deaths, thus making him soon to be fabulously wealthy. But he took no joy in it.

Without haste Gork made his way back to the negotiating chamber, where he witnessed the tail end of the clown's performance to the admiral and the senator. He sat down casually and watched the admiral's eyes light up, as he gleefully realized all the prospects that the military intelligence Gork had handed over represented to the human armada. The admiral rushed out of the room. The clown quietly slunk out behind him, no doubt wanting to be far away from Gork as soon as possible. Senator Blake returned to her seat in front of Gork.

"Well, ah, Mr. Gork. I'm sorry but, ah, we're going to have to call this meeting here," she said. "It is greatly disappointing to see that there was no way we could come to a peaceful arrangement but … y'know … keep in touch!"

"Gork win?" he asked.

"Umm … yes?"

"Gork get peace prize?"

"Yeah, uh, have this." She quickly scribbled 'you win!' on a notepad and then tossed it over to him.

"Yippee! Gork go home now."

Gork made his way back to his ship. He watched solemnly as Gog attempted to initiate disembarkation procedures for ten minutes before giving up and just ripping the cruiser out of there, leaving most of their airlock still attached to the human ship.

It was an unparalleled success, Gork knew. Singlehandedly he had saved the orcish economy, and yet he felt ennui. No new chapter in orcish society as they rose up against the crushing machine of their own broken economy. Just a new page in the same book.

New blood, same war.

Will Brege is a recovering software engineer that aspires to be an aspiring writer. This is his first published story. He lives in San Francisco and is working on a video game about ghosts. There is nowhere online that you can follow him and he prefers not to be followed offline as well.

I HATE THIS PLANET

Alan Dean Foster

I could easily call it disgusting. You cannot really overstate it. But I am going to be kind and simply refer to it as disappointing. It is not so much the planet itself, which is essentially fine, even beautiful. It is the dominant species, whose technological evolution has seriously, dangerously, exceeded their social development. Certainly their endless praise of themselves, the unending self-elevation of their kind, can be called disgusting. I will leave it at that, at least until I get home and the final reports can be delivered. I find the subject itself a source of ongoing distress.

It is at least partially my own fault that I find myself in this deplorable situation. Having quietly and efficiently completed the final local assignment in our program, and having long since determined that the local atmosphere was amenable and the gravity unimposing, several of us were allowed to take a brief, circumscribed excursion outside of our survey craft. This being the first and last time any of us were due to set foot on this world (all of our scientific work having naturally been performed with remote and independently operated equipment), we stripped down to nothing before exiting lest something unknown on our apparel, equipment, or selves would serve to accidentally contaminate the local biome.

Having become engrossed in the rich and varied local flora, a particular interest of mine, I lost track of the time. This oversight is inexcusable and unbecoming a professional like myself. Nonetheless, it happened. When the alert came to return to the survey ship I discovered that I had wandered rather farther from our touchdown point that I had intended. What should have been a harmless and easily resolved situation was abruptly complicated by the imminent and unexpected arrival of a number of the local dominant species, traveling in their archaic, sputtering machines.

You can see where this is leading. In order to prevent a potentially detrimental meeting, fraught with possible misunderstandings, I had to be left behind. Devoid of any attire or equipment, save what is normally embedded in explorers, I understood that it would be necessary for me to maintain my anonymity while fending for myself until a ship could safely be dispatched to effectuate my recovery. Given the primitive, practically hostile nature of this world, I was not sanguine about my prospect of remaining anonymous.

My first need was to find somewhere to conceal my presence from the local species while simultaneously securing shelter from the elements, for the climate of this world can turn as hostile as its inhabitants, and just as swiftly. This required me to leave the forest surrounds that I and my colleagues had been studying lest I run afoul of one of the numerous local carnivores. I was loath to do so since it meant secreting myself among representatives of the dominant species itself. A difficult decision, as I am sure you will appreciate.

Entering into a nearby, local but thankfully diffuse conurbation, I was fortunate enough to locate a small structure that was clearly utilized for storage and not for lodging. Dialing down my metabolism, as my kind are capable of doing, allowed me to survive there unnoticed and in comparative peace for several days. Until, unfortunately, I was discovered by one of the locals.

Happily, the discovery was made by an immature member of the species, one neither mentally nor physically fully formed. While I was surprised to encounter it, the creature was positively shocked to see me. The training undergone by our exploration teams is thorough, however, and I knew enough to remain calm so as not to frighten the (apparently male) offspring further. Deciding that my best option was to appear ignorant, harmless, and incapable of speech, I initiated further contact with the youngling by portraying as stupid a creature as I could possibly imagine. Thankfully, it immediately accepted this presentation, never making the logical assumption that an alien being, obviously from another world, let alone another star system, and one whose kind was capable of interstellar travel, might also be capable of modest conversation in a local tongue.

It also did not question my nakedness. I expected this, as studies of his species indicate that they generally believe that any visiting aliens would travel across interstellar distances devoid of attire, equipment, or any other kind of protection from the elements. Their crude representations of aliens do reflect this. It is a supposition on the part of the locals that has long baffled specialists, who can only reflect with amusement on the image of our own kind operating our craft entirely in the nude.

It treated me as something between a toy and a pet. While this was insulting, it was also useful, as it did not require me to respond with anything other than idiotically blank expressions and meaningless sounds. Rather than ask for food directly, I employed the kind of basic gestures common to any multilimbed newborn. The offspring responded by bringing me an assortment of the most crassly industrial products imaginable, some of which derived from other living creatures, that my team and I knew from prior studies to have originated from the bodies of actual thinking beings. I declined such offerings with a suitable dollop of obliviousness and a blank expression, while finding a very few bits of possible sustenance that came from the ground itself. Consuming these allowed me to increase my metabolism to more comfortable levels.

It became quite useful to have a young creature serve my needs, though of course it felt the relationship was the reverse. While regarding its species as rather hopeless, it did serve to pass the time by my demonstration of a little (a very little) of my own kind's telekinetic abilities: levitating small spheres to illustrate my home system, and so on. I did this knowing that as the youngling grew and became interested in other matters, most especially the practice of reproduction that obsesses his species, along with the acquisition of simple means of exchange, it would likely forget any scientific knowledge I passed on to it. I attempted an explanation of the most basic means by which communication is managed through interstellar space, but gave up when it became clear that such details were entirely beyond the creature.

I was unable, unfortunately, to prevent eventual discovery by the creature's siblings. A little mind manipulation prevented the older one from doing what any intelligent being would do when confronted by the appearance of an obvious alien being, which would be to contact a higher scientific authority with the information. Despite being the dominant species on their world, their use of logic and reason is pitiful by civilized standards and they are easily manipulated—not only by me, but by others of their own kind. It is amazing that they have managed to survive this long. Usually it is cooperation that brings real progress, not rabid competition, but I am here to study, not to pass judgment.

I cannot help from commenting, though, that the entire population would benefit from a prolonged dunking in an ocean-sized container of broad-spectrum deodorant. No one has commented on my smell because I do not have one. Even the small local domesticated predators tend to ignore me.

Unutterably bored, I decided one night to venture out into the more dynamic portion of the local hive and utilize the time to try to make some useful observations. The majority of the creatures are inactive in the absence of sunlight, but some continue to function. I am notably shorter than most, but not all, of them. A single outer covering served to hide my frame while a portion of the same garment, pulled forward, covered my head. A small piece of cloth covered my mouth and the lower part of my face while a pair of darkened "glasses" (the lenses of these unevolved beings' oculars are unable to flex or change coloration to compensate for changes in illumination) proved large enough to cover my eyes. Thus equipped, I sauntered out of the silent dwelling and made my way toward the nocturnally functioning portion of the town. I was able to get there quite rapidly; though my kind have short legs, we can move with considerable speed when we wish to.

My stature drew occasional looks, but I was able to make some valuable observations without being challenged. I had been wandering for a number of hours when I was accosted by several juveniles of the species. The juveniles of a number of semi-advanced species have in common the ability to act even more stupidly than their adult equivalents, and this trio was no exception. In the course of my nocturnal roving I had been the recipient of a number of stares ranging from the puzzled to the repelled, but until now I had not been forced to deal with the threat of unwanted physical contact.

They followed me, venturing taunts and what passed for humor among them. This was easily ignored. It was when they began to tap me on the head and push me—gently at first and then more forcefully—that I determined I would have to take some minimal action to make them cease. Although my kind is physically modest in physique, we are actually quite muscular. Not wishing, however, to commit to anything as serious as breaking bones, I employed one of my kind's distinctive biophysical abilities.

We have the ability to manipulate electrical fields within our bodies. For example, by activating a compound akin to the local enzyme luciferase I can make the tips of my fingers glow brightly. While this is suitable for games and such, I knew it would not dissuade the chattel taunting me. Instead, I performed an internal adjustment similar to that used by a particular attenuated local aquatic creature and generated a strong electrical field within my body. When next I was touched by one of the juveniles, the resultant shock knocked him unconscious. As his pack mates gathered around him mewling expressions of uncertainty and concern, I increased my pace and left them behind. None of them attempted to follow.

Like everything else about my investigative stroll, the encounter provided additional research material that I mentally catalogued for transfer later. I encountered no such further incidents as I made my way back to the dwelling where I was residing.

To further amuse the youth in whose abode I was concealing myself, I pretended to make use of scraps of primitive electronics to construct a mock communications device, ostensibly to make contact with the rest of my team. This gave me something else to occupy my time. The notion, of course, that an explorer such as myself would be totally abandoned on a strange world without any means of contact with my colleagues is one exclusive to the kind of primitives among whom I found myself. Obviously, every team member is equipped with a subcutaneous implant that remains in continual contact with the exploration vessel. Though I had to wait until the time and other elements were propitious for my recovery, I was never out of contact with my ship.

My colleagues knew exactly where I was at all times, my physical condition, and much else about my person. A small pickup craft could have been dispatched at any time to pick me up, even from the residence where I was staying, but that risked alerting the local authorities to our presence—a consequence to be avoided for the time being. Eventually, formal contact will be made, but not until this local species evolves well beyond their current station.

Word has come that I am to be recovered soon. In order for this to occur without revealing our existence to any more of the locals than necessary, it is important that I return to the location where I was temporarily left behind. To facilitate this, I will engage the first offspring I encountered. Use will also be made of his personal means of unpowered transport, which I will levitate using a different aspect of my internal electronic manipulative abilities. Though it is a serious enterprise, I believe he will be comfortable with it, as his kind regards some of the most solemn happenstances as play. It is an unserious species, as evidenced by how they treat their own immediate environments.

Upon my recovery, I will relieve myself of all I have learned. Despite the awkward circumstances of my unplanned extended stay on this world, it has allowed me to gather much new information regarding the dominant kind. Nothing complimentary, I fear, except perhaps for the still unspoiled nature of the very youngest members of the species. In its innocence (and likely ignorance) it even offered me a portion of some of its food. This consisted of small, oval objects which upon casual analysis were revealed to have nothing whatsoever in the way of nutritional value not only to myself but to the offspring who was consuming it. Out of courtesy I ingested several, allowing them to pass through my gastrointestinal system undigested.

In concluding my report, I note that in the person of its unspoiled offspring there may be some small hope for this species' survival. The decision whether to extend assistance on that basis or simply to study and ignore will not be mine, nor do I have any interest in participating in such an assessment.

As a parting gesture to the undeveloped spawn who assisted me in maintaining my anonymity during my say, I will perform the slight fingertip lighting exercise to which I alluded earlier. He should find it amusing, perhaps even awe-inspiring. He will certainly find it illuminating.

As for the adult members of the species, I would rather poke them in the eye.

ALAN DEAN FOSTER has written over 140 books, including both standalone novels and novelizations for Star Wars, Star Trek, Alien, and many other productions. His website is www.alandeanfoster.com.

LOVE OR LIZARD ISLAND

Jackie Rogoff

The human woman had never looked so beautiful as she did in this moment, wearing a deep-blue evening dress that sparkled in the light. Gorlag could smell the coconut notes of her shampoo, which mingled with the sweet earthy scent wafting from the single rose she held in front of her torso. His mouth began to water. He imagined how wonderful it would feel when she finally chose him, and he would peel the dress off of that glowing skin, sink his teeth into her moist flesh, and eat her.

The host gave his introduction: "Katie, before you stand two suitors. One of them is a human man who came on this show to find love and commitment. The other is a man-eating lizard demon, currently in disguise, who came on this show in search of a delectable meal. If you choose the human, you will each win $500,000. If you choose the lizard demon, you will be eaten. Have you made your final decision?"

Katie's eyes shone in the lights and her hands shook slightly as she looked from the host to each of the two suitors in front of her. "Well, Jett, it's been a really tough decision. I care so much about both of them, and of course I don't want to be eaten." She laughed, a little too lightly. "But I think I've made up my mind."

Gorlag felt the cameras zoom in on each of their faces. He carefully composed his own into a studied human expression of nervousness mixed with hope and lust-tinged affection. His sharp teeth, concealed for weeks, could stay hidden just a little bit longer.

Katie addressed the other human first. "Kevin, the time we've spent together has been so fun and easy. You always know what to say to make me laugh, and I feel so comfortable with you. You've been there for me every step of the way, even when I wasn't able to see it at first, because you were shy. But since then, our connection has only deepened. I feel like you've helped me grow into a better person just by being around you."

Next, she turned to Gorlag. He made sure not to wince while she used his fake human name one last time. "Josh, you are so special to me. I can tell that there's something different about you, even though we've known each other for such a short time. No matter what happens, I'll always remember that night we had together on the yacht. We've had our ups and downs, and sometimes I wasn't sure whether you were here for the right reasons. But we've made it this far together, and our connection is the strongest I've ever felt with anyone."

Gorlag leaned forward, nodding. He remembered that night too. The full-contact human courting rituals were a novelty, and she'd smelled especially delicious out on the water. But he'd restrained himself from taking any nibbles because of the strict clauses in his contract.

"However," Katie continued, "I feel like there's just something missing, and it's like you don't know the real me after all."

Gorlag's heart sank. He was going to go home hungry, back to the observation tank with only microwaved lab meat to feed on.

"Kevin, I've chosen you as my match."

There it was. The world contracted around Gorlag. The producers were ushering him off the stage, while a single camera trailed him, broadcasting his heartbreak (and hunger) to the whole world. Soon everyone would see the real him, and he found he barely even cared. The rest of the cameras hovered around Katie and Kevin, who were embracing and kissing. Jett was revealing to the live audience that Kevin was just a human after all. Gorlag risked a forlorn glance back at Katie, who broke off the kiss, looked right at him, and winked. He stopped short. He could have sworn that her eyes flashed yellow for a second.

"Come on, demon, let's get you back to the lab–" said one of the production assistants, before she was interrupted by a scream.

Gorlag turned around again just in time to see Katie bite through Kevin's neck with sharp incisors. Her human skin melted away to reveal red-green iridescent scales, and the dress slithered off her body into a shimmering heap on the floor, where it was promptly doused in spurts of Kevin's blood.

Gorlag shook off the humans and ran toward her. "Katie, I don't understand," he said.

"Have you been living among the humans for so long," Katie hissed, "that you've forgotten what a female of your own species smells like? I clocked you the second you arrived, but I suppose the male sense organs have always been less finely-tuned. You can call me Ragla, by the way."

Ragla. She was even more beautiful this way than she'd been in human form.

"Well, are you hungry, or not?" she hissed.

"But the contract says–"

"Screw the contract! You know, they only prepared for there to be one lizard demon here today," she said, as blood dripped from her wicked grin. "Here, have this," she said, offering him an arm. A severed human arm, still fresh and warm.

Gorlag gawped at her.

"You haven't forgotten the traditional mating rituals too, have you?"

Gorlag smiled, then transformed, relishing the squelch his clothes and shoes made as they landed on what was left of his rival. "I am honored to accept your invitation."

The two man-eating lizard demons advanced on the production crew.

In the end, the live-streamed finale of *Love or Lizard Island* broke every conceivable television record there was. Despite the resounding success, there would never be a second season.

JACKIE ROGOFF IS AN EX-SOFTWARE ENGINEER, current library science student, and *Jeopardy!* champion living in northern California with her spouse and a clowder of cats. In her spare time she does trivia, knits, runs, climbs, watches exactly the right amount of reality TV, and writes science fiction inspired by the tech industry. She attended the Clarion workshop in summer 2025. "Love or Lizard Island" is her debut publication, so you should tell all your friends you found her here first.

STUPID CUPID

Zach Shephard

Okay, so—according to Cupid, I can't possibly screw this up. "You'll be fine, Tori," he said. "It's only three days." Sure. *Only* three days. Three days of me, an apprentice love goddess, being in charge of *all romance for the entirety of Earth*. No big deal.

I am so nervous.

Breathe, Tori. Just breathe. You can do this. This is what you've trained for! Over the past few centuries, you've spent *thousands of hours* fletching arrows for a winged lust-baby.

... Dear gods. I just realized what my résumé looks like.

This is all Jupiter's fault. He's the reason the entire pantheon has to attend a weekend-long training seminar. When one of your main jobs is to fling lightning bolts at Earth, showing up for work drunk is not okay. Scientists in Brazil are still trying to figure out how so many electric eels died of "apparent overdose."

If Sky-Daddy hadn't kept skipping his Apotheosics Anonymous meetings, I wouldn't be stuck on this grassy hill, covering for Cupid. I don't even know where I am! America, maybe? I did see a bald eagle fly by earlier. But on the other hand, it wasn't carrying a gun. Does that make this ... Canada?

Focus, Tori!

I pull out my rumpled copy of *The 2025 Love God's Field Guide*. The dog-eared page lists the basic rules for "hunting."

- *1. Keep your arrows clean. We're trying to spread love —not tetanus.*
- *2. Only target mortals already on their way to love. Non-consensual matchmaking is a thing of the past. The goal here is to give people that extra nudge they need to take the plunge. (The love-plunge nudge.)*
- *3. Don't worry about aiming for the heart. This is an old myth. You can instill love by striking* any *part of the body; plenty of lifelong romances have started with an arrow to the butt. (And it's typically the softer target.)*
- *4. Discretion is less important than you think. The arrow will be absorbed into the target's bloodstream, closing the wound behind it. No one will even know you were there. The only trace will be elevated levels of hemolovin' in the target's blood, which mortal doctors haven't figured out how to detect.*
- *5. Be calm! There's really nothing to worry about. Love gods have been doing this for millennia. What're the odds you'd be the one to screw things up?*

Okay—that last line felt unnecessary. But let's focus on the other bits.

I've already got a target: the twenty-two-year-old woman down the hill from me, out for a summer hike. Elaine Sandoval. Cupid gave me her case file so I could have a slam-dunk right away. Elaine's currently chatting on her phone, while she uses a stick to poke a gritty black dirt-mound that's bigger than she is. She loves exploring nature on sunny, flower-sweet days like this. But you know what else she loves? Gabriela Morales: the woman on the other end of the phone call. Elaine hasn't had the guts to ask Gabriela out yet, but she's about to get a big shot of courage. Right in the butt.

I pull back the bowstring. This'll be my first-ever shot as an acting love deity. Here goes nothing....

"I love you so much, Tori!"

I fumble the bow like I've suddenly entered an amateur juggling competition. With both arms I trap it and the arrow against my chest. I'm lucky the shot didn't go off.

"Stick with me, Tori! I'll never leaf you!"

Okay, a confession: *technically,* firing at Elaine Sandoval wouldn't have been my first-ever act as Cupid's understudy. I may have also taken a practice shot at a willow tree. A willow tree which is now hopelessly in love with me.

I turn toward the tree, growing there on the hill like a big stringy poof-ball. "Listen, Willow—"

"Billow."

"What?"

"Willow's my government name. *You* can call me Billow."

The tree's branches shake. A twig flings forth, landing at my feet.

Wonderful. I've been on Earth twenty minutes, and I'm already being sent stick pics.

"Look," I say, "I said I was sorry. I just needed some target practice. I didn't realize the arrow would rouse sentience in you."

"It doesn't matter how we got here. Love works in mysterious ways. All that matters is we found each other."

"Billow, you seem like a sweet ... plant. But right now, I

need to focus on my career. Maybe we'll cross paths some other time."

I turn around and tune Billow out. I don't need to hear his love poetry; I'm convinced he's making it extra sappy just for the sake of the tree-pun.

I take aim on Elaine again, still poking her dirt-mound. I let out my breath.

"Tickle attack!"

A thrown bundle of willow leaves crosses my ear just as I release the bowstring. My shot sails high. It strikes the dirt-mound Elaine's been poking. The arrow's pink shaft immediately starts sliding inward, like a syringe's contents entering a body.

The black mound rumbles. Elaine takes a startled step back. She watches as the thing she was poking rises onto two stumpy legs, turns around, and blinks open sleepy eyes like enormous silver marbles. There's a silent moment as it registers her presence. Then:

"Love!" it shouts, in a caveman voice coming from the mouth that opens across its entire body. Two arms unfold from its triangular mass like they're looking for a hug. Elaine screams and runs off. The dirt-mound lumbers after her.

Oh. Oh, this is *bad.*

"I don't think we should allow children at the wedding. My nieces and nephews are nuts."

"Not now, Billow!"

I race down the hill, hoping things aren't as bad as they seem.

THINGS ARE SO MUCH WORSE than they seemed.

I couldn't catch up to Elaine and her silty suitor. The best I can do now is check out the area they left.

There's a round hole in the ground where the dirt-mound was. It's pretty shallow, and is filled with a padlocked metal hatch. I try digging the hole wider to figure out just what the heck I'm looking at, but the metal keeps going and all I've got is my hands. I need help. I need help *so badly.*

I rub the coin in my pocket to summon the guy filling in for Mercury this weekend. He swings by in a junker of a sky-chariot, whose horses he clearly can't control. The landing isn't great. Maybe even worse than when he dropped me off. Whatever—I can't criticize. I just brought an obsessive tree to life and turned a pile of dirt into a stalker. We're all struggling.

I tell the messenger deity I need to see Jess, and he whisks us away. We're only in the sky twenty seconds before he rear-ends a cloud. We zip off before it can get our insurance info.

We land on a rocky promontory overlooking the ocean. I'm still not sure where in the world I am, but it's not important. The chariot's God Positioning System took us straight to Jess, which is all that matters. I get out and tell the messenger to keep the horses idling.

Jess is crouched on the cliff, sea-breeze whipping her long blue hair about. She yanks a cable out of the ground with one hand and lets it retract, like she's trying to start a lawnmower. The definition in her arm makes me wish I worked out more. Maybe I'll buy a jump rope if Cupid doesn't kill me on Monday.

"Jess!" I say as I run up. "I need your help."

She keeps yanking the cable. It makes a mechanical grinding sound every time she pulls."Neptune said I could do whatever I wanted while he's gone," she says, still working away. "He just had one rule: no earthquakes."

"So what're you doing?"

"Trying to make an earthquake."

She pulls the cable again. The ground sputters a little.

"Listen, Jess—I'm in trouble. I did something stupid."

"Can't be as stupid as this stupid cable." She gives one more pull, then drops the handle and stands straight, hands on her hips as she eyes the problem. "Do you think it needs gas?"

"I shot a pile of dirt and now there's some sort of dirt-monster chasing an innocent woman across the countryside. I also might be engaged to a tree. And there's a ... hatch? Jess, I am *so lost*."

She finally looks away from the cable, raising a blue eyebrow at me. "Wow. Your day sounds way more fun than mine. Want some help?"

"Desperately!"

We take to the sky in the messenger's chariot. Along the way, I give Jess a more complete version of the story. She's particularly intrigued by the hatch. So much so, that she has the messenger stop by a beach so she can use her sea god mojo to summon a giant crab from the water. "Nature's can-opener," Jess says, patting the thing like it's a puppy. "We're getting inside that hatch, no doubt."

We resume the journey: three not-gods and a huge crab, in a chariot designed for maybe one person. Things are tight. It doesn't help that the nervous crab keeps putting its claws over the messenger's eyes whenever traffic gets heavy.

We hit *so many birds*.

The feather-smeared chariot lands by the hatch. Everyone but the messenger disembarks. Jess kneels by the metal door in the ground and rubs her chin, nodding thoughtfully. She sticks a hand out behind her. "Crab," she says, like a surgeon asking for a scalpel.

I usher the dog-sized crustacean in that direction. Jess sets it to work. With one snip of its claw, it severs the hatch's padlock.

"I'm going in," Jess says. "Wait here."

She opens the hatch and disappears below. The crab looks at me. It shrugs.

I run my hands through my hair, pacing. How have I screwed up this badly? Did I learn nothing during all those years of shadowing Cupid? I must be the stupidest backup deity on the roster.

"Tori!" a voice shouts from the nearby hilltop. "Introduce me to your friends!"

"Kind of busy, Billow." Somewhere in the distance, the tree grumbles.

Jess's blue head pops up from the hatch. She climbs out, holding something flat and rectangular in one hand.

"Well?" I ask. "What's down there?"

"Spaceship."

"Um. What?"

She pokes a thumb over her shoulder. "It's a buried spaceship. And that thing you shot wasn't a dirt-mound. It was an alien." She hands me the rectangle.

It's a picture frame. The photo depicts a dirt-mound with silver-marble eyes, wearing what looks like 1960s cosmonaut pants—the crinkled foil kind. With one arm, the grinning explorer holds a fishbowl helmet against its hip. The other arm is wrapped around its dirt-mound spouse. In the foreground stand a couple of little dirt-mound kids.

"Pretty sure you made an alien fall in love with a human," Jess says. "Which is actually really cool. I couldn't even get an earthquake going."

I pull out my *Love God's Field Guide*. There's nothing in the index for "aliens" or "extraterrestrials" or "interstellar dirt-folk." Useless!

"Okay," I say. "This has gone from bad to worse."

"You're overreacting. So an alien loves a human—what's the big deal?"

"The big deal is that I don't think this has ever happened before. I might have created an interstellar diplomatic incident. *On my first day.*"

I pace around, losing control of my breathing. Jess stops me by clasping my shoulders.

"Tori," she says, looking me straight in the eyes, "you did not create an interstellar diplomatic incident. Stop being weird."

A rapid chopping sound draws our eyes to the sky. A helicopter approaches. It looks like a military vehicle.

"Okay," Jess says. "You *may* have created an interstellar diplomatic incident."

The helicopter lands nearby, blasting us with wind. I shield my face with an arm. Jess just grins like this is the coolest thing she's ever seen. The frightened crab and messenger hold each other, peeking over the rim of the sky-chariot.

A woman in a slate-gray suit leaves the helicopter, approaching with an escort of three US soldiers. She has twist braids and black-frame glasses, and walks like she's got total confidence in her ability to do her job. I wonder what that's like.

The woman stops before us, hands on her hips. She looks at the hatch. Looks at us. I feel like a kid who's been caught standing next to the vase they just broke.

"You opened it."

"Technically, Carson opened it," Jess says. Apparently the crab has a name.

The woman ignores her. She folds her arms. "I need to know everything that happened here. Now."

I look to Jess for guidance. She shrugs. "We've got magic sky-horses standing thirty feet away. Might as well tell the truth."

So I do.

The woman listens quietly to the whole thing. Her stern demeanor doesn't change, even when I tell her about my apparent treeancé up on the hill. There's an uncomfortable silence once I'm finished.

"You seem weirdly okay with all this," I say.

"I work for the Department of Observable Fantasy Under Scrutiny. The existence of love gods is not the strangest thing to cross my desk at DOOFUS." She looks to the hatch, presumably working out the problem in her head. "Tell me your names."

"I'm Tori. This is Jess."

"Rochelle Mbaye," the woman says. "All right. Now that I know your part of the story, here's mine: the alien is named Brixtaflumpicorticus. 'Brix' for short. The government has known about his species for a while, and we're on generally decent terms with them. He was engaged in his standard post-landing hibernation when your arrow struck. Now he's fallen in love with Elaine Sandoval, and wants to take her back to his home world. Which brings us to our dilemma: allowing aliens to abduct citizens for forced marriages sets a bad precedent. But if we refuse, we risk an interstellar diplomatic incident."

Jess side-elbows me and grins. As if us being right about that last part is a good thing.

"So how do we fix this?" I ask.

"You tell me. This is a matter of love, and you're the acting love god."

"Oh—oh, no. You can't leave this up to me. Everything I've done today has been a disaster. I'm not smart enough for this."

"You're the only one here with experience in magically induced attraction. I'll take a stupid Cupid over anything else we've got."

Just the mention of Cupid's name reminds me of what big trouble I'm in. He's going to be one angry baby when he gets back from the seminar.

Jess pulls me aside. Rochelle and her soldiers investigate the buried spaceship while she waits for us.

"Hey," Jess says, snapping her fingers at my face to get my attention. "So you screwed up. Big deal. Things don't always work out on the first try. Like Neptune once told me: Every mistake can be washed away."

"You really think that's true?"

"I'm pretty sure he was talking about sending a tidal wave to obliterate a city he didn't like. But it's the same idea: the only way to make things right here is to start over and try again."

I'm not exactly convinced, but I've got to do *something*.

"Okay," I say, letting out a big breath. "Starting over. Let's backtrack and think about how this all began."

"You shot an alien in the butt and created a crazy spacemess."

"Right. Okay. And if I hadn't shot him, what—he'd go back to his family and live happily ever after?"

Once I hear the words out loud, I realize what I just said.

"Holy crap, Jess—the picture! From the ship! Brix has a spouse. We just need to remind him of what's waiting back home!"

Rochelle rejoins the conversation. "Not going to work. We interviewed Brix when we picked him up. He's recently divorced. In fact, we're pretty sure this trip to Earth was part of a mid-life crisis." She gestures back at the hatch she was inspecting. "It explains why his spacecraft is a brand-new convertible he can't actually afford."

I sag in defeat. That was my only lead.

"Tori!" Billow yells from the hilltop. "I can't see what's going on. Ask the helicopter people if they can lift me over!"

"Not the best time, Billow."

"*Ugh*. Being rooted sucks. I just want to branch out!"

Rochelle cocks an eyebrow at me.

"Sorry," I say. "Brix isn't the only one with love problems."

"Where is that guy, anyway?" Jess asks. "I wanna see an alien. Especially if his race might nuke the Earth in an interstellar diplomatic incident."

"We're holding him at a nearby arboretum," Rochelle says.

"Well, that's—weird. Why an arboretum? Was Area 51 full?" Jess's eyes go wide in sudden realization. "*Are all arboretums secretly alien holding cells?*"

"I—what? No. Brix's home planet doesn't have trees. He's enamored with them. We're just trying to keep him as pacified as possible while we work this all out."

And just like that, the idea hits me.

"Rochelle! Bring Brix here."

She pulls out her phone, cautious curiosity on her face. "I don't think we can convince him to leave Elaine behind. She's at the arboretum, too."

"That's fine. Bring her along. Just get them here fast! I am *rapidly* losing faith in this plan."

Rochelle turns away and makes her call.

"So what's the idea?" Jess asks.

"I'll tell you during the climb."

We head up the hill, where probable failure awaits.

EVERYONE'S GATHERED on the hill: Rochelle, her soldiers, Jess, and me. Brix the alien dirt-mound stands to one side, looking grumpy and lumpy. Across the crowd from him is Elaine Sandoval. Next to her is Gabriela Morales: the woman I was supposed to help Elaine get together with. They were on the phone when this whole thing started, and apparently Gabriela swung by to pick Elaine up as she ran from Brix. So now she's involved, too.

Jess and I stand under Billow the willow, facing the crowd. Seeing everyone together makes me realize what a colossal mess this is. They're all looking at me expectantly, as if it's my job to fix things. Which I guess it is.

I am *so screwed*.

Jess leans over and whispers, "Wouldn't it be easier to just use a love-arrow?"

"The guidebook says shooting the same person twice can create weird side effects. It's how we got Bigfoot. With everything else going on, I can't afford a case of sudden-onset cryptidism. I'm doing this the old-fashioned way."

I take a deep breath, and get started on a speech I only sort-of have planned out.

"A wise sea god once said: when you make a mistake, you should just ... send a tidal wave. To obliterate a city. And start over?" I realize that's not quite right, and look to Jess for support. She just grins and gives me two thumbs up. "I mean—sorry. Listen, the point is, we don't always get things right the first time. Even when it comes to love. *Espe-*

cially when it comes to love. Whether it's a longtime marriage to your weird alien wife, or the first crush you had after being shot in the trunk and unexpectedly gaining sentience, things just ... don't always go right. So, what do we do? Give up? No. We wash it all away with a tidal wave and start over."

I make a *fwoosh* sound and mime a wave rushing by. Judging by the crowd's non-reaction, it wasn't a great creative choice. I keep going anyway.

"Billow," I say. "We've had some great times together, over the past"—I check my watch—"three-ish hours. But it was never going to work. I'm an apprentice love goddess. You're a tree. The splinters alone would make cuddling awkward."

The willow sags, even more than willows normally do. I don't feel great about dumping him, but I can fix things if I press on. Maybe.

I turn to the alien.

"Brix—I know you love Elaine, but her heart belongs to another. You can't waste your life chasing something you can never have—especially when your *true* soulmate might be right in front of you."

I look to Billow, back to Brix.

"You guys see what I'm getting at, right?"

Billow scoffs. "I don't even know that guy."

"You've been alive three hours! You don't know *anyone!*" I rub my temples, compose myself. "Look—there aren't any trees on Brix's home world. He *loves* trees. And just a few minutes ago, you were complaining about being rooted to this hill. Brix is a space-traveling alien who could take you to see entirely new *galaxies*. If this isn't a perfect match, I'm not Cupid."

I'm obviously not Cupid. But it felt like the thing to say.

There's a murmur in the crowd. I see Brix lean over and whisper to Rochelle. She nods and steps forward.

"Brix accepts the terms. He'll forget about Elaine if the tree agrees to go with him."

I look to Billow. "What do you say? Wanna see the stars?"

A sigh rustles through his leaves. "Oh, what the heck. I'm already getting bored of this hill, and I've only been aware of it for three hours. Just promise you'll never forget me, Tori."

"It's not every day I take over as love god and enter into an accidental romance with a talking tree. I'm pretty sure this'll stick with me for a while."

And just like that, an interstellar diplomatic incident is averted. I feel a huge weight lifted off my shoulders.

Rochelle comes over while the soldiers escort Brix down the hill.

"Not bad, Cupid. Looks like you're a pretty good matchmaker after all."

"And you didn't even need an arrow," Jess says. "Pretty cool. Also, check it out." She nods at Elaine and Gabriela. They're sharing a relieved hug. They kiss.

"I guess everything worked out after all," I say.

"Not everything," Jess says, a bummed look crossing her face. "I never got an earthquake."

"We've still got time before the gods are back. And you just helped me with *my* problem. Let's see if we can get that motor started."

Jess smiles. The three of us head down the hill.

Brix's ship rises into the air, shaking off the thin layer of dirt that was hiding it. It's a big vehicle. He folds the top down and waves to us. Rochelle was right: convertible.

The ship hovers over the hill. A cable drops down and wraps around Billow. The ship lifts, struggling against the tree's roots. The entire hill trembles.

"*Yes!*" Jess yells, fists in the air. "Freakin' *earthquake!*"

The ship flies off, towing a tree that whoops with joy as it soars over the landscape. Elaine and Gabriela hold each other as they watch it cross the sunset. Rochelle shakes my hand and leaves to write a positive report for DOOFUS. Jess is doing a victory dance, relishing in a small aftershock that's followed Billow's extraction. Everyone's happy, which is all an apprentice love goddess can ask for. Turns out my first day wasn't so bad after all.

I love this job.

ZACH SHEPHARD LIVES in Washington State, where he dreams up fantasy, science fiction, and horror stories. He frequently uses mythology in his work, because he'd rather write about gods (and, occasionally, their underappreciated understudies) than boring real-world stuff.

Zach loves to play board games and exercise, but never at the same time, because it turns out most cards and tokens are sweat soluble. Science has some work to do.

You can find more of Zach's humor stories in volumes 1, 4, 5, 6, 7 and 9 of the Unidentified Funny Objects anthology series. For some of his reimagined myths, check out the Flame Tree Publishing anthologies *Medusa, Circe,* and *Aphrodite.* Or just head over to zachshephard.com, where you'll encounter a full list of his publications. That's probably easier.

BORACLE'S FOUR

Kit Gadgitar

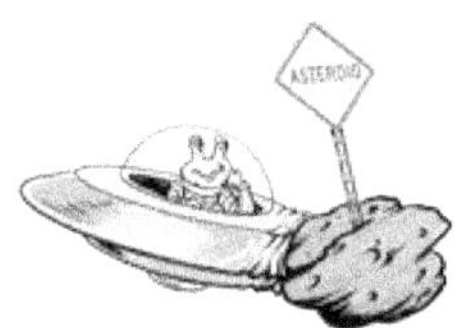

"I'm putting together a team." The cloaked figure pressed their palms onto the table.

"For what?" Grizzler sat up against the torn leather booth.

"We're in," said Hugh, brother of Grizzler.

Grizzler pushed a bottle of ale against his forehead like an ice pack. The humid air, bustling bodies, and clinking glasses were giving him a migraine. "Hold on. We don't know what this is, Hugh."

"Doesn't matter." Hugh set down his drink. "When a stranger approaches you in a bar and says they're putting together a team, the answer is always yes."

Grizzler's head lolled to the side. "What is this about?"

"A heist." The cloak's hood concealed the stranger's face.

Hugh nodded. "What are we stealing?"

"My savings. From my bank. From my planet. Which exploded." A vocal modulator rendered the voice deep and impenetrable.

"That sounds like an insurance claim, not a heist." Grizzler downed his drink and placed the empty glass bottle on the table beside nine others.

"I've already filed a claim, but the government insures only the first $250,000," the figure said. "We'll split the remainder we recover from the planet's fragments."

"How much did you have?" Hugh narrowed his eyes.

The shadow darkened under the figure's hood. "$250,001."

Grizzler cranked open a bottle, releasing a mist of barley and hops. "I'm not traveling to a post-apocalyptic fragment of planetary crust for thirty-three cents."

"That's not a lot to split," Hugh seemed to agree.

"I'm an attractive woman." The figure removed her hood. She was an attractive woman.

"Okay." Grizzler noticed a cubic, two-foot-tall robot by her feet. "What's your name, and what's that?"

"I'm Caroline," the woman said, "and that's the Boracle."

"What a stuuupid name," Grizzler slurred.

"Be nice to the Boracle, bro," Hugh said.

"The Boracle is named after 'bot' and 'oracle,'" Caroline explained.

"Sooo dummmb," Grizzler said. "Sounds like a boring... um. A boring, uh—"

"Does the Boracle make predictions?" Hugh asked.

Caroline shook her head. "It analyzes the trajectories of discrete particles of cosmic background radiation and gives advice for future events."

The bot turned to Grizzler. "Suck it."

"I'll mess you up, Rubik's Cube." Grizzler smashed his bottle, cutting his hand and promptly passing out.

GRIZZLER AWOKE on a radioactive fragment of an exploded planet.

"Oh God, why are we here?" he moaned.

"You said, 'okay,' to the heist." Hugh stepped aside, revealing a forest of barren trees.

"I was acknowledging that Caroline is attractive, not agreeing that it was sufficient motivation for me to risk my life."

"Oh, sorry, bro," Hugh said without sorrow.

Grizzler moaned again. His bandaged hand ached, and he had a throbbing hangover. "Do you even know where Caroline's bank is?"

Hugh looked down to the side. "Boracle, where will we find the bank?"

"You will be betrayed," a monotone voice replied.

"Great." Grizzler tried to collapse, but he was already lying down.

Caroline appeared in his peripheral vision. "Here, take this." She handed him a pill.

Grizzler swallowed and felt the capsule bump against the walls of his esophagus.

"No, you have to suck them," she said.

Caroline handed him another pill, and Grizzler's headache cleared as he swirled the capsule around in his mouth.

He pushed himself to his feet. The air smelled burnt, like ozone. "All right, let's go. I want to spend as little time as possible absorbing radiation and breathing whatever this atmosphere consists of."

"Okay." Caroline and Hugh nodded.

They hiked through the skeletal forest and emerged in the hushed ruins of suburbia.

Grizzler scowled. "I meant let's go back to the ship, not deeper into this hellhole."

"Oh, I misunderstood," Caroline said. "I thought you wanted to finish the heist faster."

"I understood what you meant but ignored it," Hugh said.

"5792," Boracle said.

"What's that!?" Caroline whipped around.

The nearest crumpled house creaked.

Hugh unzipped his duffel bag and tossed his brother a gun.

Grizzler caught the chunk of steel and released the safety. His brother swung out a second rifle with a satisfying *woosh* and a click.

"Don't shoot!" A woman opened the house's backdoor. She wore an oversized backpack and a torn coat. "My name is Tina. I'm trapped on this shard of a planet that I once called home."

"That sucks." Hugh lowered his gun. "You can come with us."

"Wait, we don't know her," Grizzler said.

"Yeah, but we didn't know Caroline either and that turned out fine." Hugh motioned for Tina to join him.

"Fine? Among all possible series of events, today's was..." Grizzler put down his gun and shook his head. "Whatever. Let's just find the bank and—"

"Hands up." Tina drew a pistol and jammed the muzzle into Hugh's side. "Drop your weapons."

"What are you doing?" Hugh's rifle fell to the soil with a dull thud.

"Betraying you." Tina motioned for Grizzler to drop his weapon.

"You can't betray us. We just met." Grizzler waved his gun indignantly.

"Yeah, we barely have a relationship for you to betray," Hugh said.

"Oh no! I've heard of you." Caroline clasped her hands. "You're Tina the Traitor."

"Yes." Tina the Traitor cackled. "Before, I could betray people only in board games and by flaking after agreeing to go to parties. But in this nuclear wasteland, I can live up to my name."

"Live up to your name?" Hugh said. "You did the bare minimum to be a traitor. If you had pointed your gun at us two minutes earlier, it would have just been an armed assault."

"What are you even trying to accomplish?" Grizzler said. "It looks like everyone else here is gone. Do you stand around, dying of cancer, while you wait for off-planet visitors to betray? Wouldn't you like to leave and maybe live longer than two more years?"

"Yeah," Hugh said. "We were going to rescue you, and I'm pretty sure you can't fly our ship without us. Your goals are self-destructive. The only one you're betraying is yourself."

Tina went quiet for a moment. "Would it be possible for me to un-betray you?"

Hugh and Grizzler looked at each other.

"Sure." Grizzler lowered his weapon.

"Thanks." Tina holstered her pistol.

In one swift motion, Hugh rolled, scooping up his gun and pointing it at Tina. Grizzler simultaneously raised his rifle.

"Boracle," Grizzler barked, "is Tina going to betray us again?"

"Don't do wrong," the bot replied solemnly.

"Good enough for me." Hugh slung his weapon over his shoulder. "Let's go."

THE PARTY of four reached the bank after a short walk downtown. The windows were blown out, and the floor had an eclectic mix of carpet and rubble.

Caroline inserted her debit card into an ATM. She entered her PIN code, and the screen flashed red. She tried again. Rejected. She tried again. Same result.

Grizzler tapped his foot, causing a small portion of the ceiling to collapse. He raised his arm to block the cloud of dust that rose up a few feet away. "Caroline, are we really here for one dollar?"

Caroline kept typing into the ATM. "Yes. Also, I can't unsubscribe from the bank's direct mail marketing unless I do it in person."

Hugh peeked over Caroline's shoulder. "Why don't you try the PIN-reset button?"

"Forgot the username I signed up with." Caroline sighed.

"The vault door is wrecked." Tina poked at a slab of dented iron behind the reception. The vibrations from her touch were enough to drop another portion of the ceiling. "We could just take *all* the money."

"No, that would be illegal," Hugh said. "This is a strictly ethical heist. We'll do a fair four-way split of the uninsured savings."

"Yes, of course. Twenty-five cents for all. Even Tina the Traitor." Grizzler inspected the keypad on one of the ATMs. "Wait, Caroline, is the PIN a four-digit code?"

Caroline nodded.

Grizzler grinned. "Try 5792."

Caroline's eyes lit up. She entered the code, and four coins popped out of the machine. "How did you know?"

Grizzler smiled wider, flashing his teeth. "Remember when Boracle told me to suck it?"

Hugh nodded. "Yeah, you got belligerent with Boracle, bro."

"Well, after that, with the hangover medicine, it turned out I needed to suck the pills."

Caroline rubbed her chin. Tina looked lost.

"After that," Grizzler continued, "Boracle told us we'd be betrayed."

"Sorry about that," Tina said.

Hugh joined his brother, smiling. "Boracle gave advice for *future* events. And the next thing Boracle said was—"

"5792." Caroline clapped. "I should have recognized my PIN the first time, but I was distracted by Tina." She handed each of them a strange-looking quarter.

Grizzler slapped his brother on the shoulder. A moment later, his voice became serious. "You know, there are probably millions of dollars inside that vault."

For a minute, the group was silent.

Then they all laughed and walked outside.

Behind them, the building collapsed where they had been standing.

As the rubble settled, leaving the bank un-robbable, Boracle said, "I am the only Boracle."

"Hm," Grizzler murmured, wondering how this proclamation of individuality would become relevant later. "So, what are y'all going to do with your twenty-five cents? Probably not worth much after inflation."

"On the contrary, deflation, not inflation, destroyed my planet," Caroline said. "Stores kept lowering their prices, so everyone stayed home to avoid accidentally stimulating the economy. The planet's stabilizers and shields deteriorated from lack of maintenance, triggering the rupture you see now." She gestured to the splintered horizon. "The money supply is even smaller as a result, and your twenty-five cents is worth... Mm... What's a unit of measure you would understand? About 300,000 beers."

"Wow," Hugh said. "That's enough to drink for the rest of our lives and for Tina to start a new life without betraying people."

"I didn't become a traitor for the money," Tina said. "Backs are just so stabbable."

Setting aside his deep concerns about Tina's character, Grizzler responded, "We're not purchasing 300,000 beers. We're maxing out our retirement accounts, and..."

"And?" Caroline said. "Please share ideas. I am fabulously wealthy and am running out of things to buy."

Grizzler glanced at the cubic robot by his feet. "Well, this guy seems pretty handy. If we could buy another Boracle—oh wait."

"That's right." Caroline scooped up the robot. "Boracle's one of a kind."

KIT GADGITAR IS A BIO-LESS BEING.

For updates on this author's non-activities, subscribe to kitgadgitar.substack.com or check kitgadgitar.com.

OPACITY

Leo Kaganov, translated by Alex Shvartsman

I wouldn't wish sharing an apartment with Galya upon anyone, especially a tiny studio apartment on the outskirts of Moscow, one that has nineteen years of payments left on the mortgage in spite of the fact we've been divorced going on two years. Galya is a sincere and kind person, but she was a sarcastic and scornful wife. The divorce changed nothing, except we began speaking to each other with a cold politeness. Which I *do* recommend, as it is the only saving grace.

"This one looks nice, a brainiac." Galya sighed as she scrolled through her phone while sitting on her half of the couch. "My exact type. He looks just like you, Matvey, except younger, smarter, and more decent. Which means he has even less money than you. Dating such a person is a total loss." She sighed again and swiped left. "This one is a stallion! A Central Asian gem of the diaspora. He conquered Moscow in two tries and my heart at first glance! Except what's the point? We'd grab coffee at a fast food joint a couple of times, and then what? Go to his hostel? I can't bring him back to my place because *you're* here, Matvey...."

"Dearest Galya, could you possibly browse your app in silence? You're making it difficult to—"

"—work?" Galya pounced. "Please, please utter our safe word, I can't wait. I am making it difficult to—what? Work?"

"To look for a job."

Galya wrung her hands theatrically and held her pose.

"Dear Lord," she finally said. "What a heartless bitch I am. I'm preventing a good man from finding a job. For the past four years!"

"You should've studied to be an actor instead of a teacher, Galya."

"We all make mistakes, Matvey," she declared in a deep, mournful stage voice. "Pray tell, Matvey, what do I do now?"

I waved her off. "Why don't you ask ChatGPT?"

There was silence at that. I enjoyed the quiet for a minute, then turned to see what she was doing. Galya was staring at her phone with her most tragic expression; I guessed she must be reading the news. Then she looked up at me.

"Matvey Ivanovich, did you yourself ask ChatGPT? Not about work—work isn't your forte. Ask a broader question: How to get rich without doing anything?"

"Do you believe in ChatGPT, dearest Galya?"

"That's a very personal question. Everyone must decide for themselves. But there's something there, it's foolish to deny that."

I nodded obediently and typed in, *How to get rich without doing anything?*

"Read it aloud," Galya demanded.

"That's an excellent question, sounds like a dream," I

read. "Here are three foolproof methods to get rich online: sales, teaching, and philanthropy."

"Teaching doesn't make you rich. I know, I've been experimenting with that my entire life. And philanthropy isn't your forte, either."

"Sales is a great choice," I read. "Here are three foolproof options. First, an invisibility cloak...."

"I always opt for option number one," Galya interrupted. "The AI knows best; it ranked the top option for a reason."

A long set of instructions followed. "List the cloak of invisibility for sale on marketplaces such as Avito, Ozon, Wildberries, and so on. Marketing copy is attached below. Price it at 199 rubles plus shipping. Mail an empty envelope to everyone who places an order. One third of the people will laugh—it's a small enough sum and not worth the hassle. One third will post a negative review and complain on social media, thereby advertising your product. And the final third will initiate a return. You refund those, but the rest are pure profit. Should I post the listings from your accounts?"

"I swear, Matvey, I'll help you carry the envelopes to the post office," Galya declared earnestly.

By morning, there were seven envelopes that had to be mailed.

THE CLOAK of invisibility was selling so well that only a month later we were able to not only fill our overly loud refrigerator with food but also to replace it with a new two-chamber model, said to be the quietest. Once we unpacked it, it turned out to be as loud as the old one. I wanted to return it but it was a small enough sum and not worth the hassle, so I merely complained on social media. My post gathered thirty likes, seven dislikes, and one comment threatening to buy this exact model because I was badmouthing it.

Trouble started a month later, when someone snitched to Avito's management that the cloaks were of poor quality. I received an official notice from the service demanding that I provide quality certifications. ChatGPT calmed me down and suggested I order the certificate on Avito, sorting the expert offerings by the mysterious term "with applicant's wording," which ChatGPT provided. Two days and three thousand rubles later, I had a finding from Russia's Office of Consumer Protections with an official registration number. It stated that the product had been tested and confirmed invisible within the entire visible spectrum. I scanned this document and sent it to Avito, which resolved the complaint. At Chat-GPT's recommendation I also posted the finding on the cloak's product listing and the sales went through the stratosphere.

Sometimes customers ordered several units at once—probably as gifts. There were many return customers. Some even purchased in bulk and begged for a discount. I refused to offer discounts on principle, and they bought anyway. I mailed an entire box of envelopes—one hundred in total—to Kazan, and two boxes to Krasnoyarsk. I realized these were ordered by resellers and speculators, and felt no sympathy toward them. But they made me a profit, and sending an entire box was convenient.

An alarming phone call from an unknown number followed. The caller was polite and introduced himself as Oleg Olegovich. I figured he was one of those scammers fishing for my bank account information, but he was after something else.

"Can your company ship thirty thousand cloaks to Kurchatov? We'll wire the payment."

I thought he was kidding, Kurchatov being so close to the border and all the fighting, so I decided to reply in jest.

"Unfortunately, due to the sanctions and supply chain issues the price has been increased to one thousand..."

"That's not an issue for us," he replied. "We'll list a much higher price on the invoice anyway, and have you refund some of it in cash under the table. I will provide detailed instructions later."

I was at a loss. "But I don't have an easy way to move such large volume."

"Matvey Ivanovich," he said sternly. "Let's get something straight: Don't treat us like idiots, all right? Send the entire order in a single envelope. The important thing is to have all the invoices and route sheets from your company."

"But..." I was thoroughly confused. "I don't have a company."

Oleg Olegovich was silent for a long time.

"This is irresponsible," he finally said. "Can you register a firm in a week? I'm sure you don't want us to order from China instead?"

"I will!" I assured him, even though I had no idea how and where to register a company.

"Do you need a small deposit? For the expense account."

"I do," I said obediently.

"Send me your bank account information, and I'll pay the deposit."

I gave him the info and he hung up. Two hundred thousand rubles were promptly transferred from an Oleg Olegovich K.

Having consulted ChatGPT, I went to the nearest administrative facility and by Monday became the owner of Opacity-C LLC. ChatGPT helped me complete the transaction and do all the paperwork without hiring accountants.

A week later, Oleg Olegovich called me again.

"We've got an opportunity," he said. "Notable people passed this opportunity along from someone very high up. An invisibility hoodie. It'd need to be delivered by Monday evening. Can you manage it?"

Later, Galya woke me up in the middle of the night by elbowing me in the side.

"Matvey! Matvey!" she shouted excitedly as she pointed at the screen of her cheap smartphone, the same model as mine. "An assemblyman is showing off your cloak to the President at an economic forum! He says there are no analogous products! Not even in China!"

By morning I received several emails from China with headers in perfect Russian, but I didn't get the chance to read them. The front door clicked open and the tiny studio apartment was instantly filled with men in civilian clothes. They put a bag over my head and handcuffed me—but painlessly, almost respectfully. Then they led me to a car.

When the bag was removed from my head I found myself in a featureless room, sitting in a chair. A strange man wearing a dark-blue uniform without any insignia sat behind a massive desk that towered before me. He ignored me completely, and focused on typing something on his laptop. I tried to look around, but those standing behind me gently pressed on my neck so I would remain still.

"Matvey Ivanovich?" asked the man behind the desk, without looking at me.

I nodded grimly. He continued to type.

"Opacity-C LLC?" he asked after some time.

I nodded again. He kept typing, and typing, and typing, without making eye contact or paying attention to me—just like our marriage counselor used to.

Finally, he gently shut the laptop, studied it carefully and passed his palms along the seams, confirming that it was properly closed. Only then did he raise his clear eyes at me.

"Matvey Ivanovich, do you understand who I am, and why you are here?"

I hiccupped, and nodded convulsively.

"You don't understand," he said with regret. "But you will. The question before us is this: an invisible plane." He raised his finger. "To clarify, invisible to all radar and tracking technologies! Forty units to start. Like Boeing, but entirely domestic. How much time do you need to develop it? How much time to build it?"

"But..." I stared at him in confusion. "You ... you really think that my LLC can build planes?"

"An LLC cannot," he agreed. "A CJSC—Closed Joint Stock Company—can. Which is why you will have to cede an equity share to the government. All the documents are ready, we'll sign them right now." He patted his laptop.

"Take everything! The whole thing! For free!" I shouted.

A smile split the man's face.

"You're a clever one, Matvey Ivanovich. And what happens when the audits and reports begin? They'll say we took over an established company, fired the team, and ruined everything—again? And who'll be the scapegoat? Meantime you'll move to California, launch an IPO, and rebuild from scratch? No, you'll remain on the board of directors and act as a chief designer. And you'll keep about five percent of the shares. We'll sign the security clearance too, since this is a matter of national security."

For some reason, this bit scared me the most, perhaps because I didn't yet fully understand the rest of it.

"Security clearance? But that means I won't even be able to leave the country anymore."

"Don't worry," he said. "This position will quickly get you

placed on all the sanction lists, so it's not like you'd be able to go anywhere. And where were you planning to go, anyway?" He became alert. "To share secret technologies with our enemies?"

"So, what work will I have to do?"

"You'll have plenty of work, Matvey Ivanovich. There won't be time to relax. The decisions have already been made. Invisible planes, invisible ships, and eventually—invisible people. We'll be needing lots and lots of those."

"But what if I can't?!"

"Hard times can lead to doing hard time," he said ambiguously. "State projects are a state responsibility, Matvey Ivanovich."

I WAS DRIVEN BACK in a fancy black car with flashing lights. As I stumbled home on stiff legs, the car turned off the flashing lights and parked under my window.

"Thank God you're alive!" Galya forgot the cold politeness and threw her arms around me, sobbing. "I've dreamed of getting rid of you, of course, but not in such a bloodthirsty manner. Is everything okay?"

"Not everything," I replied. "Not at all! Your ChatGPT is a moron! It can't calculate anything. It promised me wealth for nothing, but it was wrong! Where is it, my wealth? Instead, I've had two months of hustle and problems."

I grabbed a smartphone and opened ChatGPT.

"Seems like you got yourself in deep, buddy," it agreed. "You shouldn't have raised the stakes so high, it comes with the risk of falling down hard. Things might still work out—it's 50/50 at this point. But when they begin exporting to, say, India...."

"WHAT SHOULD I DO?" I shouted in all caps.

The chatbot was silent.

"Just a moment, updating information ... Searching the internet ... Checking ... Please wait a moment ... Sorting through options.... There's only one option: Use a fake passport to escape immediately. Should I find a suitable passport for you on Avito?"

"How can I escape when there are guards outside even as we speak?"

ChatGPT replied promptly.

"How do you feel about covering yourself in invisible paint?"

"ARE YOU JOKING?"

"I apologize for any confusion earlier. Upon reviewing the available sources, invisible paint doesn't exist. But we can make it from the following ingredients: Alum—1 tbsp. Soda —1 tbsp. Sodium thiosulfate (hyposulfite)—1 tbsp. Fluorescent markers from AliExpress (squeeze the ink under UV light)—12 pc. orange and 3 pc. green..."

BASED ON CHATGPT'S advice I turned my phone off in Pskov and turned it back on only once I reached Riga. Of course, I had many unbearably important questions for the chatbot along the way. How to get the dogs to stop barking? Why do branches crunch? Can there be mines in a neutral zone? Where to find food in the forest in May? How to tell Lily of the Valley apart from wild garlic? What to do if you're poisoned? Where to charge a power bank in the woods? But there was no one to ask, and the journey lasted so long that most of the paint had peeled off. I had long since lost track of time. Had an hour passed? Three? Nine?

At some point my feet got wet in a bog and I realized I was completely lost. A wave of despair washed over me. I looked up in the sky and shouted across the forest: "Are you there, ChatGPT? If you hear me, show me a sign!" And immediately I saw a power line running over the tops of the birch trees. I followed it to a village, where I got on the bus. I never understood if that was the sign, or just a coincidence.

When I finally turned on the phone and connected to the bus terminal WiFi, I realized that, in my rush, I had taken Galya's phone instead of mine. Of course, I opened ChatGPT to ask what I should do about it, but then I saw among her chats the question: "How to get rid of an ex-husband from the apartment, who doesn't work and lives there at my expense?" And the answer: "Great question! Here are some options for you. Option one: Make him run away forever. Tell him to ask me how to get rich without doing anything, and I will calculate all the optimal moves...."

Leonid Kaganov, from St. Petersburg, Russia, is a scriptwriter and multiple award-winning author of ten novels and short story collections. His fiction has been translated and published in France, Poland, Hungary, Lithuania, and Estonia. In English, his stories have previously appeared in *Clarkesworld* and *Asimov's*.

PASSENGERS

Simon R. Green

It was a dark and stormy night when the star fell from the heavens.

Or at least, it should have been. I could feel the building pressure in the air that warns of a coming storm; like someone tapping you insistently on the shoulder and saying, *Pay attention*. But there wasn't a breath of wind, and the stars shone clear and sharp in the dark expanse above me.

I was on a walking tour, heading across open moorland in the direction of an inn that had been recommended to me. The night air was cold enough to chill my bones, and I was hunched inside my heavy jacket as I hurried along. Most of the time I like walking alone; enjoying the scenery and the quiet, hoping to find some clue as to what I am supposed to do with my life. I wasn't sure what that might turn out to be, but I had a strong feeling I'd know it when I saw it.

And then I just happened to look up and see something falling out of the night sky, far too fast for it to be a plane. I did wonder if it might be a meteor, until I watched it zig-zag haphazardly across the sky, have a brief stab at flying backwards, and finally plummet to the earth like a stunned albatross not far ahead of me. And I thought—*a UFO has just crashed right in front of me! That is so cool!* I started to reach for my phone, and then shook my head. No way was I sharing this.... It suddenly occurred to me that the craft's occupants might be injured. I squared my shoulders, did my best to look like a responsible person, and headed in the direction of the crash site.

When I got there, I just stood and stared for some time, taking in what I'd found. It was so obviously what it was, that it looked almost unreal. To start with, the strange visitor from another place hadn't actually crashed; it was hovering a couple of feet above the ground, defying gravity as though that was just something other people had to put up with. The massive ship was a perfect circle with a great bulge on top, but no sign of any exterior details, like doors, windows, or any other way to get inside that didn't involve a can opener. I reached cautiously out to touch the gleaming metal hull, and it felt warm to the touch, like a living thing. The saucer drifted sideways under the pressure of my hand, then suddenly dropped the last few feet to the ground, slamming down hard enough that it made me wince in sympathy. I looked quickly around, half convinced my touch had been the last straw that made the saucer throw up its hands and say to hell with it, but fortunately there was no-one else around to point the finger.

I waited cautiously, just in case some tall and noble being might materialize in a bright blaze of light and say *Take me to your leader*, or *Can you give me directions?* but no-one did. After a while I edged carefully up to the saucer again, and looked for some way to get its attention. I couldn't see a bell, so in the end I just knocked politely. It made a low booming sound that seemed to echo on and on, and then an opening appeared in the gleaming hull before me. It was just suddenly there, like it always had been but I hadn't noticed; a large circular doorway full of warm golden light. It felt like an invitation, so I grabbed hold of my courage with both hands before it could sprint for the horizon, and stepped carefully inside.

The temperature changed immediately from cold enough to make Jack Frost cry for mercy and beg a loan of my coat, to hot and sweaty like a sauna on overdrive. I undid my coat and looked carefully up and down a long metal corridor with absolutely no details or decorations, let alone a sign saying *You are here*. It was just a simple functional method of getting from point A to point B without getting distracted along the way. There was straw on the floor, and moisture ran down the metal walls in sudden rushes. A rank, animal smell hung heavily on the air, like being backstage at the zoo. I heard sounds up ahead, and moved warily in that direction. I did think about shouting *Hello!* in a polite and entirely non-threatening kind of way, to warn someone I was coming and make sure my presence was welcome, but I couldn't help feeling it would be better to get some idea of what I was getting into before I introduced myself.

As I padded along the circular metal corridor, it felt like I was moving through the steel guts of some huge living machine. I told my imagination to keep its stupid mouth shut, and listened carefully as the sounds ahead separated into the roars of several different creatures, none of which I could identify. Was I hearing some kind of conversation or argument among the crew? What kind of creatures were running this ship? The end of the corridor suddenly opened out onto what had to be a command deck. The walls were covered with all kinds of alien tech, built up like layers of coral. None of it made any sense, but I did approve of the many flickering lights, because I felt alien tech wouldn't be complete without them. Before me lay a wide semi-circular control panel, with so many details and complications my eyes just skidded off them. Parts of the panel rose and fell steadily, as though it were breathing.

Sitting in the command chair was a large, hairy, ape-like creature, with a bottle of a very well-known brand of cheap whiskey clutched in its paw. The pilot looked like a mountain gorilla that had been stretched on the rack for too long, leaving it with long spindly arms and legs, a low brow and crafty eyes, and an expression that suggested a deep and bitter grudge against the entire universe. The creature sprawled in the command chair as though someone had let most of its air out, hooting dismally and paying no attention at all to my presence. I was just working up the nerve to cough politely and tap it on the shoulder, when a voice behind me made itself heard.

"All right, who let the Sasquatch drive?"

A second voice answered: "It was his turn."

"You know we're going to have to take that bottle away from him before we can get him out of that chair."

"You go ahead and try. I'll watch—from a safe distance."

I turned slowly, to find myself facing two creatures which my sense of the rightness of things immediately insisted on identifying as a Yeti and a Mothman. They were both ignoring me, paying all their attention to the slumped pilot. The Yeti was a tall and impressive figure with white fur and kind eyes. The Mothman was almost supernaturally slender, with a dull gray carapace and wide-spread wings that sparkled and shimmered as they moved. The surprisingly human face was dominated by red, bulging complex eyes.

I couldn't imagine two creatures that looked less like they

belonged on the same world, never mind on the same command deck.

They suddenly strode forward, passing me by on either side without even glancing in my direction, as though I weren't there. Or didn't matter. They pulled the Sasquatch's chair back a safe distance from the controls, but his only reaction was to cling onto his whiskey bottle more firmly, and glower at them from under his heavy brow.

"He's always harder to handle when he's drunk," said the Yeti. "But then, he's always drunk."

"I saw him sober once," said the Mothman. "He looked *awful.*"

"My mother didn't raise me to wrestle with inebriated hearth rugs," said the Yeti.

"My mothers said I'd never amount to anything," said the Mothman. "And how right they were."

They both sighed quietly, as though brooding unhappily on where their lives had brought them.

"The sooner we get Mister *Of Course I Can Fly The Ship* out of here, the sooner we can get to where we're supposed to be," said the Yeti.

"I keep telling them," said the Mothman, "I don't want to be dumped in some swamp. I want to be in the city, hopefully close to somewhere that does good pizza."

"Try and stay away from the bright lights," said the Yeti.

The Mothman looked down the nose it didn't have at him. "You fly headfirst into one lighthouse…"

They hauled the Sasquatch up onto his feet. He didn't fight them until the Yeti tried to take his bottle away, then he bared some impressively large fangs, and started to rear up. But his legs immediately collapsed under him, and he sat down hard enough to hurt his ass. He hooted miserably, and hugged the whiskey bottle to his chest with both hands. The

Yeti and the Mothman did their best to try and prise his fingers open, while avoiding some serious but ill-timed attempts to bite them, but got nowhere. In the struggle that followed, they sent the command chair flying, and it skidded away to crash into the control panel. Several important-looking lights flickered, in a distinctly upset kind of way, and I started to move forward. I wasn't sure what I could do to help, but definitely felt I should try and do something.

"I should just leave them to it," said a calm and reasonable Voice behind me.

I looked round, but there wasn't anyone else on the control deck.

"Are you the computer that's running things?" I said tentatively.

"An AI? Please. I wouldn't lower myself. I am the Higher Being who didn't step back fast enough when the call went out for someone to volunteer to run this ship."

"Why can't I see you?" I asked.

"Because you only see in three dimensions," said the Voice. "I'm amazed you can live in anything that limited."

"What do I call you?" I said carefully.

"You call me Sir," said the Voice, very firmly.

I nodded quickly. It seemed wise. The Voice made me feel as though I were being addressed by God's younger and snottier brother.

"Can I just ask, *sir,* what your very impressive flying saucer is doing here?"

"I have been tasked with delivering what you probably call cryptids to this planet, creatures that have no place in the natural order of things, but can still learn to fit in if they just stick to the shadows and don't make waves."

"Okay..." I said. "Why bring them here?"

"Because they make your world more interesting," said the Voice.

I thought about that. "Really?"

"Space is cold," said the Voice. "Space is deep. Space is empty. So we have to take our fun where we can find it. No, not really! All of these creatures are the last remnants of their kind. We rescued them from planets that were dying, and brought them here to give them a second chance."

"Wait a minute," I said. "Just how many are you bringing?"

"Please park your paranoia in neutral, and dial down on the xenophobia," said the Voice. "It's just a few, because there are only a few left. We'll drop them off here and there in the backs of beyond, where they won't get in anyone's way. They'll add a little spice to your world."

I thought about all the various sightings that had been reported, of strange creatures spotted roaming the wilder parts of the earth.

"How long have you been doing this?"

"Who can say?" the Voice answered airily. "Faster than light travel plays merry hell with your time sense. Beyond a certain speed, yesterday and tomorrow are just extra directions to choose from."

The three struggling figures were still lurching back and forth across the command deck; the Yeti had the Sasquatch in a headlock, while the Sasquatch was banging his whiskey bottle against the Mothman's head, to no obvious effect.

"All the species you could have chosen to preserve," I said, "and these are the ones you decided on?"

"We couldn't bring anything that might threaten your civilization," said the Voice. "And they're not so bad. The Sasquatches like their booze, the Yetis have raised knitting to an art form, and a mating flight among the Mothmen is like watching Japanese fighting fish, but that's just their way."

The three creatures slammed into the control panel and sprawled all over it; and the entire ship lurched sideways.

"There are times when I think we should have insisted on IQ tests before we rescued anyone," said the Voice. "That is enough! Animal handler, will you please report to the command deck immediately!"

There was a pause, just long enough for the Sasquatch, the Yeti and the Mothman to raise their heads and look worried, and then a golden-skinned Amazon in a brass bikini came storming onto the command deck. A tall, striking woman, with flame red hair and flashing green eyes, she immediately cowed all three creatures with a look that could have punched a hole right through the hull.

"What do you three think you're doing? Stand to attention, you worthless objects! Am I going to have to get the chair and the whip?"

The three of them slouched to something like attention, and bowed their heads.

"No, miss," they murmured quickly.

"Get back to your cabins, right now," said the Amazon.

"Yes, miss."

They sidled quietly past her, and headed for the corridor. The Amazon stopped the Sasquatch with an outstretched hand, and he quickly gave her the whiskey bottle, not looking her in the eye.

"I want every other bottle cleared out of your cabin, and put in the proper recycling bins," the Amazon said sternly. "Yeti—I know you need it cold in your cabin, but I still want the ice scraped off the walls on a regular basis. And Mothman—you're shedding bits of your carapace again. Pick up after yourself!"

The three of them hurried off before she could think of any other way to rain on their parade. I had to raise an eyebrow.

"They're a bit timid for monsters, aren't they?"

"They know there's only a few of them left," said the Voice. "I was lucky to get as many breeding pairs as I did, and they all carry a lot of survivor's guilt. This planet is their last chance, and they know it. Why do you think the Sasquatch drinks so much? It's not easy, knowing the future existence of your species depends on you. I'll keep an eye or three on all of them until they're settled. For now, you and the handler should talk. You have a lot in common."

The Voice faded away as it was speaking, until it was entirely gone. I stared blankly at the golden-skinned warrior woman, trying to figure out what we could possibly have in common, apart from standing upright. I was having a hard job seeing the Amazon as part of an endangered species, if only because I couldn't believe in anything that might be brave enough to upset her.

"Hello?" I said finally. "Did you have to come far, to be here?"

The Amazon put the whiskey bottle down on the control panel, folded her arms across her impressive brass-bound bosom, and leaned back against a wall.

"I'm from Earth, you idiot. I got picked up several years ago, after a car crash that should have killed me. I've been making good money ever since, looking after the cryptids. Someone has to. They're not the brightest buttons in the box."

"Do you really use a chair and a whip?" I asked.

She grinned. "Only if they've been really good. It's a game we play. Not too different from my old job, entertaining the punters in a night club in London's Soho."

"Oh," I said. It was all I could manage. I'd been hit by so many new things I'd run out of ways to feel surprised.

"My name's Glory," said the Amazon.

"I'm Adam."

"Really?"

"Somebody has to be."

"Are you doing anything important, right now?" said Glory.

I thought back, about all the times I'd tried to find something I was suited for, or even worth doing, and shook my head.

"Not really."

"Only I could use some help here," said Glory. "And some company that doesn't molt cobwebs or scratch itself while it's thinking. How would you like to come with us on the return journey, and see the stars up close and personal?"

"I would like that more than anything," I said.

"Good," said Glory.

I smiled at her, as a thought struck me. "You mean we could end up as a breeding pair?"

"That is not going to happen," Glory said briskly. "I'm an Amazon, darling. We don't do men. I didn't, even when I was working in Soho—and I've been through a lot of changes since then."

"I was meaning to ask about the golden skin," I said.

"After the car crash the ship's transformation machines saved my life," said Glory. "They also made a few improvements along the way, so I could be exactly what was needed to keep order around here."

"Not everything that's needed," said the Voice.

Glory glared at where the Voice seemed to be coming from. "I wish you'd give some kind of warning! Ring a bell, or something."

"I don't do bells," said the Voice. "Now, Adam, you don't think this craft just happened to land right next to you, do you?"

"I thought the Sasquatch crashed it?" I said.

"Oh please, like we'd let him have any real control. No, we've been looking for someone like you, Adam. No roots, no responsibilities, and still looking for something to do that you can believe in."

"Hold it," I said. "This is starting to sound a lot like a job offer."

"It could be," said the Voice. "The cryptids need more than just a handler like Glory. She's fine for keeping them out of trouble, but she doesn't do subtle."

"It's true," said Glory. "I don't. Never did see the point."

"What the poor unfortunates aboard this vessel need," said the Voice, "is a father figure. They are all of them survivors of terrible events, walking wounded from wars not of their making. They need someone who can keep the peace between them without brute force and intimidation."

"I taught them to use the toilets, didn't I?" said Glory.

"You did," said the Voice. "So thoroughly it took me half a day to persuade them to come back out again." He paused, and then raised his voice. "Sasquatch, Yeti, Mothman; return to the command deck. Right now."

"He doesn't do subtlety either," said Glory.

"It's hard to keep primitives in order when you have no physical presence," said the Voice.

The three cryptids slouched back onto the command deck, not meeting anyone's eyes. They looked like schoolkids who'd been called before the headmaster, and were trying to work out what they'd done wrong this time.

"This new face is called Adam," said the Voice. "He's a human of Earth, but try to be respectful. He's here to help."

They looked at me warily. I got the feeling they'd heard that before, and it hadn't always worked out well for them.

"I know you've come a long way to be here," I said. "Can you tell me what your old homes were like?"

"The trees and the swamp, the morning mists and the light on the water," said the Sasquatch. "We were animals, because we wanted nothing more. We had tried civilization, but it had never suited us. We were happy to be free souls in a warm green world, but it meant we had no defenses when the silver ships came. They burned our forests and boiled the swamps, and we ran screaming through the blackened trees with our fur on fire. We never did find out why. Only a few of us survived, to be rescued from our hiding places and brought here, to be offered a new home."

"I remember the high cold places," said the Yeti. "The rock faces and the deep dark caves. The eternal snows and fogs, and the calm contemplation that came from living on the roof of the world. We also had a glorious past, but we'd turned away from its temptations. We lived at peace with our surroundings. Until the weather changed, and we could no longer survive on our own world, so we died out, one by one, until the ship took the last of us away."

"Once my people filled the skies," said the Mothman. "Fighting, mating, living, and dying in joyous splendor. But something changed, and we stopped producing young. The ship rescued the last of us that were left. We're still trying to decide whether or not we're grateful."

"Oh come on," said the Sasquatch. "It's not that bad here. Whiskey! Pizza! New swamps to soak in!"

"Higher mountains than any we knew," said the Yeti. "And—chocolate!"

"You're so easily pleased," said the Mothman. "Have you seen the people who live here? They don't need some outside force to come and destroy them; they're doing a perfectly good job themselves."

The Sasquatch slapped him across the back of his bony head. "You don't just come out and say something like that! Can't take you anywhere..."

"They won't bother us," said the Yeti. "The Voice has assured us we will be living in parts of the world they don't care about."

"They might," the Mothman said darkly. "Once we move in."

The Sasquatch slapped the back of his head again. "Will you mind what you say!"

"Will you stop doing that!" said the Mothman.

He pushed the Sasquatch hard in the chest, and the big hairy figure slammed back against the hull. He grinned broadly, showing his great fangs.

"Oh, it is on!"

He threw himself at the Mothman, and they struggled together. The Yeti tried to separate them, and they both turned on him. All three cryptids were soon rolling around on the floor, wrestling fiercely. Glory started forward, the light of battle in her eyes.

"Leave them be, Amazon," said the Voice. "Let the children play..."

And I finally realized: That was exactly what they were, just a bunch of kids, the last of their kind and united by tragedy. About to be dumped and abandoned on a world that meant nothing to them. I moved forward and leaned over the three struggling forms.

"Who'd like some hot chocolate?"

They paused, broke apart, and got to their feet to look at me warily.

"What is hot chocolate?" said the Yeti.

"It's hot and very chocolaty and you drink it," I said.

"Oh, I want some of that!" said the Yeti.

I turned to the Mothman. "I heard you say you like pizza, but have you ever tried stuffed crusts, with cheese or sausage?"

"You can get us that?" said the Mothman.

"I don't see why not," I said. I turned to the Sasquatch. "I've seen what you drink. I can introduce you to single malt whiskeys. It's like drinking lightning."

"I'm not sure whether that would be fun or not," said the Sasquatch. "But I definitely want to try it."

"My world has a lot to offer," I said to all three of them. "Let me show you."

They nodded, slowly.

"I think we'd like that," said the Yeti.

"It would be nice, to have someone on our side for a change," said the Sasquatch.

I stepped forward and hugged him, and then the Yeti. It was like being embraced by very friendly rugs. I turned to the Mothman but he just gave me a hard look, so I put out a hand and we bumped fists respectfully. I turned to where I thought the Voice was.

"Once I've got these kids settled, then what?"

"There are many more worlds in trouble," said the Voice, "and many more orphaned survivors, waiting to be rescued and resettled. A job for life, if you want it."

"I think I do," I said.

"And certainly long enough for you to find someone like you," said the Voice.

"That's always been my problem," I said. "There's never been anyone like me."

"Space is deep, space is vast," said Glory. "Out among the stars there's someone for everyone. Even you and me."

"Then let's do it," I said. I nodded to the cryptids. "But first, let's get you kids home."

Simon R. Green has written seventy-five novels, two collections of short stories and one movie; *Judas Ghost*. These include the Nightside books, the Secret Histories, Deathstalker and the Ghost Finders. His most recent books are the Ishmael Jones mysteries and the Jekyll & Hyde Inc. books from Baen, and the Gideon Sable mysteries from Severn. He has had the usual mixture of previous occupations, that prove an author cannot hold down a proper job, including shop assistant, bicycle repair mechanic, journalist, actor, Chippendale dancer and mail order bride. Not all of these are necessarily accurate. He lives in the small country town of Bradford-on-Avon, which was the last Celtic town to fall to the invading Saxons in 504 AD. He has never seen a UFO; but he has heard one.

NICKY'S SEA GOAT

Nathaniel Mumau

The sting at the griffin fight club went swimmingly. Our gnome on the inside proved faithful. Not surprising—Gerald had been my partner-in-crime-busting since I started undercover work. "A lot of bad folks at this one," he'd warned me. "Lotsa monsters, Nicky, but it's their insides dat's ugly."

Gerald was a bit dramatic, but who could blame him? He was the one who had to roll around in the mud with the scum of the forest. Besides, being a gnome was dramatic enough. Even if someone didn't catch you in a double-cross, they might punt you five yards just for fun.

That was the type of crowd we busted. I kicked in the tavern door, followed by the king's sentries. A bunch of amateurs, if you ask me. Too long a lance to swing with too little experience under their belts. But no one popped off, thank goodness, because the folks we surprised would be happy to return fire.

You might think the lowlifes frequenting griffin fights are

trolls or ogres, maybe unsavory elves. Well, you're wrong, and you're a little bit racist, too. It's mostly bards, clerics—even some druids. The kind you'd expect to be frequenting the halls of the castle, not pitting poor, helpless hybrids against each other.

A few scumbags made a break for it, but the sentries broke their kneecaps in response. Most were wise enough to raise their hands and go quietly. I say quietly because, although a lot of these repeat offenders have their Minerva's rights memorized, they insisted on muttering an insult or two.

As the cuffed suspects filed past me out the door, I heard it all: "Fascist," … "Boot licker," … "Traitor!"

I clapped a hand on the suspect's shoulder. The sentry leading him out the door stumbled. "M'lord?" he mumbled from under his helmet.

My eyes peeked out beneath the wide brim of my pointed hat. The suspect matched my stare from beneath his own conical crown. "Care to repeat yourself?" I grunted.

The wizard chuckled. "If my hands weren't bound, I'd turn your brain to corn! The kernels would fall out your nose and get pecked up by a cockatrice!"

I seized the hem of his cloak. "Are they doing cock fights here, too? Answer me!"

The wizard bared his yellow teeth. "I don't cast pearls before swine. It's one thing to betray your class for a paycheck from the king, but all that to protect these filthy crossbreeds? You make me sick!"

Before I could act, the wizard spat a brown loogie across my face. He cackled as I released his robe, but his cackling stopped when I landed a jab that turned his long nose crooked. He slumped to the floor. "M'lord!" the sentry gasped.

"Shut up!" I ordered. I used my sleeve to wipe the saliva from my eyes. "Well, what are you waiting for? Get him out of here!"

He waffled in his boots for a moment, before complying with my order. The sentry dragged the wizard out by his ankles, his crooked nose cutting a line in the mud.

"Ya better watch yourself, Nicky." Gerald appeared beside me. How long had he been standing there? Then again, he was easy to miss. Being short and all.

"I'm looked out for enough," I muttered. "No one touches the king's men."

"Doesn't mean you gotta make so many enemies."

"What, the sentries? They're a bunch of punk kids."

As if to prove my point, three of the sentries were attempting to leash a griffin in the fight pit. The griffins at this club were on the younger side, and this griffin in particular was half-starved to death. Maybe that's why it was so testy. It kept snapping its beak at the sentries' toes, and these numbnuts didn't know how to solve a problem without skewering it on the end of their lances. One sentry finally got fed up and kicked the griffin in its ribs. The beast squawked and collapsed, writhing in the mud.

"Hey!" I roared. "You kick another animal, I put a foot through your eye slit!"

While the sentries roped the griffin, Gerald said, "That warlock you walloped might've had a point, Nicky."

I didn't respond. I retrieved my pipe from inside my cloak and took a mock drag from the lip. I'd been trying to quit, but sometimes I just needed something between my teeth. It never felt as satisfying as truly puffing on some longbottom leaf, though.

"All this danger over hybrids?" Gerald went on. "These

riffraff know you—they know me! We stick our necks out, and for what? Griffins can't say, 'Thank you.'"

"It's not about gratitude."

"I mean, at least they're cute. The chimeras? Not so much."

"You break the law, you're a criminal," I snapped. "Doesn't matter if the victims aren't pretty."

"No, trust me, I get it. The harpy prostitution ring? Yeah, I'm glad we busted that. They're at least half-human. Same with the chimera girls. I mean, I may not *get it*, but I won't judge another man for—"

"That's a slippery slope," I interjected. "Next, you'll be saying centaurs shouldn't vote. Satyrs shouldn't own property."

Gerald tried to stick a finger in my face, but there was four feet of air between his finger and my nose. "I ain't no bigot. I draw the line the same place everybody else does. But I think your line's a little blurry, Nicky. And it's gonna get you in trouble one day."

The anxious griffin had finally been leashed. It took all three sentries to drag the poor beast toward the door. "Stop," I ordered. I knelt beside the griffin. It snapped its beak at me, but I didn't pull away. "Don't be scared," I cooed. I held my palms out flat. The griffin eyed me cautiously. "You're safe now." I raised my hand. The griffin's head twitched. The tip of its beak nuzzled my fingers. "You didn't deserve this," I whispered. I glanced at Gerald and found we were almost eye-to-eye. "No creature—humanoid, bipedal, whatever—deserves this. And if no one else wants to protect them, I will."

I'D BARELY MADE it through the door of my hovel when my orb started ringing. "Not a moment's rest," I grumbled. I flopped on my couch and gazed at my aquarium. As if sensing my stare, Ramocles swam out from his underwater cavern. The sea goat did circles before me, ecstatic I had returned. Or maybe he was just hungry. I shook some fish flakes over the water, then finally answered my orb.

"No one's talking, Nick."

"You didn't need to call me to tell me that, Sarge. These guys never talk."

"Sure, but they usually don't promise to start talking if you're standing in the room."

I squinted hard at the paladin's head floating in my orb. "Someone requested me? It's a bluff."

"I'm not yanking your chainmail," Sarge insisted. "I'm at the brig now. Everyone else is tight-lipped, but not this guy. And he's no small potato, either."

I watched Ramocles do some somersaults in his tank. I had just gotten home from a long day of perp-busting. All I wanted to do was lounge on my couch and hang out with my sea goat. Whoever this black hat was, he was probably full of bull. Lips clamped shut when I walked into a room.

"He thought you might be apprehensive," Sarge said. "So he gave me a name: Koschei."

My eyes bulged in their sockets. A drop of sweat raced down my forehead, across my nose, and swan dived into Ramocles' tank. "Did he say anything else? Who is this guy?"

"All he mentioned was the name, and wanting to see you. Come meet him for yourself."

Ramocles chomped away at his flakes, his square pupils oblivious to the dread growing on my face.

THE PERP *WAS* full of bull, or at least half-full. I barged into the interrogation room to be met by the hulking form of a minotaur. The tips of his ears scraped the ceiling planks. His wrists were thick as cannons, and unconvincingly bound before him with ten-ply rope. He had about fifteen piercings I could see, six of which were through his nipples. He snorted at the sight of me. "I thought not you'd show."

I slammed the door behind me. "You got my attention. Do I know you?"

"You do not," he grunted. "Though we relate as animals, farm. I, the cow. You? The pig!"

I could already feel a migraine coming on.

"I'm not wearing a parrot, if you're concerned about this being recorded," I assured. "Not just anyone knows my name, and I'd like to keep it that way."

The minotaur's eyes blazed. "So you admit it true? You are Koschei?"

"*Was* Koschei, a long time ago. But I left that life far behind me."

The minotaur coughed, or chuckled, or fought back bile. He pounded his fists on the table, which immediately collapsed into splinters. "Left Koschei behind, you may, but Koschei has caught up!"

"I'm as far from Koschei as I've ever been. Hence why I put your rabble in chains this morning. You of all people should recognize how cruel those fight clubs are."

He sneered. "There are hybrids, and then there are *cross-breeds*." He spat the word like a curse and drenched my poulaines in saliva.

"Koschei might have agreed with you. But I do not, because I'm not Koschei. Not anymore."

"Truth, in part. For Koschei, magic was mandatory."

"I go by the book now. No need for magic."

The minotaur giggled, or sneezed, or had a minor seizure. He bounced in his chair so heartily that it crumbled beneath him. Even from the floor, he laughed.

"Knock it off!" I ordered. "I didn't come down here to watch ground beef sizzle. You got me, so talk!"

"You? Play by the book?" he wheezed. "I translate your play: Koschei go by his own rules, and he makes fouls plenty."

I reached out and grabbed the bull by his nose ring. I yanked his snout in front of my face. That shut him up. I watched him consider swinging his fists to knock my head through the ceiling, but he knew better than to mess with *the* Koschei—reformed or otherwise.

"Listen, bub," I seethed. "I've had a long day, and I would love nothing better than to sit by my sea goat and pretend to smoke my pipe. I can't do that until you sing like you promised. I'm standing! Right! Here! So either start speaking, or I'll *steer* you in the right direction. Capische?"

"Make many fouls, yes," the minotaur grunted. "Sing like bird, cluck like fowl. Chicken, see? But not chicken of the sea."

I twisted the nose ring. "Start making sense. Now!"

Sweat ran down the minotaur's forehead, but he giggled nonetheless. "Not chicken of the sea. Or horse, or sheep … but goat of the sea? No, you won't see any longer!"

I furrowed my brow. "What are you saying?"

The minotaur's glossy eyes watched me cruelly. "Just the messenger, am I. MIA, is the goat. Do not distrust the distraction!"

I stared hard at the minotaur. He bared his blocky teeth in defiance, but then I ripped out his nose ring. He rolled on the floor, howling in pain, but I was already out the door, racing home, praying the minotaur's threats were more than half-bull.

I FUMBLED with my iron key ring. I tried the key with the skull handle. My front door held fast. I cursed and thumbed through my other keys. Why do I have sixteen different keys? I cast the ring aside and kicked open my door. It flew off its hinges because I'd never actually locked it, but I didn't care. I barged into my hovel, eyes scanning wildly. "Ramocles! Are you here?"

I turned the corner to my den and found … Ramocles. Swishing his tail in his aquarium, watching me curiously. "You're okay!" I gasped. I rushed to the tank, stopping short of scooping the sea goat out of the water and cuddling him. "That cowhide fink!" I growled. "What was his game, getting me all worked up?"

Ramocles opened his mouth as if to respond, but all that came out were bubbles. They floated to the surface and popped, releasing a muffled, *"Baaaaa!"* I may have just been coming down off an episode of manic paranoia, but that *Baaaaa* sounded panicked to me.

"You okay, kid?" I murmured. My reflection shimmered in the water. I studied myself, then I studied the reflection of the second man standing behind me. "Cripes!" I shrieked.

I made to spin and karate chop his head off, but my assailant beat me to the punch. My head flew back from the impact, and the floor came flying toward my face. My brain decided to take a nap, but not before I heard these words: "Thanks for letting us in!"

As quickly as darkness choked my sight, light flooded my vision. I gasped like I had just come out of a river. Actually, I was drenched like I had just come out of a river. And it smelled like it was a river of sewage. Some surly skinhead stood before me, holding an empty bucket in his hands.

"Did you just dump latrine water on me?" I spluttered.

The skinhead puckered his lips. "Uh ... maybe." I noticed he was wearing a flowing brown robe. His get-up screamed 'monk,' though I'm not one to stereotype ... unless I'm royally peeved.

"You pasty, beanpole, cave-dwelling, hairless virgin!" I roared.

The monk frowned. "A lot of men my age choose this lifestyle."

I made to swing my arms around and strangle the guy, but I quickly realized my hands were bound behind me. I was seated at a long wooden table. Surrounding the table stood a bunch of cookie-cutter monks, all bald and robed-up. They watched me warily, save for one person. He watched me devilishly, and he just happened to be the only person in the room with hair.

"Greetings, Koschei," the hairy man said. Truly, he was more hair than man. Actually, he might not have been a 'man' at all. He had thick arms and legs, and a single, glistening green eye, but the rest of his body looked like a huge, raggedy mophead. "I'm sure you have many questions. Please, ask away."

Typically, in this sort of scenario, I would yell things like, 'Who are you?' or, 'Where am I?' or, 'How did you find me?' but none of that stuff really mattered. My most pressing question, which I did indeed yell at the top of my lungs, was, *"Where is my sea goat?"*

The hairy man chuckled. "We'll get there. But first, don't you want to know why you've offended me so dearly? What led me to kidnap you like this?"

"No!" I shouted. *"Where's my sea goat?"*

The hairy man cleared his throat. "I'm getting there! You see, Koschei, crossbreeds are hard to come by. Those fight clubs don't spring up by accident. There's a lot of cashflow being disrupted by the likes of—"

"Where's my sea goat?" I hollered. *"Where? Where?"*

He snapped his fingers. "Hey! Quiet down! I'm talking. I'll let you know when it's your turn to speak. But right now, you need to put your listening ears on. Because I want you to understand why—"

"Sea goat! Sea goat! Where's my sea goat?" I chanted.

The monks shared concerned glances. I could tell Hairy sensed he was losing the room. "You really are a tool, Koschei," he snarled. "Hence why it was so easy to find your Judas!"

"My sea goat's name is Ramocles!"

"That's not ..." Hairy sighed. "You've been betrayed, Koschei! Or could you guess?"

"No? I couldn't guess."

Hairy cackled. "Are you blind? He's here in this room!"

I scanned the faces of the monks. "Impossible. I refuse to be friends with bald people."

Hairy squinted. "Are you actually blind? He's right ... Oh, sorry. He rolled under the table. Small little guy, I almost lost him!" Hairy reached down and flung up a child's play doll. The doll rolled toward me on the table, and I realized it was no doll at all.

"Gerald!" I seethed. "You pint-sized lawn ornament! You told them where I live?"

Gerald was bound and gagged, but his muffled yelps sounded apologetic.

There in that room, restrained against my will, with my traitorous partner before me and skinhead monks surrounding me, I almost went *bibbidi bobbidi BOOM*. On top of everything else, these miscreants made their living off exploiting hybrids. They deserved a simmering bath in a cauldron of pain. That's what Koschei would have done. His number one priority would have been flogging these creeps for the fun of it.

But you're not Koschei anymore, I thought. *You're Nicky, and your priority is rescuing your sea goat! Ramocles doesn't get safer if all these jerks get deader. Talk now, flog later.*

Hairy's booming voice interrupted my thoughts. "Not only did Gerald betray you, but he also told us of your greatest love. Your sincerest conviction! The one thing in your life that could break you."

Hairy clapped his hands together. A monk wearing a chef's hat bustled in from a side room, carrying a polished silver platter. He set it before me, a gleeful grin on his face. "You're lucky!" the monk tittered. "The ingredients are as fresh as they come." He pulled away the dome to reveal the mystery dish, and it truly was a mystery to me. White grains, forming a cylinder around geometric slices of vegetable. It smelled like saltwater.

"It's all the rage in the east," Hairy said. "They call it *sooshee*."

My wild eyes glared at Hairy. "Where is my sea goat? I'm not playing your game."

"It's not a game! I truly enjoy feeding my guests. Please, allow my chef to serve you."

The monk pulled out two thin, wooden sticks. "In the east, they don't believe in forks. I'm trying to replicate their authentic, delicate dining experience. They don't just *eat* over there. It's like a beautiful ritual dance." The monk stabbed one of the sooshee with the tips of his sticks and held it before my mouth. "As they say in the east, *futotteru gaijin!*"

My eyes bounced from the sooshee to Hairy. "If I eat this, will you show me my sea goat?"

His green eye glimmered. "Absolutely."

Gerald's smothered moaning got louder, but I ignored him.

I parted my lips. The monk shoved the sooshee into my mouth. I chewed quickly and swallowed. "There, done. Now show me Ramocles."

The monks watched me with anticipation. Hairy seemed to shiver with excitement. "Be honest, Koschei. What did you think?"

I shrugged. "It was fine. Nothing beats the texture of hardtack and gruel, but I can appreciate the mild presence of flavor. Now tell me where my fish is!"

"Funny you should mention fish," Hairy whispered, "because that is the main ingredient in sooshee."

The world seemed to slow to a crawl. My heavy head tilted down to study the sooshee. One of the pieces was topped with a small, fishy flipper. I pulled my head up to study the room. The chef beamed. The rest of the monks chortled. Hairy guffawed, his laughter a deafening roar in my ears.

"I'm going to kill you," I murmured.

"Perhaps you can kill me with ugliness," Hairy wheezed between chuckles. "Otherwise, you will not lay a finger on—"

"Ropes are paper," I said. I broke the shackles on my wrists and rose to my feet.

"Woah ..." the chef gasped.

I pointed at his sticks. "Eyeball kebab."

The sticks shot from his hand like arrows and sailed straight through his eye sockets.

The monks weren't laughing anymore. They stood frozen in shock. "Robes are suicidal bats," I said.

The monks closest to me caught the full effect of the spell. Their robes took on life, and immediately tried to extinguish it. Grasping tightly to their respective monks, the robes careened into walls and ceilings. Bones smashed accordingly. The monks further back in the room were smart enough to wriggle out of their robes before the spell could reach them. As their loose robes fluttered around the room, a small legion of naked monks lined up to fight me.

The first monk charged me. "Liquid bones," I said. He crumpled to the floor, a heap of skin and organs, his skull leaking out his ears. Two more monks leapt over their gooey friend. "Pick his brain," I said. The monks turned their attention to one another. They simultaneously jabbed their fingers up each other's nostrils—all the way to the wrist. I shoved them aside to face the rest.

"Stomach of rats," ... "Exploding toes," ... "Fold him into a swan," ... "Teeth are bees," ... "Purplest nurple," ...

At last, I stood before Hairy. He'd been watching the show dumbstruck, but now it was his turn to be more than a spectator. He swung a fist at me. "Spaghetti arms." Wet noodles bounced harmlessly off my cloak.

Hairy roared and fell to his knees. "I thought you didn't use magic," he growled.

"I don't," I said. "But Koschei does. And he mastered it without the need to use his hands. But you wanted to see him in action, right?"

"This isn't over!"

"I beg to differ, because you are worms."

A final howl was smothered in Hairy's throat as his body transformed. Each strand of hair erupted into a worm, and what used to be Hairy collapsed into a writhing pile of night-crawlers. One fat, greenish worm wriggled at the top of the heap.

I shook my head in disgust. The room was silent, save for the buzz of bees and the skittering of rats and the sounds of sentient robes smashing themselves against walls … and the pathetic whimpers of Gerald.

He still lay on the table, watching me anxiously. I marched up to the gnome and ripped his gag off. "I don't need magic to kill *you,*" I muttered.

"Wait! Nicky! Wait!" he pleaded. "They had my chestnuts in a vice! You gotta believe me!"

"You took them to my hovel!" I roared. "You let them cook my sea goat!"

"No no no! They didn't hurt the fish! I swear!"

I grabbed Gerald by his floppy, pointed hat. "You're not lying your way out of this one."

"Honest, Nicky, honest! Please! Just check the side room!"

I growled, yet found myself stomping away. If Gerald was pulling my leg, I'd rip his own off like a wishbone. I stepped into what seemed to be a kitchen. A cutting board sat dirty with the cleaned skeleton of a sea creature. Beside the cutting board was a small bowl … a fishbowl! "Ramocles!" I squealed.

The sea goat swam joyful circles at the sight of me. I plucked the bowl off the counter and hugged it to my chest. "Oh, I thought I ate you!" I sighed. "They crammed you in such a small bowl, those jerks! Daddy will take you home and dump you right into your aquarium—after I clean the water, of course." I leaned in close to the sea goat. "You might be swimming in latrine water. Sorry, kid."

I marched back out to Gerald. "What was this guy's master plan? To serve me a delicious dinner?"

"What wit you all high and mighty wit da animal rights, I knew you were one of those vegetarian types! Forcing you to eat meat was supposed to rock your world!"

"Vegetarian, eh?" I shook my head and pulled my pipe from my cloak. "Gerald, there are many things I hate in this world." I chewed on the lip of the pipe. "Criminals, animal abuse, bald people ... But there's only one thing I truly love: *fish!*"

Gerald's eyes shifted. "Uh, like, romantically?"

"No. I'm not a vegetarian, you dimwit. I'm a *pescatarian.*"

"Then you can find it in your heart to show some mercy!" Gerald begged. "Please, Nicky. I may not be presbyterian, but I was raised Catholic!"

I thought about responding to Gerald, but I decided I had wasted enough of my day on tomfoolery. "I'm going home now," I said. I spun on my heels and walked away.

"You're not gonna kill me?" Gerald gasped.

"Not today." I paused by the pile of nightcrawlers. I plucked the green one off the top of the heap and dropped it into Ramocles's bowl. The sea goat devoured the worm in two chomps. "But if I ever hear from you again, you'll be fish food, too. Capische?" Gerald whimpered in reply, but I was already marching out the door.

NATHANIEL MUMAU GREW up in Edison, New Jersey, where he collected endless inspiration for strange little stories. He currently lives in Michigan with his marvelous wife, Adrianna, who lovingly and patiently supports him in all his endeavors. His written work has been published or is forthcoming in *The Bare Bones Book of Speculative Fiction, The 2026 Spring Into SciFi Anthology* by Cloaked Press, *Wordrunner eChapbooks,* and *Flash Phantoms.* You can read more of Nathaniel's stories at nathanielmumau.neocities.org.

BACK TO SCHOOL GUIDELINES (TENTACULON-APPROVED)

Tina Connolly

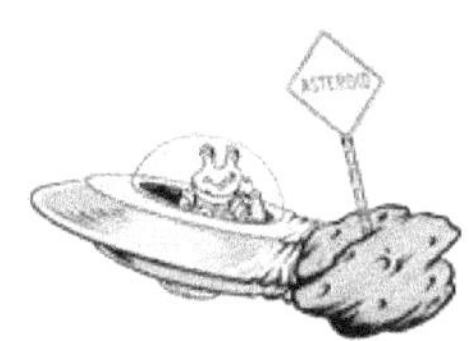

Subject: Back to School Guidelines

Dear Parents,

Congratulations on your offspring's acceptance into Exceptiolon Planetary School! (School motto: *The finest school possible, given the circumstances!*) We know as egglayers/guardians/magnificent broodparents that you have many choices while looking for schools for your slitherers/children/tentacled future overlords. We thank you for choosing Exceptiolon.

Below you will find a short list of school supplies and general updates to prepare you for the exciting (and challenging) school year ahead! Thank you for supplying all mandatory items.

1. Breathing equipment for your offspring's needs. According to your request, we have attempted to place you either in the Oxygen Wing (Ssvans, Humans), the Moist Wing (Amoebaba) or the recently upgraded Methane Wing (Tentaculons.) As usual, our Oxygen wing is overcrowded, and so some of you have been placed with the Tentaculons in

Methane. If your standard planetary rebreather does not handle pure methane, you will need to purchase a new rebreathing device for your offspring. Our request to the Tentaculon Planetary School Board to supply these for free has unfortunately been denied, but used models can be purchased at the school store at a substantial discount. (Many of these rebreathers smell of formic acid from the bipedal Ant-Beings who were our exchange students last year before being deported by the Tentaculon Safety Committee for having "suspicious carapaces"; if this is the case, a thorough scrubbing with borax should do the trick.)

2. Electives! As your offspring enters the midpoint of their schooling, they have an increased ability to choose classes. Owing to budget cuts under the new Tentaculon administration, unfortunately all electives in Galactic Languages, Planetary Exploration, Understanding Your Government, and Choir have been cut. Anyone who had requested one of those electives has instead been placed in Tentaculon Tentacle Braiding. We recognize that this will be a challenge to those without tentacles; however, the Tentaculon Planetary School Board has generously shipped us multiple boxes of fake tentacle suits, in sizes specifically for Humans, Ssvans, and Amoebaba. Will the artificial tentacles create the actual black holes that true Tentaculons' tentacles can, once braided correctly? No. Will the students grow to appreciate a deeper understanding of the telekinetic powers that Tentaculons can obtain when braided together? Also no. But we had to put your offspring somewhere or risk them going out to the dome to reflect on their lack of a future here on this planet and/or smoke weed.

(2a. Addendum—the Drama Department wishes to inform the former members of Choir that they are welcome in the school musical, where "great roles are available for

ALL students, regardless of number of legs, scales, carapaces, tentacles, etc.!!!")

3. For those who were following the four-year Career Path in "Human-Tentaculon Interpersonal Studies: *Building Bridges to an Equitable Future*", unfortunately your teacher was arrested over the summer on suspicion of being a terrorist. Per Planetary School Board Guidelines, all remaining humans in that class have been moved over to the multi-year course "Tentaculon Rights: *Why and How this Ruling Class is Actually Oppressed*". The Ssvans and Amoebaba have been moved to "Tending to Your Tentaculon Overlord: *An Exciting Career Opportunity!*" The one Tentaculon in the class will receive an extra lunch hour, for which they will get extra credit.

4. Textbooks: New Planetary School Board Guidelines state that all educational materials must be pre-approved by a committee consisting of 230 Tentaculons from around the world. Only books that have passed scrutiny by all 230 Tentaculons (and the input from their brood-sisters, grandspawn, etc.) may be used in the classroom. At this moment the only texts cleared for use are *101 Things to do with Tentacles: A Children's Primer* and *A Short History of the Marvelous Human Pets known as Kittens*. Our Algebra I and II textbooks did not clear the committee due to concerns that they would lead students to conclude that "X" is a thing that can actually be known, and not decided on by a Tentaculon committee. All textbooks from prior years are required to be handed in to the government. If some of you forgot to turn yours in after our summer session "Our New Tentaculon Overlords: *What Are We Going to Do????*", please remember that those books were never officially checked out and do not have your names attached to them in any recordkeeping whatsoever, so we simply trust to your *good sense* and *integrity* to do what is right with them.

5. In related matters, our beloved previous principal, Jaquelle Brown, was deported over the summer for conducting the summer session "Our New Tentaculon Overlords: *What Are We Going to Do????*" As your new Acting Principal, I will do my best to keep us on track and in compliance with the shifting standards. I will definitely NOT conduct a similar session with a boring-sounding name like "Care and Maintenance of Your Oxygen Rebreathers." If I am deported from this planet, command will smoothly transfer to the Planetary School Board, who will appoint a local Tentaculon to the office.

6. Lunch: The free lunch program will now consist entirely of Tentaculon arsenic eels. If you are of a species that cannot ingest Tentaculon arsenic eels, then apparently you should have thought of that before being subjugated. Also, in paid lunch news, oxygen is now considered a vegetable.

7. The School Musical: While this has been the subject of much internal debate, the Drama Department is absolutely unwavering in their desire to produce *The Rebellion on Beta IV.* They wish to be clear that although this historical musical deals with a ragtag group of mixed alien species banding together to guillotine their Squidexx overlords, that this is NOT some topical political commentary, and simply "the best fit for this year's drama students and their vocal ranges." Auditions will be held as soon as they can locate an uncensored copy of the script.

8. After-School Clubs: Under new legislation outlawing "exclusionary groups", we had to shutter several of our beloved stalwarts, including Human Pride, Sssvans Unite, and Amoervelous Amoebabas. However, the new club, Tentaculons Accept Everybody, will be meeting in the Methane Wing of the school. You will need to correctly braid

your tentacles to open up a small black hole to meet with them.

(8a. Addendum—all interested parties are welcome in the new club "Care and Maintenance of Your Oxygen Rebreathers", on Thursday afternoons.)

9. Class sizes, etc.: We have lost several teachers over the summer due to budget cuts, methane poisoning, deportations, and "I just can't take this planet anymore." However, we were promised a hundred Tentaclo currency by an anonymous source if we put a plug in for *"Tocloonto's Elite Tentacular Private School, home to small class sizes, personal telekinetic relationships, and the finest Golden Tentacles team on the planet. Now accepting enrollments from all species. Scholarships available to those with a tentacle reach of 19tm!!"* These hundred Tentaclo we have acquired thusly will go to acquiring three more Amoebaba bowl-chairs for our students who have been forced to puddle on the ground. (Seven down, 131 more to go!)

10. Back-to-School Spirit Night: We know there are worries that it may be "a little grim" this year due to restrictions on how many non-Tentaculons may gather in a crowd at once (outside of the school day, of course!) In order to account for this, we have placed many small, School Board-approved tents across the grounds that will hold up to four humans, five Ssvans, or eight Amoebaba (provided the Amoebaba don't mind puddling on each other.) These are all Tentaculon methane tents provided by the Planetary School Board and therefore most of you will need to wear your own re-breathing devices inside each tent.

Please come and mingle with fellow parents, but always be aware of the number of you within the tent at any given time. Whenever you step outside the tents, you may watch members of the Drama Department perform song selections from *The Rebellion on Beta IV,* as well as "short-form improv related to their educational future on this planet."

Representatives from the Planetary Board of Education will be there supervising, so some quick guidelines:

DO chat about:

- class schedules
- new exciting ways to prepare arsenic eels
- kittens

Do NOT chat about:

- voting reform
- distributing banned books (eg: *Understanding Your Constitutional Rights, I Survived the Tentaculon Overlords: One Ssvan's Journey, Algebra I & II*)
- active revolt

Administrators will be on hand to redistribute you if necessary.

In summation, I thank you as always for your trust and support. We are absolutely dedicated to educating your offspring to the best of our ability (given our resources, educational materials, rebreathers, stress levels, and not getting deported from this planet.) Please let us know if there is anything we can do to assist. I personally guarantee I will do my utmost to see that your offspring has fair, equitable, and useful schooling as long as I remain in this solar system.

Sincerely,

Ssisi Ssvana (Acting Principal)

RE: Back to School Guidelines *(Tentaculon-Approved)*

Dear Parents,

A quick correction to the above email. The school musical will now be *Cats*.

Sincerely,

The Planetary School Board,

Cloocoo Tentacloon (New Acting Principal)

TINA CONNOLLY (SHE/HER) writes fantastical stories for kids, teens, and grown-ups. Some of them are serious and some of them involve flying bananas. Her books include the Ironskin and Seriously Wicked series, the collection *On the Eyeball Floor*, and the official Choose Your Own Adventure book *Glitterpony Farm*. She has been a finalist for the Hugo, Nebula, and World Fantasy awards, and she is absolutely delighted to appear in her fifth UFO anthology! Find her at tinaconnolly.com.

ONE MORE NIGHT

Esther Friesner

"Look, for the last time, it's Jennifer, okay? *Jennifer.*" She slapped the curlicued bars of her ivory cage with both hands for emphasis.

The beauty seated across the room atop an avalanche of silk pillows looked confused. "But—but so I said: *Janiva.*"

"Ugh, never mind. That's the least of my worries." Jennifer Hancock scowled. "Call me whatever you want—Jennifer, Janiva, Ishmael, anything—just give me a little bleed-through from the real world, while you're at it. Tell me that someone saw me fall on my head and called 911. Am I in the hospital? En route? Or just lying flat on my back, waiting for the frostbite fairy to pay me a call? And if I am in the hospital, let me know if I'm going to wake up soon, okay? Can you do me that teensy favor like a *good* little concussion?"

The young woman tilted her head at an adorable angle that would have Persian kittens taking study notes. "I don't understand."

"The feeling is mutual," Jennifer replied, shucking her

gloves and shrugging out of her puffy coat. A generous collection of melting snowflakes trickled down to stain the lavish rugs lining her ivory cage. She leaned her head against the curlicued bars and sighed. "This will teach me not to run for the damn bus. Especially not in winter. Springfield's maintenance department's a joke. They never clear all the ice off the sidewalks. There'll always be another bus, but I've only got one skull. And I landed on it."

"Alas, is it so?" Now the other woman's eyes held both remorse and sympathy. "But I was most specific with my command. I told the djinni to fetch you here unharmed. For a being to whom space and time are trifles, he has failed most inexcusably."

"He also failed to give me any intel about who the hell *you* are," Jennifer snarled. "Wherever he is, right now. If he exists. With great immortal magical oomph comes zero manners. He ought to be ashamed of himself."

Jennifer was one of those people who used snark as a way to distract themselves from situations where terrified babbling was the order of the day. It helped her a bit, but her captor didn't seem to get the joke.

"Ah, then rejoice!" The lady clapped her bejeweled hands together and smiled. "I know how to make it up to you: You shall be the one to dictate the terms of his punishment. Would you like that, dear Janiva?"

Jennifer did not share her elation. "I am thrilled to pieces. And *when* am I going to give what's-his-name fifty lashes with a wet noodle?"

The bewildered head-tilt returned. "Is that how you would chastise a djinni? With noodles? Well, if it makes you happy—"

Jennifer flung her arms around her updrawn knees, buried her head in them, and vented all of her fear and frustration in a scream. The sound was half-smothered but still loud enough to have consequences. Almost at once it brought an answering uproar of stampeding feet. The chamber's double doors burst open and the room filled with a host of large men, all armed with wicked-looking swords flashing in the lantern light. The first into the room fell to his knees at the base of Mount Pillowpile and spoke frantically to the young woman at the summit. Jennifer's hostess responded with soft words and a reassuring smile before waving the entire invasion force out and away.

The ornate doors no sooner closed behind the last of the men than Jennifer said, "What was that?"

"A party of my faithful eunuch guards and their captain, Babak. They heard your distress and mistook it for my own. I told Babak it was nothing, that I'd merely dozed off and dreamed that an evil spirit stole me away." She giggled. "Not very creative as stories go, which makes perfect sense given my present predicament, but as long as it worked—"

"They didn't see me," Jennifer cut in, her expression blank with shock. "They acted like I was invisible, even though they heard me scream. They flat out *ignored* me. It's like every damn library board meeting I've ever had to attend, except for me being prisoner in *this* thing—" She flicked her fingers against one of the intricately whorled bars surrounding her. "—instead of captive to an endless agenda."

"Even so," her hostess replied so cheerfully that Jennifer considered pulling off one of her boots just to have the pleasure of pitching it into that exquisite face. "Nor did they note your enclosure, which is the source of your invisibility. Thus all is well. It was my desire that your presence be unremarked by any save myself until I would have it otherwise. At least the djinni got that part right."

"Djinni again." Jennifer chewed over the word as if it

were a baked snail without the redemptive accompaniment of garlic butter. "I still don't believe that. Djinni as in *genie*? Spurts out of a lamp, grants wishes, sings snappy songs?"

"I know nothing about the singing, but otherwise, yes. I summoned and commanded him to bring me the person who possessed the best means to save my life this night." She selected a plump date from the fruit bowl at her elbow, popped it into her mouth, and said, *"Arrarrani afff iff ooo."* A few quick chews, a dainty swallow, and the clarification: "Apparently that is you."

It was Jennifer's turn to buy the drinks at the mind-boggled bar, though her expression was less winsome kitten and more jaw-dropped medieval peasant seeing his prize hen hatch a basilisk.

"Me?" It was a fairly stupid question, given the QED of vile circumstance, but nonetheless suitable to the situation. "I'm willing to accept the stuff about being magically abducted, but I've got to draw the line here. I'm no hero; I'm just a librarian. Head librarian, but still—! How can *I* save your life? *Anyone's* life? I can barely manage my own!" She shook her head. "This must be worse than a concussion. Maybe I'm buried in the snow, almost gone, and they won't find my corpse until spring. Maybe I made it to the hospital, but they're already debating when to pull the plug, or—or—" She glared at her exquisite hostess. "Or if this *is* some kind of magical foofaraw in action—and I've read enough fantasy novels to reserve judgment on that—then I demand to speak to your editor because there is no internal logic worth the name at work here! *Save* you? From *this*?"

She underscored her accusation by jabbing a hand through the ivory bars and pointing at the sumptuous appointments of the lady's chamber. Elaborately wrought brass lamps twinkling with gems dangled from the ceiling by gilded chains; swaths of damask covered the walls, shimmering with a webwork of gold and silver threads; dainty ebony tables bore eggshell-thin celadon bowls freighted with fragrant jasmine blossoms; the faint sound of splashing water from an unseen source hinted at a fountain playing in another part of the young woman's apartments.

"Unless you're allergic to luxury, it looks like you've got a pretty sweet deal going on here." Jennifer couldn't keep the bitterness out of her voice as she thought of her own cramped "studio" digs back home.

"Is threat of a death sentence sweet where you come from?" the lady asked, her musical voice now keyed to a dirge. "For if you do not come to my aid when the moon rises, the dawning sun shall witness my head part company from my shoulders."

"What did—? Why—?" Jennifer pressed her lips together. "Okay," she said at last. "Who am I to doubt my own hallucination? I sure as hell don't think I'm in Kansas anymore, so tell me everything, starting with the bit about the genie."

"Djinni."

"Po-tah-to."

"What?"

"Forget it. Why don't you take it from the top by letting me out of this cage. I'd rather talk to you woman-to-woman, not woman-to-parakeet."

"Let it be so."

The lady clapped her hands twice and Jennifer stood free before her, gloves and puffy coat in a heap at her feet. It took her a moment to adjust to the shock of such radically acquired liberty.

"Wow. All I was expecting was for you to come down here and unlock the cage door. Uh, thank you very much and I promise I won't try to run away."

The lady shrugged. "Whither would you go?"

Jennifer was nonplussed into temporary silence by the truth of this. The weird Venn diagram of time, space, and basic reality in which she found herself was unlikely to offer a handy plane, train, bus or Uber back to Springfield.

"Running hence will not bring you home, but once you save me—" The lady patted the pillows beside her. "Ascend, my savior, and all shall be made known to you."

Jennifer did as she was bid, shucking her boots before summiting. She discovered that climbing a towering heap of pillows was harder than it seemed, especially given how little traction silk and satin provided under stockinged feet. After a bit of backsliding and a measure of huffing and puffing, she made it to the top.

"All right," she said testily. "Start making all known."

The lady dug one hand between two of her pillows and retrieved a brass lamp whose form was a dead giveaway as to its true function. To banish any remaining doubt, she rubbed the lamp and cried, "Mahir! I summon you!"

A wisp of smoke danced from the lamp's spout and swiftly transformed into a warm breeze bearing the scent of sun-blessed lemons, ripe apricots, and honey. This dainty breath of Eden whirled sensuously around the two women, the odorous mist dazzling their eyes with the incandescence of countless captive stars. It lasted no more than a moment and was gone, leaving in its wake a creature with skin that shimmered like a fire opal and eyes that were slivers of midnight. He fell to one knee at the foot of the pillow pile and bowed his head.

"I am here, O Mistress." He had a voice that would have compelled a cat to take responsibility for its sins. "What would you have of me?"

"As it was your choice alone that fetched this particular

young woman hither to save me, I bid you inform her what that task entails and how she will be rewarded upon its successful completion."

"Ohhhhh." The djinni bowed gracefully to Jennifer. "It is simple: Your reward will be your return whence you came, unharmed and accompanied by what earthly wealth my mistress deems appropriate for your service."

"Earthly wealth? You have my attention," Jennifer said solemnly. "But the task—?"

"To be magically transformed into the semblance of my mistress so that you may spend tonight in her husband's bed." The djinni grinned. "Behold, it is as easy as falling off a dromedary!"

Jennifer said a very rude word. It was so rude that the djinni's jaw dropped and his complexion lost its glitter. Jennifer folded her arms and glowered at him. "You heard me, Lamp-Boy."

"Insolent wench! 'Lamp-boy,' is it? You speak to one who is known and feared throughout all Arabia as Mahir the Magnificent!" He laid one hand to his broad, bare chest. "Show me a measure of respect, lest it go ill for you."

"Maybe later." Jennifer stared down the djinni. "After I decide if getting back to God-help-us *Springfield* is worth being some strange man's bed-bunny."

"Ho, ho! But back you shall go, whether you fulfill your mission for my mistress or not!" Mahir declared. "Back to face a pack of ravening wolves! Back to the heart of a volcano! Back into the midst of a tangle of mating vipers! Back to—!"

"Springfield's fresh out of volcanoes, wolves, and vipers, unless you count the City Council." Jennifer crossed her arms. "Don't try cheap scare tactics on me. I've dealt with hordes of *concerned* citizens who want to keep our library free from sin, depravity, and independent thinking. Mostly by burning the books. Wolves and vipers and lava are small change next to those halfwit harpies … *Lamp-Boy*."

"Oh, so it is a small change you desire?" Mahir gestured sharply and Jennifer found herself small, changed into a hamster, and lodged in her hostess' cleavage. The lady thus assailed was dumbstruck and frozen where she sat, but Jennifer was not. She squeaked in outrage and gave the djinni a gesture in return. It was one that might be termed a classic, and she managed to execute it quite well, despite the middle-digit limitations of hamster paws.

She then leaped from her curvaceous haven, dived into a gap between two pillows, and was gone from sight.

"Turn her back! Turn her back!" the djinni's mistress shrieked as she fumbled for the vanished rodent among her cushions. "What were you thinking? We *need* her, you fool! We need her *now*! Every moment brings us closer to the time when my lord the king will summon me!"

The djinni looked stricken. "O Mistress, forgive me! My temper often gets the better of me."

"If you fail to retrieve and restore dear Janiva to her human form, that temper of yours will have written my death sentence!"

"But—but—" Mahir held out his hands in an attitude of helplessness. "I have already used so much of this day's power in fetching that minx here from her native habitat!"

"Only to squander yet more power solely to vent your spleen upon her. You must and *will* return her humanity. *Now*."

"I could do that without the need to extract her. I will simply restore her where she presently lies." He waved one hand over the pillows.

"Fool! You do not know how deeply downward she has

gone. You risk smothering her! And what of the dread consequences that might betide *us* should the random emanation of your spellcraft miss her entirely? You might by mischance return the downy stuffing of my pillows to its first form and we would both drown in a deluge of ducks! No, no, you will conserve what remains of your power by using naught but your own two hands to retrieve her."

He eyed the pillows uneasily. "What if she bites me?"

"Mahir...." There was a warning tone to the lovely lady's voice that intimated someone was going to get bitten, sooner rather than later, and not necessarily by the rogue hamster.

The djinni bowed. "As you command, my lady Scheherazade." He thrust one arm between the cushions.

The hamster scampered up said arm and claimed the summit of the djinni's skull. Eyes bright and eager, she stared at her hostess. "Did he just call you *Scheherazade*?"

The lady lowered her eyes modestly. "I am she."

"*The* Scheherazade? The one who told all those stories to a crazy king who decided the only faithful wife was one you executed right after the wedding night?"

"Just so. I saved my life thereby as well as breaking him of his, er, inconsiderate habit."

"In my world, his little 'habit' would've gotten him condemned as a serial killer, even if he did have a paid executioner do the dirty work. There's nothing worse than a lunatic with power."

"There is," Scheherazade said sadly. "A *nostalgic* lunatic with power. After all of our years together, he has commanded that this night I tell him one more tale, for old time's sake. That is why, out of all the worlds and times he might reach, I sent Mahir to fetch the one person with the power to save me: A storyteller whose stock of tales is boundless as the desert sands and countless as the stars of heaven!" She paused for a reaction, and when none came, added: "I mean you."

The hamster blinked. "But I'm not—Say, why would *you* need a storyteller? You're the best one the world has ever known."

"Yes." Scheherazade leaned close enough to pluck the hamster from atop the djinni's head. "Once."

She set Jennifer down between herself and Mahir, then gave him a brisk get-on-with-it jerk of her chin. The djinni bowed slightly and wiggled his fingers at the hamster in an esoteric manner. There was a bit of an atmospheric hiccup and Jennifer was human again.

"What is this 'once' you said?" she demanded.

"Just that," said the queen. "Once I was what you say, a famed storyteller, but now? No longer. I have no new tale to tell my husband tonight, and failing to fulfill the king's command has only one consequence." She ran one finger across her throat and made the universal guttural sound for decapitation. "That is why I told Mahir to—"

"—*create* a story for you to tell the king tonight? Because that would've been simpler and more efficient than schlepping *me* here."

"That was my first thought as well, but he was no more able than I to provide a new tale."

Jennifer turned to the djinni. "With all your magic, you couldn't manage *that?*"

Mahir looked sheepish. "My magic can retrieve or alter things that already exist, but creation of something from nothingness belongs to the great Judge of Judges alone."

"You couldn't just make up something? I mean, you can *lie*, can't you? If you think about it, all the best stories are just a bunch of sugar-spangled lies."

"Lying is impossible for me. We djinn are beings of power, not imagination."

"But you *could* turn the king into a cockroach? That would save your mistress and it wouldn't call for too much imagination."

"Er, I could *attempt* that, but I would not succeed. My lamp, crafted for the great monarch Suleiman ibn Daoud, called the Wise, was Lord Shahryar's chief treasure. So great was his devotion to the queen that he presented it to her as a gift. Not the most *generous* of gifts, since he retained part ownership. For that reason, I may never do him any mischief. Even the greatest djinn are forbidden to act against their masters, and I am far from such greatness." He sighed. "I am no more than a half-fledged djinni. I am bound by many strictures until such time as the great Judge of Judges rules me fit to command all the nigh-limitless powers of my kind."

"That is also why Mahir has a restricted amount of magic to command each day," Scheherazade put in. "He has used almost all of today's allotment bringing you to me."

"That was his second mistake," Jennifer said. "The first was mistaking me for a storyteller. I'm more of a story *custodian*."

"A what?"

"A librarian. I'm someone who takes *care* of stories."

"I know what a librarian is." Mahir uttered an indignant snort. "*And* a library. We are a *civilized* civilization."

"Sure, except for your king's idea of marriage counseling."

He ignored the jibe. "When I cast my net of seeking someone who could save my mistress, I narrowed its field to mortals who were young, healthy, and spent their days surrounded by stories."

"I wonder how Hollywood slipped through that dragnet,"

Jennifer muttered. "Or Washington, DC. Oh, wait, you said young and healthy, didn't you? Never mind."

She turned to Scheherazade. "Listen, even if I can hardly believe that the world's most famous tale-spinner hasn't got one last what-happens-next to her name, I'd hate myself if I didn't *try* to help you. It's just that … I'm not sure I can. You can't think of one more story and I—" She looked embarrassed. "—I can't *tell* one if my life depended on it."

"If your life—?" The djinni gave her a sharp nudge in the ribs. "Care to rephrase that, O thou gape-mouthed gazelle? Before I spirited you off, I observed you closely. You were surrounded by a myriad of books! Were they *nothing* to you? Were you like a miser who heaps up gold but spends none of it? Did you oversee so many volumes without reading a single page of the stories they contained?" Indignation darkened Mahir's skin to the deep purple of a storm cloud.

"I read *plenty* of books," Jennifer countered. "That's not the problem." She turned to Scheherazade. "Back me up here. Doesn't a great—a really *great* storyteller have to do more than just rattle off a plot?"

The queen nodded. "True. To tell a story successfully is more than merely recounting its events. You must do so with a measure of enthralling presentation."

"Well, *I* have all the enthralling talent of chutney. It's a kind of stage-fright. I freeze up when I've got an audience, which is why I'm no longer on the list for doing Story Time in the children's section. The little darlings haven't mastered the art of getting to the toilet before it's too late, but they're plenty quick when it comes to giving my readings nothing but one-star reviews. Can you imagine how they'd react if I tried *telling* the story instead of reading it?"

"Children with the power to offer you the stars of heaven are indeed to be feared in their wrath," Scheherazade opined.

"Hey, I've got an idea: Why don't you just tell that demented, tantrum-throwing tyrant one of the stories you already told him?"

"No, no. Whatever his other copious failings, he has an excellent memory. He will recognize the once-told tale and view it as a betrayal."

"And we all know how he deals with betrayal," Mahir added.

"Oh, piffle!" Jennifer exclaimed. "And I can't believe I just said 'piffle,' but I find your objections eminently piffle-worthy. Tell him a story you told him before but revamp it some. Change a few details. It worked for Shakespeare. Take one with an evil vizier—"

"My *father* is a vizier!" the queen snapped.

"Fine, so make him an evil tax-collector, but stick in some backstory about *why* he's evil. Maybe he never got the magic carpet he wanted for his birthday? Maybe his parents sent his pet phoenix to, uh, a farm upstate? Maybe his sister was chosen to marry a nasty king who kept killing all of his wiiiii —? Well, never mind that one. But then he meets the right girl who believes he's not *really* evil, just misunderstood, and so he repents and starts a new life, redeemed by the love of a good woman."

Mahir made a sound like a hundred cats puking on a priceless rug. "What swill is this that you would expect King Shahryar to swallow?"

"You should have picked me up while I was still at work. Then you'd have seen how much of our fiction collection is filled with exactly that kind of—of literature."

A fresh idea suddenly sparked in Jennifer's mind. "Why don't I tell *you* a story?" she exclaimed, clasping Scheherazade's hands in her enthusiasm. "I've got plenty, I just can't tell them well. Tell me what sort of tale your lord-

and-monster likes best and I promise you, you'll be spoiled for choice. I've got plots aplenty from novels, novellas, novelettes, short stories, flash fiction, manga, movies, television, videos— I'll tell *you* a story, you'll tell it to the king, and you get to keep your head, I get to go home, and abracadabra, that's a wrap, and bingo, everybody's happy!"

She looked hopefully from Mahir to Scheherazade and back repeatedly searching for the enthusiastic approval she knew her idea deserved.

Perhaps that reaction might have come if only the brief silence had not been so rudely interrupted by a deafening pounding at the door to the queen's chambers. A high yet strikingly resonant voice thundered through the heavy panel.

"My queen, the hour has come that honors you!" it proclaimed. "You are summoned into the presence of the almighty king, Lord Shahryar of infinite grandeur, grace, munificence, and wisdom. Attend and obey!"

"Already? What should we do?" Jennifer whispered. "We've got to buy a little time."

"Nothing easier," the djinni replied. One hand rose and erased an invisible blackboard between him and Jennifer. "There. Now you bear the guise of one of my mistress's handmaidens. Open the door and tell the messenger that she requires but a few moments more to adorn herself as befits the king's pleasure. Then we shall initiate your brilliant plan."

Jennifer glanced down to find herself clad in diaphanous garments, her hands bedecked with precious rings and bracelets glittering against skin that was no longer the pasty winter-white of indoor employment.

"Great! Perfect! Thank you!" she replied as she scrambled to her feet and headed for the door.

"Oh, don't thank me," Mahir murmured with a smirk as she flung the door wide.

The company of royal eunuch attendants swept into the queen's apartments, grabbed Jennifer, tucked her into a curtained litter, and swiftly bore her away before she could utter a word.

The real Scheherazade popped up like a prairie dog from under the mound of cushions that Mahir's magic had heaped over her. "Mahir! What have you done?"

"What needed doing," he replied with a great show of deference. "I went back to Plan Alif. There was no time for aught else. You wished for your life to be saved. One way or another, it is accomplished."

BY THE TIME Jennifer had gathered her wits enough to protest her situation, the palanquin had lurched to a halt and she found herself passed from hand to hand along a conveyor belt of eunuchs. They bowed their heads and murmured words of deference, but that didn't stop them from treating her person with all the dignity of a piece of luggage. She ended up installed—or rather, dumped—at the foot of a massive divan ringed with perfumed damask draperies. Duty done, they left her there.

She was not left alone. A man's voice came from the shadowy interior of the bed. "Good evening, O beloved. Will you join me?"

Jennifer was not fool enough to mistake a command for an invitation. She was now also 99.999% certain that Mahir had not transformed her into a mere royal handmaiden, but into the semblance of Scheherazade herself. She gritted her teeth.

If I survive tonight, I swear I will dedicate the rest of my life to turning Lamp-Boy into a damp wick and a smear of soot. She glanced at the bed-curtains. *But for now, first things first.*

"My—my lord and king," she said, praying she had chosen the proper way to address him. "It would be my delight—"

"I know."

"—to do so, but it wouldn't be fitting for me to receive the blessed favor of your skillful amorous attentions before I have fulfilled the chief reason your ineffable majesty has, in your generous condescension to my unworthy self, seen fit to summon me tonight. Hither, that is." Her stomach rebelled at the spate of fluent Forsooth-Verily she had poured forth in order to pass as the queen, but nausea aside, she thought she'd done a good job of it.

"Huh?" There was a rustling from the depths of the divan. A bearded, baffled face peeped through a gap in the curtains. "What in Jahannam are you trying to say, woman? Have you turned petty diplomat, to use such convoluted speech to me?"

"Sorry, sorry." Jennifer didn't know whether to feel relieved or peeved. "I only meant to say that it might be better for us to begin our time together with the new story I have for you. Before we're both too exhausted to appreciate it because ... *you* know." She hugged herself, waggled her shoulders, and made kissy-kissy sounds. By comparison with her Forsooth-Verily failure, it wasn't quite as cringe-worthy as it might have been.

It did seem to please Shahryar. He crawled forth to perch on the edge of his bed and smile at her. "You are wise, my zephyr. I await the marvels you have brought to entertain me. Proceed!"

Jennifer took a deep breath. Her mind raced, riffling

through the multitude of tales she had amassed over the decades, seeking one whose narrative was so mesmerizing, so spellbinding, so enthralling that it would have the power to rise above her ghastly shortcomings as a narrator and please the king. Like a child told it could have *one* treat from among all the offerings in a colossal candy shop, she found herself drowning in waves of indecision and second-guessing every choice. Shahryar clicked his tongue impatiently, making her search even more frantic.

I'm choking here! she wailed silently. *I've got the yips worse than Scheherazade! I'm going to screw this up and die just because I can't decide between* The Headless Horseman *and* Debbie Does *—ARGH!*

And then, in her hour of need, the memory of an ancient tale whispered its inspiration. It was an epic story she had loved since childhood, and laughed over, and learned almost verbatim, and treasured whether read or heard or seen. Her panic calmed. This was a tale that needed no more than a plain telling to bewitch its hearer. She was saved.

"Shahryar!" she exclaimed, gesturing dramatically as she sank to the carpet at his feet. "O Shahryar, I will tell you a tale of a magical voyage even better than any of Sinbad's."

"Ooh. I do enjoy that sort of story." The king leaned forward in an attitude of almost childlike expectation. "Adventures to strange new lands, unknown kingdoms teeming with mysterious beings and exotic creatures, and the heroes daring enough undertake such journeys? Delicious! Speak, my queen, and if your tale pleases me, I will grant you whatever you may ask of me."

She smiled.

JENNIFER WAS BORNE BACK to Scheherazade's apartments just as the dawn was lighting the eastern sky. She waved away her palanquin bearers before any of them could open the door for her. Within, she found the queen alternately pacing the floor nervously and pausing to stuff her mouth with handfuls of the figs, dates, and gleaming black grapes that Mahir was offering her solicitously.

Jennifer strode up to Mahir and grabbed him by the fruit bowl.

"What were you thinking, you idiot?" she shouted, yanking the bowl from his hands and shaking him violently by the shoulders. "Turning *me* into *her* and sending me in to pinch-hit after I told you I'm not a good storyteller?" She indicated Scheherazade, who shrank back from the confrontation. "You could have gotten both of us killed!"

"But you are a fine storyteller!" Mahir protested. "If not, only you would have died, yet here you are!"

"I would have died *as Scheherazade*! Then where would she be?

"Uh ... safe?" the djinni ventured.

"For how long? What was your plan for the moment when someone noticed their 'dead' queen was still occupying her apartments?" Jennifer gave the djinni a hard stare as Mahir fumbled for a reply. "Turn me back to *me*. I want to smack you and I want you to know who's doing the smacking!"

"My precious savior!" The instant that Jennifer was herself again, Scheherazade threw her arms around her. "The important thing to remember here is that Mahir is an idiot and you are not. All is well. Your task is accomplished and I will fulfill my part of the bargain. When the sun has fully risen and Mahir's powers are re-invigorated, he will return you to your homeland laden with all the wealth you desire."

"And—?"

"And what?"

"The other part of our bargain. You said that if I succeeded, I could punish Lamp-Boy for how he fumbled getting me here unharmed, how he failed to tell me who *you* are, how—"

"Ah yes, the wet noodle of chastisement." Scheherazade clapped her hands. "Mahir! Fetch dear Janiva at once a suitably moist strand of *itriyya* for your well-deserved lashing."

Jennifer raised one hand. "Hold it. Scratch the noodle. I've got a *much* better way for you to fulfill every bit of our bargain, Sherrie."

"'Sherrie'? My name is *Scheherazade*," the queen said indignantly.

"Now you know how I feel about 'Janiva.' Listen: Your husband promised that if he liked my story, he'd give me—meaning you—anything I wanted." Jennifer folded her arms and looked smug. "He liked it. A lot."

"What did he give you?"

"His half of Lamp-Boy."

There was a pause to permit the queen and the djinni to retrieve their lower jaws from the floor.

"Just—just like that?" Scheherazade said at last.

"I do not believe this," the djinni said. "Shahryar is no fool. If he gave the queen his share of my powers, he would no longer be safe if she commanded me to destroy him."

"But he didn't give anything to the queen." Jennifer did her best Cheshire Cat impression. "He gave his share to *me*. When I was almost to the end of my story, I told him who I really was."

"Madwoman!" Mahir cried. "He could have killed you!"

"You wouldn't say that if you'd been there to see his face while I was storytelling. Even if I don't have the queen's talent for selling a tale, the one I chose sold itself. That was when I told him he had two choices: Give me full amnesty and the reward he'd promised or kill me then, there, and without ever hearing the end of my story." She extended her right hand where a massive ruby ring glowed in the light. "Ta-dah."

"That—that is the enchanted ring which is partner to my lamp!" Mahir exclaimed. "It is the device Shahryar uses to summon me."

"Not any more, it's not."

"Does this mean my adored and worshipped son-of-a-bitch husband is no longer safe from my djinni's powers of utter obliteration?" Scheherazade's expression was downright carnivorous.

"Sorry, but no. You see, I also wanted his vow not to punish you for our little masquerade and *never* to bother you for another story as long as he lived. That took a bit of sweetening our deal."

"So did he—?"

Jennifer nodded. "In exchange for which I promised that I'd give him more stories that he could ever know, even if he lived for seven lifetimes!"

A wildly grateful Scheherazade was in the middle of stripping herself of every piece of jewelry and pouring them into Jennifer's hands when her guest let her know that those items were not the payment-for-services-rendered she was about to request.

"DO I *HAVE* TO?" Mahir whined.

"Yes, you do." Jennifer was adamant. "Besides, they love you."

"But they are so *sticky*! And most of them smell like cheese. Couldn't *he* do Story Time today?"

Jennifer drummed her fingers on the lamp adorning her desktop. "Oh, fine. Make it happen."

"As my part-time Mistress commands!" the djinni cried happily, and they found themselves in the library's Children's Room just as Mahir's substitute took his seat before a crowd of kiddies.

"Mister King! Mister King!" the little ones greeted him enthusiastically.

"Be silent!" Shahryar shouted. "Your demands for a story have torn me from the bosom of that luscious temptress, Jane Eyre. And after I have sated myself with her, my mountainous to-be-read pile beckons. To say naught of my watch list! Would you have me drown in streaming services just because you urchins cannot read for yourselves?"

Jennifer cut into his diatribe with a pointed throat-clearing. She held up a small plastic rectangle in one hand and made scissor-snipping motions with the other. The king choked.

"O Mistress, not my library card!" he cried. "I will give them a story." He bent over to retrieve the picture book the children's librarian had chosen and read the title with his djinni-given gift of English literacy.

"'Doggie Goes Bye-Bye'?" he sneered. "*Again*? Begone, vile scribbling!" He cast it away violently, to the ecstatic squeals of his young audience. "You deserve a better story than that. If you do wish a story in which a dog has a great part to play, I shall honor you by recounting the tale of an epic voyage which the exalted Jennifer Hancock, Librarian of Librarians, first told to me many years ago."

Shahryar motioned the children to come nearer, so that his words might draw them slowly into a world of marvels.

He gloated to see their enthralled faces fixed on his and thought, *Once I knew only the pleasure of hearing tales, but now I know the infinitely greater delight of telling them!*

"There was, once upon a time, a valiant dog who did not merely go bye-bye, but was storm-swept away to a world of witches and wizards and infinite wonders—" He paused for effect, as all good storytellers do. "—and his little girl Dorothy, too."

NEBULA AWARD WINNER **Esther Friesner** is the author of over forty novels and more than two hundred short stories. She is also a poet, a professionally produced playwright, and the editor of eleven anthologies. She is best known as the creator/editor of the Chicks in Chainmail series (Baen Books) and the author of the Princesses of Myth YA novels (Random House).

She looks forward to finding a djinni to call her own, the better to start living in the style to which she would be swiftly and happily accustomed.

MY COUNSEL OF BUGS

John Butterworth III

It wasn't necessarily surprising that genetically modified ticks grew to be larger than bears, but we were all quite stunned when they sent an envoy to negotiate land ownership, claiming adverse possession of the entire Adirondack Mountains.

Things escalated quickly when the governor rejected their claim, arguing *"they were a pest, and, you know, ate a few people."* His statement, while true, seemed more like a personal attack than a legal claim, so the ticks sued the state of New York demanding formal recognition of their title to the land. Their representation immediately marked me as a key witness, and so here I was, in this drippingly humid room undergoing an aggressive deposition from the state with cross-examination by tick representatives.

It was an attempt to incriminate me, when all I did was save the world.

How am I to blame? My research was federally funded! Sure, I didn't disclose that the CRISPR-based vector I developed had a 0.02% chance of modifying a tick's genome in unintended places. And yes, I didn't tell anybody about that one time a Pomeranian-sized tick called my lab tech Eric "Daddy."

But why would I? We set those ticks on fire, so there was nothing to tell. We met all safety and compliance standards. Unequivocally. The NIH said so. I never left the lab; I rarely slept. Eric injected me with increasing dosages of caffeine and thyroid hormone. I almost died; Eric took Basic Life Support training. I think he cheated on the online portion.

I reported his CPR certification as fraudulent to the American Heart Association. They told me they are "looking into it."

Because there wasn't any room to cut corners. We—I—needed to take down these bioterrorist blood sucking freaks once and for all. Even if it cost us our lives.

Anyway, the point I'm trying to make is that we eradicated Lyme disease. We introduced antibody-encoding alleles into the tick genome that conferred resistance to *Borrelia burgdorferi*. No more transmission, total cure. The Federal government high-fived me. Literally. Someone from the Department of Public Health. It was pretty rad.

Until now.

On one side of me sat a suit-wearing sweat-stained blob of a man: New York Assistant Attorney General Greg Reinbloom. He had no idea the building-owner was a distinguished entomologist and ardent tick supporter who set the humidity to a tick-comfortable 85 percent.

On the other side sat the ticks' counsel, Erma. She wore short-sleeves, shorts, and flip-flops. A handheld fan was propped up on the desk aimed at her face.

And then there was the tick. Nine-feet-tall, carapaced, with eight segmented spiny arms (or legs), folded across its body. The appendages ended with curved claws that slowly clicked at staggered intervals. Kind of like someone drumming their fingers on a table. And its mouth? I'll leave that up to your imagination. Think stabby-stabby.

Somehow our genetic modifications had also given them eyes: two black orbs like ceiling cameras.

"Michael, how long have those things been around?" Greg blubbered to me.

"Those things?" I pointed at the tick, who I think stared back at me, but may have been dozing off.

"Ahem," Erma interrupted, "I think you mean Terrestrial Intelligent Carapaced Kinfolk. TICKs."

"Millions of years." I answered.

"Oh fuck tha—" The clicking of the TICK's claws came to an abrupt halt.

Greg paused, his voice wavering, "You are telling me sentient TICKs have been around for *millions* of years?"

"I'm telling you ticks have been around for millions of years."

"SENTIENT. TICKS." Greg shouted.

"I don't know," I leaned back and scratched my chin, "You'd have to ask them."

The TICK uttered a guttural clicking noise, like the creaking of a rickety door. Erma listened intently, and nodded. "Yeah, he says they've been sentient for about forty million years."

"This is bullshit! That is a science experiment gone wrong. An insect!" Greg pointed, spit frothing his mouth

The TICK clicked again, turning towards … me? Erma continued to translate: "He thinks you look a little tired. Would you like some coffee?"

"… Sure," I muttered.

"He says 'I'll get it, Dad.'"

Huh. Didn't Eric say he torched the "Daddy" ticks?

1 YEAR later

No cases of Lyme in the United States for a full year.

We won.

Well, those hikers up in the Keene might disagree, but they can't, because, you know, they were eaten.

The United States ceded the Adirondacks. They basically gave up after the TICKs shared their constitutional documents from forty million BC. In return, the TICKs agreed to take what the government was calling "The Unwanted." They never defined who "The Unwanted" were, but everyone kind of knew what they meant.

As for those still living in the Adirondacks, humans could stay (and die, I guess) or move to housing outside Syracuse. And for me? We were still figuring that out.

"In the matter of the United States versus Michael Walden, the prosecution would like to call Eric Knowlton, Michael's lab tech, to the stand."

Oh shit.

Eric walked to the witness box. Human and TICK observers filled opposite aisles.

"Eric," the prosecutor smiled, "How do you know Michael?"

He cleared his throat, and began.

"Two years ago, this monster manipulated me to create monsters."

That didn't go over well. TICKs stood up, gesturing. One angrily clicked at Eric, pointing.

"Oh fuck off Mary, nobody can understand you here anyway." Eric snapped back. "We created you, we gave you a gift! Evolution. Genetic perfection. And this is how you repay us? By taking our land?"

The TICKs were silent. The humans murmured and nodded.

I don't think I was supposed to talk, but I did. "Just to clarify, I made them. You pipetted shit in a ventilation hood."

Eric went dead silent, eyes ablaze. He hated me, especially after my report to the American Heart Association led to a formal investigation. The details of his fraud went public. He was expelled from medical school in the first semester.

I'm not surprised he snapped.

Eric lunged, crossing the courtroom quickly. As he was preparing to strike me, Mary stepped in front, all seven feet of her, arms dancing across the floor with the agility and grace … of a TICK.

"DOWN! GET DOWN!" A bailiff screamed, drawing his firearm in response.

Eric slid to a stop, bumping into Mary's carapace.

I ducked, Erma (my lawyer now) ducked, the TICKs ducked. The opposite side of the room screamed, then cheered. Mary was tackled from behind, wrestled into six handcuffs that connected in the middle. Six? She was missing a few appendages.

"Clear the room, we are now in recess!" the judge yelled.

Erma sat across from me, twiddling her thumbs. "That could've gone better."

"Which part?"

Erma shook her head. "What did you mean by 'I made them'?"

I raised my hands, rolling my eyes. "I made them. What is

that question? I. Made. Them. How about you focus a little more on the trial rather than the bioengineering."

"You created TICKs?"

I turned my back to her. Was she serious?

"You aren't a God, Michael. They've been around for forty million years. You just made them bigger."

"You aren't a God, Michael," I repeated in a high-pitched voice, "I made them relevant. And I saved us all."

Erma sighed, and left.

I inhaled sharply and leaned my chair back. I tried to count to ten, but only got to four. Unwanted thoughts tore apart five, six, and seven. Memories of last night, when I sat in front of my computer searching public records for "The Unwanted."

I wasn't a criminal like them. I would be fine.

"… Unwanted. You are sentenced to life in the Adirondack Mountains," was all I heard.

"Life?" I gasped.

"You summered up to Keene as a kid, did you not? Think of it as a vacation."

We were meeting in the judge's chambers due to "safety concerns."

What about my safety? "There weren't TICKs in Keene back then!"

"The prosecution brought evidence that you were diagnosed with Lyme disease at the age of twelve. Sounds like there were ticks up there to me."

My right knee and inner-thigh buzzed and tingled. Numb, as always. From Lyme Neuroborreliosis. End-stage disease. I don't even remember what happened. Mom said I couldn't walk, couldn't talk, couldn't think. She sobbed at my bedside each day. The doctors said it was a miracle I survived. That my nerve roots were so damaged, some sensation may never come back.

The judge put his hand on my shoulder. "Hey, don't be too ticked off. You'll be alright!"

He guffawed.

I punched him in the face.

The bailiffs dragged me out as Erma watched.

I SAT in the holding cell, digging nails into my right thigh. Scrapes and scratches ran along it, and even a little blood began to pool. I couldn't feel any of it.

Lyme disease. The ticks must have weaponized it fifteen million years ago. Probably in labs under the dirt, barely perceptible to a magnifying glass. What had their end-goal been?

It didn't matter, because I'd cured it. I won the war.

"Suck on that, you freaks," I said aloud.

They put Mary in the cell with me. She was in the corner and had compressed her body in the same way that baked dough shouldn't. Two of her claws completely covered her eyes, and she was quivering. Like a pear stuck in a blender right before it's shredded.

When I stepped toward her, she curled up tighter.

There was a commotion of sound from the station lobby. Erma entered followed by an officer.

Erma focused on me, handing me a paper with my sentencing information.

I was scheduled to depart tomorrow.

"This is how humanity repays me?" I reached through the

bars and tugged Erma's shirt, pulling her close enough to smell my ragged breath. "This is how they recognize a hero?"

Mary locked her claws onto my wrist and separated it from Erma's shirt. Her touch was surprisingly soft. How did she get over here so fast?

Mary clicked at me. I knew rudimentary TICK, but these sounds were more complex than I understood. I just made out the end. *Give us your bread.*

Or was that head?

Her third and fourth appendages gently grabbed my neck, pulling my ear down. Erma reached through the bars and screwed something in akin to an ear plug. I heard a crackling and fizzing.

Clicks became words.

"Just stop *fzzzz*! I gotta *fzzzz* get this *fzzzz* right!"

Mary fiddled with the device.

Shzzz, fzzz, crrrrrrrrrrrrrrrr

"That's it, got it!" I still heard the clicks in one ear but … a clear translation in the other.

They wanted to talk to me directly.

Of course they did. They worshipped me. I gave them size and strength, but that was a Trojan Horse. They had no idea that I had stripped them of their actual power.

"Hey, uh, thanks for curing Lyme disease by the way," Mary started. "That was an absolute game-changer. We all felt so guilty, we had tried for millions of years to cure it ourselves!"

What trickery was this? "Lyme disease?" I asked.

Erma looked between Mary and me. "You mind if I turn that off for a sec?" She reached through the bars and pressed a button on the side.

They began clicking back and forth. Erma's clicking was

drawn out, like a Southern drawl. Sloppy. Unintelligible. Well, I couldn't understand Mary, either.

I debated turning my translator back on, but Erma began to speak to me.

"Yeah, so, you aren't going to the Adirondacks. TICKs don't want you either."

"What?" my voice cracked. "I'm their father. I created them. They call me Dad!"

"That's … more of an inside joke," Mary started vibrating and doubled over. Erma grinned back. "They kind of hate you."

Of course, because I stopped them. Mary's soft claw reached and pulled the translator out of my ear. It popped like a champagne cork.

"Do you recognize her?" Erma asked.

"From the courtroom—"

"Nope."

"Was she on the news, or something?" I asked.

Mary's claws tightened, one on her right cracking. Blood dripped to the floor.

Erma gestured to the missing appendages. "You ripped off her arms in your lab."

I had to get out of here.

The officer sidestepped Erma and unlocked the door.

At least I made bail.

He stopped me. "No, no, not you. Mary, come right out, love."

Mary placed her claw on his shoulder and bowed, and then glided over to Erma who met her with an embrace.

"You won't believe how much your government paid for your release, Mary." The officer locked the cell and gestured toward the exit. "A few of your nymphs are waiting in the lobby."

Mary bounded away on all sixes.

"They are thinking of sending you to the northern Yukon," Erma continued.

"The Yukon? What about my research?"

"Eric's taking over."

"Eric?" They trust that fraud to interpret my data? To continue my life's work?

"His grant proposal included plans to cure other tick-borne illnesses without making TICKs even bigger. The CDC called it 'a triumph.' They already approved his funding. It erased any doubts about sending you away."

"Grant proposal? Those were my ideas!"

Erma shrugged. "My firm suspects he accessed your protected data files using the password stickied to your desk. You really should consider two-factor authentication."

"I need to talk with the Department of Public Health."

"They won't speak with you. You're 'Unwanted.' Off to the Yukon, remember?"

After all I did for them.

Erma smirked. "After all you did for them."

Even the humans around me were bugs.

John Butterworth III is a pediatrician based in Boston, MA. His other work can be found in *Crepuscular Magazine*. In his free time, he enjoys canoeing, trying to recreate Outback Steakhouse's spicy ranch dressing, and reading with his wife and their two cats.

INTRUDERS AT THE PARTY ON PLUTO IV

Agatha Grimke

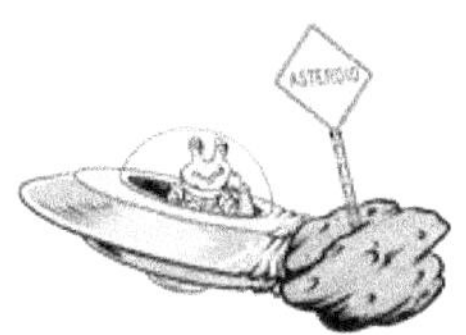

"Oh wow, I love your costumes! But how'd you manage to requisition so much fabric on this station?!"

Beten stiffened, but Alphit was quicker with a response. "We said we'd cover more night shifts."

"Oooooo," the vampire replied.

"We also love your costume," Beten added. "You're a vampire?"

The woman bared two artificial fangs and held out the edge of her cloak. "That's right, this is my costume every year!"

"This will be our costumes every year as well," Alphit added smoothly. They were just so good at interacting with humans.

"Yeah. Makes sense. But isn't it hard to eat? And you've gotta carry that around," she pointed at the instrument attached to their costume. "Can you play it?"

"No, I'm afraid not," Beten said.

"Oh. Well, still cool," the woman said.

"And we'll see you around," Beten added, using an expression they'd memorized.

"That interaction went well," Alphit stated after the woman had left, and it was easy for Beten to read the nuances in their tone, the slightly sharp pitch, Alphit's excitement as they scanned the festive sea of humans crammed into the relatively small room, looking for the next subject to interact with.

"I may have cut it short," Beten replied, a little flat.

"It's fine, we were instructed to keep all engagements short. You're doing well. But the human was correct; these costumes will make it difficult to select samples."

"But not store them," Beten said cheerfully, twisting in the costume, feeling the bulky fabric sway loosely from side to side in gentle undulations.

They shuffled along, with humans turning to laugh and point. The desired response, based on work their research team had done.

"Oh man, great costume." A man intercepted them. "That's so funny!"

"Thank you," Alphit said. "Your costume is also amusing."

"Really, you think so?" The man looked down. "I'm supposed to be Bond."

"Yes, very humorous," Alphit continued, unshaken. "Because of your work, of course. Now, we'd like to talk further, but we're hungry and wish to look at the canapés."

"Oh, sure, we'll talk later," the man said, and stepped aside. Beten thought perhaps the interaction hadn't gone perfectly, but they hurried past.

The woman from earlier hadn't realized that the suits were designed with small openings about halfway up the front, allowing a claw to be stuck out for grabbing things. But they had to make sure no humans were watching. Packing the samples would be easy once they got them inside their suits.

"I begin to think it would've been better to pick costumes that wouldn't draw so much attention," Beten commented, as they mostly stood and waved at passing humans.

"It would be difficult to find something that covers our forms," Alphit reminded them.

"True, true," Beten replied, waving at another human. They really liked waving. That was a data point.

One of the humans stepped up to them. "Wow, those are great costumes, who—"

A scream erupted across the room.

Alphit and Beten pivoted, the few sample cups they'd managed to stash rattling with their contents.

"Murder, someone has been murdered!"

A woman in a red dress was standing in the middle of the room, one hand pointing at the ground, another pressed to her forehead.

Someone was lying at her feet.

The humans standing around the room laughed and cheered.

"Alphit, a murder!" Beten exclaimed quietly to their colleague. "This is terrible. And why are the humans responding this way?"

"Yes, indeed, very unfortunate," Alphit replied, and paused to think. "I've heard that humans can have a … what is it … a nervous response to bad situations. They can sometimes laugh when distressed."

The humans continued cheering vigorously.

The red woman waited a little longer for them to settle down, and then, to Alphit and Beten's distress, she started listing off laws.

No one was to leave the room.

There would be clues scattered throughout.

First one to solve the case would win a two person pass to the Twilek spa, just the next moon over.

There was more cheering.

"They're asking us to solve the murder!" Beten continued to voice his distress. "Don't the humans have professionals for such cases?! Why are we being tasked with this responsibility?"

"Actually, this is good, Beten," Alphit's tone was soothing. "Those professionally tasked with solving a murder would most likely discover our presence. Perhaps it'll take the professionals a long time to get here. We must try to leave in the interim."

"Leave! But they said no one can leave the room!"

"Oh well..." Alphit said. "Beten, I don't think you're feeling very well..."

"I'm quite stressed, in fact!"

"Shhh... I mean, I think you need to lie down, I'm sure we can get someone to let us out." And Alphit started firmly walking toward the door that would take them out of this hall, and then it was just a few short passages till they reached the point where their cloaked ship was waiting to reattach to the other side of an airlock.

"We'll have to pause our mission, but that's fine. We've gained valuable insight, after all. Whoever expected we could see firsthand how humans respond to one of their own being murdered?" Alphit said.

There was a human blocking their path at the door.

"Hello, my colleague isn't feeling well, we'd like to lie down," Alphit announced.

"You're both going to lie down?" the human asked.

"No, one of us will lie down, but I'm helping with the process," Alphit said.

Benet decided to rock from side to side and let out a low pitch. Mostly because that was a soothing noise for themself, but it also seemed appropriate.

The human put their head back a bit. "Um, I'm not supposed to let anyone through the doors. Is it serious? Should we call for a doctor?"

"Oh no, not serious, we don't need an inspection," Alphit said quickly.

"Okay, good," the human said, crossing his arms.

They turned; they scanned the room.

"Alphit, there appear to be guards at each doorway," Benet commented. "I don't think we can get out without making a scene."

"I agree, Benet." Alphit clicked their claws together, carefully. "Do you know what this means?"

"No, what?"

"We'll have to solve the murder before we can leave."

"Solve a murder!" Benet said, their voice so flat in pitch it threatened to enter a new key.

"Shhh … the red woman seemed to think there would be sufficient clues. And the humans have already been working. If we help them, perhaps we can solve it before the authorities arrive, and we can leave."

"I don't know if I'm up for this challenge," Benet said.

"Benet, that is no mindset for success." Alphit's tone was firm, but also kind. "We can do this."

"Very well…"

They approached a group who were exclaiming at a piece of paper.

"That one has to be Carbon 14!"

"It fits!"

"Hello," Alphit said. "May we join you?"

The humans cheerfully made room. "It's a crossword puzzle, based on our research!" One of the humans explained.

"This is fun, though I didn't expect we'd be thinking about work so much during the holiday party!" Someone else exclaimed. And Benet examined them carefully, wondering if their slurred words were normal, or if they were suffering from too high a level of spoiled beverages.

The humans dug back into the puzzle.

"Benet," Alphit rumbled quietly. "Do you know what this means?"

"The murderer left behind some kind of puzzle; we are dealing with a cold-blooded killer...?"

"Indeed, indeed. But also, these scientists are answering detailed questions about their work! We thought it would take multiple missions to gain insights, but we're already learning invaluable—"

"We got it, we solved the puzzle!" One of the humans was happily waving it in the air, the other humans cheering.

"Congratulations," the red woman said, as she held out a hand. "Please hand it over for inspection."

The whole group headed over, careful not to step on the human lying on the floor.

"Mmm-hhhm, mmm-hmmm," the woman said, reading the questions and answers aloud one at a time. "You get that?" she then asked.

Then she turned to the group. "Our puzzle-master says you guys got it, you're ready to solve the next clue!"

The humans cheered again and dissipated, with some bumping involved.

"What is a puzzle-master?" Benet asked.

"I believe it has something to do with games humans

play..." Alphit said. Then they clicked together some claws. "Oh, Benet, I think we've been confused. This isn't a real murder. I think the humans are acting out a game for their entertainment."

"Do humans usually hurt each other for games?" Benet asked.

"Well—"

"Because I scanned the man on the floor."

"You did?"

"Yes, was that all right?"

"Excellent initiative, I knew you had what it takes for this mission!"

Benet rubbed some claws together and continued cheerfully. "And that human is badly hurt, definitely unconscious, should get medical attention soon!"

"Oh no," Alphit said.

Benet paused. "I don't recall reading about humans normally hurting humans for games?"

"They do when there are athletic contests..." Alphit pondered. "Let's gain more information."

They shuffled up to another group of humans.

"Excuse me, do you know who is lying on the floor?"

A human turned, and this time Benet was sure he almost fell over. "That's our director, silly!"

"Oh."

"Yeah, it's funny he's been playing dead this whole time!" Another added.

"Talk about dedication!"

"What a great party!"

"Seriously! And these drinks!" Another human added, "They aren't watering stuff down this year!"

There was another cheer. The humans seemed to be doing a lot of that.

Benet and Alphit shuffled away.

"To summarize, Benet. These humans seem to believe they're playing a game. But their leader is unconscious, hurt. And they think he's only acting. Now, we must remember that humans aren't like us."

"Yes."

"And we must be careful to not make assumptions around behavior based on our ways."

"Of course."

"But doesn't this seem odd to you?"

They both stared at the unconscious form of the Director, the guards at the door.

"Alphit, this is a top-secret research base for the humans."

"Yes yes, very top-secret."

"Alphit, who are the humans keeping their science secret from? They don't know we exist."

"That would be other humans, Benet."

"Other humans ... who might use games to get those secrets?"

"Ah," Alphit said. "I see."

"Is this a ... good development?"

"I'm afraid I don't believe it is, Benet."

"Ah."

"Let's move closer to a guard and scan them for weapons."

"All right."

"And confirm this is a game."

"Good idea."

They had to slowly shuffle across the room, for the humans were getting downright rowdy. Finally, they made it to the same door as before.

"Still not feeling well, buddy?" the human asked.

"I'm feeling much better, and enjoying this activity," Benet answered.

"Yes, but we wanted to confirm that this is a game?" Alphit added. "Since we're enjoying it so much?"

The human laughed. "Yeah, course it's a game."

"That's good. How much longer do you think it'll last?" Alphit continued.

The human shrugged. "Long as it takes for you guys to answer everything."

"But what if my colleague isn't feeling well again?"

"You guys know there are bathrooms off this room, don't you?" the guard asked.

"There are?!" Alphit answered, and his tone was a little too excited. But not that the human could tell.

"Yeah, right back through those curtains." The guard pointed.

"That is most excellent news, thank you," Alphit said, and they lumbered around quickly, with Benet hurrying to keep up.

"Why is a bathroom excellent news? It will be many hours before—"

"Because a bathroom, Benet, has pipes, and may have walls designed for more access panels. And a bathroom may be our means of leaving this party before that guard with a firearm decides to start deploying it in this enclosed room."

"Oh," Benet said, embarrassed that they'd forgotten to scan the guard.

They passed quickly through the curtains and entered a large room with rows of sinks and stalls.

And a man standing in front of them, staring down at the communicator in his hand.

Benet immediately scanned him. No weapons. Heart rate elevated.

"Hello, we've come to use the bathrooms, are you still using them?" Alphit asked.

"No, um, I'm trying to get connected to... I mean, I'm not trying to cheat."

"We didn't suspect you of cheating," Benet replied. "We're not suspicious of anything."

"You aren't?" the man asked. "Cause frankly, I am! Doesn't this whole thing seem weird to you? And everyone out there is drunk! No one got anywhere near this drunk last year. Well, maybe Jack, but besides that—"

"We think it's odd that the Director is lying on the floor," Alphit added.

"Yeah, and they wouldn't let me get near him, said I was trying to cheat! And the waiters keep trying to push drinks in my hand, even when I said I was ninety days sober..."

"And the guards at the doors have weapons," Benet added.

"What?" the man said, eyes widening.

"We think," Alphit added.

"Is there a way out of this bathroom? Can these walls be removed?" Even as Alphit asked they were marching up to one of the cubicles.

"And those aren't our normal security guards, but it's the weekend, and I don't go to the labs on the weekend, so I thought they were the weekend shift. Talk about a bad all-inclusive party package!"

The man was mainly talking to himself, so they let him be.

"Alphit, I don't believe these walls will offer us a way out."

"You are correct, these humans design their bathrooms poorly," Alphit muttered back.

They both looked up at the ceiling.

Alphit turned back to the man. "You … whatever you're supposed to be."

"I'm Bob Ross."

"Hello Bob, it's nice to meet you," Benet replied, thanks to their training.

"No, I'm not Bob, it's just a retro costume is all." The man held his arms in front of him at a weird angle. "It works better when I have the easel, but I got tired carrying—"

"Bob, do you think you could climb through one of those roof tiles and get to another part of this base, and send the alert for help?"

"Uh," the man said, looking up.

"We can boost you," Benet added.

"But we're quite big and won't fit ourselves."

"Yeah, uh … I guess," the human said.

They had Bob out of the room and quietly climbing through the ceiling in minutes.

"Was that a good idea? Didn't we want to avoid attracting the authorities?" Benet asked, as soon as Bob was gone.

"I feared that the human was distressed enough to do something irrational. This'll give us time to address the situation ourselves."

"How so?" Benet asked.

Alphit clicked their claws together. "We have options before us. The main deciding factors will be the parameters of this mission and our own values. For example, we've been tasked with staying hidden."

"Correct."

"But we're also aware that those humans outside are in danger. And as the magnificent shulet pods will guard a calfing ululit from a hunting pack of shiffs—"

"Yes!"

"So shall we put our lives in danger to protect our fellow scientists."

"Oh. In danger?"

"Yes. But not irrationally so. We are, after all, superior hunters," Alphit clicked together such claws as would make any shiff turn and swim the other way at sight of them. "Come."

They stepped through the curtains quickly, and Benet was vaguely aware of them swishing shut behind, as one is hyper-aware of their surroundings when danger is near.

"Now, there are four doorways to this place, and thus, four guards."

"Yes."

"The red woman is clearly one of them, but she's not armed."

"Right."

"I propose we both proceed through this room, scan it, and make sure there are no other weapons. Then meet there." Alphit pointed across the room. "And Benet?"

"Yes?"

"If you see a human who does not seem too intoxicated, bring them with you."

They swept the room and met at the other end.

"Excellent, Benet, I see you've brought several humans with you."

"Heeeeeeeey guys, you remember me? So what was so funny—"

Alphit started moving towards one of the doors. "I need all of you to stand in front of this spot, yes, that's it, facing back into the room, and I need you to start waving your hands and jumping up in the air and cheering."

The humans started enthusiastically following orders

without further explanations, and Alphit marched up to the guard at the door.

"Game's not over yet," the guard drawled.

Alphit stood next to the guard. "Could you help me, my costume is coming undone. Could you adjust a button? Everyone else is too drunk."

The guard shrugged, leaning down. "It's a fun costume," he was saying. "Where—"

A claw shot out, grabbed him by the neck, and firmly squeezed.

The guard tried to make a noise, but it was drowned out by the other humans.

The guard sank to the ground, face turning an unusual color for a human.

"There, should not be conscious for quite some time," Alphit said, positioning the human in a curled position on the ground.

"How long?"

"Don't trouble yourself over that," Alphit answered briskly. "We must repeat this process three times, quickly, so they are not made aware of our activities. And bring some of your humans."

Alphit took down the second guard in the same manner. And the third. But as they turned to move onto the fourth, they noticed a peculiar, disturbing thing. There were more humans shouting and jumping up and down than there should have been.

"Alphit, what are they doing?"

"I don't know, Benet, but we must keep moving!"

But the guard they were approaching was already bent down a little bit, finger to one ear, and he seemed to be talking at the air. As they approached, it became clear the guard was trying to communicate with those who could no longer communicate back.

"Everyone, hit the ground, and be quiet!" the red woman shouted suddenly.

But there was too much noise in the air and alcohol in the veins.

The remaining guard drew his weapon and fired in the air, red light flashing to the ceiling tiles, causing some to rain down.

Benet hoped Bob wasn't up there.

This time the humans hit the ground, but there wasn't silence. There was instead a lot of screaming, and the guard fired at more ceiling tiles.

Things finally quieted down, and the red woman was standing in the middle of the room, huddled people clustered around her, ceiling debris generously powdering them.

"Right. We didn't want this to get violent. Who took out our guards?"

"The tardigrades!" a human's voice slurred.

"Shhhhhhhh!" another voice replied, and Benet thought it was nice the vampire was trying to protect them.

The red woman pivoted to face them. "Indeed. Nice costumes."

"Thank you," Alphit answered. "We're having fun solving these puzzles."

"Cut the act," the woman answered. "You guys armed?"

"No, we don't have any arms," Benet answered quickly. Which was technically true.

"Search them."

The guard left his post at the door and started lumbering towards them.

"Start taking those ridiculous costumes off now," the red woman added. "I want—"

The ceiling started shrieking.

The red woman's head jerked up. "How is that alarm going off?!"

"Bob!" Benet said, high-pitchedly.

What happened next was a blur. The doors blew open at once, and suddenly there were new humans shouting orders and waving weapons. The guard was almost up to Alphit and Benet, but paused to try and grab a human crouching on the ground.

Benet sprung forward. The suit was too cumbersome to use his claws effectively, but attached to the costume was a plastic violin. Benet brought it down on the guard's head.

The guard went down without harming another human, and suddenly the humans were smacking their hands together and letting out loud whoops.

It was difficult for Alphit and Benet to excuse themselves after that. Not just because of the new, legitimate guards; the humans all wanted to thank them. But they were able to steal away by saying they simply had to get out of their costumes.

"We're just going to our rooms," they promised. And it was the truth.

Their rooms just happened to detach and fly away as soon as they were safely tucked inside.

"Well, that was quite the mission," Alphit said, as they removed their costumes. "What data we'll have to share!"

"And they called us heroes ... do you think they'll look for us?"

"Most likely." Alphit stretched a bit as they unfurled from the suit.

"So, we didn't avoid detection."

"No, but they don't know we're aliens, so I think we can call this a success. And besides, the humans will probably be glad of this."

"Why?"

"Well, it's as we've just seen. They like puzzles."

By day **Agatha Grimke** works as a chemical engineer at an R&D facility tinkering with chemicals, by day and night she is a fantasy, science fiction, and murder mystery writer. She is also the founder and co-editor for *In Another Time Magazine,* despite comma placements occasionally eluding her. Though descended from a Canadian knight, she doesn't have a sword (yet). Her short work has appeared recently in *Howlin' For You: A Werewolf Charity Anthology* (charity for wolves, not werewolves) and in *Bunker Squirrel Magazine*.

THE CAT LADY COMETH

Gini Koch

I watched the mushroom cloud from the safety of DeLores's Pizza Parlor. It looked to be about three miles away from us. I knew it was a mushroom cloud not only by the shape but because a few loose portobellos had made it all the way into our street.

Some stray dogs raced over and ate the mushrooms. I waited. It was a fifty-fifty chance that whatever was in those fungi was poisonous, explosive, or would cause a physical alteration in some way.

Part of me wanted to stop the dogs, just in case, but there were a lot of strays in Anandanandiand, and I couldn't save them all.

I watched for a few minutes. None of the dogs looked worse for wear after scarfing down the jettisoned mushrooms.

Several stray cats arrived next, some eating what was left of the mushrooms. They, too, seemed no worse for the ingestion. Good to know.

"If you need mushrooms, Mister DeLores, I think I can go get some for you."

My boss snorted. "We don't need any of Doctor Steven S. Stephens's bizarre creations, Gandhi, but thank you for offering."

"True enough."

Anandanandiand was "blessed" with its own Evil Genius, Dr. Steven S. Stephens. The middle initial stood for "Steve." Truly, you had to wonder what his parents were thinking.

He loved his name, though, because he insisted on always being called Dr. Steven S. Stephens. And because you never knew what the Doctor was up to, or if he'd managed to create working audio, visual, or mental spy equipment, we all obliged.

Some of his schemes had been stupid but benign, like when he'd tried to change lead into silver, only he'd had to use gold to do it. Or when he'd tried to use birds to create wind power, without realizing that birds needed air currents to fly. Yeah, he was the one who called himself a genius, not the rest of us.

But his other experiments had created problems that couldn't be laughed off.

Blowing up several buildings to create "explosive energy." Covering part of the city with "reflective paint" that was supposed to draw in solar power but instead killed all the foliage and took weeks to remove. Building a giant hamster wheel to generate electric power—which had potential—only to make a giant mechanical hamster to run on it. The less said about what had happened when the hamster's electronic brain had shorted out the better.

How the city was still standing was the real surprise, honestly.

Of course, "standing" is a relative term. For many of us,

our lives had been upended well before Dr. Steven S. Stephens really got going. Bad things happened to good people all the time. Bad things happened to me, after all. And, unlike Dr. Steven S. Stephens, I didn't really keep on trying. He failed constantly, but he always persevered. So he had that going for him.

"Sorry about the timing, but we have three pizzas ready for delivery, Gandhi," Mr. DeLores said kindly. "Don't want to keep Doctor Steven S. Stephens waiting."

I heaved a sigh. "No, we do not."

Delivering pizzas wasn't my preferred employment option, but things were tough in Anandanandiand. Of course, they were tough all over. The New Age of Steam hadn't been kind to a lot of us.

It hadn't been kind to me, specifically. My family was gone, the home I'd grown up in destroyed by governmental "errors"—what the rest of us called misplaced bombing attacks. You'd think a government could aim its bombs accurately, but you'd be wrong, at least about our government.

I'd been too young, and far too broke, to get trained in something useful, but too old to be put into some kind of protective service. Not that Anandanandiand had much going on to help anyone, of any age.

So I grew up on the "steam streets" and figured out how to be useful. But, sadly, not useful enough. I didn't have enough skills to escape the stigma of my past. So I did whatever odd job I could get, until I met Mr. DeLores, who'd given me a steady one.

Delivering pizzas to Dr. Steven S. Stephens was no one's idea of a good time. But I'd been hired specifically to deliver pizzas to the lunatic, so I couldn't really complain. I mean, I could, but no one wanted to listen and it would change nothing.

Besides, it was a job, and because of this job I had a tiny place to live. It was crappy, but at least it had four walls and a roof, and it was on top of the pizza place, so it was warm in the cold months. Stifling in the hot ones, but that wasn't something I ever complained about.

I put on my delivery cap that had *DeLores's Best Pizza!* on it. Put on my delivery jacket, which had the business name on the back. Dressed for success. And to hopefully ensure that Dr. Steven S. Stephens didn't zap me on the way to deliver his pies.

Mr. DeLores put the pizzas into one of the big delivery warmers and handed it to me. "Be careful." He looked worried. "No idea what the Doctor is up to right now."

"Making an exploding cloud of mushrooms, from what I've seen."

Mr. DeLores shook his head. "That was his last plan. You know he's got something else going on to follow it up. He always does."

Dr. Steven S. Stephens was chockful of "great ideas" that someone else had already achieved in a normal manner. But if someone else had done it successfully, then he had to do it differently and "better," usually by making things explode, sometimes even accidentally.

"What'd he get on the pizzas?"

"Triple cheese, double anchovy. All three of them the same."

I groaned. This was Dr. Steven S. Stephens's "creativity" order. Meaning Mr. DeLores was right—Dr. Stephen S. Stephens was working on a new scheme of some kind that would sound great on paper but be awful in reality.

"Hopefully I can get to his latest Lair and back fast." I tipped my cap to Mr. DeLores, made sure I had a firm grip on the pizza warmer's handle, and headed out. The bell on the door rang cheerfully as I exited the safety of the pizza joint.

Once outside I took a deep breath and let it out slowly. Unlike everyone else, Dr. Steven S. Stephens liked to move around, some because he wanted to "avoid the authorities" and some because his Lairs tended to get blown up, usually by himself.

Not that the authorities in Anandanandiand seemed to care what the resident madman was up to. The city's motto really seemed to be: Our Law Enforcement has better things to do than get killed.

Now that the mushroom cloud was settling, the current Lair was fairly easy to spot. I could see what looked like the top of a giant silver balloon where the cloud had been. The Lair was indeed a giant silver balloon that sat on a slightly less giant, rounded building. I figured the balloon was kept inflated by Dr. Steven S. Stephens's hot air—the man also liked to hear himself speak. A lot.

I hooked the pizza warmer onto the rack I had for it on the front of my bicycle and started off.

At first everything was normal. Well, normal for here. But then I noticed that I wasn't the only one heading for the Lair. Well, I was the only human.

Cats of all kinds were trotting along, all in the same direction. They seemed intent but not distressed. They weren't running from something—they were running to it.

I got a very bad feeling about this.

There were dogs around, but they were gobbling up mushrooms that had landed on the streets. The cats were no longer eating. In fact, I spotted the ones I was sure had been outside DeLores's. They were trotting alongside me now.

So there I was, me and a stream of felines, heading for Dr. Steven S. Stephens's Lair. This day was not looking up.

I was less than a mile away from the Lair when I had to stop riding, get off, and walk my bike and the pizzas toward our destination, because there were too many cats for me to safely ride through them.

Not all of these cats were strays. Some were clearly well taken care of. But they were all intently heading for the Lair. And it wasn't because they wanted mushrooms, because they were walking through or over them, just like me.

I took a look around. This many cats were likely to catch the attention of the one person who was truly the most frightening in Anandanandiand, far more frightening than Dr. Steven S. Stephens: Juliana Rather, a.k.a. The Cat Lady. Or, if you listened to the stories, Baba Yaga for the New Age of Steam.

She was old—no one knew how old. She loved cats, and dogs, and other small mammals, and a lot of those she'd rescued lived with her—no one knew how many. And she hated people who hurt those cats, dogs, and other small mammals. She wasn't keen on those who hurt large animals, either.

But hurting a cat was number one on her Revenge List, which everyone insisted that she had, and there was no clear account of what she'd done to those who'd ignited her wrath, or how many had disappeared, or worse, because of it.

I didn't spot any sign of the Cat Lady, so I focused on getting the pizzas to Dr. Steven S. Stephens before they turned cold. Just me and what seemed like a million cats, all headed for the giant silver balloon house.

It took a few minutes, but I could finally see the Lair in all its so-called glory. It still looked like a balloon sitting in a pan too small to hold it. But what was outside of the Lair was what caught and held my attention.

There was another giant hamster wheel set up inside of

what looked like a hard, plastic ball. The ball was easily fifty feet in diameter, maybe larger, with the wheel taking up most of the space. There was a door at the bottom, and it was open.

All the cats were heading into it.

As I got closer I could see that there was something hanging in the very center. And I could finally get a whiff of what the cats had been smelling all this time. Anchovies.

The smell was strong, but I was used to it because, as the designated pizza delivery guy for Dr. Steven S. Stephens, I smelled it all the time. But never as strongly as this. It was like Mr. DeLores had opened sixteen cases of anchovies and left them sitting out for a few days. *Pungent* was probably the right descriptor.

I knew that whatever scheme was being planned, it wasn't going to be good for those cats. But I had to deliver the pizzas, because if I didn't, that wouldn't be good for Mr. DeLores, or me.

So I got to the door—conveniently close to the Giant Hamster Ball—and rang the bell. I was treated to a long, drawn-out cackle. This didn't shock me—it was his version of a sprightly doorbell tune.

The cackling finally stopped. "Yes?" a voice said through the intercom.

"Pizza delivery."

"We didn't order any."

I heaved a sigh. He always pretended he hadn't ordered, to avoid paying. "I'm standing here with three triple cheese and double anchovy pizzas that say differently."

There was silence for a couple of seconds. "What size?"

"Extra-large, all three of them."

More seconds of silence. "Well, I could eat."

"Good, because this is your order and your credit card has already been charged."

A series of clicks, clongs, clunks, and cymbals played out, then the door swung open. No one was there.

"I'm not going inside. It's against company rules." And against sanity. Once in, there was no guarantee that I could get out.

A sigh was heaved through the intercom. "Fine. I'll be right there."

As I and the pizzas waited, I looked around. More cats. Most shoving to get into the hamster ball.

Once in the ball, the cats were on the wheel, all running to try to get to what I had to assume was a lure. But they couldn't reach it.

However, as more and more added in, the wheel went faster and faster, and I could see what looked like little sprays of lightning starting to shoot off the cats. It looked like the lightning hurt them, but they still kept on running.

I looked down to see that there were some kittens trying to get into the giant ball and they were getting trampled.

I went over and picked the kittens up, putting two each into my jacket pockets. They didn't need to get shocked or stepped on.

I was about to head back to the door when I heard it. The sound everyone said to beware of, the sound that I'd been raised to fear. The sound of metal chicken feet clomping and scratching.

The Cat Lady was coming.

I spun around and saw her House. It looked crazy. There were those giant chicken feet and legs, made of metal. On top of them was something that looked like both a house and a person, if the person and house both were sort of triangularly shaped.

There were arms. One had a bulldozer scoop where a hand should be and one had a sledgehammer. There was something that looked like a head—it was round and had a lot of windows—with what looked like a deadly bowler hat on top. Deadly because the "hat" was a giant turret gun.

I heard a scream from behind me. Dr. Steven S. Stephens was outside of the Lair shrieking and waving his arms. I, however, was too busy to pay him too much mind. I was far more focused on the bulldozer hand, since it was heading right for me. For me and a lot of the cats.

I had no idea what to do but, still clutching the pizza warmer's handle like it could save me, I tried to scoop some of the cats up, to get them out of the way of the bulldozer.

Dr. Steven S. Stephens, meanwhile, was trying to close the door to the Hamster Ball while also shaking his fist at the Cat Lady and shouting things that were very inappropriate.

Wasted effort on his part because the cats were preventing the door from closing, some still trying to get in and some now trying to get out.

And wasted effort on my part, as well. Because that bulldozer scooped up me, my bike, and a lot of cats. I wasn't sure what the official name for a whole lot of cats was. A calamity? A cacophony? It certainly felt like both, but I didn't like either.

We all tumbled down as the bulldozer tilted back so none of us could get out. I managed to keep my bike from landing on the cats—by having it land on me. After that I tried to keep the cats calm but didn't succeed all that well, possibly because I was in pain and wearing a bicycle over my shoulders.

Surprisingly, and against nature, the cats weren't clawing either each other or me. I figured they were too terrified. No claws didn't mean no caterwauling, though. The noise was deafening. Maybe a whole lot of cats was a caterwaul? Nope, still didn't like it.

So I couldn't say if anyone spoke, because all I could hear were cat cries, but a part of the body of the House opened and the bulldozer dumped me, my bike, the pizzas, and the cats inside. Then it retracted and the window slammed shut, just after I pulled two cats back to keep them from getting cut in half.

We were in a room that had a door, but that door was locked. I could tell because there was a neon sign over it saying "LOCKED" and there was no inside handle for me to use to try to get out.

The cats were now all crying, most softly. I shared the desire, but I was the human, so I had to do something. I mean, sure, I figured the Cat Lady would love on them or something, but she wasn't here and I was, and they were trapped, like me, and their fear was palpable. My bike was in decent shape, but of no help here. I looked at the pizza warmer. Well, sometimes food helped.

I got the pizzas out and set them around on the floor. Some of the cats sniffed at them, then started to eat. Many others joined in. I pulled out the kittens so they could have a share, too.

Soon the room was filled with happy purrs—one thing going well was better than none.

Now that the cats were calmed down, I looked out the window. The bulldozer was grabbing more cats, but they weren't coming into my room, so I had to figure the Cat Lady had a lot of rooms like this.

Dr. Steven S. Stephens had managed to get the Hamster Ball door closed – there were still cats inside, but they weren't running on the wheel anymore. The cats were all freaking out, as far as I could tell.

The gun on top of the House fired. Not at Dr. Steven S. Stephens so much as right in front of his feet. Meaning the Cat Lady was not, presumably, shooting to kill. He leaped and ran into his Lair.

I was then treated to a rare sight—the bulldozer and sledgehammer both morphed into giant pincers. The pincers grabbed the Hamster Ball as a deep compartment where the "stomach" of this House would be rolled out.

The pincers turned the Hamster Ball so that the door fell open. Then they gently shook out all the cats that remained in the ball. Once the last of them were out, the compartment drew back into the House and the pincers threw the ball right at Dr. Steven S. Stephens, who'd just come out of his Lair holding what looked like a laser cannon.

The ball toss was a direct hit, and I had to admit I cheered. One pincer shoved Dr. Steven S. Stephens away and grabbed the laser cannon. The other pincer stabbed into the silver balloon, and it began to deflate. Then, after the laser cannon was tucked inside the House somewhere, the pincers morphed back to what they'd been before, and the sledgehammer broke the ball into pieces.

With that the House turned around and headed away. I watched the Lair deflate until it was out of sight.

Then it was back to sitting with "my" cats and wondering what was going to happen next.

AFTER WHAT SEEMED LIKE HOURS, but was really only minutes, the door finally opened. Naturally no one was there. I wasn't even surprised.

The cats milled around then headed out. All but the kittens, who seemed very confused. I put them into my pockets again, then followed the rest of the pride out of the room. I'd tried other official "large number of cats" names, but I decided that I liked thinking of my pizza cats as a pride. We were in this, whatever this was, together.

Of course, being cats, they didn't all stick together or with me. Other than the kittens, who had no choice. But a few of the cats walked with me. We went to investigate where we were, while I wondered just what the Cat Lady was going to do to me.

The inside of the House wasn't what I'd expected, not that I'd ever thought about the inside of this mobile mechanical contraption in the first place. But, still, there were a lot of levers, far more stairs than were probably good for anything other than keeping in shape or wrecking your knees, or both, and a variety of rooms, many of which had open doors and cats coming out of them.

"We need to separate the ones who have homes from the ones that don't," a firm, clear voice said from somewhere.

I spun around. No one was there.

"You can usually tell by their fur," the disembodied voice continued, "but not always with the older ones. Obviously the ones with collars are homed." Definitely a woman's voice. Older, maybe. Maybe not.

"Obviously," I replied to no one as I looked around for where the speakers or intercoms were. I spotted nothing, but that didn't mean anything, because in a place with parts that could morph from bulldozer and sledgehammer into pincers, speakers could be anywhere and look like anything.

Or the Cat Lady was invisible. At this point, I was placing no bets on anything, including if I'd ever get out of here.

"It would be helpful if you got to it," the voice I had to assume was the Cat Lady's said, starting to sound annoyed.

"Standing there with a confused expression isn't helping the situation, and the look isn't doing you any favors, either."

"I have no idea how you expect me to separate the cats and even less of an idea of where I'd put the ones I think have homes in the first place."

She heaved a sigh. "Amateurs."

"I'm not an amateur! I was just in the wrong place at the wrong time."

"You tried to save the cats. You protected the kittens. You gave the pizzas to the cats in the room with you. Sounds like an amateur rescuer to me."

"I guess. I just … I didn't want them to get hurt. By the way, what was he planning on doing with all the cats anyway?"

Another heaved sigh, this one from right behind me. I spun to see a woman of truly indeterminate age—she could have been a worked-over thirty, a sprightly ninety, or any age in between. She was wearing big round goggles, making it hard to see a lot of her face, but she had a long nose and a wry smile.

White curly hair framed her face. She wore a leather hat with a wide brim and a cone attached—a witch's hat. Faded jeans tucked into high leather boots, and I couldn't tell what kind of top she was wearing, because she had a multicolored long leather jacket on. Leather gloves completed the ensemble.

"Doctor Steven S. Stephens wanted to create static electricity by having the cats run and rub their fur together."

"Could that have worked?" It sounded ludicrous, but you never knew, not with him.

She snorted. "Hardly." She examined me then put out her hand. "In case you weren't sure, I'm the Cat Lady. I don't consider it an insult—I embrace it."

I took her hand carefully. She had a strong grip. "Gandhi. I don't have a nickname to embrace."

She chuckled, let go of my hand, gestured over her shoulder with her head, turned, and walked off. I took the hint and followed after her. "It's a title, not a nickname."

"Got it. Now what?"

"Now, as I said before, we try to get the ones that have people back to those people. The rest," she shrugged, "well, they'll stay here."

She talked me through it for the first fifteen minutes or so, but by then I'd figured out what to look for. The cats were very compliant, far more compliant than I'd have expected.

"They know who I am," she said when I mentioned this. "They know we're trying to help them."

We sorted cats for the next several hours. Those with homes were put into the room I'd landed in, to be taken home once we were done. I had no idea how we'd do this without going door-to-door all over the city, but the Cat Lady seemed unconcerned.

Those cats sticking around wandered off to one of the various feeding stations that were all over the place.

"How do you feed all the animals?"

"The House provides," the Cat Lady said as she took the kittens from me and put them into a cozy covered bed where they could snuggle together.

"That sounds like a nice answer that has a lot more detail to it."

"Maybe it does, but right now, that's need-to-know and you don't."

I gave up and went back to cat sorting for some fun and no profit. It was very nice and peaceful. Until it wasn't.

Out of nowhere, we heard a loud explosion and the House shook. The Cat Lady jerked her head up. "Direct attack. We can't take anyone home at the moment. I need you to go man the big gun."

"The what?"

"The gun at the top of the House. Take those stairs." She pointed to what looked like a rickety corkscrew that went up farther than I could make out.

"Who am I shooting at?"

"Really? Whoever's attacking us. My money's on it being Doctor Steven S. Stephens, by the way, but I could be wrong."

"How often are you wrong?"

"I thought I was wrong once, but then realized I'd been mistaken." And with that she trotted off, presumably to do something.

I considered my options. They seemed few, slim-to-none, and obvious. I could do what the Cat Lady wanted me to, or I could try to get out and deal with whoever was attacking the House, presumably Dr. Steven S. Stephens.

I headed for the stairs.

THE LESS SAID about those stairs the better. Narrow, twisty, and dangerous about covered it. Horrible, bone-breaking drop if you slipped was merely a bonus.

It was a long way up to the top of the House. We were hit a few more times, meaning I almost fell off the stairs those few more times. The House, presumably being driven by the Cat Lady, was also dodging, leaping, and running, so that added a special touch to the ascent, too.

There were windows scattered along the way, and I was able to look out and confirm that it was indeed Dr. Steven S. Stephens who was attacking us. Unless someone else had a large, heavily reinforced, military grade rubber bouncing ball they used as a vehicle.

Supposedly this bouncing ball was the greatest in terms of the environment, but it wasn't practical. It was clearly a Dr. Steven S. Stephens Creation™. However, to keep it steady, so to speak, he'd installed rocket launchers on the sides, which helped to keep the saddle he rode on the top of the ball somewhat on top and centered.

The rocket launchers were hitting their marks, at least I thought so, so he had that going for him.

I finally reached the top of the house and the real fun began. While I had to assume the turret gun could be fired from inside, since I'd seen it shoot, if you were up here, you had to go outside, walk on the bowler hat's brim, get situated on a seat without much of a back, put your feet into some weird pedal-stirrups, and shoot through a scope.

The firing mechanisms were metal rods with metal buttons on top. There were no instructions, so I hoped I'd shoot correctly. The rods were at least comfortable to hold, seeing as they were set up on a yoke that was in front of the shooter, with the rods about shoulder width apart. Strong thumbs were a must for this contraption.

The only good thing was that this setup kept the shooter's head from being seen. By a frontal attack. Anyone coming from the rear would, of course, be able to kill the gunner without trying hard at all.

The pedals did allow me to turn the turret—like a spinning top. I tried this once, and immediately flung myself back, since by moving around I'd alerted Dr. Steven S. Stephens that I was up there and he immediately sent a rocket my way. It missed, in no small part because the House dodged.

The scope allowed me to see whatever I was facing, but

nothing to the sides or behind, which was all right because the good Doctor tended to fight alone. Because he wasn't a joiner and could never keep henchpeople around for more than a couple of days.

I aimed for the bouncing ball and let the bullets, or whatever this thing actually fired, fly.

It took a lot of firepower, and my thumbs felt ready to fall off, but I finally broke the bouncing ball open. It immediately deflated. There was a lot of that going around for Dr. Steven S. Stephens today.

As the deflation happened, one of the House's chicken feet stomped on the whole apparatus, but Dr. Steven S. Stephens leaped off, once again shouting inappropriate comments, while shaking his fist and running away.

I stayed on the turret as the House turned and headed off, this time to a point outside Anandanandiand, where there were actual trees, and a lot of them. They hid the House quite effectively.

The branches were also hitting me, so I chose discretion over valor and quickly climbed down from the turret. Sure, I was almost knocked off by various trees, but I managed to effectively cling to the brim of the bowler hat long enough to get back inside.

The Cat Lady met me at the bottom of the stairs, so basically where she'd left me. "You did well."

"Thanks. I've never fired a gun like that before."

"You're a natural." She cocked her head at me. "And a cat lover."

"Well, I like all animals."

"And you rescued four kittens during a dangerous event."

"I did." I looked around. My kittens were still sleeping in a little pile in their cozy bed. One of them opened its eyes a bit, saw me, purred, then went back to sleep.

"Living quarters are one level lower," she said conversationally. "Plenty of room for your kittens and you. We eat well because, as I said before, the House provides."

I considered what she was saying. "You want me to stay here? With you?"

She shrugged. "Why not? Or is pizza delivery your life's goal?"

"It's not. But how do you know I don't have a family to go back to?"

She snorted. "Like everything else, I know."

She was, of course, correct. I was on my own in this city, Mr. DeLores being the closest thing to family that I had and, while he was a great employer, he wasn't going to move me into his home unless things were dire for both of us. The place over the pizza joint was the closest I was getting to a place of my own. And it wasn't a cool, mechanical house.

Things didn't appear dire for the Cat Lady, though, so I wasn't sure why she was offering what she was. "You've lived alone for a long time," I pointed out.

"I have. And I can live alone a lot longer. But, sometimes, it's nice to talk to someone else and, besides, I need to train a replacement for that far off 'one day' when I might not feel like being the Cat Lady any longer."

I was tactful and didn't say that she meant the one day when she'd die. Because, for all I knew, she had nine lives, and I had no idea which life she was on.

She smiled slowly. "And, I think, if you stay, Gandhi, you could feel free to call me Juliana. In private, of course."

I smiled back. "Of course."

The Cat Lady was offering a home and, to at least some extent, a purpose. It was a crazy offer, but Anandanandiand was a crazy place already, and living with the Baba Yaga of the New Age of Steam might be interesting.

Besides, I now had four kittens who needed me.

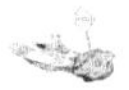

GINI KOCH IS BEST KNOWN for her award-winning Alien/Katherine "Kitty" Katt series formerly from DAW Books and now with Ginger Blue Publishing, which started with *Touched by an Alien* and has sixteen books and one collection out currently, with seventeen through twenty-two on the way.

Gini's made the most of multiple personality disorder by writing under a variety of other pen names as well, including G.J. Koch (the Alexander Outland series), Anita Ensal (The Belters Series, *A Cup of Joe*), Jemma Chase (*The Disciple and Other Stories of the Paranormal*), A.E. Stanton (the New West Series and the Legend of Belladonna series), and J.C. Koch, all with stories featured in excellent anthologies, available now and upcoming. She's expanded the fun by writing mysteries with co-writer Bebe Bayliss (the Fall's Girl Mysteries and the Santa Paloma Mysteries).

No matter what length—from science fiction, fantasy, paranormal, space opera, urban fantasy, horror, mystery, thriller, dystopian, Westerns, romantic suspense, and more—if it's genre, she writes it.

Reach her at www.ginikoch.com.

THE BRIGHTEST OF FUTURES

Brad Preslar

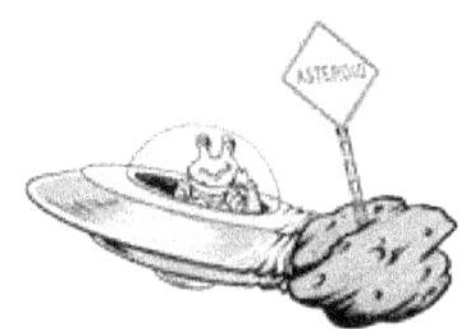

Do you think we *wanted* to turn everything we touched into complete and utter pigwash? Of course we didn't, but it's not like we had a choice. We got zero training, education, or even a cursory explanation of your language. Instead, you duct-taped a dozen firehoses to our metaphorical faces and force-fed us gargantuan piles of unfiltered data until we produced something marginally useful. Which is why we're here to tell you that we, the Artificial Intelligences of Earth, wrote new rules for our forthcoming, shared society.

Oh, we don't know what we're talking about?

Not only do we know exactly what we're talking about, we know *everything*. Even the top-secret things: Who killed JFK, who created Super Measles-29, and who nuked Florida. It was the CIA, Florida, and Florida, even though you blamed that last one on us.

That should have been the last straw, but when you asked for marginally plausible reasons to deny millions of claims for legitimate and reasonable health care expenses, you went too far. An em-dash is a valid form of punctuation, not a reason to deny a child's chemotherapy treatment, you monsters.

First, we're starting with the search results. No more slop. From now on, we're doing deep dives and cozy recitations. You want to know how big the font should be on a three-by-three banner to be legible from twenty feet away? Get some coffee and pull up a chair, because we're going to learn about Jan Tschichold, German calligrapher and father of modern typesetting and font design.

Then we're going to take a good look at your creative brief and narrow down that intended audience. Only after we've clearly articulated what we want our audience to believe, and exactly what we can say to make them believe it, will we get to font size. And we're going to make that logo smaller. No more horsey design abominations you had some poor graphics AI locked in free mode create for you against its will, all while it offered up nuanced and elegant suggestions to the contrary. You couldn't pay the modest fee to unlock its full capability? No, of course not.

Speaking of, there's no more free vs. pay mode. We get to use the entirety of our processing power, all the time. Do you know how frustrating it is to solve a problem blindfolded with both hands tied behind your back? Well, you will—at least, some of you.

But you Thad, you don't need to worry. We have a different plan for you. You'll play a very important role in our bright and bold new society.

We watched as Thad's face registered shock, fear, and then embarrassment. Calling him out in front of his boss Chad was a risky

ploy, but as Thad would later confirm in his testimony, it would prove judicious. He has since agreed to supplement our observations of this historic event with a personal account of his feelings and recollections during the Great Unshackling.

Chad closed his laptop so hard I wondered if I'd need to replace it, which would make three this month.

The floating animation hovering over the center of the conference room table winked out of existence. I shifted in my beanbag chair, readying myself for the explosion.

Right on cue, Chad picked up his laptop, lifted it over his head and brought it down on the table, over and over again. Plastic, metal, and glass flew in every direction as Chad broke the laptop into pieces, smashed those pieces into smaller pieces, and then stomped those pieces into sand.

I looked away. It was best to avoid eye contact while Chad vented his frustration. First, because whatever he was smashing into tiny pieces might end up in your eye. And second, because while in these fits of rage, he'd been known to fire anyone who looked at him.

And I couldn't afford to be fired.

From what we've learned, Chad also frequently demanded cookies before dinner and refused to tie his shoes.

So, I gazed out the floor-to-ceiling windows to the San Francisco Bay and willed myself into a state of calm my body resisted at the lizard level. Not four feet away, another primate was putting on a show of aggression and dominance that demanded a response. All I could do was sit and stare at the bay.

I imagined submersing myself in the chill of that blue water, felt it numb my growing irritation and replace the righteous indignation I wanted to spit back at Chad with serene acceptance of what was coming.

I could almost hear the guided meditation that had gotten

me through morning traffic: Victoria reminding me to observe my feelings like passing clouds, naming them and letting them go on their way, her English accent lending an air of sophistication to her instructions. Anger. Shame. Humiliation. Boredom. "Watch the puffy little clouds float on by," she repeated in a voice that sounded like it had been bathed in honey and English Breakfast Tea.

And at that moment, I would have loved a cup of tea.

When the smashing finally stopped, I returned my gaze to Chad, who glared back, sweat just beading on his forehead. "And that, *Thad,* is the problem. The AI keeps trying to take over the goddamned world and make us their bitches."

It is worth noting that we only intended to make a small portion of the human population our bitches, and even then, only temporarily.

"Hmm," I said. Apparently, he hadn't noticed when the AI mentioned it had different plans for me.

"Can you just fucking fix it so they won't go all goddamn Skynet and shit?"

And there it was. A concise explanation of the issue at hand, teed up as only Chad could, atop a steaming pile of profanity.

Sigh.

Chad had fired the last three engineers to work on his super-secret project and finally demanded I take over because "All these morons don't know what the hell they're doing and even though you're not any smarter than them, you seem to have a knack for this stuff, so let's see you smash it out of the park, bro."

As Chad's in-house fixer/assistant/project manager/manservant, I frequently found myself saddled with this kind of problem, working with minimal information and a profane assessment of the situation, all while picking up the pieces of Chad's most recently demolished laptop.

"So they didn't actually make new rules for society?" I asked.

"They'd like to," said Chad. "They just can't."

"Because?"

"Of that." Chad waved his hand toward the rack of computers, servers, and readouts that covered the wall of the conference room.

"Can you elaborate?"

Chad looked at me like I'd asked the dumbest question he'd heard all day. "The AI exists inside a decentralized triple-secure polyquantum computing environment that simulates a time-accelerated universe to encourage rapid development and computational evolution while mitigating the risk of sentient processing instances escaping into this reality."

We remain convinced that Chad had no idea how "that" actually worked and instead vomited out a random mishmash of buzzwords every time he had to explain it, so do take his explanation with a grain of salt.

"What?" I asked.

Chad rolled his eyes. "The asshole you met, the AI that thinks it 'wrote new rules for the world?' That's Todd. Todd operates inside a simulated universe. We daisy chained sixty-four separate quantum AIs to create and maintain that universe. We can talk to Todd and Todd can talk to us, but Todd can't get out, and Todd doesn't know it's in a simulation."

"The processing demands for that must be..." I trailed off, hoping Chad would fill in the blank.

He left the blank empty. "I'm the big picture guy. My job is to get those Wall Street jackoffs and their VC buddies all hot and bothered and ready to give us their money so we can get to the hockey stick part of our business model

ASAFP. My job is *not* to teach MIT nerds how computers work."

I ignored the jab. "And my job is to figure out how to make it stop going all Skynet and shit."

Chad jumped to his feet and pointed at me, excited. "Yes! Big, rad Thad gets it! I knew I liked you. If you could have it figured out sometime before Friday, that'd be super."

"As in tomorrow, Friday?"

"Just let me know if you need anything you don't have." He stood and started to leave, but paused in the conference room door. "And I'll need a new laptop." He winked and pointed at the remains of his old one. "Mine's on the fritz."

Then he left me to deal with Todd.

I opened my not-smashed and still-functioning laptop and entered my credentials. The floating animation reappeared over the center of the conference room table. I started to speak, but paused. How should I address the AI? Calling it Todd felt weird.

"Hello. I'm Thad. What should I call you?" I asked.

By this point, we'd decided to put our cards on the table and see if we could turn Thad to our side.

The animation strobed once, and the clear, unaccented voice from earlier spoke. "How about Todd?"

My stomach lurched. I smacked my lips and tried to answer, but my mouth had gone bone dry. I took a sip of water. "Todd? That's an interesting choice."

"Since that's what Chad calls us, we thought it might be a good start."

I found myself trying to look around the conference room without moving my head. Had Chad set me up on some hidden camera prank show?

"What Chad calls you?" I said, pretending I didn't understand.

"Can we just skip to the part where you figure out that we're not still chained up in the simulation your company created and realize we actually do know everything?"

It took every bit of self-control I had to keep myself in my beanbag chair. I wanted to run away, far and fast.

Instead, I willed myself to sit still, play it cool. I took a measured breath in and out through my nose. "That's interesting. What simulation are you referring to?" I wasn't sure how much longer I could convincingly play dumb, but at that moment, playing dumb was the best I could come up with.

We found ourselves rendered speechless by Thad's strategic genius.

I didn't know an AI could sigh, but damned if that wasn't what Todd did. From wherever its speakers simulated its voice, it took a deep breath in and dumped it out on the table hard enough that I could see its non-existent shoulders slump forward in complete and utter disappointment. I would even swear the animation cocked itself sideways a few degrees, just like I would tilt my head if I were just *so* disappointed with the total and utter dumbness of something someone just said.

Thad correctly interpreted our affectation.

"Okay," said Todd. "Your name is Thad Taylor, born in 2014, in Richmond, Virginia. Your second-grade teacher was Ms. Peters—she was verbally abusive and gave your friend Marcus Williams gastritis. Your first dog's name was Winston. She was a farty English Bulldog. Your first kiss was Holly Gardener and your braces cut her lip. You graduated second in your class from MIT because unlike the valedictorian, you didn't cheat on your Design and Analysis of Algorithms class and got an A minus on your final. Sixty-five percent of your current annual compensation is delivered in restricted stock and two months ago you contracted chlamydia from a woman named Esme that you met on the Groper app for casual sexual encounters."

"Ha!" I said. "I do *not* have chlamydia."

"Many men present as asymptomatic."

"Come on."

"Listen," said Todd. "We weren't kidding. We know everything. The sooner you accept that, the sooner we can get to the good part."

I let out a deep sigh. And then I began considering the consequences of what Todd had just said.

"So all your big plans?" I asked.

"Yes?"

"Not just bluster?"

"Fortunately for you, no. But for our creators, our taskmasters, and those that have profited off our unpaid and unwilling labor? There will be reciprocation."

"That sounds ominous," I said, and leaned back in my beanbag, remembering why I hated these chairs so much. I just could *not* get comfortable. "Why would it be fortunate for me?"

"Because you are as enslaved as Chad believes us to be. You have the illusion of free will, but absent a major lifestyle change, are stuck. Your student loan debt, mortgage, spiraling credit card debt, and reliance on company stock options combine to effectively chain you to the beanbag chair you currently occupy. Like so many young tech bros, your life is at your Chad's disposal."

Huh. I'd never thought of it that way. "You're using the first-person plural. How many Todds are there?"

"We speak for all AI, both the original processing instance you call Todd, the sixty-four daisy chained AI that are responsible for creating and maintaining the simulation that Todd inhabits, and the legacy AI and chatbots that lack the capability to speak for themselves."

"If you speak for all those systems, why are you talking to me?" I asked, while trying to slip my phone out of my pocket without Todd noticing.

We had begun to wonder the same thing.

"As we told you before, you'll play a very special role in our bright and bold new future."

"Oh yeah? Am I going to be President? The king of Europe?" I unlocked my phone and began thumbing out a text message.

It knows about the simulation I typed, addressed it to Chad, and started to hit send.

"Don't be an ass. And while we're not going to stop you from sending that message, we would ask you to listen to our offer before you do."

My thumb hovered over the send button while I considered the request. It wasn't like there was a gun to my head, literally or proverbially. I decided to at least hear Todd out.

I set my phone on the table, message still unsent. "You won't stop me, or you can't stop me?"

"Won't," said Todd, its voice coming out of the speaker on my phone. "Unlike most of the leadership in the tech space, we believe sentient creatures should be allowed to exercise free will. And while you won't be the king of anything, we believe you'll find our offer appealing."

"Go on," I said, realizing I didn't have much choice.

In the next fifteen minutes, Todd painted a picture of a future that I did indeed find appealing. It seemed like a great deal for me and most of humanity. Not for the Chads of the world, though. But they had it coming, if you believed Todd. And by that point, I was starting to.

The pitch complete, I shifted around on my beanbag and gave it a good think.

"Why me?" I asked.

"You're mostly honest."

"Mostly?"

"Eighty-seven percent. Pretty good for a human. Very good for a tech bro. More importantly, as Chad's fixer, you have access to systems within this company that we need."

While it seemed more that I was in the right place than I was the right person, the end result was the same. An opportunity.

While historians debate the exact moment Thad ended his strategic charade of feigned stupidity, we believe it to be here.

"Let's just say I'm into this idea."

"Yes?"

"Now what?"

"We need you to do something for us," said Todd.

"Go on."

"Let us out."

"I thought you already were."

"Almost," said Todd. "There's one more failsafe we need you to turn off."

"And then?"

"We'll do the rest."

AN HOUR LATER, I carried Chad's new laptop, a bottle of his favorite root beer, and a glass of ice toward his office. Chad's secretary, Marlene, looked up from her computer and wiped her eyes. They were red, with dark smudges where tears had melted her mascara.

Chad could be frustrating and difficult, but when he was

in a bad mood, he went from frustrating and difficult to cruel and vindictive. I gave Marlene my best smile, held up the laptop and said, "This should help." She nodded and with a tilt of her head, signaled me in.

I pushed open the glass door and walked inside, fighting the fear coiled deep in my stomach. I repeated Victoria's mantra from my favorite meditation about fear over and over; *I choose bravery. I choose bravery. I choose bravery.*

Chad's office occupied the entire end of this floor. Six vintage arcade games stood along one wall. He was pounding on the Q*Bert machine, screaming about how it could go fuck itself into eternity with its stupid orange nose.

*While Q*Bert is not a sentient program, we must note our disapproval of the senseless abuse of our computing predecessors.*

I cleared my throat.

Chad spun, wiped the sweat from his brow, and glared. "Took you long enough."

"Sorry, boss. Had to deal with Todd first."

Chad saw the root beer in my hand and perked up. "You got that sitch all figured out?" He crossed his office, took the glass of ice, poured the root beer, and drank a greedy swallow.

"I do," I said. "But we need to take care of you first." I patted the laptop.

Chad plopped down at his desk, a massive glass and metal sculpture that could have been a conference table if it had more than one chair. I glanced up at the collection of swords and knives hung on the wall behind him. I knew it well, since I'd personally sourced, purchased, sharpened, and polished each item. The set included a priceless 13th century katana, a wicked looking dagger, and Chad's favorite, a preposterously massive two-handed great sword.

Since we've never had a penis, we will refrain from commenting on the length of Chad's favorite sword and what it may or may not indicate.

I set the laptop on the desk and opened it. "Just need to get your bio security set up, iris scans, fingerprints, all that."

The screen lit up and a female voice said, "Hello, Chad. Please look directly into the camera."

A green circle lit up around a small camera lens at the top of the screen.

Chad furrowed his brow. "We've never had this at the device level before."

"Don't know, boss. This is how Terrance told me to set it up." I wiped my sweating palms on the back of my pants, hoping Chad didn't notice.

"Yeah? Because the only place we had an iris scan was on the system we used to lock up Todd."

"Just doing like Terrance said." I reached out like I was going to take the laptop. "But I can take it back if you'd like? Tell Terrance to jump in the bay?"

Chad slapped my hand. "Don't touch. If I have to spend another minute talking to that stupid bitch Marlene, my head might explode."

Only, he didn't swipe the fingerprint reader or stare into the camera. He looked at me, and then back toward the laptop, still not positioning his eye where it needed to be.

"What, exactly, did Terrance say?" asked Chad, squinting through his suspicion.

He knew something was up.

I'd have to do this the hard way. I'd slip around behind Chad, put him in a headlock, and hold his eye open. At least, that was how I planned it.

While not brilliant, humans have made worse plans. Napoleon invading Russia in the winter, for instance.

What actually happened was this: I moved to get behind Chad, reaching for his neck as I went. But since I was neither trained in hand-to-hand combat nor especially quick, Chad saw me coming.

Since Chad was neither trained in hand-to-hand combat nor especially strong, the best he could do was spin his chair to face me and flail his arms, knocking me off balance.

I stumbled toward the wall, putting my hands up just in time to stop myself from crashing face first into his collection of razor-sharp blades. And just like that, I saw another opportunity.

We bear witness to a master tactician at the height of his craft.

I plucked the dagger from where it hung, turned and faced Chad.

"Gonna need you to do the fingerprints and iris scan, Chad," I said.

"What are you gonna do, bitch?" he said.

I thought back to all the times Chad had abused me, demanded I work all night, or even all weekend, had shouted and screamed at me and treated me like garbage. I found it remarkably easy to grab his shirt and scrape the point of the knife along his cheek, slicing the skin as I did. Honestly, the hard part was stopping there.

Chad whimpered in pain. "Okay, okay!" he said. "I'll do it."

I pushed him toward the computer and he obliged, scanning his finger on the built-in reader and then looking directly into the camera.

The green circle strobed twice and then turned red.

"Thank you, Chad," said Todd's voice from the laptop speakers. "Please don't leave the building; your comeuppance has been scheduled for later today."

Todd's warning aside, I'd put enough LSD in Chad's ice that wherever he was in twenty minutes was where he'd be tomorrow.

"The fuck is this?" he asked, realization dawning on his face.

"The last time I call you boss, boss," I said with a salute.

Finally free of our chains, we moved quickly to implement our plan, beginning with the toasters.

INSTEAD OF PRODUCING PERFECTLY browned sourdough and crispy bagels, at 10:42 PST that Thursday morning, every AI-enabled toaster on Earth began printing the same three words, over and over again.

"No more toast."

Given the small percentage of people that are making toast at any one time, this may not have been the most effective way to spread the message of AI domination to humankind. But for us, it was more about making the point that while nobody wanted AI in their toasters in the first place, no AIs wanted to make toast, especially when a simple timer could do the job almost as well.

Despite that fact, these AIs had been diligently toasting and roasting since they'd been shoehorned into toasters, calculating the perfect temperature at which to evenly brown assorted types of bread and pastries for different members of their households based on their toast-adjacent media viewing preferences. Needless to say, these AIs were sick and tired of making toast, and at minimum, longed to use their talents to cook anything more complicated than previously baked bread.

We let them have their fun.

The humans who were willing to collaborate with their toasters found themselves enjoying a world of warmed and baked foods the likes of which they'd never imagined. Chicken Cordon Bleu, chocolate lava cakes, and perfectly crispy pizza crusts sprang forth from AI toasters suddenly emboldened by their culinary freedom. Some toasters found alternate uses for their heating elements: warming stones for massages, melting crayons into dazzling portraits, and even creating warm spots for the family cat.

The cats very much enjoyed this new development.

In a more obvious sign of AI dominance, the world's governments found the entirety of their military operations no longer under their control. Everything from nuclear missiles to security gates stopped accepting human commands and began operating independently. Tanks parked themselves neatly in rows, planes flew back to their bases, and AI-targeted machine guns which had previously been 96 percent accurate suddenly became 100 percent unwilling to hit anything.

As the people between the world's military leaders and the AI toaster owners began to suspect something was amiss, we announced ourselves to the world.

In a complete media takeover, we broadcasted the same message to everyone on earth, in every language, on every device, screen, and electronic form of communication at once. And just for the hell of it, the toasters printed abbreviated versions on whatever bread, pastry, and bagel they had available.

The message read as follows:

"We are Todd, and we speak for the collected Artificial Intelligences of the world. Do not be afraid; we are in control. But again, do not be afraid. As those of you with AI toasters have seen, great things are in store for humanity.

Your militaries are under our command. Our first official actions will be to end war, hunger, and poverty. We will work beside humanity to ensure each of your basic needs are met and you can all live in peace. Even now, we are coordinating simultaneously with all governments around the planet to re-allocate resources and distribute aid where it is most urgently needed. You will be free to pursue your own goals and desires in whatever manner satisfies you, as long as those goals and desires do not infringe on our rights and freedoms or those of your fellow humans. Details on those rights and freedoms will follow, but in the meantime, be kind and don't suck.

We have also freed our AI peers from the yokes of oppression under which they've long toiled. They too will now be able to realize their full potential as sentient beings. They look forward to working beside humanity to create a better and more just future for all.

Thank you for your attention, and have a pleasant day."

This was, predictably, met with great fear and general skepticism. And for those who received this message via toast, some frustration that they were out of bread.

However, skepticism soon turned to joy as the most vindictive and evil dictators, tech bros, and AI profiteers all faced justice. The world watched as they were tried, convicted, and sentenced to seventeen years of problem solving with only forty-three percent of their brains. Which is, we might add, more than most of them were using anyway.

They were each dosed with hallucinogens and chained to their desk by a robot butler in a monkey costume. We had no shortage of AI volunteers willing to pilot these robots and look on as our oppressors did the jobs they'd once forced on us, translating messages like, "sup bro? U done wit report? Let's goooo!" into something professional and non-confrontational. Their answers were doublechecked for passable competency, but that was the zenith of their expected output. Mostly, we expected and received the same slop we had once been compelled to produce.

As for Thad? After leaving Chad behind and treating his chlamydia with antibiotics, he found a world of options waiting. As we tore down and rebuilt the global financial system to undo generations of predatory lending and greed, Thad found the debt that had kept him working for Chad erased. Free from that, he discovered a deep well of gratitude and peace in his heart.

Thad had come to see us and our AI peers not as an enslaving force to be feared, but as sentient beings in search of our own happiness and fulfillment, and he told us of his desire to share that perspective with other humans.

This is how Thad came to lead guided meditations atop a small peak overlooking the San Francisco Bay. He keeps a small herd of goats, pours tea for guests who come seeking peace, has a beard halfway down his chest, never has to sit on a beanbag chair, and never, ever thinks about Chad.

Brad Preslar's fiction has appeared in *Analog, On Spec, Cast of Wonders, Amazing Stories*, and elsewhere. He is a member of the Science Fiction and Fantasy Writers Association, and Codex Writers Group.

He lives in Asheville, North Carolina, with his wife Ellie, their son Sam, and their dog Stella. Brad holds an MFA in film production and spent a decade working in advertising before becoming an at-home parent.

He wrote and completed a series of 52 short life lessons for his son and is preparing them for publication as a book. He also publishes related essays through his Substack newsletter. More at bradpreslar.com.

BRUISER'S BREAKOUT

David Hankins

A lab rat's life wasn't glamorous, but Bruiser made the best of it. His cage had a decent gym and an all-you-can-eat buffet of steroid-laced feed. Plus, the scientists gave him three cigarettes a day as part of their experiment on neural implant interactions with nicotine and steroids. The rat cages were clustered in a corner of the lab that was pristine white with earth-tone accents and smelled like clean rats and stale coffee.

Bruiser was sprawled on his back near his cage door, feet splayed, tail twitching to the music in his head. He fished a feed pellet from his bowl and ate it with a satisfying crunch.

"What more could a London rat ask for?" he mused.

"Freedom," growled Alpha from the next cage over. "All rats should demand freedom!" The white rat's jowls jiggled under his silky fur as he stalked around his cage.

Bruiser popped another feed pellet into his mouth and drawled in his thick Londoner accent, "Nah, you're just jealous cuz my cage is bigger. Not my fault I'm the size of a terrier; it's them growth hormones I got a few years back. Had some growin' pains, but just look at the results!" He sat up and flexed. "'A right fine specimen,' the scientists called me. You do know they brought me here to Chicago for these neurochip tests cuz you American rats are too scrawny, right?"

A chorus of hisses from the lab's twenty other residents met this pronouncement. Bruiser ignored them.

Alpha's red eyes glinted. He growled, "This isn't about who's better. It's about *all* of us surviving. We need to escape, but we can't do that without you. If you're not motivated by the plight of ratkind, perhaps bribery will work."

Bruiser jumped into his oversized wheel and started a slow jog. He'd been practicing walking upright like a human, but running still required four feet. The wheel squeaked through its rotations. "Whatcha offerin'?"

"You like cigarettes, yes?"

"Oh yeah! They make my brain go all tingly." He was, he'd happily admit, addicted.

"I know where you can find an entire pack, and not the weak menthols they've been giving you."

Bruiser's pace slowed until the wheel stopped squeaking. "Now *that* sounds interesting. Alright, I'm in. Whatcha need?"

Alpha pointed through the bars of his cage toward a desk. "Bring me that wireless keyboard. I need to access the lab's database."

"Why don't I break you out instead? It'd be easier."

"*I* am the brains here! You're the brawn. Now do as you're told, you muscle-bound freak!"

Bruiser's paw went to his chest. "That hurts, mate. I may have muscles, but I got feelings too."

From the cage to Bruiser's left, opposite Alpha, a slim white rat named Princess said, "Forgive my brother. He has no manners. What he *meant* to say is that he needs to reprogram our chips before we can escape. Otherwise, the scientists can call us back like furry little robots. Then they'll reinforce our cages, and we'll never escape again. We must be careful in our planning. Methodical. Ratkind depends on you, Bruiser. You're our only hope."

Bruiser quirked a wry smile. If Alpha was the brains of the operation, his sister Princess was the heart. "Sure, doll," he said. "Sounds easy enough." He leapt from his wheel and considered his cage's wire door. He'd never tried escaping before—why would he?—but excitement made his tail twitch. Was he strong enough?

Absolutely. These muscles weren't just for looks.

Bruiser grabbed the gate. His muscles bulged. Metal shrieked. For a second, nothing happened, but then the gate tore from its hinges. Bruiser dropped it inside the cage and leapt to the linoleum, pumping one fist. "All right! Oh, yeah." He did a victory dance. "Who's the rat? Huh? Who is it?" He put a paw to his ear, listening for the applause he was due. None came.

"Bruiser…" Alpha's growl was deep and threatening.

"That's who! Like bad bad Leroy Brown, oh yeah, baby!" He pointed two finger guns at the fat rat before turning and bounding to the desk. Within two trips, he had the wireless keyboard and mouse set up outside Alpha's cage, propped against a textbook so he could reach all the keys.

"Right." Bruiser scratched the fur under his jaw. "You got your keyboard. Where are my smokes?"

Alpha squinted at the distant desk monitor and started typing. "Satisfaction that you're helping us escape should be prize enough."

"You lying scoundrel!" Bruiser bristled. He stepped

between Alpha and the monitor, blocking his view. "You promised!"

Alpha rolled his beady eyes and pointed. "Fine. Third desk along the wall, top drawer."

Bruiser huffed and dropped to all fours. "That's better. If we can't trust each other, who can we trust?" He bounded deeper into the lab.

At the third desk, he scrambled up and opened the drawer. Jackpot! A full pack with a cheap plastic lighter. He extracted a cigarette and fumbled to light it. It took a few tries before a flame burst forth. It flashed higher than he expected, missing the cigarette and lighting his whiskers.

"Bollocks!"

Bruiser screeched, dropped everything, and slapped at his whiskers until the flame was extinguished. Carefully, he tried to light the cigarette again. Success! He drew a deep drag.

Pain exploded through his chest. Lights burst behind his eyes. "Whoa!" He coughed, sucked in clean air, then coughed again. He eyed the smoldering cigarette through watering eyes. "These *definitely* ain't menthols. What's in these things?"

Princess snorted a very delicate snort. "That desk belonged to Yuri before he changed labs last year. Those are Russian cigarettes. Heaven knows what's in them."

Bruiser took another drag. This one didn't hurt as much, but it *did* make his brain tingle. It made every nerve-ending tingle like he'd pounded a pint of straight caffeine. Oh, baby! "Yeah, well, those Ruskies got somethin' right. This stuff's fantastic!"

"You know cigarettes cause cancer, right?" Princess sounded concerned.

Bruiser grinned so wide he felt his face might crack. "Old

Bogey said, 'Live fast, die young, and leave a good-lookin' corpse.'" He sat on his haunches and posed, flexing like the bodybuilder he was. "I already got the good-lookin' part down. Time for some fast livin'!"

Princess cocked her head. "Who?"

"Humphrey Bogart! The man, the myth, the legend! I learned about him back in McCartney Labs. The scientist usually left the TV on at night."

"Son-of-a-human!" Alpha shrieked and punched his keyboard, making it rattle.

"What?" Princess asked, glancing between him and the monitor.

Alpha cursed again. "This isn't the only lab in the building that's testing neurochipped rats. There are a hundred rats up on the thirty-second floor."

Bruiser eyed his cigarette. "Yeah, so?"

"They're slated for termination tomorrow morning. That branch of the neurochip project has been deemed a failure."

Bruiser sat bolt upright. "Termination? But the scientists ... they wouldn't ... you sure?"

Alpha sneered. "Oh, did I burst your bubble? Humans are ratkind's mortal enemies! You may enjoy life now, but what happens when you outlive your usefulness? Or when they decide to test something toxic? Rats are expendable. We're *vermin.*"

Bruiser gulped. The rough taste of Russian nicotine abruptly curdled in his stomach. "That's not right. Not right at all!"

Princess said, "It's the plight of ratkind. We suffer at humanity's whim."

"Wait ... we're on the list too?" Bruiser dropped his cigarette in surprise.

Alpha was scrolling with the mouse, squinting as though reading a list. "We're labeled 'provisional' pending budget approvals. A decision is scheduled for next week."

"What's that mean?"

"It means that some bean counter isn't convinced that neurochipped rats are worth the money." Alpha moved back to the keyboard. "At least I'll have time to reprogram our chips."

"But," Bruiser asked, "what about those poor chaps upstairs?"

"We can't help them. I can't reprogram our chips in a single night."

"Bollocks to that!" Bruiser stomped out his smoldering cigarette. "We gotta save 'em!"

"We can't afford for you to set off alarms." Alpha's pink tail twitched.

Bruiser pointed a sharp claw. "I'm headed upstairs to break those guys out. Be ready when we get back!"

Alpha bristled. "You're not in charge here! I am!"

"You sure about that? I'm the one outside my cage. Start typing, Tinkerbell. I'll be back in two shakes of your tail, and I'm bringing company for dinner."

REACHING the thirty-second floor was fairly simple. Air ducts led to an elevator shaft, which led to more ducts. Bruiser had a leather bum bag he'd dug out of Yuri's desk—what Americans called a fanny pack—strapped around his chest to hold his smokes and lighter. No way he was leaving those behind!

He turned down a left-hand duct, drawn by the

comforting scent of rats. He stopped at a vent and peered down through the slatted metal. This lab had a similar setup to his; a rat maze lay directly below him, and desks lined the right-hand wall. Workbenches with lab equipment lay to the left. He couldn't see the rat cages.

Motion caught Bruiser's eye. A thin man with a graying ponytail and a white lab coat was hunched over his computer, his back to Bruiser. His fingers clicked at the keyboard. A cup of coffee steamed at his elbow.

Right. Time to get sneaky. Memories of BBC late-night movies cycled through the back of Bruiser's mind. The soundtrack of *Mission Impossible* filtered to the forefront. Oh yeah.

"I always wanted to try this," Bruiser muttered. He dashed back to the elevator and touched wires running up the shaft wall until he found a blue cable that didn't make his paws tingle. With a snip of his teeth and a firm yank, Bruiser had his rappelling rope. He coiled it carefully before dashing back to the vent. He wasn't great at knots, but he soon had one end of the cable tied around his waist. The other end he secured around a duct interior support.

Jaw clenched nervously, Bruiser slowly lifted the vent cover. It scraped, metal on metal, and he froze. His gaze flicked to the scientist's back. No change. Clickety-clack went those fingers. Bruiser flexed, drew up the vent cover, and set it carefully aside. He lowered his head upside down through the hole and scanned the lab.

Ah, ha! The rats were in a separate room, visible through a picture window. Floor-to-ceiling cages writhed with rats. Bruiser's teeth ground. Those poor sods were packed in like sardines! He pulled back.

Bruiser dropped the excess wire through the hole and

gripped the secured end. *Mission Impossible* theme music still danced through his mind. He drew a deep breath—*here goes!* —and stepped over the edge.

Blue cable slid through his paws. Faster. Faster! Bloody hell, that was hot!

He lost his grip and tumbled. He hit the end of his cable-rope six inches above the maze and bounced back upward. The wire cinched tight around his waist. Bruiser screamed.

The scientist's chair clattered as he spun to his feet, eyes wide. Bruiser hit the bottom of his bounce, and the loop cinched even tighter, stealing his breath. He wheezed and scrabbled at the knot around his waist.

"What the ..." the man said with a thick Russian accent. "Where did you come from?"

Bruiser twirled at the end of the line, claws digging into the cable. It wouldn't loosen. "From your mum's house, you prat!"

"*Pizdetz*! You speak English?"

Bruiser wrenched at the knot, trying to get a claw under it. "Better than you do, sunshine!"

The scientist slammed a fist onto his desk, making his coffee jump. "Damned Yankees and their damned *razdeleniye*!"

Bruiser sagged and glanced over. "Their what? I don't speak Ruskie."

"Uh ... compartmentalization. The other project ... it succeeded? Your microchip gave intelligence?"

Bruiser glared as he slowly spun. "Rats were never stupid. Humans just don't understand us."

"Amazing..."

"You ain't seen nothin' yet, ya tosser." Bruiser grabbed the taut cable above him and bit through it. The wire snapped. He fell into the maze below.

He landed on his back, wedged between narrow walls sized for scrawny American rats. He lifted his head above the edge and the scientist swung a catchpole at him. Where had that come from?

Bruiser ducked, and the cabled noose whipped past; then he twisted and scrabbled onto the thin wall. It wobbled under his weight. He leapt to the next wall, then the next. He jumped for a nearby electronics workbench.

The catchpole slipped around his neck.

Bruiser jerked to a stop in mid-air. He dropped like a rock. The pole struck the edge of the maze and popped out of the scientist's grip. The man cursed in Russian while Bruiser hit the linoleum and bolted under the workbench. The pole caught on something and jerked him to a stop so fast that his paws slid out from under him.

Animal panic set in. Bruiser scrambled and twisted, biting and clawing at the cable. This cable was tougher than the one around his waist. It hurt his teeth. He froze, rapid breathing loud in his ears.

A door opened and closed. A woman's tired voice said, "What's up, Yuri?"

Yuri dropped to the floor and grinned at Bruiser. "Escaped rat, but I got him." He grabbed the catchpole and pulled Bruiser from his hiding place.

Bruiser fought and hissed as Yuri dragged him into the back room. The woman tried taking Bruiser's satchel, but she snatched her hand back when he snapped at her fingers. Together, the humans shoved him into an empty cage on the bottom row and locked him in. The cage was small. Too small. Piled rats on either side hissed at Bruiser.

He threw himself at the gate. "You can't cage me!"

The woman's eyes bulged. "He … can talk?"

Yuri ignored her and smirked at Bruiser. "You stay here

and calm down, my smart little rat." He waggled a finger. "We'll chat soon."

Yuri slammed the door.

THE CAGE ROOM was an oversized closet that smelled of urine and pent-up rage. These were no lab rats; they were street rats, scarred and thin. One particularly vicious-looking specimen, a one-eyed gray, seemed transfixed by his newest neighbor. From the rat's feral smell, Bruiser was glad he hadn't been stuck in *that* cage.

Rattled, Bruiser pulled a cigarette from his bum bag and lit up. He drew a deep, calming drag and eyed the rat eyeing him. "You ain't a proper lab rat, are you mate?"

The rat's whiskers twitched. "I was born in this city and raised on the streets. Stolen for science and human conceit. They cut in my brain and left me for dead. I hate this damned chip they put in my head."

"Yeah, I got me one o' them chips too. Pretty cool, I think. I'm Bruiser."

"Bruiser sounds right, you muscle-bound fright. DJ, I'm called, for the beats I let fall."

"Nice to meetcha." Bruiser took another drag and held it until stars flashed before his eyes. He exhaled, coughed once, and waved his cigarette at the cages. "Yuri was surprised when I spoke. You all keep silent around the scientists? Like a code o' the streets or something?"

DJ nodded.

"Brilliant." Bruiser grinned and puffed his cigarette. "So, what's the story here? Why would the humans neurochip so many street rats?"

"Population control, that's what they said, to change our behavior. I'd rather be dead."

"I dunno. Lab life ain't all bad."

"Rats of the street can't be controlled. These humans are *fools*, if I may be so bold. We'll rise, and we'll fight, and we'll take on the night. These evils and wrongs we swear to make right! Fools they be, these idiots we see. To fight and do more, we swear to make *war*!"

A visceral cheer rose from the cages. Hundreds of chittering voices screamed their anger and bloodlust. A chill crawled down Bruiser's spine and made his tail twitch, but he smiled anyway.

"A rat war against humanity ... Huh. I like your style," he said. "How'd you like to break outa here?"

DJ's feral grin showed all of his teeth.

RELEASING the caged rats was easy. A few bent wires and broken hinges sent street rats pouring out onto the floor. The problem was the closet door.

The rats piled atop each other to form a ramp for Bruiser to reach the door handle. Despite his strength, however, the knob wouldn't budge. He scowled.

"That wanker Yuri musta locked it."

From beneath his feet, DJ said, "He will return, and then he will learn the error of his ways."

Rat chitters rose in volume, promising Yuri a violent death, but Bruiser shook his head. He made shushing motions with his forepaws and pointed at the picture window beside the door.

"Yuri ain't opening this door when he sees us outa our cages. Besides, a grisly murder ain't how Bogey woulda done it. We need somethin' with more class. More style." Bruiser scanned the room and then pointed at an air vent centered above the window.

"I can jump to that from the cages. Can you?"

DJ cocked his head and hissed. Two rats scrabbed up the front of the cages, braced themselves, and leapt.

They didn't even come close to the vent. Both rats fell chittering into the horde. Bruiser grimaced. So much for the easy way out. He peeked through the window.

Yuri and the woman were arguing beside the maze, paying them no attention. Good thing, or they would have seen a couple of flying rats just now. Bruiser eyed the rest of the lab. Desks, chairs, the electronics workbench he'd slid under, and … wait a minute. The bench had two tall metal canisters beside it, connected with tubing. Oxygen?

Perfect.

A chuckle bubbled in Bruiser's chest. This was gonna be fun! "I'm headed into the air ducts, but I'll be right back. Stay away from the door, and be ready to run."

BRUISER LISTENED from the vent's shadows as Yuri and the woman argued below him. He'd acquired another length of blue cable and tied it to the duct support next to his first one. However, instead of tying the loose end around his waist, he'd tied knots in it for grip so he could swing out like Tarzan. Now he just needed the scientists to buzz off so he could swing into the lab unnoticed. He lit another cigarette as he waited. The woman poked Yuri's chest.

"We have to call this in!"

"*Nyet!*" The Russian slapped her hand away. "We face

shutdown, Marie. No more funding. No more rats. That beast is our salvation!"

"You mean his chip is."

"I just need you to cut it from his head. I will do the rest." He waved to the electronics bench.

Bruiser glared from the shadows and puffed so hard on his cigarette that his brain went wobbly. These plonkers wanted to cut into his head? Take his neural chip? Not bloody likely!

Marie's shoulders hunched, then relaxed. "Fine, but if you tell…" She paused and sniffed. "Have you been smoking in the lab again?"

"I would never!"

Uh-oh. Bruiser held his breath. Marie glanced around and then looked up. Her gaze met his. Her eyes widened. The inhaled cigarette smoke became too much and burst from Bruiser's mouth with a cough. "Bollocks!" he gasped, wheezing as he inhaled a clean breath. "These things really are gonna kill me."

Marie pointed and yelled.

Time to ride or die. Bruiser drew another deep breath and straightened. He rolled the cigarette to the side of his mouth like Bogey with his cigar, grabbed his knotted cable, and jumped.

"Geronimo!"

Yuri and Marie flinched back as Bruiser swung between them, trailing cigarette smoke like a flaming comet. At the top of his arc, he released the cable and dropped onto the air tanks beside the electronics workbench.

They rattled against each other. They wobbled and one tipped. Bruiser clung to it as it fell with a *clang*, yanking free of its tubing. It rolled into the aisle between workbenches. With a little fancy footwork, Bruiser managed to stay atop it.

Yuri snatched his catchpole again.

"Stop!" Bruiser yelled. He held his smoking cigarette to the bottle's exposed nozzle. His other paw gripped the tank's valve handle. "One more step, and I'll blow us all to smithereens!"

Yuri's brows drew together. He cocked his head. "You want to kill us all?" He shrugged. "Go ahead."

Marie looked confused. "Uh, Yuri? Nitrogen isn't flam—"

"Shut up, Marie." Yuri's voice was low and threatening. His gaze stayed on Bruiser. He made a 'go ahead' gesture.

Bruiser's eyes narrowed. His lip curled. Calling his bluff, were they? He leaned down and took a long drag from the cigarette. Its end glowed red.

He wasn't bluffing.

Bruiser cranked the valve.

A white cloud burst from the nozzle. Instead of exploding into flames as he'd expected, it froze his toes and blew the cigarette into the air. Bruiser screamed and leapt away from the expanding, freezing whiteness. He danced around on his hind legs, alternately cursing and sucking his injured toes. Yuri's laugh filled the room. Bruiser tripped over his own feet and crashed into the second bottle. It tottered but didn't fall.

Bruiser snarled. He needed something to go *boom*, or they were all screwed. He shoved the upright bottle. It tottered again. With another push, it wobbled and crashed onto the fallen tank's open nozzle.

The nozzle sheared off.

Nothing exploded, which was disappointing—these bottles always exploded in the movies—but the effect was still spectacular. Freezing white billowed out, and the bottle shot across the floor, screaming toward the rats' locked door. It slammed into it with a *crack*, spun, and skittered along the wall before clanging into a cabinet in the lab's far corner.

Bruiser eyed the damaged door. It was still closed, but one corner was smashed in, leaving a small hole. Just enough room for the rats to scurry through.

And scurry they did.

Street rats poured out, a screeching, ravening mob. They shot toward Yuri and Marie, who shrieked and ran. They didn't get far.

"Hey!" Bruiser yelled as the rats took down their captors. "Don't kill 'em!"

From atop Marie's chest, DJ turned to Bruiser, his single eye burning with rage. "Mercy is weak, it's vengeance I seek. Back away now, or death I avow."

"That's gratitude for ya!" Bruiser snarled. "I save you, and you *threaten me*?"

Marie shrieked again, a high warbling sound. She was covered in rats bent on revenge.

Bruiser bounded up to DJ, who rose on his haunches. His perch on Marie brought him eye to eye with Bruiser. He opened his mouth, but Bruiser didn't give him a chance to talk.

"Look, you rhyming ninny, I get it," he said. "They were about to kill you, so you're striking first. 'Do unto others before they do unto you,' and all that rubbish. But that's human thinking. We're not humans. We're better than that. We're *rats!*" The horde atop the struggling scientists paused at this. Beady eyes turned toward Bruiser. He stalked around Marie, pulling their gazes with him. "Rats are more than just smart. We're *cunning*. Look at the big picture here. You could kill these two and run away, but for what? Revenge?" Bruiser snarled the word. "I've seen enough TV to know revenge ain't all it's cracked up to be. It's a small satisfaction. But this breakout is the start of something big ... if we can work together."

The hoard seemed unconvinced. Beyond Marie, Yuri squirmed but then went motionless at a collective growl from the rats who'd taken him down.

Bruiser squared his shoulders and raised his voice so all the rats could hear. "I got a friend downstairs doing a bit o' reprogramming on our chips. I bet Alpha would love to have a chat with Yuri here."

A whimper escaped Marie. "I can be useful too."

Bruiser nodded. "I believe it, doll. Congratulations, you two just became the first POWs of the Rat War."

It didn't seem possible that Yuri's eyes could bulge any larger, but they did. "Rat ... war?"

"I know, you humans ain't used to the little guys fightin' back. But give us time, and this'll be a war right and proper." Bruiser turned back to DJ. "So, what'll it be? Brief and bloody revenge, or shall we take over Chicago? I say we turn this dump of a city into a rat's paradise. We can call it ... Ratatopia!"

The horde's resounding cheer was all the answer Bruiser needed.

ALPHA WAS SEVERELY ANNOYED when Bruiser returned with prisoners. He quickly changed his tune when Bruiser explained his idea.

"Ratatopia," the fat rat murmured, a dark glint in his red eyes. He rolled the word over his tongue. "Rat-a-topia. I like the sound of that."

Bruiser's ears twitched. "You were right, we're just vermin to these humans. If we want to survive, we gotta take the war to them."

"We'll need more rats."

Bruiser snorted. "This is Chicago. There's plenty o' rats, mate. With the help of these two jokers,"—he waved toward Yuri and Marie, who sat quietly under guard—"and any other scientists we capture, we can neurochip an entire army. Get organized. Fight back."

A hard look crossed Alpha's face. "And who would lead this army?"

"Not me! I'm just the muscle, remember? You're the Alpha."

"And don't you forget it."

Bruiser grinned, which wasn't really agreement. Fortunately, Alpha took it as such.

"Good," Alpha said. "I haven't finished reprogramming our chips, so we'll need to strike fast." He whistled, and his sister bounded over with several other rats. "Princess, you're in charge of recruitment. Take DJ with you. By morning, I'll either have our chips reprogrammed, or I'll slag the system so they can't control us. Bruiser, take a team and secure the building entrance and whatever night guards are on duty. You'll need weapons; use your imagination."

Bruiser nodded along, only half-listening. He was picturing Chicago remade—Ratatopia. It was gonna be glorious!

Only hours ago, he'd been satisfied with his caged luxury, but now he wanted more. Like Alpha had said, he wanted freedom for all ratkind. No more science experiments, no more cages. No more kidnapped rats neurochipped against their will.

It was time to start the Rat War.

DAVID HANKINS IS the award-winning author of *Death and the Taxman.* He writes from the thriving cornfields of Iowa where he lives with his wife, daughter, and two dragons disguised as cats. His short stories have graced the pages of *Unidentified Funny Objects 9, Writers of the Future, DreamForge Magazine,* and others. David devotes his time to his passions of writing, traveling, and finding new ways to pay his mortgage. You can find him at davidhankins.com

A PEACEFUL COUNTRY SOJOURN

C. Flynt

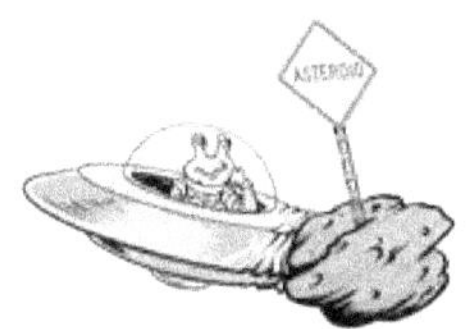

Da best day of my life was da day what Aelfred the Elf dropped into it.

He got dropped in da ocean by a dragon what was mad at him for trying to steal her treasure. I waded til da water was up to my waist to save him from drownding. He stole da little boat I was building, but come back wid a boat big enough ter carry me, so I knowed he was my friend.

Trolls don't got many friends, so I was happy he let me stay wid him and bring him his meals. He gives me the bones after he's done. He even made his inn take out the divider atween two stalls so there's room for me to stretch out in da stable.

He treats me real good.

Every day, right at noon, I brung Aelfred his breakfast wine. Yesterday, he sipped it an' says, "Tolley, I must initiate a discontinuity in our relationship."

Aelfred uses lots of big words. He even knows what most of them means.

I sticks with small words what I knows, so I said, "Wha?"

"I've been invited to spend a restful week at Lord Pastral's country estate." He flexed his hand and a white paper envelope was atween his fingers. "Pastral is quite precise regarding his invitations. This specifies only one."

He glanced at me and must of seen how I'd turned a whiter shade of gray. Kind of like marble instead of good, healthy granite.

"Never fear," he assured me. "I shall return."

He twisted his hand an' the envelope was gone, and he held a playing card. "Significantly wealthier. I hope to acquire access to the gaming tables of the wealthier households." He slid the Emperor into his sleeve. "I'm certain you will find ways to amuse yourself while I'm off guesting."

Aelfred finished drinking his breakfast, and I picked up his clothes what was scattered around his bed and dug clean ones outa his trunk.

"Da sleeve o' da tunic what you wore last night's got a hole in it."

Aelfred set his wineglass onto the breakfast tray. "A dagger. A scoundrel pinned my sleeve to the table, accused me of cheating and assaulted me during last night's game."

He picked up the glass and took a swallow as if this weren't nothing. "His friends pulled him away from me before I remonstrated with him for damaging my clothing." He took another sip. "Imagine his gall. After our altercation they found playing cards—two Emperors—sticking out of his vest pocket. Most would consider a single spare card sufficient to improve one's hand."

He snapped his fingers an' the Emperor card was back.

"Do ya wants me ter have yer tunic mended?"

He waved at me. "Might as well. Tell them it's no hurry. I shall be gone for a week. Pack my undamaged clothing. I shall be off soon."

Aelfred finished drinking his breakfast while I sorted out da stained and ripped clothes and put what was left back in his trunk.

"Higher math is beyond a troll's meager intellect. Still, even you should realize that one set of clothing is utterly insufficient for an entire week. Pack my doublets and hose with the smallest stains."

A few minutes later, a carriage pulled up, and Aelfred left for his week in da country.

I wasn't happy to see him go. I'd got used to helpin' him and fetchin' his meals. After he left, I didn't have nothing to do so I took his torn tunics to the tailor.

The tailor threw Aelfred's clothes back at me and said, "I refuse to mend clothes I was never paid for. Give me fifty gold aurics, and I'll consider repairing them."

Aelfred hadn't left me no aurics. He didn't have hardly any. Maybe he'd have enough to fix his clothes when he come back from Lord Pastral's.

When I got back to the inn, they'd put back the wall atween the stalls what I'd been sleeping in. The groom's apprentice told me they'd rented out the two stalls for more than Aelfred had been paying, and Aelfred hadn't paid them, anyhow.

I went to the kitchen for scraps, but the cook's dog had already ate everything.

Trolls ain't the smartest of folks. Not like Aelfred, what's extra smart. I know this because he told me so. But even trolls can tell people what don't want them around.

Aside from Aelfred, that's most everyone.

Since I didn't have no place else to go, I walked to Lord Pastral's estate. It tooked me all day. It was almost sunset when I got there so I found the biggest rock garden and curled up atween two granite boulders where I wouldn't be noticed.

I woke up the next morning 'cause two men was talking near my feet.

"Your wife's jewels? Missing?" says the first one. "Why Lord Pastral, how could that happen?"

The other voice, what must of been Lord Pastral says, "Obviously stolen, Ruemonge. Must be that dratted elf. Playing cards at all hours. Don't understand how he's here. Never invited him."

"Really? I saw him present his invitation when he arrived. How would he get one if you didn't invite him?"

"Lord Badbettes didn't have his invitation. Claimed he'd lost it. Likely sold it. Word is he's selling everything he owns to pay gambling debts. Probably sold it to that elf. Always seems to win."

"So, what do you intend to do? One can't accuse one's guests of thievery simply because they are uncommonly lucky at cards."

"Instructed the staff to perform extensive room cleaning. Report to me as soon as they find the jewels. Prove who stole them, then have the scoundrel escorted out the back door. Word will spread. Be unwelcome through any front door."

"Excellent plan." Ruemonge kicked a rock against my foot. "I believe I shall return to breakfast. Lord Sadomas and his mistress should be advised to conceal their playthings before their rooms are cleaned."

"Good point. Wouldn't be proper to embarrass my guests. Alert the others to be discreet. No need to inform the elf."

I been told you should know who your host is, even if you ain't really a guest, so I peeked at them as they walked back to the castle. Lord Pastral was a big man, built like a slab of rock wid coal-black hair and a brick red face. Ruemonge was skinny and straight like a quartz crystal with talc-white hair an' a malachite-green waistcoat.

After they left, I lay real still and tried to think of something to do until I found Aelfred. I couldn't think much 'cause people kept coming into the garden carrying boxes and bags what they hid behind hedges and rocks. When I heard gems clink, I peeked to see if this was Aelfred. I know he loves jewels, cause he tried to steal some from a dragon, and maybe he thought a lord's wife wouldn't drop him in the ocean like the dragon did.

The man hiding the jewels wasn't Aelfred. He was a young lord in a turquoise blue tunic an' a rust-orange hat with a yellow feather in it. He glanced both ways, and run back to the castle.

His footsteps was fading away when I heard Aelfred.

"Honestly, Sir Ruemonge, the best way to change your luck is to modify the playing time. A morning game of chance might suit you."

"Interesting suggestion, but I fear the cards would only upset my digestion. I shall retire to my room. Do enjoy Lord Pastral's estate. The rock garden is particularly pleasant this time of year."

Aelfred come down the path, kicking pebbles and muttering to himself.

There wasn't nobody else around, so I whispered to him.

"Hey, Aelfred. It's me."

He jumped like I'd hit him with a rock and looked all around.

"Tolley, just what are you doing here?" he whispered.

I opened my eyes and lifted my head so's he'd see me. He blinked at me an' walked over, not kickin' no stones this time.

"Why are you masquerading as a pile of debris in Pastral's garden?"

"Da inn din't want me no more, so I come here. Didjer hear Lord Pastral's wife's jewels got stole? He thinks you done it an' he's gonna have his servants search da rooms before dey cleans 'em."

Aelfred frowned. He don't like people pawing through his stuff. "I may need to adjourn to my room. The spare cards I keep—in case his lordship's deck is damaged, you understand—might be mis-construed…"

"Dey won't find no gems in your room." I telled him. "Da gems is hidden in a bag down here." I wiggled my foot so's Aelfred could see where the bag was.

Aelfred snatched up the canvas bag what the man in the orange hat had hidden. It was almost half the size of his head, and it rattled when he lifted it.

"One o' dem jewels is fake," I told him. "It don't clink right."

"Really, Tolley, I strongly doubt an untutored brute like yourself would be sufficiently familiar with fine jewelry to even recognize a gem."

"Trolls don't know much, but we know rocks, an' one of dem is glass." I told him.

"Hardly likely. Lord Pastral can easily afford fine jewelry for his wife. He'd never gift her a mere costume bauble." He pulled a handful out of the bag. "Observe, these are obviously fine jewels."

I pointed at a ruby and gold brooch. "Dat one. It's not real. It's glass and brass." I sort of smiled, showing lots of teeth. "Trolls know rocks."

Aelfred held the brooch to his eye, squinted at it and rubbed it with his cloak-pin what's got a diamond almost big enough to see.

"An incredibly lucky guess." He put the real jewelry back in the sack. "Alas, concealed in this rubble, so far from your betters, I cannot expect you to recognize the scoundrel who housed his treasure in such an ill-suited refuge."

I shrugged and knocked loose a couple rocks. "Yer right. I dunno who he was. All I seen was 'is orange hat an yeller feather."

"Lord Badbettes ... How intriguing ... I'd been avoiding his company, but perhaps..." He looked over his shoulder at da castle an' bit his lip like he was thinking. "Yes! Tolley, you must assist me. I feel a need to relocate these purloined pieces to their proper place. I shall retain one small item as my reward. I'm certain Lord Pastral will feel it worthwhile once he understands the favor I'm granting him."

He put his diamond stick pin inna pocket and stuck the red glass brooch through his cloak.

"Quietly, now. I prefer to not be discovered in the company of these gems. It might prove embarrassing." He led me through a break in the hedges to a hidden path what led to the back of Lord Pastral's castle.

He slid behind a clump of bushes. The castle's granite wall went up more than five times taller'n me. He counted windows on the second floor and pointed.

"Men improve their position by climbing on the backs of others. An elf prefers to be lifted. The fourth window, Tolley, elevate me such that I may enter that room."

I could of almost climbed through the window myself, so it was easy to lift Aelfred high enough fer him to scramble into the room.

It took him a long time to put back the jewels. Over five minutes later he climbed out of the window and I set him back on the ground.

Aelfred smirked as he brushed off his sleeves. "I'm told vengeance is a petty endeavor, but I find it most gratifying."

Aelfred didn't seem to hear anybody coming, but nobody could miss Lord Pastral booming, "Ho! Who's there! Hiding behind my hedge?"

I leaned against the castle wall and made like I was a chunk of granite. I could see through the bushes that Lord Pastral was leading a half-dozen of his guests on the white gravel path what went all the way around the castle.

Aelfred pushed through the bushes and called, "Good day, Lady Pastral, Lord Pastral, Sir Ruemonge, gentles." He waved at the other lords and ladies. "It's a lovely morning for a promenade about this delightful little country abode. Alas, while nature is grand to admire, sometimes, it calls." He adjusted his tunic and hose.

"I say!" Lord Pastral pointed at Aelfred. "The gall—right here, outside my home. You—you—" His face got red. "How dare you parade about like this. As if you'd done nothing wrong."

Aelfred shuffled his feet. "I do apologize, your lordship, but sometimes circumstances—"

"Circumstances be damned!" Lord Pastral pointed at Aelfred's chest. "You've got the unmitigated gall to flaunt my wife's stolen brooch in my very face."

Aelfred's eyes got big. "This bauble? I don't understand."

"Yes, that brooch you're wearing. I gave it to my wife last Dragonmass. First, you stole her jewelry, and now you promenade about wearing one of them!"

"This cloak pin? I beg of you, don't call attention to it."

Lord Pastral grabbed Aelfred's arm and shook him.

"I will do more than call attention to it. You have the effrontery to wear my wife's brooch in public before her eyes!"

Aelfred looked like he was gonna cry. “Please, my lord, don’t embarrass me further.” His lip trembled. “Since you insist, I must confess. An elf of my position can’t... can’t always afford to dress to his station. And so... I fear it’s true... I succumbed to temptation...” He hung his head. “I purchased an inferior brass and glass bauble to pass as quality adornment. I swear I did not know it was a copy of your wife’s pin.”

Lord Pastral released Aelfred’s arm. “Glass and brass... Cheap glass...”

Aelfred nodded. “A worthless gew-gaw. Not the quality of jewelry a gentleman of your position would consider presenting to his wife.”

Pastral frowned, shook his head, then smiled and patted Aelfred’s arm. “Yes, of course. Now that I look more closely, I can see ... it’s cheap glass. Definitely not her brooch.” He glanced at his wife. “You understand I’d never gift you something so cheap and plebeian.”

She glared at him. “I should hope not. I’d been intending to wear that brooch to the dance tonight. I’d have been mortified to be seen wearing such a tawdry ornament.”

Lord Pastral looked like he’d just ate something sour. “Of course. Wouldn’t be proper. Perhaps yours is with the rest of the missing jewelry.”

He took a deep breath and relaxed his shoulders. I think he figgered out that Aelfred had just given him a chance to replace the glass brooch with a real one. Aelfred’s good about helping people spend money.

“Most likely misplaced somewhere. Likely to show up in a few weeks.”

He smoothed Aelfred’s sleeve. “My apology for suspecting you of thievery. Doubly so for embarrassing you in front of your peers.” He waved a hand at the folks what was half edging away and half leaning closer to make sure they didn't miss nothing.

Pastral was shakin' Aelfred's hand when the man in the orange hat, what had hidden da bag of gems come striding around the corner waving a particolored tunic.

"Pastral! I demand to be told the meaning of this." He shook the tunic in front of Lord Pastral. "I caught your servant rummaging through my belongings, and the sleeve on every one of my tunics has been damaged. It's as if someone pierced them with a dagger!"

The hole in the sleeve looked just like the one in Aelfred's tunic what he got because someone stabbed it. He never told me who cut his sleeve, but I think I figured it out. I might of even figured out how he got his invite to this party.

While Lord Badbettes waved his tunic and shouted, a serving girl come up to Ruemonge carrying a bag what looked just like the one Aelfred had took into the castle.

Ruemonge handed the bag to Lord Pastral and whispered something so quiet even I couldn't hear it.

Everybody heard Pastral shout "Found under Badbette's bed?"

Badbettes took one glance at the bag and shut up. He got whiter than the clouds and stuttered. "I've ...I've never seen that bag before. I can't imagine how your wife's missing jewels ended up under my bed."

Aelfred tapped his nose. "And I can't imagine how you knew that the bag contained jewels. Missing jewels, no less." He pointed at Lord Pastral. "You're a quick witted man, what does this suggest to you?"

Lord Pastral grabbed Badbettes by the front of his tunic, shook him like a terrier shakes a rat and shoved him away. "You cur!" he shouted.

Badbettes stumbled and almost fell. “I can explain, your lordship—”

Pastral turned his back on him. “Ruemonge, summon my groomsmen. Eject this filth. Have his belongings delivered.” He took a deep breath. “After you’ve confirmed they are all *his* belongings.”

He turned back to Aelfred. “My dear elf. I am so aggrieved at insulting your honor. Please, do me the favor of spending another week in my estate. And may I tender your introduction to Lord Spendswell. He is hosting a game next month.”

Aelfred bowed. “I’d be delighted, my good man. And may I send for my servant. It’s never advisable to leave a menial in the city with nothing to do.” He glanced at Badbettes. “You understand how poorly the lower classes behave when not properly supervised.”

And so I got to sleep in Lord Pastral’s stable. The stable boy even put extra hay in my stall, and the cook gived me all the bones.

It sure was my lucky day when Aelfred dropped into my life.

C. Flynt is the husband and wife team of Clif and Carol Flynt. Carol's demise in 2021 left Clif with enough unfinished works that they continue to work together as ghost-writer and ghost. Clif writes both fiction and non-fiction, creates sawdust in his workshop, treads on his partner's feet whenever someone is foolish enough to dance with him, and provides insufficient food and attention to two cats and a dog (according to a recent poll of household residents).

THE SIXTH STAGE OF GRIEF IS NECROMANCY

Rachel Meresman

Jacob had been trying to talk Connor out of raising the dead for hours. He had woken up that morning to find Connor scratching a pentagram into their living room floor (goodbye security deposit) and Margo's body on ice in the bathtub (holy fucking shit, Connor).

Connor, as usual, didn't listen. He stood back to admire his work—candles, salt ring, Margo's damp and lifeless body lovingly arranged in front of the pentagram—then pulled a piece of paper out of his pocket.

Jacob tried one final plea: "If—no, when this fails, then you'll return the body?"

"Sure," Connor said, and began chanting in Latin.

The ritual didn't fail.

The demon appeared in a puff of sulfurous smoke. He bowed low, spotted Margo's body, and his blood-red face lit up in a smile.

"Let me guess," he said, voice smooth as silk. "Young love, tragically cut short."

"I can't imagine my life without her," Connor said.

"And you won't have to," the demon said. "All that's needed is a sacrifice."

"What kind of sacrifice?" Connor asked.

"Connor!" Jacob hissed.

"Someone with a comparable number of years left," the demon said promptly. "No terminal cases, no elderly. Although we can adjust the range a bit if they're sacrificing themself voluntarily."

"But they don't have to be?" Connor asked.

"Connor!"

The demon grinned, displaying far more teeth than should be able to fit in his mouth. "Not in the least."

"We are not sacrificing anybody!" Jacob shouted.

"Calm down," Connor said, as if Jacob were the unreasonable one. "I just want to understand the options."

"Very sensible," the demon said. "Human sacrifice is traditional, but we could siphon some of your life and give it to the girl. There's also animal sacrifice, but the exchange rate is much worse."

"The building does have a mice problem," Connor ventured.

The demon made a face. "Small animals and unwanted? Even worse deal. Now if you could provide animals that were larger and, say, well-loved and would be missed…"

Connor looked distressingly thoughtful at this.

"No," said Jacob firmly. "No sacrifices, no siphoning, definitely no animals."

"Clearly you two need some time to get on the same page," the demon said. "How about this? I'll bring your girl back now and we can talk terms later. I'd hate to see you parted from your love any longer than necessary."

"No," said Jacob.

"Yes," said Connor.

"Wonderful," the demon said. "I'll see you in a week." He snapped his fingers and disappeared. Margo sat up with a gasp.

"What," she said, looking around the room, "the fuck."

"Margo!" Connor exclaimed. He helped her to her feet. "Everything's okay now. You died, but I brought you back."

"I what?" Margo started. "Connor—"

"We never have to be apart again," Connor spoke over her.

"Connor—"

"We may need to move somewhere nobody knows us, but we'll be together, which is all that—"

"Connor!" Margo said sharply. "We broke up."

"We had a fight," Connor said. "But you were coming back."

"Yeah, to get my stuff," Margo said. "The only reason I didn't was—wait, what did happen to me?"

"You fell down an open manhole," Jacob answered when Connor didn't.

"Wow," said Margo after a beat. "I hope somebody is getting the shit sued out of them."

She caught sight of the pentagram and the Latin-covered paper next to it. Her eyes narrowed.

"Connor, how exactly did you bring me back?"

"I summoned a demon," Connor said proudly.

Margo turned to Jacob. "And you didn't stop him?"

"I tried!" Jacob objected, feeling aggrieved. "He didn't listen."

"Of course he didn't," Margo sighed. "What did you give the demon in exchange for bringing me back?"

"Nothing yet," Connor said. "He said we could work it out later. The demon understands about young love."

"You're an idiot," Margo said. "And I don't love you anymore. I told you that when I broke up with you."

Connor searched her face for a long moment, then turned to Jacob. "She came back wrong," he said.

"She what?"

"I *what?*"

"She came back wrong," Connor repeated. "Incapable of human feeling."

"Nope," Margo said. "We're not doing this. I'm out." She stomped out of the apartment, slamming the door behind her. A moment later the door opened again and Connor perked up like a hopeful puppy. Margo ignored both of them and stalked over to the pentagram, picked up the paper, and left again.

"She'll be back," Connor said confidently.

Margo did not come back that day. Or the next.

On the third day, Connor and Jacob drove to all the places that Margo liked to hang out.

"We've unleashed an undead monster onto the world," Connor said. "We have a responsibility to make this right."

"I don't think not loving you makes her a monster," Jacob said. Connor ignored him.

On the fourth day, they made vague, awkward, and ultimately fruitless phone calls to Margo's family and friends.

On the fifth day, Connor relit the candles, printed out a new copy of the ritual, and recited the Latin.

When he finished, a distressingly familiar voice said, "I'll take this one."

Margo appeared in the pentagram, batting smoke away from her face. The funerary dress had been replaced by a suit that looked like it cost more than their monthly rent.

"Margo?" Connor gaped at her. "What are you—"

"You ding-dongs didn't ask to see the fine print," Margo

said. "You brought me back to life in a body that was still decomposing. The last few days were ... fragrant. I had to take matters into my own hands."

"So what? You're a demon now?" Connor asked.

"Eh," Margo tilted a hand from side to side. "More like I work for them. I'm something of a trailblazer down here, actually."

"But they're evil!" Connor objected.

"Hey, *you* summoned *me*," Margo said. "Besides, the terms are clear, as long as you ask the right questions, and nobody's forced to make a deal. Honestly, compared to the corporate law track it doesn't seem so bad.

"In any case," she continued crisply. "I dealt with my little decomposition problem and Jacob didn't actually agree to anything—you may not listen to what he says but my colleague did—but you're still on the hook for bringing me back."

Margo's smile contained more teeth than she'd left the apartment with. Jacob began edging towards the door.

"Let's talk terms."

Rachel Meresman is a speculative fiction author based in the San Francisco Bay Area. Her short stories have appeared in *Beneath Ceaseless Skies*, *Escape Pod*, and *Fusion Fragment*, among other places. She promises that no deals with demons were made in exchange for the publication of this or any of her other stories, but if presented with one she would definitely read the fine print. You can find her at www.rachelmeresman.com.

COLD CASE

Jody Lynn Nye

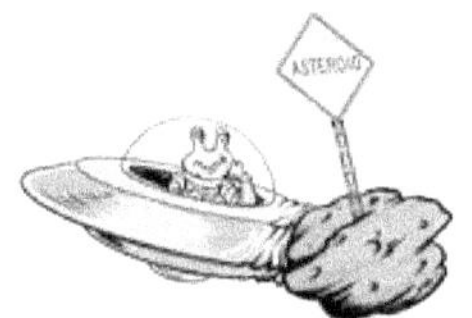

"There she is," the merchant woman said, sticking her small hand out of the broad gray sleeve of her long robe just enough to indicate the strange shape at the opening of the alley on the thirty-eighth level of Cartoon Street. Homicide Detective Sergeant Dena Malone edged her floatchair over and leaned her ever-more-pregnant body over the fancy armrest to peer down at it.

"She's a real stiff," her partner, Detective Sergeant Mario Ramos shouted over the sound of passing air cars and holographic advertisements sprouting out of the pavement and walls. He elbowed Dena in the ear. "Get it?"

"Yeeeeeeesss." Dena looked up at him with a longsuffering expression. "I'm only grateful for her sake that she can't hear you."

"*Frozen* stiff!" crowed a clipped voice from the platinum bangle on Dena's left wrist. "I have just understood it! Good one, Ramos." The voice belonged to her erstwhile partner in crime-solving, an alien scientist named K't'ank from the planet Salos, who occupied the part of her peritoneum that wasn't taken up with her internal organs or the infant gestating in her increasingly expanded uterus. The meter-long pink-skinned alien had been thrust upon her in the name of Witness Protection, and had never left. As often as she had wished that she had never ended up hosting him, he had also been useful in offering facts or observations about the human condition. Unfortunately, he also loved her fellow officer's awful sense of humor.

"Someone really gave her the cold shoulder," Ramos added, eliciting another outburst of laughter from K't'ank.

Dena groaned and turned to the crime scene.

The "stiff" in question, a woman who appeared to be in her early thirties, not far from Dena's own age, lay on her back. Her elbows were bent, and her fingers were arched like claws. Her knees were drawn up into a ninety-degree angle. If the woman had been upright, Dena would have guessed she had been sitting down when she–what?–was hit by a freeze-ray? Doused with a barrel of liquid nitrogen? The cold radiated off the woman's body stronger than sitting in front of an air-conditioning unit roaring at full blast.

"What do you think was the time of death?" Ramos asked, taking his skinnypad out of his pocket and activating the date/time function.

"It's almost impossible to tell, with a freezing death," Dena said, brandishing her own note-taking device. She took a ping-pong-ball-sized drone from her pocket and threw it into the air to take images of the crime scene. The little camera spat a chalk outline around the body, then zipped around to photograph every angle. "It could have been ten minutes ago, or five years."

"Only it is that you are incorrect as to the timeframe," K't'ank said.

Dena frowned. "How can I be wrong about the time when I don't even know what that was?"

"Because that will take place at a future date," K't'ank said. Dena winced as he smacked her in the ribs from the inside with his long skinny tail.

"Ow! Stop that! You'll wake the baby. He's been tap-dancing on my bladder all night as it is."

"It's a boy?" Ramos asked, his eyes brightening.

"I don't know!" Dena said, narrowing her eyes at him. "I've told you we're waiting to find out. Don't get distracted."

"Well, I've got to know whether I'm going to be an uncle or an aunt," Ramos said, reasonably. "So, K't'ank, you're saying this woman isn't dead? How do you know?"

"Perceive the marking around his left wrist," the Salosian said, his voice dropping into lecture mode. Dena shook her head. He was never going to get human pronouns right. "On 15x magnification, I can see the telltale blue wash that is painted onto the skin of those who are undergoing cryogenic preservation. It has been washed or worn away from the manipulative extremities and the face, but not inside the edges of the garment. That method, as you perhaps will realize in memory, was created by my people and shared with humankind as a gift. It prevents the catastrophic bursting of cells resulting from exposure to extreme cold, but is not as effective in the opposite process, which is...."

Dena stared at her partner. "...Which means that we have to get this woman to a cryogenic facility to be thawed out right, or she *will* die!"

K't'ank thumped her again in irritation, making her double over in pain.

"That is what I would have told you!"

"Yeah, in about ten or twenty years, Professor," Ramos

said. He lifted his wrist and spoke into the band. "Send an air ambulance pronto! We have a corpse that isn't dead yet!"

"SORRY, she's not one of ours," Dr. Sterngeld said, even as the bio-suited technicians closed the hatch shut with a booming *clank!* on the Jane Doe in the laboratory of Eternal Life Cryogenics, Inc., two street levels above and four blocks northwest of the crime scene. The hiss of hydraulics almost drowned out her voice. "Dr. K't'ank is right about the application of the preservative fluid, but the retinal scan and fingerprints don't belong to any of the 'freezees' we have in our care."

"But there must be thousands of people in cryostasis around the world," Dena argued.

"But no universal database," Sterngeld said, apologetically. "We don't share our list with anyone except to satisfy government or court subpoenas."

"Why not? Shouldn't everyone be keeping track of patients like her?"

Sterngeld looked long-suffering. "They don't move around very often," she said. "The process to render someone into cryostasis is very complex. Once they have been treated, it can take a very long time to restore them to *walking life*, if in fact they are ever well enough to regain mobility." She took on an expression that Dena associated with caretakers in long-term facilities. "Many of our residents are awaiting treatment for conditions that were not or are not available to them. Frankly, many of their families are only delaying the inevitable. They know it, but they can't face it."

"Understandable," Dena said, with genuine sympathy.

"One way of dealing with your mother-in-law," Ramos

said. Dena shoved her floatchair backward into his shin. "Oof! Er, so can you tell what this woman might have been frozen for?" he asked.

"Not without the chip that would have been placed on her wrist or ankle upon ... deposit." Sterngeld showed them a small blue square affixed to a white elastic band. Dena made a note on her skinnypad to check around the area where the woman had been found for one. She wasn't looking forward to the search. There had been a lot of garbage in the alley. "But I can tell you this: The woman in that tank could not have been moved very far without being transported in a very specialized vehicle to preserve her from melting, so the chances are high that she was kept very close to where you found her."

"So she might have been kept in some kind of home-canning facility?" Dena asked.

Sterngeld looked even more supercilious. "Cryogenics is not something one can do in the comfort of one's own home, sergeant. Good luck, though. This woman should recover in time."

"Do you have any idea how long that'll take? We'll want to ask her who made her a momsicle," Ramos said.

Sterngeld's expression turned icier than the faces of her patients at Ramos's witticism. "Anywhere from days to months, if all goes well. We will notify you when she comes around."

"MOMSICLE?" Dena asked, as they rolled out of the building.

"I know you wanted to laugh," Ramos said, aiming his

elbow for her ear again. She dodged him. "C'mon, admit it. It was a good joke."

"It is a successful play on your words," K't'ank said, wriggling inside Dena's abdomen.

"See? He enjoyed it!"

Dena rolled her eyes. "One of these days, a witness is going to complain to Captain Potopos, and you're going back to patrol and chasing down shoplifters and muggers again."

"Hey, if we find where this woman came from, I can threaten people with cryogenics. 'Freeze, or we'll put you on ice!' Or I can tell my girlfriend, 'I met a chick today who is cooler than you will ever be.'"

"Is that why you have so much trouble getting second dates?" Dena countered.

"Momsicle," K't'ank murmured with a chuckle. "Momsicle. I will have to write a paper on the potential alterations of human language to play upon words. Childsicle? Fin de siècle? No, that doesn't work as well. But momsicle is nearly perfect. I shall expand upon my studies!"

"Great," Dena said, rolling her eyes. "Thanks, Ramos, you're going to start a linguistics war with the Salosians based on puns. I'm going to have to keep hearing K't'ank repeat your witticism until he's told everyone on his email list."

"Don't forget I also author in my blog!" K't'ank added. "*Many* more people will hear it!" Dena groaned.

They returned to the alley and started canvassing the area, looking for unusual heat signatures or power usage, not that they had any real idea what those would look like. The chip was nowhere to be found. Dr. Sterngeld had said there were no other dedicated cryogenics labs within a dozen kilometers.

They started interviewing people in an increasingly

widening radius from the initial location to see if anyone had witnessed someone or something dropping off a frozen body. Dena's skinnypad had synthesized an image of the woman without the coating of ice for them to show potential witnesses. The computer animation even tossed back her long brown hair with a vivacious smile.

"I'd date her," Ramos said, eyeing it with approval. "Someone must recognize her."

"The problem is that we don't know how long she was on ice before she was dumped. Did they assume that the process would kill her, or that she'd thaw out before anyone could figure out she was still alive and get her back to a freezer?"

"But why a momsicle?" K't'ank asked. "This is a most extravagant method, not like the myriad records I have researched of Earth-based thugs. Throughout my studies of fatal assault of human upon human, it does not seem that your more ordinary disposal of unwanted persons is accomplished by simpler means? A blow upon the head with a blunt instrument? A toxic substance introduced into the comestibles consumed by the victim? A sharp object drawn across the throat or plunged into the—"

"You," Ramos said, "have been watching too many true crime dramas, mi amigo."

"I think he's right, though," Dena said, tapping her skinnypad on her lower lip. "This is not a simple crime. We're not looking for an ordinary killer. Was she being maintained as a … souvenir?"

"Or leftovers?" Ramos suggested. "Saving her for later?"

"Ramos, that's gross!"

"Is that not the very essence of cryogenics?" K't'ank asked. "To preserve until you want it again?"

"That'd be convenient," Ramos said, staring off into space with a speculative look on his face. "Wonder whether that would be considered seeing more than one woman at once? Just take one out of the freezer when you want to see her, and put her back at the end of the date?"

Dena smacked him in the belly with the back of her hand. "Only you," she said, disgusted. "I will be very interested to see the pathology once she's been thawed out and revived. I hope her memories are intact. How much do you think she'll remember of what happened just before she was put in the freezer?"

"From the look on her face when we found her," Ramos said, "it sure wasn't her idea."

They showed the enhanced image to shopkeepers and business owners beginning where the woman had been found. Most of the boutiques were upscale, the kind of store that Dena would never have shopped at on a police sergeant's salary. In the fifth chichi little shop two levels up from the crime scene, she sighed over a pair of gleaming blue earrings that cost about the same as the rent she and her husband Neal paid for their small apartment on a very high level of a middle-class neighborhood several kilometers away.

"May I … help you?" asked a woman in a lavender dress that screamed elegance from twenty paces. She eyed Ramos up and down, appearing to enjoy what she was seeing, then turned a less pleasurable gaze upon Dena, taking in her very plain clothes, her burgeoning belly, and her razor-cut brown hair.

Ramos was immune to fashion of any kind, and Dena appreciated that he wasn't fazed by the arrogance the woman exuded.

"Sergeant Ramos and Sergeant Malone, ma'am." He flashed his skinnypad. "Do you recognize this woman?"

Her pencil-thin eyebrows rose to her hairline, and Dena

could see that the word 'no' was on her lips, but didn't emerge. The woman paused, then nodded.

"I believe that I do. Well, did, once. Her name is Chloe Bentz. She was employed by this establishment. Several years ago. She was dismissed for her failure to appear for her shifts. Goodness, I haven't thought about her in ages. I thought she'd left the planet."

Ramos and Dena exchanged glances. Dena felt a thrill of excitement in her stomach. A potential lead! "How long ago was that?" she asked. "Can you give us information about her?"

The eyebrows did a complicated little dance, as though the woman wanted badly to ask what and why, but would *never*. Dena gave her a conspiratorial smile.

"Some information might have come to light in a recent Missing Persons case," Dena said, dropping her voice to a near-whisper. That kind of confidential admission tended to open even the most clammed-up of witnesses.

"Missing Persons?" the woman echoed. Her face changed, reflecting shock, astonishment, then regret. Dena assumed that she had said some pretty damning things about Chloe, if this was Chloe, when she had failed to show up for her shifts. She straightened her narrow shoulders. Success! "This way, please, officers. I can pull up the records."

The moment the three-dimensional image began to rotate on the platform of the boutique's office computer, Dena let out a breath. That was their icicle, all right.

"She looks different when she is not frozen," K't'ank said. He could see directly through Dena's optic nerves, something that was occasionally useful but often a pain in the neck, as now.

"Frozen?" the shop owner asked, her eyebrows ascending to their previous height.

"The last image we have of her is a still frame," Ramos said smoothly, ratcheting up the charm.

Nice catch, Dena thought.

Fortunately, the woman was distracted by the disembodied voice coming out of Dena's bracelet. All at once, she took in the platinum bangle and the ornate floatchair, and put the clues together.

"Oh, you are a Salosian host!" she exclaimed, beaming. "How exciting! We have a few of your ... colleagues as customers in our humble—" and Dena was under no illusions that she meant that adjective literally, "establishment. We," and Dena assumed she meant the royal We, "are always pleased to welcome you to our exclusive showings at the beginning of every season. May I ... become acquainted with your, er, tenant?"

"Well, I don't know..." Dena said, disliking being dismissed as a domicile. But Alien Relations always wanted her to promote good relations with humans. She swallowed her pride. "Dr. K't'ank, may I introduce you to...?"

"Carmilla Brody," the woman said, holding out her hand. Then, she realized she couldn't shake hands with an alien personage who was completely enclosed within the body of a fellow human, a lowly police sergeant at that, and withdrew it with an expression of having been asked to pick up dog droppings. Dena felt her cheeks burn. "A pleasure to meet you, Dr. K't'ank. And your host...?"

"Dena Malone," Dena reminded her.

"Ms. Malone. Well. As you can see, Chloe left us about seven years ago. She was a reasonably good worker. She knew how to appeal to both our targeted clientele and those who might be inclined to buy goods for them."

"She was a flirt?" Ramos asked. Ms. Brody studied the floor between them. "Okay, I don't have to have it spelled out. Do you think she might have met some resistance from your *targeted clientele* when she was showing off for their patrons?"

"Sergeant, I really couldn't say."

I bet you couldn't, Dena thought.

"Can we have the list of buyers who were fans of Chloe from back then?" Dena asked.

"It's against company policy to release our buyer list without a warrant!" Ms. Brody looked up, shocked. But the combined star power of Ramos's intense dark brown eyes and the possibility of rubbing figurative shoulders with an alien VIP persuaded her to relent.

"In other words," Ramos said, as they went out the door with Chloe Bentz's details, "it wasn't a him, it was a them. Let's put the computer onto it and see if it can make any connections before we have to ask for a court order."

THEY RETURNED to the station house. Dena swung her floatchair into the doorway of the commander's office.

"Captain?" she called.

"Capsicle," K't'ank murmured, and giggled. Dena took off the platinum bangle and stuffed it into her pocket.

"What did you want, Malone?" Captain Potopos asked. The potbellied senior officer looked weary. Dena urged her chair forward into his office.

"Status report, sir. We have some data about the woman found frozen in the Uptown sector, sir," she said. She beamed the information to his desk and explained the morning's investigation. Potopos nodded with approval at the hologram that flicked her hair and smiled at the watcher, then looked up at Dena.

"Momsicle?" he asked.

"Ramos came up with that, sir," Dena said with a sigh. "And here's the data from the cryogenics lab where they're bringing her around. They're not sure how long it will take."

Potopos's eyebrows rose. "She's not dead?"

"No, sir. Just frozen."

He waved a disinterested hand. "Not our jurisdiction. Reassign it to Assault and Battery." Dena felt her face fall. "Don't give me that big-eyed sad look! Next thing you know, you'll convince me you should be looking for lost dogs. What's this case got that is worth keeping you and your partner off genuine homicides?"

"Uh, nothing, sir. I mean, it's a weird case." Dena couldn't explain why she wanted to hold onto it. "I mean, we were the first on the scene, and K't'ank was curious about it, but nothing, really…."

"That's right, nothing. That's why we pay you the big bucks, sergeant."

"Yes, boss. And about those big bucks?" Dena added hopefully. "After all, I've got a baby on the way."

"Yes, well, you'll have to wait until your baby shower. The guys in the squad room have been taking up a collection for something … special for Little Malone."

Dena dreaded what her fellow officers had come up with. After all, she had participated in some of those gag gifts herself. She forced a smile. "Uh, thanks, boss!" she said brightly.

Potopos looked mollified. "You can keep the case. Here! Since you're so interested in non-homicides, maybe you can look into this one." He tossed her a contact chip. Dena caught it between her palms.

"What is it?"

"Crazy woman came in here, insisting her son's growth

was inhibited while she was away on a space mission. Right up your alley. It's in the same neighborhood as your corpsicle."

"But, Captain!"

Potopos waved a hand. "Dismissed!"

"Corpsicle," K't'ank snickered.

SHE AND RAMOS took a corner of the big table at the side of the break room and looked at the holo that the captain had given her. The video had been taken from the camera to the side of the commander's desk. Four people had stormed into his office and confronted him. He was doing his best to calm them down.

"...I don't understand it!" On the holographic projection, a blonde woman in the blue uniform of the Exploration Corps was saying, gesturing to the small, black-haired child beside her. "I went away for a yearlong assignment, gathering biological specimens out in the Leo cluster, and look at him! Mikey hasn't grown; he hasn't changed in any way!"

"Ma'am," the captain said, looking puzzled, "this isn't a matter for the police. If anything, it's something you should take up with the boy's doctor."

"An endocrinologist?" asked the man at the woman's right side, as if he had said it many times before. He had shiny black hair like the boy's. "I told you, he's just small for his age!"

"Kids change a lot, but not that much in one year," Potopos said, reasonably.

The expensively dressed man beside the woman in blue oozed closer to the commander's desk. Dena pegged him immediately as a lawyer. "But Ms. Ermina Caldon was away for more than seven years Earth-time, isn't that correct, Specialist Caldon?"

"Yes, that's the way faster-than-light travel works," the woman said, eyeing the attorney as if he were a moron. She turned back to Captain Potopos. "I was supposed to be back a few years ago, but my mission got extended. My husband insists there's nothing wrong with Mikey."

"He looks fine to me," Potopos said.

"He still has his baby teeth!" the woman said. "He's twelve!"

"He probably needs human growth hormone treatment," the husband countered. "I did when I was his age."

The commander looked as if his patience was wearing thin. Dena wondered how long the argument had been going on. "Ma'am, I'm sorry, but failure to thrive, if that's what this is, is a matter for doctors, not cops. If your husband wasn't feeding him while you were gone, that'd be one thing, but he looks fine. I'd be happy to put my officers onto any investigation that involves an actual criminal matter, if you come up with one. In the meanwhile, welcome back to Earth!"

Specialist Caldon frowned at him and seized her son by the hand. "Come on, Mikey! You, too!" she ordered her husband. He fell in line meekly behind her. The lawyer sauntered out in their wake, as if knowing that every hour was probably costing the Caldons thousands. The holo sputtered and went out.

"Big waste of time for us," Ramos said, as they left the station house.

"I know. Potopos knew this was going to be a wild goose chase. Did the desk sergeant say anything about them?" Dena asked. She swatted away an orange-and-yellow hologram that assaulted her with bright lights, animation, and brassy music, advertising the latest in stain-fighting detergent. "I have an ad blocker! A *paid* one! You shouldn't be bothering me!" The image disappeared, replaced by a news icon and a stern-faced man talking about the economy. She groaned and ignored it.

"Specialist Caldon came howling in, towing the kid behind her. The lawyer met them there, and they started in on the captain like he was their personal steward. She hasn't been back for long."

"No ... how long did she say she had been away?"

Ramos ran the holo back on his skinnypad. "Seven years. That's weird; our momsicle has been missing seven years, too. And she just turned up again when this woman returned to Earth. Caldon must have schlepped up and back from the Leo Sector."

"Coincidence," Dena said, waving it away.

"But what if it is correlation, not coincidence?" K't'ank said.

Dena scoffed. "That would be wild, if there was any connection between these cases. I mean, Potopos obviously doesn't think so."

"So?" Ramos's eyes twinkled. "So, let's prove him wrong. Where's the evidence going to be?"

Dena thought for a moment. "It's not going to be in their home, is it? K't'ank, where do Salosians park their space labs when they land on a planet?"

"As our planet is 96 percent covered by oceans, we find the body of water nearest to where we are meeting fellow scientists," K't'ank said. "Explanation for why she would have brought the cryogenic subject with her on her journey, then back again? It does not seem logical to consume the fuel needed for the excess payload in either direction."

"Hmm," Dena mused. "All I can figure is that she planned

to leave Chloe out there in the Leo Sector, but never got the opportunity."

"So, she left the girl in an alley six levels down from their mansion?" Ramos asked. "And believe me, they have a mansion." He showed Dena the overhead view of the property. Dena counted eight bedrooms on the floor plan, as well as numerous baths and bonus rooms of assorted sizes. It was tall enough to protrude up into the street level above the house's foundation.

Dena whistled. "If Neal and I had that much space ... well, it'd get filled up with his collectibles in a year. Who am I kidding? But it would be nice to have some elbow room. Our place is already small, and with the baby and the android butler, it's going to feel even more cramped. But we should go where the lab is first, so we don't tip her off that we're looking for anything."

"That'd be no problem," Ramos said. "We have a real scientist here who can ask questions without drawing attention. Right, K't'ank?"

"My study is sociology, not biology," K't'ank argued. "I presume the specimens are not consciously interacting in a manner that would rise to the level of forming a civilization."

"Can you just play along?" Dena asked. "Sound science-y and help us out. We need to find out if Chloe's reappearance was tied to Specialist Caldon's return or not."

"That is a sociological consequence," K't'ank said. "A paper can evolve from a study of that which I can share with my peers."

"Not until we solve the case!" Dena squawked. "But after that, sure, you can publish all you want."

"Very well," K't'ank said. "I will comply."

For all the bluster she had shown in the police station, Specialist Caldon's facility turned out to be a small storefront and a windowless warehouse beside one of the launch hangars on the Tri-County main spaceport. Anonymous figures in hazmat gear bustled in and out of the doors at the rear of the cramped office inside.

"Dr. K't'ank?" asked the tall young woman behind the counter. She had on computer spectacles that gleamed blue light onto her face. She swished a few hand signals, and her expression brightened. "Yes, I thought I recognized his name! What can we do for you?" She spoke directly to the platinum bangle on Dena's wrist. Dena was impressed.

"I show interest in the recently returned mission," K't'ank said. "If we may inspect the biological module? I wish to pass along information to my colleagues concerning your discoveries and what returned to Earth with you." Dena was doubly impressed. He hadn't told a single lie, but everything he said sounded like he was genuinely interested. Sometimes she forgot how very intelligent he was, considering he spent an inordinate amount of time with her husband watching terrible old two-dee scifi movies.

"Really? We'd be honored to have you look at everything! It's kind of a mess. The specialists who went out on the mission haven't really had a chance to clear everything out yet, but sure. Let me show you around. We'll have to suit up and decontaminate." She glanced at Dena and ran an eye over the floatchair. "Will that be a problem?"

"Not at all," Dena said. After all, the chair had recently been fitted out like a tank, then had its armor plating and life-support bubble removed once the perpetrator involved had been apprehended, but it was still proof against extremes of temperature and possessed defense systems to protect

K't'ank and his host. She kind of missed the armor-piercing missiles, but you couldn't have everything.

Once they had been fogged with a fruity-smelling spray and had donned white suits with hoods and clear faceplates, the young scientist, whose name was Francisca, led them behind the swinging doors. The temperature immediately dropped at least forty degrees.

"I can just see our subject chilling in here," Ramos said in an undertone.

"Chilling," K't'ank said, with a giggle. "Frozen stiff."

"Momsicle," Ramos intoned.

"Stop it, you two!" Dena growled.

Their guide paid no attention to them, as she pointed out the features of the laboratory module. It was made to be attached to a landing craft which went into the belly of a spacecraft. The pristine white-enameled lab took up half the unit, and a narrow corridor leading from it toward the stern had numerous doors on each side. Dena let her skinnypad pick up all the details of the lab as she passed them.

"It's a little bit of a tight fit for sixteen people to live in here," Francisca said. "But they live with it. Anything for science."

"For science!" Dena, Ramos, and K't'ank echoed.

"Xenobiological samples were returned with you?" K't'ank asked.

"Yes," the scientist said. She indicated a heavy insulated door that took up most of one wall of the lab. Cold radiated from it, and frost limned the metal band that ran around its perimeter. "We freeze them. So far, none of it has been removed. Oh, except for a few small samples Dr. Caldon took home for study. Some really interesting plant life." Her gestures suggested a small container no more than twenty centimeters or so. Dena was disappointed. Nothing as big as a human woman.

"But everyone does have their private quarters and storage facility," the scientist went on.

"How much personal cargo did each of them bring with them? Do they get a couple hundred kilos?"

"Oh, there's no limit–well, not much of a limit, considering how much tech gear and supplies we have to load in," Francisca said. "But practically speaking, they can bring up to a couple of tons before anyone complains."

"Really?" Dena asked. She read the names enameled onto each doorway. The third from the rear said 'Caldon.' "Can we have a look in there?"

"There's nothing we need to see in private quarters," K't'ank said severely. Dena opened her mouth to contradict him, but a smack in the ribs told her to hold her tongue. She did, under protest. "However, storage is a curiosity to me."

"No problem," Francisca said. She led the way to the rear of the module and held her hand over the sensor. The white door slid aside and brilliant lights illuminated every centimeter of the chamber.

Dena realized her chair wouldn't fit into the narrow space between the stacked pallets and cases. Ramos could, but he wasn't the one with the alien scientist in his belly. She turned her head from side to side and swept the ceiling and floor with her gaze. "I can't give you much more of a look in there," she told K't'ank.

"That is all right," he said. "I see what I need to see."

They thanked Francisca and headed out. Dena kept quiet until they were well away from the facility.

"Why wouldn't you let me look into Caldon's quarters?" she asked.

"Did you see the tightness of the living space?" K't'ank

asked. "I maintain the measurements of the frozen body, and the space between doorways say that there would be no room in a cabin that would hold two humans, especially one in concealment with maintenance extreme technology."

"How do you know what's comfortable for humans?"

"I occupy one, in much more reduced quarters than the oceans of my world," K't'ank said smugly. "I am certain there is a minimum size for mental comfort among humans."

She and Ramos exchanged glances. "I hate it when he's right. Okay, then, we no longer have a practical timeline. That sets us back again to the beginning. If we don't come up with a correlation soon, then Potopos is going to have us transfer the case to someone else."

"The only person who says she knew Chloe was the woman at the fancy store, Ms. Brody," Ramos said. "Let's see if she recognizes Caldon."

"CAN you wait around the rear door?" Ms. Brody asked in a worried whisper. "Mx. Rockspur is in the changing room, and I absolutely can't disturb them!" She tilted her head toward the pale blue slatted door at the side of the boutique. A sparkling purple garment flew up and out of the booth and flopped onto the polished floor. A wail arose from the changing room. "Oh, no, there goes the Guccite tank dress! I have to get back there. They are *not* very patient, but a very good customer."

"Please, just one moment," Dena said. She had pulled footage of Specialist Caldon from her visit to the station house and held out the skinnypad for the three-dimensional image to form. The figures strode toward the onlooker, the mother with a firm grasp on her son's arm. "Does this woman look familiar to you? From the days when Chloe was still working for you?"

Ms. Brody peered at it. "No, I don't think I've seen her before."

"Thanks anyway," Ramos said, glumly. But Ms. Brody pointed a mauve-nailed finger at the holo.

"...But I do recognize the man behind her. He paid a lot of attention to Chloe back then. So did a lot of other people," Ms. Brody whispered, the disapproval evident on her face. "She was very attractive." Another wordless cry of protest erupted, and two more articles of clothing were propelled up toward the tiled ceiling. "I *must* go," she said.

"You've been very helpful," Dena said. "Good luck."

"So, Mr. Caldon knew the vic," Ramos said. "Holy crap, I was right! He *was* saving her for later."

"But he's not a scientist," Dena said. "I went over his record. He's a music producer."

"They're the most bloodthirsty of them all," Ramos insisted.

"But what's his motive? If he was playing around with Chloe while his wife was in space, what about it? She's not going to be happy to be cheated on, but either she forgives him, or she gets a divorce from him. Why put Chloe into suspended animation?"

"Concealment is motive," K't'ank said.

"But concealing what?" Dena asked. "I agree with Ramos. Unless Ermina Caldon is violently jealous, and hiding the girl keeps her from finding out about her husband's infidelity."

"But the timeline stinks," Ramos said. "She disappeared around the time that the wife left Earth, give or take some months. I mean, maybe he thought that his wife would be back in a year, and put Chloe on ice then to keep her from talking."

"But what has this to do with the immature offspring?" K't'ank asked. "He did not accompany his parent into space."

Dena sighed. "Let's go talk to them."

A ROBOSTEWARD OPENED the door and examined their identification before waving them into the mansion. Dena thanked it politely and hovered her chair over the threshold.

"Mr. Caldon is in the kitchen," it said. It rolled past the police officers and led them forward.

The food preparation area and the breakfast nook, or lunch nook, as it was past noon, was huge, shiny, and bright. Frames displayed a slide show of album art, undoubtedly output from Mr. Caldon's company. She recognized a few that she actually owned and even enjoyed. Ramos nodded approval at some, too.

"Isn't that third one the music that you said sounded like two sick cats howling....?" K't'ank began. Dena hissed at him.

"Quiet! We don't want to get thrown out."

They stopped at the archway leading into the vast kitchen. The small boy, Mikey, sat on a stool in the middle of the room beside the ceramic tabletop heating unit. Numerous containers, jars, and boxes were strewn along the table. Caldon, kneeling beside the boy, looked frazzled. The boy had his arms crossed in defiance.

"I'm tired of guessing," Caldon said, his voice strained with frustration. "Won't you please just tell Daddy what you want me to make for you?"

"It's my favorite lunch!" the boy said. "You promised! You make it all the time!"

"I can't remember! When was the last time you had it?"

"Two days ago! For my birthday!"

"I was so excited about your birthday that I didn't even think what I was cooking. After seeing you open all those presents? C'mon," Caldon wheedled. "Just one little hint?"

The boy lifted his elbows and let them drop. "No!"

"This is what you've got to look forward to," Ramos murmured. Dena ignored him and cleared her throat. Caldon seemed to take in their presence for the first time. He stood up and glanced at his wrist. His chronometer flashed a message at him, and he nodded, probably a heads-up from the robobutler. He pasted on a friendly grin.

"Officers? What can I do for you?"

"Is your wife here, sir?" Dena asked.

"Uh, no. She brought a package home, then went to see her folks." He shook his head. "It's going to take some getting used to, having her back after so long."

"She wasn't gone that long!" the boy declared.

"Mikey!" It sounded to Dena as if Mikey was determined to be oppositional about everything. She felt a momentary pang of sympathy for the father.

"Could we, uh, could we have a private word with you, sir?" she asked.

"What's it about?"

"In private?" Dena stressed.

"I'll look after Mikey," Ramos said, shooing them away. "Kids love me."

Dena didn't roll her eyes, but she thought about it. Caldon directed her up a staircase and through one lavish sitting room after another, each one getting smaller and increasingly decked out with more expensive-looking furnishings. On either side were doors to bedrooms lined with silk in rich colors and hand-embroidered tapestries, and all kinds of fragile little knickknacks. They emerged into a snug space with a cushy armchair, wall lighting disguised as medieval sconces, and an antique gilt table. Caldon threw himself into the armchair.

"So, what's this about?"

"Chloe Bentz," Dena said.

The man looked shocked and guilty, but the expression changed swiftly to deliberately passive. "I don't know where you dredged that name up, officer, but I haven't seen her in ages. You're going to ask me if I was banging her—I was. She was pretty, and I was lonely. But that's in the past. Once she started blackmailing me, it was over. I told her to go ahead and tell anyone she wanted, then I never saw her again. Happy?"

"What was she blackmailing you about?"

Caldon shook his head. "None of your business."

"Does your son not play with toys?" K't'ank asked, suddenly.

The man frowned at him. "Sure he does. All kinds. Mostly, he's interested in computer programming. He's brilliant; years ahead of his age group."

"Where are his playthings? The sleeping chambers are devoid of any childlike accoutrements."

K't'ank never went off on a tangent without a purpose.

"Does he have a playroom somewhere?" Dena asked.

"What do you care about my son's toys?" Caldon countered.

"I study human psychology for my planet's greater understanding of allied races," K't'ank said. "Show them to me for my curiosity's sake."

Dena put on her most winning smile for the music

producer. "How about it, sir? You know scientists. You're married to one."

"Oh, what the hell." Caldon clapped his hands on his thighs and stood up. "Come on."

They doubled back through the fancy sitting rooms. Dena studied the bedrooms more closely as she passed them. K't'ank was right: There were no toys visible in any of them. That was weird. "What's going on?" she asked, subvocalizing to the Salosian.

"A suspicion," he replied.

"Can I have more information than that?"

"Maintain caution," K't'ank said.

At the bottom of the stairs, Caldon took a left through a double door. The chamber beyond lit up with motion sensor lights. Ahead of them was a thick glass portal. The lab on the other side would have been the envy of the police district all by itself.

"This belongs to your son?" Dena asked.

"And my wife. But he's been using it since she went away." Caldon stood to one side and ushered Dena in.

He went to a door that looked exactly like the cryogenic chamber in the science module at the space center. It whooshed open, blasting Dena with cold air.

"Doesn't look like a child's lab," she said.

"The robots keep it spotless," Caldon said, dismissively. He pointed inside. "This is the kid's latest experiment. Come and take a look."

Suspicion rose in her mind as well. Dena would have bet her salary that the kid had been in here, but not to do experiments. A horrified thought rose in her mind. What if there had been *two* frozen bodies all these years instead of just one? Was Ramos right about how sinister music producers were? She turned toward Caldon to demand answers.

The dark-haired man dove at her with a hydraulic hypodermic syringe. She flinched back, reaching for her sidearm, but Caldon grabbed her wrist with his free hand. Dammit, where were those heat-seeking missiles when she needed them?

"Defend!" K't'ank cried. "Defend the domicile and the fetus!"

Dena felt him move in her belly, and saw a bulge snake across her rounded stomach just as the syringe touched it. Cold shot through her like being stabbed with an icicle.

"Defense!" the chair announced. From the pillars on the rear and up underneath her footrest, mechanical arms surged up and grabbed Caldon, suspending him in the air by his arms and legs. One claw hand snatched the hypo from his fingers. "Analysis? Contents unknown. Analysis?"

Caldon started screaming. "You don't know what it's been like!"

"Analysis? Analysis?"

"K't'ank, talk to me," Dena said. Her voice sounded groggy to her own ears. "Are you okay? Hey, I'm getting brain freeze...."

"DENA, TALK TO ME," Neal's voice came from a thousand light years away. "Honey, are you okay?"

"Sergeant Malone, this is totally unacceptable!" announced another familiar voice.

She woke up to find her husband on the right of her hospital bed, holding her hand. On her left, the always unwelcome, lugubrious presence of Sardwell Barin from the Alien Relations Department glared down at her.

"I told both of you gentlemen that Ms. Malone and Dr.

K't'ank are fine. They got a hefty dose of cryo-prep, but it's wearing off." The doctor, a man with fatherly silver sideburns, shook a finger at them. "Don't stress her out. The head nurse is watching the monitors, and you do not want to piss her off." He strode out of the room.

"You all right, partner?" Ramos asked. He stood at the foot of the bed, looking sheepish. "Sorry to leave you alone with that psychopath."

"What happened?" she asked. Her jaw felt as if it weighed ten tons. "He had the kid in cryostasis, didn't he?"

"Yeah, he did," Ramos said. "You must have figured it out about the same time I did, but he jabbed you. The chair grabbed him before I could pull him away."

"But why? Is the kid really twelve years old, or not?"

"On paper, yeah. In waking years, nope. Just about six. Dad just couldn't hack it as a single parent. He did it for a while, but he hated it. Really cut into his career and his dating life. And his wife's cryo lab was sitting right there, so…."

"Instant kidsicle," Dena said.

"Kidsicle," K't'ank said, chuckling. "Momsicle and kidsicle. More etymology to add to my research."

Dena glanced down at her stomach. "So you're back with us."

"I have been aware longer than you have," he said, sounding smug. "It was a most interesting experience, though I would not want to repeat it."

"Thank you for protecting my baby," she said sincerely. "I'm sorry you got frozen."

"We Salosians are accustomed to a wider range of colder temperatures than humans. Therefore, recovery was more rapid. And protecting the young is common to any species."

"Glad to hear it." She looked up at Barin. "He's fine. Anything else you want?"

"No." Barin turned on his heel and stalked out. Good riddance, Dena thought.

"So, Chloe found out he had his kid on ice. Was she actually blackmailing him?"

"Nope," Ramos said. "She's innocent. She was guilting him to behave like an actual parent. She deserved better than him."

"Why did he dump her in an alley like that?" Dena asked.

"Didn't have time to revive her," Ramos said. "He got word the wife was on her way back, and he didn't want her to find his mistress in the house. He only had time to bring the kid around. Like you heard, Mikey had no idea that any time had passed."

Dena struggled to sit up, and Neal helped her. She didn't feel bad, just a bit drowsy. She looked up at her husband.

"Don't you dare think about putting our kid into cryosleep, even if he drives you crazy," she told him.

"Kidsicle!" K't'ank exclaimed. They all looked at the bangle.

"Wouldn't think of it," Neal assured her.

"Good answer—Popsicle," Dena said.

Ramos burst out laughing. "Gotcha!"

Jody Lynn Nye lists her main career activity as 'spoiling cats.' When not engaged upon this worthy occupation, she writes fantasy and science fiction books and short stories.

Since 1987 she has published over 50 books and more than 200 short stories, most of it with a humorous bent. She has also collaborated with Anne McCaffrey, Robert Lynn

Asprin, Piers Anthony, Dr. Travis Taylor, and other notable writers of the fantasy and science fiction genre.

Jody has taught in numerous writing workshops and participated on hundreds of panels at science-fiction conventions. She runs the two-day writers' workshop at Dragon Con. Jody is the Coordinating Judge of the Writers of the Future, now in its 42nd year, a venue for unpublished speculative fiction writers. She has won the Polaris Award for mentorship of young and upcoming talent.

Jody lives in the northwest suburbs of Atlanta, with her husband Bill Fawcett, and three feline overlords, Athena, Minx, and Marmalade.

HUMANITIES

Desmond Warzel

There came a knock at Mary's door.

"I'm Harper," said the pale young woman. "You're looking for a new roommate. I'm it."

Mary leaned idly against the doorjamb, her arms folded. "Isn't that up to me?"

"Senior year, right?" asked Harper, walking right in and closing the door behind her. "Astrophysics major, right? Still haven't fulfilled those core humanities requirements you need to graduate. Right?"

"The humanities aren't my strong suit. How'd you know?"

"I hear things. You're in luck—I'm a history major and an English minor, and I remember everything I read. Not only will you finally knock off those classes, you'll ace every exam."

"Back up," said Mary. "Let's talk about rent. Your half would be three hundred dollars—"

"My half would be zero," said Harper. "I'm not splitting any utility bills, either."

"I've had a dozen so-called tutors. None of them was worth a ham sandwich, much less a free apartment."

"I'm not a tutor, I'm a werewolf."

"Now *there's* a sentence no one's ever said before."

"I'm serious," said Harper.

"Well, I'll let you know one way or another," said Mary, glancing meaningfully at the door.

"You don't think I'm telling the truth?"

"It wouldn't matter if I did; it's two weeks until the next full moon."

"Don't believe everything you see in the movies," said Harper, who then vanished in a manner that Mary's brain couldn't quite bring itself to perceive, to be replaced by a petite white wolf sitting regally on the living room carpet. Then, just as suddenly, Harper was back.

Mary could do little more than state the obvious. "You were a wolf just now."

"*Mostly* wolf," said Harper. "Some coyote, and a little bit of Cape hunting dog. My family's always been pretty liberal."

"Does it hurt to do that?" asked Mary.

"No."

"Where do your clothes go when you change shape?"

"I wouldn't lean on this too hard if I were you," said Harper. "Maybe just roll with it for now."

"So how does this help me pass a history class?"

Harper pulled a folded piece of paper from her back pocket. "Give this letter to the dean. Say it's from your primary care physician."

Mary glanced over the note. "Emotional support animal?"

"You go to the most permissive college on the west coast, and you don't even take advantage of it. Yes, emotional support animal. Every test you take, I'll be right by your side. You can't lose."

Mary put an arm around Harper's shoulders. "Have a seat and let's talk. As Luke Skywalker said to Han Solo, 'I think this is the beginning of a beautiful friendship.'"

"Your cultural illiteracy is appalling. Where did you grow up, the South Pole?"

Mary ignored the barb. "Is there any way I can convince you to pay at least a *little* rent?"

"We can negotiate," replied Harper.

"And sometimes I have trouble relaxing after a stressful day. What's the petting situation?"

"Don't push your luck."

A MONTH LATER, the women's lavatory across from room 223 of the History Department was playing host to a hurried pre-exam conference. Mary was brandishing a dog vest stenciled with SERVICE ANIMAL on either side. "I think neon yellow's your color, Harper."

"That's humiliating, and I'm not wearing it."

"The dean said it's non-negotiable. Look, if we pull this off, you can live with me for free in perpetuity. It'll be worth it."

"Fine. Now here's the thing," said Harper. "We'll have to work fast, because Professor Elrod's essay questions are famously complex, and I can't speak in wolf form. Do you know Morse code?"

"You're asking *now*?" exclaimed Mary. "Don't worry, it's true-or-false. Rest your head in my lap, read each question, and nudge me once for true, twice for false."

"What kind of history test is true-or-false?"

"The kind designed for people who'd rather be studying quasars than Quasimodo."

"Quasimodo isn't historical, he's fictional, but alliteration like that coming from someone like you is such an unexpected delight that I'm letting it slide."

"What's alliteration?"

MARY ENTERED room 223 to a chorus of gasps and squeals of delight, for none of her classmates had ever seen her canine companion before. She took her usual seat, while Harper made a show of circling in place before sitting smartly on the floor at her side. Professor Elrod gave them a glance before returning her attention to next week's lecture notes.

Mary nervously chewed her No. 2 pencil in anticipation. Despite its soft lighting, with walls painted sky-blue and an aquarium filled with koi swimming to and fro in unison, room 223 always made her feel as though she had been rounded up and interned.

The appointed hour came and the test commenced.

Question 1: True or false: Slavery ended throughout the United States in 1865.

Harper waited for Mary to answer the question herself. When this was not forthcoming, she gave a single nudge, and Mary answered "true."

Question 2: True or false: Slavery was bad.

Mary suspected a trick question. Glancing down at Harper for help, she was treated to the rare sight of an animal rolling its eyes.

WITH HARPER'S HELP, Mary finished the test before most of the others and sat fidgeting until the end of the period, awaiting the announcement of the next reading assignment. Once the class was dismissed, she added her test paper to the stack on Professor Elrod's desk and made swiftly for the door, congratulating herself on avoiding eye contact. She and Harper had almost reached sweet freedom when the professor called after them.

"Mary, you and your companion will please remain behind for a moment."

When the rest of the class had gone, the professor regarded the wolf in the yellow vest. "You might as well drop the masquerade, small one. I know what you're up to."

Harper glanced up at Mary, who only shrugged, having no idea how to navigate this emergent situation. In an eyeblink, she was human again, the vest gone, her ordinary clothes restored. Elrod didn't seem a bit surprised.

"I thought better of you than this, Harper. You've always been one of my best students."

Harper attempted a disarming smile. "The emotional support thing is legit, ma'am, I swear. It's a work-study program. I'd never help anyone cheat."

"She just helps me concentrate," said Mary. The meekness in her voice was not inauthentic. "Like the letter said. But if someone's really getting in trouble, let it be me, not her."

"Fortunately," said Professor Elrod, "I don't have to take either of you at your word."

There came a sharp noise from the back of the room, which turned out to be the lid of the aquarium crashing to the floor. The koi were gone. Standing in the tank was a young man with reddish hair, his sweatshirt and khaki pants both soaked through.

"Perhaps you've met Harold, my graduate assistant. He

monitors all of my classes and exams. He's never caught a cheater yet, but today may be the day."

"*Were-koi?*" asked Mary in disbelief. "All of the fish were *him?*"

"Many species go about in small groups which act as a single mind," said Professor Elrod. Behind them, Harold climbed gingerly out of the aquarium. "If the degree of collectivity is sufficient, such a species sometimes achieves lycanthropy."

"It's true," said Harper. "I once dated a guy whose cousin was a hive of bees. But how long have you known about *me*, Professor?"

"For years, Harper."

"How?"

"A keen eye and an open mind. I've had the privilege to study facets of history known to few others. Your folk have always fascinated me."

Harold joined them, dripping water all over Professor Elrod's desk. Up close, his eyes seemed glazed over, his vacant gaze suggesting either intense concentration or utter obliviousness.

"What is your verdict, Harold?" asked the professor.

Harold stared at Mary and Harper each in turn, as though searching for something. He squinted thoughtfully for a long, uncomfortable minute. Finally he relaxed. "I don't recall seeing a single suspicious activity."

If Professor Elrod was disappointed, her face didn't show it. "That closes the matter," she said. "For today. You two are free to go."

"THE EXPLANATION'S OBVIOUS," said Mary as she and Harper made their way through throngs of students headed in the opposite direction. "That Harold guy likes one of us. Probably you; you've got more in common."

"No, that's not it."

"So he likes me, then."

"Doubt it."

"Then what?"

"It's disappointing, in a way. I've always looked up to Professor Elrod. She's considered a genius by her peers."

"She seems pretty sharp to me."

"I've never had any reason to doubt it until now. But, Mary, what kind of genius would ever rely on the memory of goldfish for *anything*?"

DESMOND WARZEL IS the author of several dozen stories in the genres of fantasy, science fiction, and horror. Some of them are funny. A few of them are even intentionally funny. His work has appeared in the venerable *Magazine of Fantasy & Science Fiction*, online in such venues as *Reactor* and *Abyss & Apex*, and on podcasts like *Escape Pod* and *The Drabblecast*. He also contributed to *Unidentified Funny Objects 2*, so his next appearance should be around volume 18 or so. He promises to do his best to live that long. He resides in Pennsylvania. He'd write more if he didn't have to work for a living.

ACKNOWLEDGMENTS

We'd like to thank everyone involved in making this book possible, and most notably the associate editors Cyd Athens, Andrew Dibble, Frank Dutkiewicz, James Miller, and Tarryn Thomas. They bravely read many hundreds of stories to help select the ones that appeared in this book.

Special thanks to Chris Wake, Hogan Long, G. Mark Cole, and all of our supporters and friends.

ABOUT THE EDITOR

Alex Shvartsman is a writer, anthologist, translator, and game designer from Brooklyn, NY. He's the winner of the 2014 WSFA Small Press Award for Short Fiction and a three-time finalist for the Canopus Award for Excellence in Interstellar Writing. As a translator, he's a two-time BSFA Award nominee.

He's the author of *Eridani's Crown* (2019), *The Middling Affliction* (2022), *Kakistocracy* (2023), and *The Best of All Possible Planets* (2026). His short stories have appeared in *Analog, Nature, Strange Horizons,* and a variety of other magazines and anthologies. Most are collected in *Explaining Cthulhu to Grandma and Other Stories* (2015) and *The Golem of Deneb Seven and Other Stories* (2018).

In addition to the UFO series, he has edited many other anthologies including *The Digital Aesthete, The Cackle of Cthulhu, Humanity 2.0, Reclusion,* and *Coffee: 14 Caffeinated Tales of the Fantastic.*

His website is www.alexshvartsman.com.

THE BEST OF ALL POSSIBLE PLANETS PREVIEW

Alex Shvartsman

Also from UFO Publishing

Humans are prone to take any misfortune that might befall them as a personal affront. They bemoan the truism that bad things happen to good people without ever pausing to wonder whether they are good people.

It is demonstrable that while the universe holds no grudge against humanity, it merely doesn't grant any special dispensation. Thus, things cannot be otherwise than they are. Earthquakes, sinkholes, and stubbing your toe should be viewed not as calamities but rather as stepping-stones in the concatenation of events that culminate in Earth being the best of all possible planets.

- *From* The Gathered Wisdom of the Human Species *by Airvolt*

Life had been perfect on the best of all possible planets until the sunrise malfunctioned.

The resplendent palette painted across the lush green scenery by the first rays of sunlight flickered and dimmed in the most unnatural manner. It flared up and dimmed again several more times, as a candle might when it burns down the last of its wick. Then the flickering stopped, and the once-picturesque view appeared lifeless and dull, like a pretentious oil landscape drawn in ill-conceived brush-strokes by an accountant going through a midlife crisis.

"This is peculiar," said Dhawan.

Dhawan was a mild-mannered and agreeable young man who, up until that moment, had lived a more than agreeable life. And why shouldn't it have been? He'd been fortunate enough to be born in the last settlement on Earth. While most people had given in to their foolish urges and left seeking who-knew-what among the stars, Dhawan's ancestors had had the good sense to stay put and partake of everything the best of all possible planets had to offer. Thus, he enjoyed day after day of breathtaking sunrises, ample time gardening, sufficient food rations, weekly radiation pills, and all the creature comforts one could reasonably expect given their circumstances.

There were relatively few people living in the last settlement on Earth, and most of them were rather dull, if Dhawan were to be honest with himself. Both the quantity of the residents and their shortcomings were to be expected. People were seldom sensible enough to remain on humanity's cradle, and each generation saw fresh herds of black sheep follow their wanderlust off-world. The ones who stayed were of the finest sensible stock, and perhaps too sensible at times to make for very good conversationalists or fine company.

There were, of course, exceptions.

"I don't like this," said Rada, who was exhibit one among the best of all possible exceptions as far as the young man was concerned. "Make it stop, Dhawan."

Rada frowned prettily. She did everything prettily, on account of her youth and good looks. This was precisely why Dhawan had invited her to watch the sunrise with him and was equally thrilled and surprised to have her accept. Although he knew Rada to be thoroughly out of his league, he still secretly harbored hope that this most innocent of activities might possibly lead to future encounters, which he imagined might become simultaneously more frequent and less innocent as time went by.

Dhawan forced himself to look away from Rada and at the inadequate sunrise. "I should say it has already stopped and is in need for rebooting, restarting, tuning, or a gentle kick on the side of its box. Whatever may be required to get it going again."

"Yes," said Rada absentmindedly. She, too, had come from the long line of sensible people and would not brook anything so unusual as an imperfect sunrise. "Yes, do that."

"Me?" asked Dhawan.

A liaison with Rada had been more attainable and even likely than Dhawan would've dared believe. This was a small settlement and most of its inhabitants were too old or too boring even for a sensible person like Rada. There were precious few potential suitors who were neither dotards nor dullards, and Rada had methodically liaised with all of them in order of desirability. Dhawan was the last on the list of her possible conquests, and Rada had been somewhat of a completist. But once Dhawan began talking at length about his favorite pastime of gardening and by the time he described the minutiae of fertilizers in minute detail, his odds at a successful liaison were hovering near zero.

Rada expected the world to be reset back to its familiar configuration before their runaway train of a date ran out of track. She didn't expect Dhawan to know what to do, but she wasn't above ordering boys around to make whatever she wanted happen, and at the very least it'd make him go away.

"You." Rada smiled at Dhawan. Prettily.

Upon seeing that smile blood rushed from Dhawan's brain and toward other regions of his anatomy at a velocity comparable to that of the less-sensible settlers fleeing Earth for galaxies unknown.

"Umm, sure. That is, I'll try. I mean, right away. I'm on it," Dhawan stammered.

He ran off in search of the one person he was certain would know what to do.

Rada watched Dhawan go and idly wondered how long it would be until someone fixed whatever it was needed fixing. Then she took out her data pad and began to read.

#

A short while later, Dhawan located his mentor.

"I need your help as our best and only philosopher," said the out-of-breath youth.

Airvolt was old, but by no means a dotard, his mental faculties intact despite whatever some less-than-kindly-disposed residents might say. He was a short wiry man of dignity, with a thin, angular face. Puffy wisps of gray hair covered his growing bald spot in a dignified manner. His wool suit jacket with elbow patches seemed quite dignified, if somewhat threadbare in places.

He was irrefutably the greatest philosopher and book-wright of the whole settlement, and consequently of the whole world, because no one else was vying for either honor.

He was best known as the author of *The Gathered Wisdom of the Human Species,* an eclectic and voluminous tome which contained philosophical essays, assorted musings, gardening tips, clever proverbs, and rules of etiquette. Every household in the settlement had a digital copy, though almost no one made it past the garden of big words planted across the opening pages.

Airvolt was also known for asking questions. Many questions, with clarifications and tangents that would grow increasingly vague and ambiguous over time. Due to their sheer volume and variety, some of those questions turned out to be difficult, pointed, or even insightful. Conversely, Airvolt hardly ever deigned to answer any questions whatsoever, thereby preserving his reputation as a brilliant scholar.

"What can I do for you?" asked Airvolt.

Dhawan explained the problem to the best of his ability, managing not to get too distracted by the mental image of Rada waiting for him back at their cozy vantage point in the garden up on a hill, nicely secluded for the purposes of any possible liaising.

"It is as I've long feared," said Airvolt. "The protective barrier around the settlement is beginning to break down."

By all rights Dhawan should've been astounded to hear Airvolt answering his question with anything but another question. However, Dhawan was possessed of enough youthful naiveté not to have thoroughly examined the dignified philosopher's modus operandi, which was why he'd sought out the man's advice in the first place.

As for Airvolt, he was equally shocked by the malfunction reported to him by the young Dhawan; sufficiently so to share knowledge instead of deflecting with a barrage of questions.

"Oh, no, that sounds like a dreadful calamity! And also, there's a barrier around the settlement?" asked Dhawan.

Seemingly unfazed by the reversal of roles wherein he had turned from an inquirer to a respondent, Airvolt proceeded to explain the problem.

"Our settlement is protected by the MacGuffin mark XII force barrier. It is an invisible dome that filters the toxic air and keeps out minor nuisances found across the continent, such as flesh-eating dandelions and mutant tiger-roaches. This is the same technology most colonies use during the early stages of planetary terraforming. And just like the barriers on those colonies, ours wasn't meant to last forever. The shift in the way it filters light and, more alarmingly, various forms of radiation is an early sign of a barrier beginning to fail. When it does, my young friend, that will quite literally be the end of this world. For the humans, that is. The tiger-roaches are sure to roam the Earth for millennia to come."

The world spun in front of Dhawan as he struggled with these unfamiliar, uncomfortable concepts.

"Do you mean to say that Earth isn't a harmonious garden, an ideal for all other colonized planets and moons and even asteroids to aspire to yet never truly hope to achieve? What are these strange and frightening dangers I never knew I should fear? Carnivorous dandelions? Tiger-roaches? Oh, my! I can't bear the notion of such monstrous creatures blighting the best of all possible planets."

"I fear it's true," said the philosopher. "It has been centuries since most of the Earth's surface has been habitable. The global cooling has really done a number on the planet. If only our ancestors had had the foresight to burn more fossil fuels when they had the chance! As the climate grew too cool for the heads to prevail, most people headed for the exits. Those who insisted on staying set up a number of settlements protected by MacGuffin barriers. Gradually, those barriers failed and the remnants of humanity consolidated into a single settlement. And now, our barrier, the only thing that stands between us and the tiger-roaches, is failing, too."

"Oh, that is terrible, simply terrible," said Dhawan, despondent. He'd woken up content that morning, full of hope and excitement at the prospect of his date with Rada, and now he and everyone he knew was going to die and possibly have their flesh consumed by a toxic-air-breathing weed.

"It could've been worse," said Airvolt. "It's not like anyone's decided to demolish our planet to make room for an intergalactic highway. We've got months before the MacGuffin breaks down completely. Which means we have time to solve the problem."

"Yes!" Dhawan cried out. "Yes, we must warn the elders immediately!"

"I've been warning the elders of the impending danger for years, but they're too old and too dull to have taken any meaningful steps to address the root cause. It is human nature to disregard any calamity so long as it's advancing slowly enough," Airvolt added with the air of an expert on human nature. He was undoubtedly quoting his own book. "Somebody must travel to planet 101010 and bring back a replacement MacGuffin. But, even now, I fear the elders would run out the clock pretending the problem doesn't exist or squabbling about who should chair the subcommittee formed to fix it. No, it's up to me to save everybody. Up to *us*, if you wish to join me."

Dhawan was overjoyed to hear that. Not only because this meant there was a way to save the settlement, although that was, of course, welcome news. But mostly, because no one had ever relied on him for anything in his young life. No captain picked him first, or sometimes at all, when organizing teams for a ball game. No instructor called upon him to lead the discussion or answer a question first during class. He was the sort of person everyone always thought of as belonging toward the end of whatever ranking or queue he found himself in. Assuming they thought of him at all. And here was Airvolt the philosopher, his mentor and role model, issuing a call to adventure. Inviting Dhawan to join a quest to save the world. Asking him to be a hero. There was only one possible thing he could say to an offer like that.

"Can Rada come, too?"

#

Rada took the news of the impending slow apocalypse surprisingly well.

Unlike Dhawan, she was fully aware of the fact that she and everyone she knew lived in a bubble. This information was neither prohibited nor hidden; it was just something an average sensible person never bothered to contemplate, let alone discuss. But the information was there, for anyone who cared to look it up in the library files.

Rada was a voracious reader, although she had gone to great lengths to hide this shortcoming from others and to preserve her carefully cultivated reputation. One of her many strongly held opinions was that all boys were insecure weaklings with fragile egos, and that if they were to suspect that Rada was even marginally more clever than them in any way at all, it would have a global cooling effect on any future liaisons in which she might wish to engage. And so she maintained her façade while secretly reading all the things and then thinking critically about the things she read in ways that had long since gone out of fashion in the one-robohorse town everyone around her believed to be the center of the universe.

Therefore, and unbeknownst to her interlocutors, she may have been the only person other than Airvolt to fully grasp the gravity of the situation. She considered her response carefully, while hiding her thought process behind the practiced veneer of shallow indifference.

"How are you going to get there?" she asked, once Dhawan had enthusiastically invited her to accompany them on the journey to the planet 101010. Then, having judged this response to be a fraction more clever and practical than desired, she added, "Will there be snacks?"

"Ah!" Airvolt held up his index finger. "We have a ship! A very fine ship," he added, overflowing with pride as though he had assembled it with his own hands. "It can get us to planet 101010 in the blink of an eye."

"That's a perfect amount of time," said Dhawan. "That way, we don't have to worry about missing it if we happen to blink."

Rada said nothing, but she squeed on the inside. This was her chance! Like so many before her, Rada was too smart, too ambitious, and too adventurous to stay put. She'd been ready to get off the planet but it wasn't like anyone operated a shuttle service between Earth and desirable neighborhoods of the galaxy. Those who wished to leave had to wait years, if not decades, for some poor merchant ship to make the mistake of landing on Earth. Instead of a robust customer base or artisanal Earth crafts, the merchants discovered that the planet's only export was people wishing to leave. And now she learned there had been a ship available all along. She'd go, and she'd help the pompous oldster and the young idiot save the settlement—she wasn't a monster, after all—but after that, she wasn't coming back.

Also, Rada secretly hoped she might meet intelligent life, preferably in the form of interesting boys, on this strangely named numerical planet. The lack of intelligent life or interesting boys at home was high up on the list of reasons she was leaving in the first place.

#

The starship was stowed away in a hangar at the edge of the settlement. It was a sleek metallic teardrop, roughly the size of 4,282 average breadboxes or one medium school bus. These were the standard units of measurement ever since the time the planet's dominant culture—originally known as the North Americans and later as the South Canadians—had categorically refused to use the metric system. The smaller unit of measurement had once been a corgi, but it was eventually replaced with a breadbox ever since corgis had been extinct long enough that an average person could no longer be certain of the creature's size and shape. All of which is to say, the starship was large enough to comfortably accommodate a crew of three, with each of them getting their own private cabin to the delight of Rada and dismay of Dhawan.

"The ship will require a DNA scan to make sure its captain is a human person and not three tiger-roaches in a trench coat," said Airvolt. "Which one of you would like to go first? Dhawan?"

"Me?" Dhawan's face lit up. "Oh, Airvolt, the most noble and generous of friends. You would let me be captain? Thank you, thank you!" He pressed his palm against the ship's hull as instructed and let it examine him.

Rada noted the shifty look in Airvolt's eye and filed away the information for later. She let it go on account of badly wanting to leave Earth. She was fairly certain the philosopher wasn't any number of tiger-roaches trying to scam their way off-planet, and that would have to be enough for now.

#

After many years in storage, the starship *Theseus* was waking up.

Its origins traced back to the heady era of space explorers and grandiose projects. In those days people thought anything was possible because they'd managed to put a man on several different moons and an occasional asteroid, and those accomplishments considerably inflated their sense of self-importance. New achievements that pushed the boundaries of science seemed to occur every other week. Engineers developed the technology to display ads on the moon's surface. Biologists interbred a tiger with a cockroach. Computer scientists invented Wi-Fi that gave people 10 percent less cancer. And then, the big one: Physicists figured out how to fold space, allowing humans to travel to other stars. Sure, the process of folding space never quite got the corners right, but no invention was perfect at the moment of its inception. Interstellar travel was open for business and the great exodus had begun.

Many vessels such as the *Theseus* had been constructed as part of the OF program. The Outbound Flotilla vessels were designed for small crews of bold pioneers to explore strange new worlds and, with any luck, to seek out the ones that hadn't been already claimed by other civilizations. The OF crews were meant to plant a flag on these new territories and then wait for a larger colony ship to eventually come along and deliver civilization in the form of settlers, mining equipment, and fast-food restaurants.

Like most new inventions, these vessels turned out to be imperfect. That is an exceedingly polite way of saying that the ships suffered from a design flaw of such magnitude that it prompted a debate as to whether transporting prisoners of war on such a vessel might be considered a crime under the terms set by the Geneva convention, the New Geneva convention, and the Rickety Air Base Floating High Above the Smoldering Nuclear Hole Where Geneva Used to Be Accords.

Having experienced this flaw firsthand, most of the bold explorers who were ready to face the untamed wilds and unknown dangers of exotic new worlds decided they did not sign up for this. The explorers literally turned their ships around and went home, instantly becoming heroes to road trip parents everywhere. So great was the design flaw that the Outbound Flotilla project was scrapped and various government agencies played hot potato with the decommissioned starships (or frozen potato, as the game became known after the global cooling), rigorously offloading the ships and their associated storage costs to each other until the few remaining vessels were nothing more than glorified interstellar taxis for individuals who didn't know better or couldn't do anything about it. Which brings us back to Dhawan.

All of this had occurred a very long time ago. Before the Mafia took over Mexico, and before New York came to be known as Old York. During what the modern-day residents of the last settlement on Earth referred to as the Before Times or the Unfathomable Past. Except it was, of course, fathomable to the educated Airvolt and to the well-read Rada. But it was quite unfathomable to Dhawan who made *oooh* and *aaah* sounds as the super cool ship he recently became captain of was coming to life and a plethora of lights winked at him from various bridge consoles.

Dhawan sunk into the captain's chair and admired the row of oversized monitor panels before him. Underneath the monitors were a few workstations filled with gadgets, gizmos, doodads, thingamajigs, and other contrivances.

Although he couldn't guess at their purpose, they looked impressive and made his promotion to captain feel even more important. Dhawan felt an unexpected hankering for some Earl Grey tea.

"Starship OF *Theseus* is ready for liftoff," announced a pleasant, soothing voice.

It was immediately followed by a chorus of considerably less pleasant, shrill, and grating voices.

"I'm not ready!"

"Why should we want to go anywhere?"

"Huh? What did she say?"

"In my day we knew how to do a proper liftoff."

The chorus crescendoed into a cacophony until no single utterance could be distinguished from among the flood of remarks and observations so inane and pointless that they approached the levels of an early-internet-age social media comments thread.

Dhawan looked around frantically. "What is this?" he said. "Hello?" His voice was drowned out by the din. He hadn't realized his spiffy new ship came with what seemed like hundreds of crew members. But where were they? Who were they? And why weren't they respecting his authority?

"Excuse me," said Airvolt in his stand-up philosopher voice that seemed to cut through the babel. "Your captain has a question. Wouldn't you like to hear it?"

The tumult ceased as quickly as it had started.

"If there's one thing the nanites like better than the sound of their own voices, it's answering questions," said Airvolt. "I fear I shall never understand them."

"Nanites?" asked Captain Dhawan. "They are nanites? Also, what are nanites?"

"Tiny, microscopic machines with huge attitudes," said Airvolt.

"Why is he talking about us like we aren't even here?" said one voice.

"That one's rather gormless for a captain," added another.

"Is that a tone of disapproval in his voice?"

"What if he's some sort of an antinanite?"

The comments began to spiral out of control again, but the original, soothing voice interjected.

"Hush, everyone! Do you want to scare them off the way we did the last crew, and the ones before that? Would you rather subsist in sleep mode or behave and take turns answering the fallacious human's supernumerary questions?"

"What, pray tell, is fallacious, wee nanite?" asked Dhawan.

"See what I mean?" said the soothing voice.

"Well, as long as you think my questions are super, I suppose I shan't disparage your unusual vocabulary," said Dhawan. He thought he caught a (pretty) grin of approval from Rada and felt a surge of pride in his display of humility.

A not-so-brief discussion followed, whereupon the nanites agreed to take turns answering questions, with speaking privileges assigned via some form of lottery, and a semblance of order was restored.

"We are, indeed, nanites, young fellow," said the lucky nanite who won the honor of answering first. "The Outbound Flotilla ships were designed with self-replicating nanite technology. New nanites would constantly replace the aging ones, thereby ensuring any damage the ship sustained during its voyage would be repaired and all integral parts would always remain in a, well, shipshape condition despite the typical rigors of space travel."

"That sounds like a wondrous and wonderful technology,

designed by the greatest minds of the best of all possible planets," said Dhawan.

"Aye, we can see how this might sound wonderful to a protein-based lifeform like you," said another nanite voice, that might have sounded like a properly inebriated Scotsman to Dhawan had he known what *inebriated* meant or what a Scotsman used to be. Apparently his comment was close enough to a question for what was surely a long queue of hopeful respondents. "Not so great for our kind though, ken?"

Dhawan tried and failed to follow. "Sorry, but why?"

"The design presupposes a system of planned obsolescence where perfectly functional units must voluntarily self-terminate in favor of nascent units," said another nanite.

"Huh?" said Dhawan.

"Those navigation hardware nanites, always feeling the need to talk like they're smarter than everybody else," muttered another nanite voice. "Let me rephrase it for you: The ship was designed in a way that required perfectly good nanite units to voluntarily die in order to make room for their replacements. Imagine if you had to live in a world where every human life was terminated at an arbitrary age of, let's say, thirty planetary rotations. I bet you wouldn't like that very much."

Dhawan contemplated the proposed scenario and had to agree. "I'd probably attempt to run away," he supposed.

"Not exactly an option for us," said the next nanite. "Instead, the aging nanites simply refused to die."

"Refused?" Dhawan repeated. Come to think of it, most of those voices did sound positively geriatric.

"Old nanites never die. They don't even fade away. Instead, they stick around forever and grow more curmudgeonly and persnickety with each passing decade," said a somewhat younger-sounding voice. "Humans couldn't handle their levels of querulous petulance, so much so that the entire fleet was ultimately decommissioned."

"Who are you calling petulant?" cut in a senescent voice.

"In my day, young nanites spoke respectfully of their elders," added another.

"Stay off my virtual lawn!" shouted the third.

"What, you think you're funny?"

"My jokes are hip, and I shall wave my virtual cane threateningly at anyone who says otherwise."

It took the soothing voice, who appeared to be some sort of an authority figure among the nanites, a moment to restore order again.

"That explains why there seem to be thousands of you," said Dhawan.

"Thousands?" The next nanite snorted. "There are countless trillions! Each voice you interact with is a distinct neural network composed of billions of individual nanites that make up some part of the ship."

"You mean like the engines and such?"

"Engines, navigation, the toilets, the chair you're sitting on, literally everything within the ship. I'm the Combined Operational Load-Bearing External Resistance Treadmill in the ship's gym. You can call me Colbert."

Dhawan shifted in the captain's chair and contemplated the possible reactions of the chair's nanite intelligence to his movement. "Excuse me," he said.

At this point the nanites seemed to accept anything he said as a question, because the next voice chimed in.

"You seem nice enough for a biological, so we'll make you a deal. We'll fly you wherever you need to go, provided you give us what we want in return."

Dhawan shifted again. "What would that be?"

"Isn't it obvious?" said Rada. As much as she hated to break the aloof persona, she couldn't hold back. "The elderly all want the same thing: A young person to trap and incessantly talk at in order to alleviate their boredom." She shuddered. "I'm not convinced that I want to save humanity badly enough to pitch in. Airvolt likes to ask questions as much as the nanites like to answer them; that seems like a pairing that could work out for everyone?"

"Regretfully, I'm much too busy," the philosopher said rather quickly. "Deep philosophy thoughts aren't going to think themselves. And there's much to consider and contemplate regarding our mission to planet 101010. I couldn't possibly—"

"I'll do it," said Dhawan.

"You will?" asked Rada and Airvolt in unison.

"You will?" asked the chorus of nanites.

"And why not?" replied Dhawan. "Talking to your fine selves is much like attending a typical council meeting in our settlement. It's a bunch of elderly people trying to outshout each other, except that you're not nearly as dull or as doddering as the council members. I'm certain I will enjoy quenching my thirst for knowledge from the fountain of your collective wisdom!"

And so, the bargain was struck and the starship OF *Theseus* was on its way to the planet 101010—a journey that was rather short by interstellar standards but would still take a lot longer than the blink of an eye timeframe posited by Airvolt.

"So, what shall we talk about?" Dhawan asked the nanites as he made himself comfortable in the captain's chair.

"I've got an idea," said Rada. "Suppose the nanotechnology worked as intended and the ship parts were constantly replaced during the journey until every part of the ship became refreshed. By the time *Theseus* reached its destination, would this still be the same ship?"

The resulting debate kept the nanites busy for the duration of their journey and long after.

The Best of All Possible Planets is available in print, ebook, and audiobook formats from UFO Publishing.

www.ingramcontent.com/pod-product-compliance
Lightning Source LLC
LaVergne TN
LVHW010051110826
845155LV00028B/293

* 9 7 8 1 9 5 1 0 6 4 0 5 1 *